Danarko

Maxina Storibrook

Cover Design
by
Marienixza Midaliz Diaz

ISBN-10: 1539929914
ISBN-13: 978-1539929918

DEDICATION

If it wasn't for my mother, I would have never been brave enough to write. If it wasn't for that bravery, I would have never written so many drafts of this book. If it weren't for all of those drafts, it would have never turned into the pearl it is today.

Here's to you, Mama.

ACKNOWLEDGMENTS

My mother has endured so many drafts of this book –
most of them not so great. However, despite this, she
still encouraged me to keep writing and to keep
improving. She is my first reader, editor, critique, and
fan.

I would like to thank all of my family and friends for
supporting me in my endeavors to put pen to paper.
It really means a lot to me; every comment and word
of encouragement helped me get closer and closer to
this goal. My father, especially, has been a huge silent
support for me; I look up to him and highly value his
opinion, so his approval for me being a writer means
a lot to me.

Here's just a few of the people who have supported,
helped, and encouraged me through this wild, crazy,
amazing adventure that is my writing: Christine
Stayrook, Amanda Prisbe, Danielle Friend, Becca
Farabaugh, Hannah Brown, Rachel Kiggins, Nathan
Wind, Annslee Oaks, Tyler Williamson, Linda Bell,
Jordan Trigler, Anne Kraft, and John Patrick Bray.

I would like to thank all of my creative writing and
English teachers/professors throughout my life. They
all saw something in my writing and helped me grow
not only as a writer but also as a person.

Now for a little story about these two ladies I met
back in November 2015; I had joined a NaNoWriMo
group on Facebook. One day, I had commented on a
post. The person I was commenting to was being
rude; a lady, Adele, private messaged me, wondering

if I was okay with her saying something to him about it. I told her no, it wasn't worth it. After that, we got to chatting about writing and other things we have in common. Now, she is a good friend and beta reader for my books.

As I was perusing the group's newsfeed on a different day, I noticed a writer had posted some fan art done by a friend of hers. I followed the links to the artist's page and fell in love with her work, deciding then and there that this person will do the cover of my book. As you can see by the cover art, Ryou (Marienixza Midaliz Diaz) did a fantastic job!

These two women – Adele and Ryou – have become really good friends of mine and have provided excellent, in-depth feedback on my books. If it wasn't for Adele, I don't think I would have been able to write the version of Danarko you are reading today. If it wasn't for Ryou, I probably wouldn't have this unique (and epically awesome) cover. Thank you, ladies.

If you would like to show my cover artist your support, her Facebook page is www.facebook.com/Clockworkjoker/ and her Patreon page is www.patreon.com/Clockworkjoker

CONTENTS

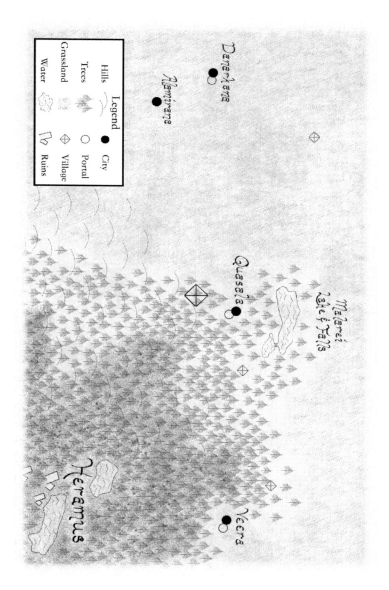

viii

CHAPTER 1
RED BLOOD, BLUE FLOWER

"Stop." Mara flicks her chestnut hair out of her tanned face and gold eyes, widening her stance on the mats covering the floor of the pseudo-dojo. She looks calm and ready, like a cougar waiting for its prey to step in front of her.

Standing across from her, Justin awkwardly straightens from an improper roundhouse kick, his beefy frame looking odd against Mara's tall, lean build.

"What did I do wrong?" he drawls in a heavy Southern accent, raking his fingers through his mousy brown hair.

"Lift your ankle and straighten your leg more," Mara advises him, enunciating each word precisely – not condescending or teasing, just factual.

Her high-ranking brown belt shifts over her white Judo uniform as she executes a perfect roundhouse kick as an example, her leg arcing out, up, and around in a graceful, dance-like move. Her foot barely makes a sound as it lands onto the padded floor of the gym-sized room. Her willowy frame straightens, bringing her back to her full height of nearly five and a half feet tall.

The dojo's instructor, Ronny, claps his weathered hands together as the creases around his eyes wrinkle in amusement. "Excellent, Mara. Class, that will be all for today."

"Arigatou, sensei," Mara thanks the instructor in Japanese, pressing her palms together and bowing deeply from the waist.

Mr. Ronny bows back. "You're most welcome. I look forward to your assistance next time, as well." He turns to the football player beside her. "Justin, please say hello to your father for me."

"I will, sir." Justin bows.

Mara walks to the entrance, stepping off the training mats onto the wooden floor by the shoe racks and cubbies. She methodically slips her feet into her socks and tennis shoes as Justin fumbles with his giant boots.

"Hurry up," she says, grabbing her plain black bag from a cubby and gliding to the door. She mulls over the ancient Chinese meditation-in-motion martial art and philosophy, t'ai chi ch'uan, and some new patterns she had learned today from her instructor.

Jogging after her, Justin grabs a sports bag with an image of a football and the name "Guntos" on it. They exit the building into a sparsely populated parking lot in front of a little strip mall that is the only place to shop in that small, rural corner of Tennessee. The mid-summer heat beats down on them. "Hey, do you think she noticed?"

She pauses at the passenger door to Justin's old, hand-painted blue and red Chevrolet truck. "I believe she was training, as well, so she may not have seen you," she comments as they climb in. "You did pretty good today."

"You think so?" he asks rhetorically, his cheeks flushing a bright pink.

Mara smirks. His crush is a pretty girl with dark brown hair and a petite build; he had joined the dojo just to get closer to her, but instead, he got closer to the mats. "Your form could use a bit more work, but you're getting somewhere with it. Where's your dad today?"

Justin grins. "He didn't want me tellin', but he got your mom a gift and took it straight over."

She fingers her elongated ears, her face twisting in disgust. "Maybe we could hang out at your place instead."

"What, don't want to be siblings?" he jokes as the truck tumbles to life. "You can't avoid it forever, especially now that school is out."

"It's not that..." Mara mumbles. Bryce, her mother's boyfriend and Justin's father, is a football coach at their school. His wife had died of cancer around the same time Mara and Ezra had moved into the area. Ezra and the coach had met through a support group for widows two years ago and grew closer over time.

Mara stares at her hands, remembering her father's large, callused fingers turning the pages of his worn yet detailed sketchbook as he told her and Codi stories about a fantastical engineer designing cities and academies; it was one of her favorite memories of her father and adopted brother. A painful twinge shoots through her heart as she remembers her brother who had vanished five years ago.

Maybe Dad's sketchbook is still on the bar, Mara thinks, distracting herself by rubbing circles into her bag's soft strap with her callused thumb. *Maybe Justin will play Siege with me...*

The truck leaves the small town and bounces down the country roads, the trees zipping by in a green and brown blur. The thirty-minute drive passes by in comfortable silence.

Justin turns onto a gravel road that curves up a small hill and stops next to a quaint house made out of brick and wood. A huge tree in the front yard shadows the SUV and pickup truck parked under it, and a wooded area surrounds the little plot of land. Despite living there for two years, they haven't made it look very lived-in yet.

Mara lands softly on her feet as Justin thuds to the ground. They walk towards the house, Mara's stride graceful and elegant next to Justin's blocky, slouched gait.

"Want to play Siege?" Mara asks as they walk into the house. They drop their bags by the bar stools next to the bar. She fingers the large sketchbook on the marbled surface, opening it onto the blueprint-design of a labyrinth city. A Ziploc baggy containing the little homemade markers of different abilities rests in the middle of the drawing.

Justin rolls his eyes. "You *always* wanna play Siege." His eyes twinkle as an idea comes to his mind. "Maybe we could change the rules – "

Mara laughs, shoving on his shoulder. He barely budges. "Not a chance. Last time we did, you came up with some crazy rule that the mages couldn't fire over buildings – which makes no sense as the buildings were built for mages to be able to shoot over them."

Justin huffs. "Seriously, though. How did you and yer dad come up with something so complicated?"

Mara sometimes wonders the same thing; she had been so young when her father had sketched out the city, traced over immovable areas in pen, and then created the tabs for barriers, illusions, and other defense systems. Shrugging, she admits, "I don't know."

Justin snorts. "I bet Settlers of Catan or Risk wouldn't be on your wish list for your birthday, would it? They ain't nearly as hard as this."

Mara raises an eyebrow, smirking at him. "I love all strategy games, even Battleship."

A challenging grin lights up Justin's face. "Just you wait, I'll surprise you with the best gift ever this June!"

Mara props her chin on her hand and strokes a signature in the bottom right corner of a picture that reads, 'Shokain Danarko.' Absently, she flips through a few pages with a smile on her face, revealing an intricate drawing of a labyrinth city, a crystalline castle, and a ruined town. Justin looks at the drawings with her.

"Yer dad was really good," he comments, examining the picture of the ruined town. The picture had been shaded with graphite, although Mara remembers the description: red trees, orange-brown grass, and blue opaque glass-like structures that had been broken over centuries of just lying around.

"Yup." She flips back to the aerial view of the town. "Wanna play, then?"

"If I win, you gotta start calling me brother," he bargains, grinning lopsidedly.

"When I win, you should ask Claurice out," Mara shoots back, and snickers at Justin's reddening cheeks.

Thump.

Mara and Justin glance deeper into the house. "Mom?" Mara calls out, but there is no response. She glances at Justin before stepping into the kitchen.

He follows her. "Hey, I think we should just leave them alone," he hints as Mara examines the state of the kitchen. Cooking appliances and dishes litter the island counter, and a thawed lamb leg package floats in a pool of lukewarm water. Ezra must have been preparing dinner.

"Maybe..." Mara murmurs out loud, turning back to the living room. She doesn't want to think about what her mother and her boyfriend are doing in the back room. "Let's turn on some – "

Bang.

The sound of the gunshot ricochets through the house. Mara whirls around, staring down the hallway. Justin shifts closer to Mara, fear and concern warring on his face. She glances at him, and they slowly approach the door at the end of the hallway. She stares at the handle, unable to reach out and grab it.

Within the room, something crashes to the hardwood floor and shatters.

Mara's hand whips out and turns the knob, swinging the door open. The master bedroom is nearly as big as the living room, hosting a queen-sized canopy bed with a beautiful red and gold comforter. The short dresser, two end tables, and vanity bordering the room are all made out of a dark wood. Two mid-height shelves on the walls support pictures, knick-knacks, and Shokain's elegant katana.

Bryce clutches Ezra's honey-blonde hair, shoving her against the wall near the door. She squints her vivid blue eyes at Mara and Justin, urging them to leave with a glance as she fights to breathe.

"Wha'daya think yer doin' in here?" Bryce slurs, the stench of something sickeningly sweet wafting off of him. He shakes his oily brown hair out of his face. There is no flash of recognition as he glares at Mara and Justin, his brown eyes dead and slightly unfocused.

Mara stares at the silver pistol in Bryce's hand. Small, but so deadly. She chokes on air, the sight of the weapon filling her whole vision. Images flash through her mind of her father lying on the ground, bleeding to death.

It will kill me.

"Dad! Let her go!" Justin yells, his voice trembling slightly. Mara snaps out of her phobia-induced daze in time to see Bryce knock the gun's barrel against Justin's cheek. The quarterback stumbles and clutches the edge of the dresser next to the door to stabilize himself.

Mara steps forward and performs the same kick she had been praised on just earlier that day. Her foot connects with Bryce's forearm, knocking the gun to the side. It skitters across the floor and thuds against the dresser.

Justin takes this opportunity and tackles his father, knocking the big man off-balance and twisting his arms behind him. Mara performs several moves against the restrained man.

Uppercut. Straight punch. Right hook. Sweeping kick.

Bryce slumps to one knee.

Mara jabs her knee into his torso. He rams his head forward and clips Mara's hip with his skull. She winces, pulling back slightly.

Bryce surges from the floor, his muscles bulging as he pulls free from his son. He swings around and backhands Justin, sending him flying. He crashes into the vanity on the other side of the room, blacking out from the impact.

Mara's eyes widen. Justin had been boasting just earlier that week about how he could lift the same amount as his father now. However, based off that move, Bryce seems much stronger than his son.

Her left foot a blur, Mara performs a swift roundhouse kick, aiming for Bryce's neck.

He catches her foot.

Examining the ankle he now tightly holds, he grins dementedly and swings her towards the dresser.

"Ah – !" Mara's shriek is cut off as her back slams against the wall, her breath whooshing out. She slumps onto the dresser, dazed and gasping for air.

Bryce stalks towards her, but a short, sturdy wooden stool splinters over his head. Ezra stumbles backwards, her face pale yet set with determination. "Don't touch my daughter," she threatens, her voice as slick and cold as Vaseline on ice.

Bryce, too fast for Mara to comprehend, grips Ezra's neck and throws her across the room. Her head strikes the wall and she slumps to the floor, knocked out.

Mara leans forward, needing to be on her feet before he comes after her again. This isn't the Bryce they all know and care for. Bryce owns hunting rifles, not a small pistol. Bryce doesn't know any self-defense, yet he fights like a professional. *Assassin*, crosses Mara's mind, but she shakes it off. Ridiculous.

In a blink of an eye, he stands in front of her. His gun points at her stomach.

Startled, Mara stares into his eyes. His pupils are dilated to the point that the brown iris is barely a thin line bordering the whites of his eyes. "A ik'te Essence fora'ring?" he asks in a strange accent, heavily rolling the consonants while clearly pronouncing the vowels – definitely not a Southern accent.

All she catches is 'Essence,' which makes no sense, and 'for a ring.' A ring? He's looking for a ring? "Bryce – " she starts.

His hand crushes her throat, shoving her back into the wall over the dresser. "A ik'te Essence fora'ring?" he demands, his voice louder. The barrel jams above Mara's left hip.

She fights to breathe as she tries pushing him away, but he is much stronger than she had ever thought possible. Not even the pressure points on his arm work. She fumbles along the dresser, trying to find something, anything, to defend herself with.

Bryce pushes a little harder against her throat, and blackish-red spots cloud her vision. He repeats the same phrase in that flat tone, the point of the gun digging into her stomach.

Her fingers wrap around a cold, rectangular object.

"Screw... you," she forces out and swings the heavy steel jewelry box against his head.

Bang.

Bryce staggers back. Blood drips down his face from where the box had gouged him.

Mara instinctively wraps her hand over her abdomen. She grits her teeth and looks down at the red flower blooming above her hipbone. She trembles violently as the death of her father flashes through her mind.

Mara sobs. "Mom..." she cries softly, her fist clenching over her wound as she slumps off the dresser, fighting to stay conscious.

Bryce towers over Mara as blood flows in a steady stream down her side.

Groaning, Justin rolls off the broken vanity and stares in horror at Mara. Yelling in rage, he tackles his father, sending him back several steps.

Ezra, coming to her senses, shakes her head to clear her thoughts. Seeing the boy trying his hardest to fend off his own father, she stands up quickly. The room spins slightly as she hurries to Mara's side.

"Get out of here!" Justin says over his shoulder, landing a kick between Bryce's legs. "Sorry," he mumbles as his father hunches over in temporary pain.

Ezra drapes Mara's arm over her shoulder and hoists the girl to her feet. She grabs the now-dented jewelry box and heads to the door.

"No," Mara gasps, straining to look over her shoulder as Ezra drags the girl out of the room. "Mom, we need to help – "

"There's nothing we can do!" Ezra cries. Mara glances at her mother, seeing a tear slip down her mother's cheek. "We need to leave, now."

Mara bites her lip, reminded of what had happened to her father. Again, she is useless; she can't help her friend in the state she is in. She follows after her mother, gasping as her side throbs painfully.

"My-my bag has a first aid kit," Mara says as they pass by the bar. Blood still pours freely from the wound, coating her hip and leg.

Ezra quickly snatches the gym bag and tosses it over her shoulder. Mara grabs the sketchbook off the counter, clutching it to her chest as if it would save her. *I wish Dad were here*, she thinks, desperate. In her condition, she knows she cannot protect her mother.

Heavy footsteps emerge from the hallway. Glancing back, Mara watches Bryce approach them, his gun raised. Her eyes widen in horror. "Justin – "

Ezra yanks Mara out the front door, dragging the girl behind one of the vehicles. They collapse against the side of the SUV. Feeling as if there is still something in the wound, Mara gasps for air as she tries to settle her nerves and evaluate the situation.

Her eyes sting as the events of what had just happened replay in her head. *What happened to Justin?* She closes her eyes and covers her mouth with the back of her hand, holding down the bile threatening to come up from the shifting object in her stomach. *More importantly, why is Bryce trying to kill us?*

Ezra flips open the lid of the decent-sized jewelry box with nearly enough force to break the hinges. The box is crammed with items; a strange metal contraption looking vaguely like a small pistol and a blue flower with yellow-green leaves in a vial stand out the most. Five oval sandstones just a little bigger than her thumb rest beneath the odd contraption and vial, each painted with different colors and patterns. Shokain's sunstone ring glints forlornly in the corner as if it had been abandoned and forgotten in the clutter. No wonder the steel jewelry box had been heavy.

The screened door of the house creaks open. *I meant to oil that today*, Mara thinks to herself, her mind going numb. Bryce-but-not-Bryce calls out in the foreign language, but all she recognizes is "Danarko."

Ezra's head snaps up, her breath stopping as she listens to the man's words. Biting her lip, she takes out the metal contraption and shoves the box at Mara.

"Snap one of the stones in half," she whispers at Mara, holding the palm-sized contraption. Mara has the crazy idea it is a laser gun; it definitely has enough cooling elements to keep it from overheating. "Any of them will do." She rushes out from behind the vehicle.

Mara tries to go after her mother, but a painful jab in her side takes away her breath as something slices her from inside. She nearly throws up from the sensation, wanting to claw the bullet out of her.

A strange *zzst* sound is closely followed by the *bang* from Bryce's gun.

Mara covers her ears, trying to block out the sounds. *She's going to die,* she thinks, tears pouring down her face. Her side throbs sharply as she tries to limit her movements, unable to stand the feeling of the bullet shifting under her skin. *She's going to die, just like Daddy did.*

Opening her eyes, she stares into the box at the sand-colored stones. One of them has purple and blue swirls painted on it, reminding her of her father's friend who used to tell stories to her and Codi. After her father's funeral, she had said some terrible things to him out of frustration and grief, yelling at him to never come back. He hadn't.

Fingers shaking violently, she reaches forward and picks up the sandstone. She uses the rest of her strength to snap it in half.

A high-pitched whining sound pierces the air. She drops the two halves and slaps her hands over her ears, but it doesn't help.

In front of her, the air warps, forming a slit and then expanding into an oval big enough for her to step through. The air within shifts, looking like a hazy picture of a clock tower. A man with lavender hair, purple eyes, and pointed ears steps through, his features looking too perfect and eerily beautiful. He wears a blue tunic and beige cloth pants with a belt fastened around his waist, still looking the same age as when Mara was a little girl – about twenty years old.

Mara's vision blurs as she stares at the man. "Star," she chokes out Aeserast's nickname, the memory of the blue-eyed, purple-haired man's devastated face flashing through her mind. He looks different now, but she definitely recognizes him. "I'm sorry... I'm sorry..."

"It's all right," he consoles her, quickly kneeling beside her to take her hand. His breath hitches at the sight of Mara's wound as his eyes widen in horror. "Who-who did this?"

"Bryce." Mara tilts her head to the side of the vehicle. "Mom... Mom's fighting him."

Aeserast's eyes sharpen and his jaw tenses. The muscles around his eyes twitch into a deadly look. It was the scariest expression she had ever seen on anyone; for a split second, Mara wonders if she really does know this man.

"Stay here," he commands. Even his voice is cold. Sticking his hand through the warped air he had appeared through, he withdraws a giant crescent-shaped blade nearly the same height as himself. He stalks around the corner just as the oval shrinks and disappears.

Stunned, Mara stares straight ahead, unsure how to take what had just happened. *Bryce is acting like some trained assassin, Mom has a zapping gun, and Aeserast just appeared out of nowhere looking as if he had been at a convention and hasn't aged a day.* Mara stares at the jewelry box in a daze. *What is going on?*

As soon as she finishes that thought, Ezra skids around the corner and collapses next to Mara, fumbling with the vial containing the flower.

"Mom," Mara says in an oddly calm voice. Ezra freezes, staring at her daughter in horror. Mara's head spins slightly from the blood loss. "What... just happened?"

Ezra swallows hard, refocusing her attempts to take off the lid of the vial. Aeserast, striding around the car empty-handed, calmly takes the vial from her and pops it open with one finger. He gazes at Mara, concern and worry warring on his face with barely contained fear.

Ezra pulls out two blue petals and holds them near Mara's lips. "Eat this," she orders, her voice trembling.

Mara continues to stare at her mother, clenching her jaw. *I want answers,* she demands with her eyes.

Ezra grits her teeth in frustration. "Mara, you'll bleed out if you don't eat this right now."

Mara slowly parts her lips. Ezra crams the flower into Mara's mouth, not giving the girl time to change her mind. Startled, Mara snaps her teeth shut around the petals.

They dissolve in her mouth, reminding her of some nasty medicinal tablets she had to take once.

Ezra sighs in relief. "Aeserast, there should be a boy in the back room. Can you – "

"Of course." He jogs around the vehicle. Not even a second later, Mara hears the screen door screeching open.

That was fast, she thinks drowsily as her breathing deepens. She frowns slightly. "Did you... drug me?"

"You're bleeding too much," Ezra dodges the question, lifting the hem of Mara's stained dojo uniform and staring at the bullet entrance. She prods Mara's back and frowns. "The bullet is still inside."

"Could have told you that..." Mara mumbles, her eyes sliding shut. "It feels like it's cutting me..."

Ezra's breath hisses in. Her mother's warm hands press against her wound, and Mara groans as the bullet shifts.

"The boy is fine, merely unconscious. Is Mara all right?" Aeserast asks. He leans over Ezra's shoulder, examining the bullet wound.

Mara opens her eyes, wondering how he had gotten back so fast. *Maybe the drug is warping my sense of time...*

"Th-the bullet. I think it had neivir shards within it, and they broke free when Mara was shot." Ezra bites her lip again, snapping the lid of the jewelry box closed and stuffing it and the sketchbook into Mara's gym bag. "Aeserast, I can't do this here. I need to go home."

Aeserast nods as Mara's eyes slide closed again. He says something to Ezra, but Mara is having a hard time following their conversation. She feels as if she should be paying attention, but the petals had done something to her.

Mara's eyes fly open when Aeserast picks her up, her left side jarring sharply. She moans, her face twisting in agony. "I apologize, Mara," he whispers. "This will probably hurt."

Mara's breathing hitches in alarm as he walks towards a warped oval of air. Her mother is nowhere in sight. "Ah... No..." she says weakly as her head thumps against Aeserast's shoulder. She squeezes her eyes shut, not wanting to go through whatever that thing is but not having the strength to push away from Aeserast.

Mara has the odd sensation of cool water passing through her entire being. It rips something out of her, something that had been keeping *it* repressed. A blinding silver light flashes through the darkness of Mara's mind.

She screams.

A strange warmth spreads through her body as something floods all of her senses. For a split second, she could feel, taste, hear, smell, and see her surroundings through a surreal view from above Aeserast and Ezra; a colorful, thick fog swirls around them, reacting to the storm of silver lightning bolts and black tendrils wrapping around Mara's body.

Overwhelmed, Mara blacks out.

The autumn-colored leaves sway in a small breeze as eleven-year-old Mara picks wildflowers in the field behind her parents' house. She hums her father's favorite lullaby, smiling slightly. "Mama will like these," she murmurs to herself, plucking a daffodil from its stem.

Three strangely-dressed men emerge from the edge of the woods, holding shotguns and adjusting their orange hunting vests uncomfortably. They murmur to one another in a foreign language. One of them sees Mara and hushes the others.

"Who are you?" the man asks, frowning slightly as he takes in the little girl's blue T-shirt and jeans, hazelnut hair, sun-kissed skin, and burnt gold eyes. "Where are your parents?"

Mara backs up, clenching the flowers in her hand. She glances between the three men, wary. "This is our property," she says firmly, keeping the tremble out of her voice the best she can. "Please leave before I call the cops."

She reaches into her pocket to pull out her cell phone. The man who had spoken quickly holds up his hands, laughing nervously. "We're just a little lost. No need to – "

An arm wraps around her middle and yanks her backwards. She squeaks, alarmed, as her father, Shokain, drags her up the slope. He narrows his dark gold eyes, his long hazelnut hair pulled back into a ponytail.

"Hey, you! Stop!" the man calls out. He says something in a foreign language.

Bang.

Shokain jerks, falling to one knee. "Run, Mara," he rasps, pushing her away from him. Blood blossoms from his shoulder, forming a red bud right above his heart.

"No!" Mara screams, holding her hands over where he had been shot clean through his shoulder. She tries to heal him like the people in all his stories had done, but nothing happens. "Daddy!"

He strokes her face. "I love you, Mara," he whispers. He coughs, and blood trickles out of his mouth. "Don't allow this to consume your life. Remember what I taught you."

He pulls Mara against his chest in a tight hug, blocking her vision as he takes off his sunstone ring and presses it into her palm. He speaks in the same foreign language as the men, and their screams echo through Mara's head before they suddenly... stop. When Shokain releases her and she looks around, they are nowhere to be seen.

"Daddy, let's go home," Mara begs. Shokain collapses onto his back, still coughing up blood. His eyes dim. "Daddy? Daddy!"

"Don't... cry, Mara..." he murmurs, his fingers briefly tightening around hers. "Don't... forget..."

He trails off. Mara holds her breath, waiting for him to finish, but he doesn't. "Don't forget what?" she asks, tears streaming down her face. "Don't just say something..." Her voice catches as she chokes on a sob. "And not finish it. It's... not nice..."

She rests her head against his chest, inhaling the sharp coppery twang. She doesn't hear his heartbeat. "Daddy... Come back..." Her tears mingle with the blood.

CHAPTER 2
FAMILY

Mara's eyelids flutter. "Daddy…" she mumbles.

Opening her eyes, she blearily looks around the room, disoriented. Expensive-looking pillows and blankets cradle her on top of an Egyptian style futon in silver and blue colors. A dresser and vanity nestle in one corner next to an open door leading to a toilet and old-style bath with a shower nozzle. On the other side of the room, a sliding door remains tightly shut. Dimly glowing orbs float over their stands, reminding Mara of some lights she had seen in an ad just the other day. Something about reverse magnetism keeping them afloat or something; it had advertised them as being the 'new future for lighting rooms.'

She frowns slightly. *Where am I? This isn't a hospital…* Voices outside the door draw her attention.

"… spoke Xharos, so she didn't understand it."

Mara frowns, focusing on her mother's voice. *Sha rose?* She repeats the unfamiliar word phonetically, not recognizing it. *Is that what Bryce had been speaking?*

The next to speak is Aeserast. "So that bullet was meant for you."

Startled, Mara glances towards the door. She prods her side gingerly, looking for bandages. She doesn't find anything.

Sitting up in bed, she nearly misses Ezra's next words as she yanks the unfamiliar shirt up to examine her side. "Most likely. It had neivir shards in it just like the one that had killed Shokain."

Stunned, Mara stares at the two-inch-thick scar running horizontally just above her hipbone where the bullet wound should have been. It looks more like she had been stabbed instead of shot. *What's neivir? What does it have to do with Dad?* Staring at the scar, her mouth goes dry as a more important question runs through her mind. *How long have I been unconscious?*

Mara nearly does not catch another man's hanging question due to the sound of her pounding heart. "Does Mara know about...?"

Mara remembers her mother's face when she had explained the situation to the eleven-year-old Mara. *You were always keeping something from me, Mom,* she thinks, holding her breath as she waits to hear her mother's answer. She hopes her suspicion is wrong.

"No, and I want to keep it that way."

Her mother's statement makes Mara's heart drop. They tell one another everything; there are no secrets between them. Now, though, she just learned that the woman who had raised her had kept the biggest secret imaginable.

Surprisingly, her mother continues. *She had sighed,* Mara knows intuitively. "I don't know if that will be possible, though, since both of our Sources are no longer being repressed and hidden. The paro'ki will be able to find us so easily now – and I'm not sure we can survive another assassination attempt."

Assassination. That word rings in Mara's head, and she connects the dots despite the unfamiliar words and terms. *Dad was assassinated. But... why? He was just a creative goofball who had started up and taught self-defense classes in a small Tennessee town.*

She misses the next part of the conversation as a spark flashes in her peripheral. Startled, she glances to her right in time to hear a crackly noise by her ear. Passing it off as static electricity, she takes a deep breath to steady her nerves.

She needs to figure out what is going on. Why did Bryce attack them? Why didn't he recognize his own son? What did he say to her in that weird language? What was that hole in the air? How did Aeserast just... appear like that? What was up with that giant curved blade?

Aeserast doesn't even look a day older than five years ago – earlier, even. She takes another deep breath to keep her emotions in check. He has always had lavender hair, but why did he have those weird ears and purple eyes?

The door opens. Aeserast and Ezra walk in, a man and a woman following close behind them. The man has dark, grey-streaked hair and brown eyes while the woman has exquisite yet soft features that compliment her honey-blonde hair and blue eyes. All four of them look as though they had pulled an all-nighter, complete with drooping eyes, messy hair, and exhausted expressions.

Ezra rushes to Mara's side and sits on the edge of the bed, clasping the girl's hand. Despite her tiredness, she forces a reassuring smile on her face. "How are you feeling, sweetie? Do you hurt anywhere?"

"I..." Mara touches her side, a bit overwhelmed by everything that had just happened. "No..." *I wonder what she would do if I just ask her about Dad,* she wonders, and decides against it. Instead, she opts for safer questions. "Who are they? Where's Justin?"

Ezra's smile is a little bit stronger. "This is your Uncle Jonan and Aunt Surana. We're going to be staying with them for a while. Justin... will be all right."

"It is good to see you made it through the surgery well," Jonan says roughly, looking a little embarrassed at being called uncle.

Aunt and uncle? Mara stares at them. She saw no family resemblance between the supposed brother and sister. *That's right... she's adopted,* Mara remembers. *Mom always said we didn't have enough money to visit. How did we even get here? Why did she evade my question like that?*

"How long was I out?" Mara asks instead as she brushes her hand over her side again. She wonders if she missed her birthday; an illogical thought in a time like this, but it was better than focusing on some of the other things she had overheard. "The wound..."

Ezra takes a deep breath. "Mara, you... you were shot yesterday."

Mara stares at her mother. The light globes in the room flicker slightly. "Quit joking, Mom."

Aeserast kneels next to the bed. "She is not joking, Mara."

Mara stares at him. She remembers him walking through the warped oval and then pulling the giant crescent-shaped blade out of thin air. "How did you appear like that?" she asks, her voice shaking.

"Mara, you need to calm down," Ezra says simply, as if that one single phrase holds all the answers.

Mara stares at her. "Calm down?" she repeats, incredulous. "Bryce attacked us. He didn't even recognize Justin. Dad's friend appears out of *nowhere* and you..." She shakes her head. "You had me break a rock and fed me a blue flower."

"Mara, I can explain – "

"Why didn't you tell me Dad was murdered?"

Mara interrupts, a tear slipping down her cheek.

Ezra's hand flies to her mouth as she stares at her daughter in shock. "You... heard us..."

"Yeah." Mara glares at her, an old anger rising to the surface. However, this time, it is directed at her mother. "Why would you keep something like that from me?"

Ezra's face crumples. Jonan steps up and rubs Ezra's shoulder, giving Mara a stern look. "Your mother was only trying to protect you, Mara."

"From what?" Mara cries, frustrated. "Who's trying to kill us?"

Everyone is now staring at Mara. "Do you want to tell her, or should I?" Aeserast asks.

"Oh, please do," Mara snaps, her temper flaring. The lights blink in and out. "Just like all of your other stories." She knows her words are hurting them, but she can't stop. She is nearing her patience level. If there is much more beating around the hedges of questions, she might punch something.

"Mara Ariela!" Ezra snaps, glaring at her daughter. *Oops,* Mara thinks, cringing. "Do not talk that way to him. Apologize right now."

Mara doesn't meet Aeserast's eyes. "I'm sorry."

"It is quite all right." He gives her a kind, forgiving smile. "You were always so fiery when younger, too. I can't believe how much you have grown."

Mara's cheeks flush a faint shade of pink. Despite always thinking of him as family, she couldn't help but be charmed by his ethereal beauty.

"As for your question... your father somehow incurred the wrath of the paro'ki, or tyrant, of Saheir." Aeserast says this with a straight face, not faltering once in his kind, gentle expression.

Mara's eyes narrow. "What is... Saheir?"

"A continent. It is one of five major ones on Blazhreia, this world," he explains simply. "We are currently in Veera, one of the easternmost cities to the capital."

Mara opens her mouth to berate him, but a flicker of silver catches her attention. She glances down at her lap, her breath catching in her throat. Silver lightning bolts dance across her hands.

Freaked out by the light show, she moves as if to rub off the sparks.

The flickering light globes shatter at once.

Aeserast grabs Mara's sparking wrists as the others duck and shield their heads. She sees him wince as the bolts shock his hand, and she tries to pull away. "No —"

A wave of calmness washes through her. She gulps one huge lungful of air after another as if she had been holding her breath underwater until now. All the tension and frustration from the conversation washes away and she feels lightheaded from the sudden change in her.

"Nnngh," she moans, slumping forward.

"Whoops, too much." Aeserast quickly catches her before she can fall off the bed and leans her against the headboard. She stares up at him, dazed and sleepy.

"Wha' did you do to me?" she slurs as he perches on the edge of the bed, now holding only one of her hands. A silvery spark flashes across her freed right hand, marking the end of the light show.

Jonan, Surana, and Ezra slowly sit up, glancing around the room. The only light comes from the door into the hallway. "I'll get more globes," Surana volunteers, carefully picking her way across the glass-covered floor.

Jonan and Ezra glance at Aeserast. Seeing that he had calmed Mara, Ezra begins clearing away some of the bigger pieces of glass as Jonan opens the curtains next to the bed, letting in some early morning light. They murmur to one another as they work together.

"Star..." Mara murmurs, leaning her forehead against his shoulder. She fights to keep her eyes open. *All he did was touch me... Maybe I'm dreaming. That would kind of make sense.*

"Hmm?"

"I'm sorry for yelling at you after Daddy's funeral." She closes her eyes, taking another deep breath. He smells of mist and darkness, along with something sweet.

Aeserast chuckles, reaching over and patting her head like he used to do when she was a little girl. "It is quite all right. Are you feeling better now?"

"Yeah... what were those little silver lightning bolts?" she asks, raising her right hand. Nothing abnormal about it.

"It's your Source," he explains simply. "Do you remember that story I told you about the chemical spill on another world?"

Feeling a little more awake, she sits upright, blinking. "Yeah," she finally says, watching her mother create a pile of broken glass. She racks her brain, thinking back to that story. She had been... nine. Aeserast had even drawn diagrams. That was when she had fallen in love with science. "Something about the biochemical affecting the people's genetic makeup..."

"Yes." He lets go of her hand and pats it gently,

shifting around so he is facing her. "The biochemical had altered the people and fused with their genetic code."

Mara mulls over this, frowning slightly. "Did the people ever manage to get it out of them?"

Aeserast chuckles. "No. They learned to use it. They call it Source."

Mara takes a deep breath as she connects the dots, feeling her anxiety slowly return. "That's crazy. I don't have anything like that." She clenches her jaw, staring hard at Aeserast. "What did you do to me? How did I suddenly get so calm?"

"I helped your body mass-produce serotonin and dopamine until you calmed down."

Mara giggles at this ridiculous response and suddenly stops, realizing that's exactly what it felt like. Suddenly alarmed, she looks down at her hands, seeing tiny silver sparks igniting over her hands.

"If this... Source stuff is real," she begins warily. Ezra pauses, glancing over in surprise at her daughter's words. "Why couldn't I use it earlier?"

Why didn't it work when Daddy died? This is what she really wants to ask. When she was younger, she had been like any other kid who had believed in magic. However, when her father had died, she had tried the 'healing spells' he had told her about. Not even the one that causes flowers to grow had worked. Ever since that day, she has been convinced both her father and Aeserast had lied to her, telling fictional stories to a little girl without explaining that they weren't actually real. She had rode on that anger, using it to mask her grief at losing her father.

Aeserast sighs and glances at Ezra. "I will leave this one to you," he says, standing up and helping with the shattered glass.

Ezra sits back, chewing on her lip. Mara recognizes her mother's habit and is instantly suspicious. Silver lightning bolts play across her hands. "What did you do, Mom?"

"Ah..." She stands up and carefully brushes off her hands, procrastinating. "Well... when we went to Earth, we needed to hide our Source, as Naiya could have tracked us that way. So we... blocked and repressed your Source."

Mara stares at the lightning bolts. *So... those stories were real,* she realizes, her vision blurring. *If it hadn't been blocked, maybe I could have saved him.*

Ezra lightly touches Mara's shoulder. A tear spills over and races down the girl's cheek. "Don't blame yourself," Ezra murmurs, hugging her. "You wouldn't have been able to do anything."

Mara wraps her arms around her, allowing the hot liquid to pour down her face in the safe, hidden confines of her mother's embrace. "I miss him," she breathes, barely audible.

"I miss him, too," Ezra admits, stroking Mara's hair. She closes her eyes, trying to keep her own tears at bay so she can remain strong for her daughter.

"Codi, Mom told you not to barge in!"

"Is she awake?!"

Mara's head whips around at the two new arrivals. The one who had spoken first is a girl with honey-blonde hair and sky-blue eyes. Her smooth features and thin frame look like Surana's, although she does not seem like an exact carbon copy of the older woman.

As soon as Mara sees the boy who had demanded to know if she is awake, her breath hitches. Despite the growth spurt, lack of baby fat, and a five-year timespan, she recognizes her adopted brother. His messy, wavy black hair is cut and styled nearly exactly the same way as five years ago, and his moss-green eyes expose undisguised concern. He had never been able to hide his emotions well.

"Codi?" Mara's voice breaks on the last syllable. "You're... alive."

His eyes shine with unshed tears. He vaults across the room, scooping up her hand and clenching it tightly. She could see on his face that he is scared to hug her as he repeatedly glances at her side. "You're the one I should be saying that to! You, Mom, and Star – "

"Aeserast," Aeserast corrects, sighing as he stands up. "That nickname is never going away."

" – You just appeared in the foyer." Codi clears his throat, disguising a sniffle. "Are-are you feeling all right?"

"I feel a little dizzy," she admits, smiling faintly. "I might be getting sick."

"Your body is adjusting to your Source," Aeserast explains just as Surana returns with four small egg-shaped glass pieces in her hands. As soon as she walks in, they instantly light up and expand. Aeserast leaps forward and catches two that tumble from her grasp.

A man and a woman dressed in plain clothes follow her, carrying brooms and dustpans. Jonan quickly moves out of the way, and they immediately begin cleaning up the shattered mess of glass on the floor.

Codi lightly tugs on her hand. "Come on, Mara," he urges, flashing a brilliant smile at her.

Ezra chuckles. "Wait just a moment, Codi." He lets go of Mara's hand, pouting slightly. Ezra picks up a stack of clothes off a chair and beckons to Mara. "Come into the bathroom, sweetie, so I can check your side."

Mara follows her mother into the little room perpendicular to the bed, her head still spinning. Ezra closes the door behind them and reaches for the shower knobs. "This one is hot water, and this one is cold. You have to turn both of them to get to the temperature you want."

"Mom..."

Ezra turns to Mara and lifts the shirt's edge, looking at the scar running over Mara's hipbone. She frets as if wishing she could do something about the white mark.

"Mom, why won't you look at me?"

Ezra's eyes are shining with tears. "I'm so sorry, sweetie. It shouldn't have scarred..."

Mara grabs her mother's hands and yanks them away from the blemish. "Mom, it's okay," she reassures her mother even though she still doesn't fully understand what is going on. "You know I've never cared about scars."

Ezra strokes Mara's hair and gives her a wavering smile. "I know." She kisses her daughter's forehead. "I'll let you get cleaned up. Here's some of my old clothes; Jonan and Surana never got rid of them, and they're about your size."

She escapes the bathroom before Mara could stop her. Sighing, Mara turns on the faucets, playing with the heat until it is at a comfortable temperature. She takes a quick shower, noticing only a slight ache in her side as she moves around.

Now dressed and clean, she steps out of the room. Codi turns around from talking with Ezra and grins. Mara's breath catches in her throat and she nearly bursts into tears again; she never thought she would see her brother again. She hugs him tightly.

He pats her back, chuckling. "Come on; we'll show you around."

"Kim," Ezra calls to the blonde girl, smirking at the reunited siblings.

The girl forces a tense smile. "Please, Aunt Ezra, I... really don't like being called that."

Ezra covers her mouth, her eyes wide. "Oh, I'm sorry. Could you keep an eye on them, Kimala?"

Kimala beams at Ezra. "Of course, Aunt Ezra!"

Codi grins and grabs Mara's hand, pulling her out the door. Mara chuckles at his eagerness. Kimala follows them down the hallway. They pass by fantastical pictures of odd-shaped flowers and colorful sceneries along the walls. Silver trees, red bushes, house-shaped brown flowers, and many more fill the spaces within the frames.

Kimala's mood shifts as soon as they are out of earshot from Mara's room. "Codi, slow down. She could still be injured," she says sharply, all sense of respect gone from her voice.

"Kimala, don't be mean," Codi tells the girl. To Mara, he not-so-subtly whispers, "She's upset because Mom called her Kim. She hates that nickname."

"It doesn't even sound like my name," Kimala grumbles, glaring out the bay windows along the hallway. "It's Kee-mala, not Kim-ala."

"Oh." Mara is still struggling to get used to the idea that all of her father's and Aeserast's stories were real, let alone trying to understand why Kimala wouldn't like that particular nickname. "Where are we going?"

"I say we go to the garden," Kimala suggests, her voice cold. "No Source globes to shatter there."

Source globe… that must be what those glowing orbs were. She stares at a flickering one as they continue down the long hallway.

Codi stops and turns towards her, looking as though someone had broken his favorite toy. He drops their linked hands. "I thought we could play a strategy game," he admits, shuffling his feet nervously. "No one else here likes them."

So he still does that adorable pout, Mara thinks, smiling. "Yeah, sure." Her smile slowly disappears as she stares at her brother. *He looks so happy here…* "Did you… run away?" Mara blurts without thinking, a twinge of jealousy spiking through her.

Codi stares at her, appalled. "And leave behind such a cute little sister? No! I was kidnapped."

Mara freezes, stunned at Codi's nonchalant way of saying it. He sulks down the hall, frowning slightly. "Who kidnapped you?" she finally asks, taking deep breaths to keep herself calm.

He waves his hand in the air, dismissing the question as she follows him. "It doesn't matter anymore; they died of some disease I carried over from Earth. The Brunets found me after that, so I've been here since then." Mara recognizes her mother's maiden name.

Codi pauses in front of a set of gilded wooden doors and grins at Mara. "You're going to love this," he murmurs, throwing the doors open with a dramatic push.

Kimala rolls her eyes. "Show-off." However, she

smiles a little bit, amused at Codi's exaggerated movements.

Mara stares in amazement at the huge library stretching to either side of the double doors. The ten-foot bookshelves touch the ceiling of the gym-sized room, every shelf completely stocked. Genre labels classify the different sections. Reading niches and tables are scattered throughout the maze while huge bay windows with window seats are spread along the three walls, allowing ample amounts of natural reading light.

"Amazing," Mara breathes. She wanders to the nearest window, staring down at a field that has sparring dummies and a little cluster of trees before reaching a short wall probably only three feet high. A town spreads out past the mansion's little wall, splayed almost haphazardly with alleyways and crisscrossing roads. A fifteen-foot wall towers in the distance, forming a circle around the town with the mansion at the epicenter. It looks to be about three miles away.

People in an assortment of odd clothes walk along the litter-free streets; some even wear different colored robes, leather vests, or glistening armor. Weapons – some bladed and others like Ezra's laser gun, only bigger – are carried openly. There is no sign of electrical poles, vehicles, or even streetlights – just hovering globes over some platforms sticking out from the sides of the oddly shaped buildings. Some of the houses have rounded rooms like hobbit homes or greenhouses sticking out from them; others have roofs with upturned edges to catch water for the gardens on them. A few houses have no corners other than the roof, made entirely of curves and soft edges.

It is definitely not Earth.

If what Dad and Aeserast had said when I was younger is true, then I guess being on a different world isn't too far fetched... A million questions flit through her mind. Do they have plumbing and sewer? What about electricity? Vehicles? What do they do for food – is everything fresh or do they package and can certain goods? She narrows her eyes, her mind on overdrive as she thinks of endless possibilities. Finally, she turns to Codi.

"What can you do with Source?" she asks. She glances at her hand, watching a silver lightning bolt dance across her fingers in response to her excitement. Maybe she can find a use for this new ability. If there is a possibility to use it in a field she likes, she will leap on the opportunity.

"Oh, all sorts of things. You can build bridges, make weapons, become a medic..."

Wrong question, Mara realizes, glancing at the bookshelves. "Is there a book about it?"

Codi nods excitedly. He rushes to a shelf and tugs down two books, handing them to her. They read *The History of Voyana on Blazhreia* and *The Basic Control Techniques of One's Source*. Before he could start rambling again, she sits down and opens the history book, assuming she should understand what it is before she can learn how to control it.

Kimala smirks at Codi. "Looks like your game is on hold."

Codi yanks a book off the shelf and collapses in the seat next to Mara. "Shut up, Kimala."

The blonde-haired girl storms away, snatching a book from a shelf and curling up in a windowsill.

After a while, the sun peers through the window

and lights up the table as Mara frowns slightly at the book. "Hey," she gets Codi's attention, pointing at a line. "This says the Voyana stuff can be used to split apart molecules and reassemble the atoms into other elements. Does this mean it reduces molecules back to their atomic state only to restructure them within only a few seconds as different elements off the periodic table?"

Codi nods. "It's a bit confusing if you're only just now learning it, but yeah, you got it."

Mara shakes her head. "Splitting them might be easy, but restructuring it with just Voyana sounds a bit... sci-fi-ish." She fights her urge to laugh. "I mean, what do you do, think your way into turning lead into gold?"

Codi shrugs. "There are some who study alchemy, but most just deal with relevant stuff, like the medical or scientific field."

Mara leans forward, fascinated. "Wait, is there a whole school dedicated to this magic stuff?"

Codi sighs. "I thought it was magic when I first got here, too, but it's not," he says. "It's – "

"A biochemical, I know. It just seems so... magic-like." Mara flips back to the first chapter. *The history sounds pretty similar to Aeserast's and Dad's stories. I guess they were trying to teach us of this world in a subtle, roundabout way.*

Codi rests his chin on his hand. "Voyana is an energy supply to the world. It's used in place of other things, like gasoline. Better?"

Not really... Mara thinks to herself.

Kimala, who had been studying in the sun with a medical book, huffs and repositions her long legs. "Voyana means energy, Mara, not magic," she explains matter-of-factly. "It's a multi-function biochemical energy source that can be used for a multitude of things. For example, medics use it to look at internal wounds and clear out debris without ever making an incision. Being a microscopic atomic particle, it can pass through nearly any material, so all of the debris is broken down and then restructured to be helpful instead of harmful to the body. The rest is filtered out through the pores before clumping into a disposable solid."

Mara tilts her head to the side, contemplating. "So... what about me?" she asks, thinking of her scar. "Why does it look like I got stabbed?"

Kimala stares out the window. "There were... complications. There's an illegal material called neivir commonly used among assassins and murderers of other countries. The only way to remove it is by pulling out the shards by hand, which is dangerous because the neivir can slice through the tools like butter."

So that's what they had been talking about, Mara realizes, rubbing her chin thoughtfully. *Dad had been shot with a similar bullet...*

Codi's head pops up. "Wait, you understood that?"

"Yeah." The history book snaps shut and Mara rests her long fingers on the cover. "It's some advanced invasive biochemical from another world that some radiated species decided to dump here." She tosses the book at Codi and he catches it. "Of course I would understand jargon like that."

"If you want something harder, try *Alkina's History of Science,*" Kimala murmurs absently, resuming her studying. "You'll probably need the Earthling-to-Xharos language dictionary, though. That will be five rows down, to the left along the wall between the two bay windows in a group reading area."

"Thanks," Mara says, surprised at how helpful Kimala has been this afternoon despite her cold attitude towards Mara.

"That's super-hard stuff!" Codi hisses.

Kimala shrugs, twirling her honey-colored hair around her finger. "She didn't grow up here, so she needs a crash-course. Simple as that." She snaps the book closed and stands up, giving Mara a sickeningly sweet smile. "Have fun, Earthling."

Mara watches the girl sashay out of the library. She smiles slightly and stands up.

"You're not seriously going to take her suggestion, are you?" Codi asks, incredulous. "She's trying to make a fool out of you."

"Oh, I know." Mara goes to the history section and pulls down the 'recommended' book. She smirks at Codi. "But imagine her face if I *don't* make a fool out of myself."

Mara reads to her heart's content, eager to learn anything she can about this new world. She does not want to be caught unaware by her cousin's spontaneous quizzes, such as what the social ranking system is or how Voyana was created; anyway, it is too fun seeing Kimala's stunned face whenever Mara is able to answer the girl's questions correctly.

Surana insists on making custom clothes for Ezra and Mara. Unsure how the process went, Mara just tells her aunt what she likes – non-binding clothes, earthen tones, nothing flashy, fully practical, deep pockets – and left it at that. She ends up with several different types of outfits, but Mara's favorites are the snug yet non-binding sets that she can train in.

Mara likes the reading niches in the windows, enjoying the view and the sunlight as she scribbles away in the little notebook her mother had given her. However, after she finds the garden maze made out of lattice walls and ceilings, she lounges outside and plays strategy games with Codi in the dappled sunlight as Aeserast sits nearby and sips on his tea. As soon as Ezra permits it, Mara helps Codi with his self-defense in the mornings; he had gotten rusty after not having a proper sparring partner. He fumbles through the moves, finally having to work for a win with her. Mara is happy to just have her brother back again and thoroughly enjoys reconnecting with him over their old habits.

Mara is stunned to learn Jonan, Surana, and Ezra are tein'fu, the equivalence of a duke or duchess in this world. Mara, Codi, and Kimala are tein'stra, or the children of that rank. She is shocked yet again when she finds out her mother had been a high-ranked medic and the assistant of the head of the medical facility in the capital of this continent, Quasala, and that she had been considered one of the best on all of Blazhreia. The lack of formality baffles Mara; people would greet Ezra like an old friend, not paying any heed to her old title as medic advisor or as tein'fu.

Mara feels as if she is learning of a side of her mother that she never would have known about if they had not come back to Blazhreia.

CHAPTER 3
CONTROL

Over a week passes by, and Mara grows accustomed to her new life. On the first of the next month, Tora, she joins her recently reunited family in the garden for the 'New Year's Feast,' a luncheon on the first of the new year - the dead of summer, oddly enough. The wooden lattice-style awning, archways, and walls create an exquisite maze out of the private garden in the rear field of the mansion. Its various 'sections' offer a perfect opportunity for one to get lost in the beauty of the tamed plants. Vines coat the awnings and thread their way through the lattice. The fragrant blue, purple, yellow, and red flowers splash the garden with color.

A long table made out of dark wood that could sit twelve is nestled within the heart of the garden. A lavish array of fruits, vegetables, meats, and cheeses decorate the surface in swirling patterns and designs. The chairs have plush cushions on them and the backrests curve slightly to provide a more comfortable seated position.

Mara sits down with the others, glancing around the table. She still finds it funny that her brother wants to be a guard, and she can't see Kimala being a medic with her bedside manners.

"Where's Star?" Mara asks, curious. She knows he isn't actually family, but he had been around these past few days answering any questions she had about the books she has been reading; he seemed to have everything memorized to the letter. She wanted to ask him a bit more about Cerlail Academy and what is taught there.

Ezra chuckles at Mara's innocent-sounding question as the Brunet family stare at her. "He had to run some errands. He will be back soon, don't worry."

"Good," Mara grumbles as everyone dishes out what they want from the wide array in front of them. She follows suit.

"When is your birthday?" Surana asks, smiling kindly as she starts the small talk.

"It's – " Mara pauses, her mind blanking. *Ah, shoot. Codi helped me convert it earlier. What is this month called again?* She could already see Kimala smiling in satisfaction.

"The twenty-seventh of Tora," Ezra chimes in, smiling reassuringly at Mara. "She will be turning sixteen, so it will be a big year."

Mara pales. She hopes her mother does not want her to wear a dress this year.

Silverware clatters onto the table as Surana, Jonan, and Kimala gape at Mara. "No way," Kimala breathes, appalled. "I share a birthday with her?"

Mara glances at her, surprised at the weird coincidence.

"But you were pregnant several weeks after me," Surana says quietly, her eyes wide.

"Oh, what shall we do…" Jonan murmurs, already trying to work out some problem. "Two in the same night…"

Codi focuses on his food, trying to remain inconspicuous.

"Don't worry about me," Mara quickly cuts in, finally regaining her composure after her mother's statement. "I don't like big events, so Kimala can have her extravagant party while I do my thing."

"No, Mara," Ezra states firmly. "You are celebrating this year. On Blazhreia, sixteen is considered an adult and is cause for celebration."

Mara recognizes that tone in her mother's voice. She stares at her plate and sinks in her chair. "Yes, ma'am," she mumbles reluctantly. "Just... no gifts."

Ezra chuckles and Codi smiles slightly as the other three merely continue staring at Mara as if she had just sprouted horns. "No gifts?" Kimala mutters. "Who wouldn't want gifts?"

Mara ignores her. *I guess it's like having my eighteenth birthday come two years earlier.* She frowns slightly, an unpleasant thought coming to mind. "What's the legal drinking age here?"

Kimala, Surana, and Jonan give her matching quizzical looks, not recognizing the term. Ezra chuckles. "When you turn sixteen, you are allowed your first alcoholic beverage, so long as it is light like ale."

Mara wrinkles her nose in an almost cute look of disgust. "So there will be alcohol."

"You do not have to drink if you don't want to," Ezra reassures her.

Kimala's eyes widen. "Why wouldn't you? It is tradition to have a drink on your sixteenth birthday." She smiles encouragingly at Mara.

So you want to play that way? Mara thinks, returning the smile. *You will lose.*

Ezra opens her mouth to speak, but then notices Mara's small smile. She narrows her eyes, wondering what her daughter is up to.

"I do not believe in intoxication; it sets one up to be taken advantage of." Mara stares straight at Kimala, her eyes glinting. "I also do not appreciate someone trying to convince me otherwise just because it is traditional."

Kimala shrugs. Mara can tell she is rattled, but she doesn't show it as she says almost flippantly, "Do whatever you want." She sits back, daintily plucking a piece of cheese off her plate with a little stick and popping it into her mouth.

She's like Wendy, Mara realizes, thinking back to her last semester at high school before summer had started. The pompous cheerleader had made straight A's and thought she was the smartest, most important person in the world. Mara has to fight her smirk, remembering what her constant rebuttals had done to the poor popular girl. Kimala will be fun to tease.

Ezra restrains her chuckle, knowing what the situation between the two girls is now. She smiles at Surana, bragging, "Mara has always acted older than her age. She was a year ahead in school and studied Academy-level textbooks in her spare time. As a hobby, she stayed up to date on everything in the scientific field on Earth. I am sure she won't have much trouble adjusting to Blazhreia's and Alkina's way of thinking."

Surana's usual kind smile twitches. Surprisingly, she responds, "They might get along, then. Kimala is a prodigy in the medical field; once she attends Cerlail Academy, she will be testing to go straight into interning with a field medic. She has been studying her whole life, preparing herself for complete success in the medical field." Kimala straightens, and Mara could see the girl mentally preening her ego-feathers.

Jonan sighs and glances at Codi. "Would you like to join me in the office, Codi? I would like to speak with you a bit about the upcoming trip."

Codi quickly nods, eager to get out of the tension-filled garden.

< * >

Mara takes a deep breath, centering her mind and body as the early morning rays kiss her skin. Her sleeveless black top frees her arms for easy movements while the black slacks end right below her knee, allowing for quick kicks and low crouches. Her toes sink into the soft ankle-high grass. Her ponytail sways with each smooth glide and turn.

I wonder if Sta – Aeserast would teach me how to control these weird sparks since he seems to know a lot about it, she wonders, allowing her thoughts to drift to what had happened that morning. She has been having a lot of nasty dreams lately, and just that morning, she had woken up in a cold sweat with the little lightning bolts flickering around her. All the Source globes had shattered again for the fifth time since she had arrived in Veera almost three weeks ago.

She exhales slowly as her arm moves around and her leg shifts positions. She clears her mind, performing the t'ai chi ch'uan martial art movements in a slow, therapeutic rhythm.

She flows from one pattern to the next, gliding through the grass like an exotic dancer. Her breathing parallels her movements, her mind synchronizing with the stable, calming pattern. She closes her eyes as she touches the sun's rays and twists in the warm breeze's arms.

She hears the soft rustle of the grass as two people approach her. Opening her eyes, she turns around. Aeserast's expression is filled with awe and amazement, his light hair pulled back with hairpins. His plain clothes compliment his fair features.

Slinking behind him, a young man looking the same age as Aeserast appraises her from head-to-toe, smirking suggestively. His gold eyes have vertical pupils like a cat, and two oddly shaped ears poke out from his red-streaked spiky black hair, reminding her of a lynx. She has the insane urge to touch one of his ears to see if it is real but squashes it instantly. Freckles sprinkle across his face, somehow reminding Mara even more of a feline. He is dressed in a button-up shirt where half is red and the other half is black, the first three buttons undone and exposing a key hanging by a black string around his neck. His black pants look snug yet comfy, allowing for quick movements.

Mara fights not to stare. *I want to duel him,* she catches herself thinking, and immediately has to redirect her thoughts before her cheeks turn red. Why does she always think that when she sees a cute guy?!

"Good morning, Mara," Aeserast greets her, smiling as he leans in and gives her a quick hug.

The hug surprises her, but she complies. She had always hugged him in the past, after all. "Good morning, Aeserast."

Aeserast's eyes glint. "So you *do* know my name," he says, smiling slightly.

"Of course I do." She examines the young man, taking note of his fluid movements. She holds out her hand. "I'm – "

He gives her a wicked grin and bows over her hand, kissing the back lightly. "Tein'stra Mara Danarko," he purrs, a hint of respect and playful teasing in his voice as he straightens, still holding her hand. "A pleasure to make your acquaintance."

Mara's cheeks turn a soft pink as she yanks back her hand. She still doesn't quite know what to do with the information that she is nobility. Wondering if it is normal for him to do that, she glances at Aeserast. She doesn't want to flip his friend in case it is actually the norm; he did, after all, use the honorific title on her.

"I told you not to do that, Shaniel." Aeserast shakes his head, sighing heavily and rubbing his temple. "Mara, do not be afraid to take action against this man if he makes you uncomfortable."

"Whaaat?" Shaniel grins, exposing sharp canines. He winks at Mara. "She's a noble, so I have to greet her properly."

Mara steadies her breathing. "Please do not do it again," she requests, glancing at Aeserast. "Were you looking for me?"

He nods. "Ezra said you are wanting to learn how to control your Source. Do you have any questions?"

A fiery light sparks in Shaniel's eyes. He claps his hands together, leaning forward excitedly. "Ooh, how much do you know?"

Mara frowns at him. She doesn't quite understand why he is so excited. "I've only read about it so far. I haven't put any theories into practice."

"Aww, so cute!" he exclaims.

He vanishes.

Mara glances around, startled. An arm drapes over her shoulders just as a husky voice murmurs next to her ear, "Can I teach her, Aeserast?"

Unsettled by his proximity, Mara reflexively grabs the arm and yanks Shaniel over her shoulder. His arm twists in her grip as he flips around, barely managing to land on his toes. A single hand on the ground helps him balance as he stares into Mara's eyes, only centimeters away.

His grin widens, a wild look barely contained in his gaze. "You'll be fun."

Mara's breath catches, excitement building in her. She doesn't know how, but he had seen through her move. Her lips quirk up as she wonders if she can learn anything from this young man. "You're interesting."

"You're the interesting one," Shaniel breathes, smirking.

Aeserast sighs. "Do not kill one another. I will be in the garden. Join me when you're done with your scuffle."

Mara twists the arm she is still holding. Shaniel effortlessly flows with the movement, grabbing her arm and dragging her in closer. He strikes out, flat-palmed, towards her chest.

She easily deflects the wide-open move, raising an eyebrow at him. *You're better than that,* she challenges silently, bringing her knee up. Being so close-ranged, she should be able to get in a hit —

He sidesteps it and leans in, his nose brushing her ear as he whispers, "I know *you're* better than that."

Mara's breath stops. She has never liked anyone getting so close. She pulls her arm back for a quick punch to his side; he definitely won't be able to dodge this one, not with his other arm still tightly clutching Mara's.

He stops it with his hand just as his lips press against hers.

Her knee flies upwards, aiming between his legs. Surprised, Shaniel jumps out of the way. "Wha – "

Crunch.

Shaniel howls, clutching his nose. Quivering with embarrassment and anger, Mara glares at him, her cheeks bright red. Her fingers remain clenched in a tight fist, silver sparks flitting over her as she fights to reign in her emotions.

She stalks to the private garden, deducing she had inflicted enough damage. She hopes his nose heals crooked. She finds a calm Aeserast sipping delicately at a cup of bluish-purple tea in the first niche of the garden, extra cups and saucers stacked neatly next to the flower-printed teapot.

Shaniel storms in after her, pointing at his crooked, bloody nose. "Bloody Mavi, Aeserast, she *broke it!*"

"That's what you get for trying to kiss every cute person who talks to you," he responds smoothly.

My first... to a playboy! she mourns, collapsing into one of the chairs and slumping until her head is against the back of the seat. She covers her face with her hands.

"Touch her and I am certain you will get more than just a broken nose," Aeserast warns, and Mara's eyes fly open to see the young man leaning towards her. She glares at Shaniel just as one of the silver bolts zipping around her crackles ominously. Surprisingly, the blood on his face is gone, although his nose is still crooked.

Shaniel's eyes widen as he quickly backs up. "Whoa, easy there. That couldn't have been your first, right?" He laughs awkwardly, trying to lighten the mood. His face pales when Mara's murderous look doesn't change. "It was. Carc'ra. I apologize."

At his tilted ears and wide eyes, Mara cannot help but be reminded of a cute cat being chastised. "Some moral code you have there," she grumbles, wrapping her arms around her legs.

"Actually, yes." He perks up, hopping into a chair and perching in it cross-legged. He holds up his hand and raises his fingers as he ticks off his rules. "I don't mess with intoxicated individuals. I don't get involved with couples or grievers. I don't take first kisses unless given permission. I don't do anything with my students, and I stay away from groups."

He winks and sticks out his tongue, looking ridiculously adorable.

"Ah." Shaniel slaps his fist against his palm. He puffs out his chest as if proud with what he is about to say. "I also have nothing to do with anyone considered a minor."

Aeserast and Mara stare at him with deadpan looks.

Shaniel glances between them, confused. "What?"

"Mara is fifteen," Aeserast points out bluntly, sipping his tea.

Shaniel's face turns so white even his freckles pale. He clutches his hair, breathing out slowly. "Oh, no... Ezra will kill me. I swear, Mara, I thought you were seventeen or eighteen... Please, please, *please* don't tell your mother. She will gut me." He closes his eyes. "I deserve it, though... fifteen. What have I done?"

Mara stares at him, baffled. What happened to the flirty playboy from just a moment ago?

Aeserast finishes his tea and sets the cup down. "He takes his rules very seriously," he explains to Mara softly as he stands up and moves behind Mara's chair. "Shaniel, her sixteenth birthday is this month, so Ezra will not kill you."

Shaniel peeks out from between his fingers and watches as Aeserast gently sets his hands on Mara's shoulders. "Wait, you let him touch you?" he asks, jealous.

"He's not assaulting me," she snaps back. As Aeserast rubs circles into her tense shoulder muscles, she feels herself calming down. "You're doing that weird thing again," she says in a mellow voice, her neck relaxing underneath his fingers. "I was controlling it on my own..."

Aeserast chuckles as her eyes close. "Not quite."

Ezra walks around the corner with a book tucked under her arm. Her eyes widen at the sight of Shaniel pouting in a chair and Aeserast kneading Mara's shoulders. "What happened here?" Ezra asks, concerned.

The two men glance her way. "Mara broke my nose," Shaniel whines, pointing at the crooked feature. Mara shoots a half-disinterested, half-angry glare at him.

Ezra glances warily at Shaniel. "Knowing you, you probably deserved it." She approaches him and raises her hand near his nose; it glows a soft butterscotch color. When she pulls away, his nose is straight.

Mara stares at Shaniel's nose, wishing it had stayed broken just a little while longer. She is still getting used to seeing her mother use Source, but after watching her heal a broken wrist just the other day, she figures there are weirder things one could do with the strange energy.

Ezra hands the book to Mara, and the teenager sees it is her book on controlling Source. She immediately opens it to where she had left off and tunes out the others as Aeserast returns to his chair.

"Mind if I join you?" Ezra asks, gesturing to the seat next to him.

"Of course not." Aeserast lifts the teapot. "Tea, anyone?"

Several hours pass by underneath the garden canopy. Mara squints at the blue sky through the leaves twining in the lattice above her, guessing it is around lunchtime by the position of the sun. Straightening in the chair as she closes her book, she catches sight of Aeserast and Ezra murmuring to one another in two small chairs at the other end of the small 'room' created by the lattice walls.

Mara's stomach rumbles as she stretches.

Shaniel skips into the little garden cove, carrying a tray covered with food. "I snatched some lunch," Shaniel says cheerily, setting the tray down on the little table before plopping in a chair.

Mara stares at the food warily, wondering if he did anything to it.

Aeserast sighs heavily, rubbing his forehead. "Did you steal from the kitchens again?" Shaniel grins sheepishly at him.

Mara snatches a cracker and a square piece of cheese without looking at the cat-eared man.

Ezra stands up, gesturing to Shaniel to follow her. "Shaniel, I would like to speak with you inside." Her serious expression spoke trouble for the flirty cat-eared man.

Sighing, Shaniel rises to his feet and reluctantly follows her. "You're gonna lecture me, aren't you? Got your laugh, now I'm in trouble…" he grumbles, disappearing into the garden's maze as he and Ezra head back to the mansion.

"How are your studies?" Aeserast asks with a small smile on his lips, distracting Mara.

Mara shrugs. "Good. Alkinian history before Voyana is a lot easier to digest. It's a pity their advancement had to stop so abruptly just because that biochemical destroyed it." She pauses, thinking about last night. She had taken the Alkinian book Kimala had recommended to her room and fell asleep while reading it. "Voyana means energy, and Source is someone's personal energy, correct?"

Aeserast nods as he walks over to a Source globe stand. He lifts the softly glowing orb out of its floating position and sits across from her, holding the globe in the palm of his hand. It slowly shrinks to reveal a piece of frosted glass shaped like a duck egg.

"This is what an inactive Source globe looks like," he explains. "Only someone who has Source can cause it to glow."

The glass duck egg suddenly glows and expands into a spherical orb the size of Aeserast's palm.

Mara stares at the orb. She examines it from as many angles as she could. It is definitely not static electricity or heat-sensitive, but it is not big enough to hold batteries, either. Curious, she asks, "How did you do that?"

Aeserast's brows twitch together, and the fist-sized globe shrinks, going dark. "I focused my Source – the energy I was born with – towards the globe. It reacts to even the smallest bit of energy, but the more it receives, the larger and brighter it will become."

Mara tilts her head to the side as she recollects all she had learned on Source so far. "So because you were chemically altered by the biochemical, you can now control the biochemical, correct?"

Aeserast chuckles. "Yes. Here." He takes her hand and presses the smooth glass egg into it. It lights up before it even touches her skin, and within a handful of seconds, it is bigger than her palm.

"Wh-what did I do?" Mara asks, uncertain. The globe pulses and strains to grow even more. A black hairline fracture appears, accompanied by a sharp noise sounding like superheated ice crackling.

"Mara, look at me." Mara focuses on Aeserast's calm expression. She can tell he had expected the orb to do this. "You need to figure out what is causing your anxiety. Your Source and emotions are very closely related; once one is out of control, so is the other. Think of it like a chain reaction. Try some of your meditation techniques."

"What exactly do I need to do?" Mara asks, already regulating her breathing.

An ominous crack emanates from the globe.

Aeserast sighs. "What is bothering you?"

A black line appears just underneath the surface of the globe. She stares at the fragile orb in her hand. "How do I keep it from breaking?" Mara murmurs, a small frown creasing her brow. *How is it even doing this? Is it those little lightning bolts?* She squints at the orb; sure enough, little silver sparks are racing across the glowing off-white surface.

"Focus, Mara. Pinpoint where the problem is," he reiterates, guiding Mara in a calm voice.

Mara closes her eyes and focuses inwards. She settles her racing thoughts, shoving them into their respective categories. Years of training and meditation – both with her father and through all of her defense classes – had taught her this level of control over her mind.

Somewhere in the deep, deep recesses of her mind, she feels an odd pressure and discovers silver sparks smothering a core of black, writhing tendrils. Mara takes a deep breath, calming her nerves. Both of the colors settle down.

Mara frowns, trying to figure out what this blob is. *Is this Source? How am I supposed to control it?* she thinks to herself, suddenly uneasy. The silver sparks and black tendrils strike against one another in response to her sudden distress.

An irrational, volatile thought crosses through her mind. *Maybe… maybe they're right. Maybe it* is *reacting to my emotions.*

The orb explodes.

Glass flies past her face, grazing her cheek. The memory of a broken window and men ransacking the house flashes through her mind almost too fast for her to comprehend. She doesn't remember anyone breaking into their home, though; it is as if the memory is not her own.

Aeserast wraps his fingers around Mara's wrists, turning her cut palms toward him. Calmness seeps into her as he delicately plucks the glowing glass shards out of her hand. "Are you all right?"

"I-I think so," she whispers. He glances up, and his purple eyes trap her in his gaze. She swallows, trying to ignore their proximity. "What just happened?"

Aeserast's eyes crinkle slightly as he smiles, and he suddenly looks older than twenty. "You are learning how to control the power you were born with."

Mara takes a deep breath, knowing he is helping her regulate her churning emotions. "What if I can't control it?"

He holds both of her hands, covering the wounds. His warm fingers glow a soft lavender. When he pulls away, the minor scratches are completely healed while the bigger cuts have stopped bleeding. His smile is soft and trusting.

"You are a Danarko," he says simply, waving his hand over the orb. A nearly transparent purple mist slowly collects the shattered fragments and coalesces them into the small egg-shaped glass. "You will figure it out."

He sets the fixed Source globe on her healed palm. It glows brightly.

< * >

Mara easily slips into a routine at the mansion. In the mornings, she trains with Codi; occasionally, Shaniel will pop in and comment on their form, giving them tips. Mara notices he is overly cautious around her as if afraid she will punch him and cannot help but antagonize him a bit by throwing some wild punches or kicks his way which more often than not results in her flat on her back, glaring up at her superior.

Before or during lunch, she will go a round or two of a strategy game with either Codi or Shaniel – and with this one, she more often than not metaphorically puts *them* on their backs.

Her afternoons are dedicated to studying or working on Aeserast's exercises; she has finally stopped shattering the orb every single time she holds it, but she is having trouble keeping it a stable size.

About two weeks after she had started training with Aeserast, Mara sits cross-legged with a glowing, distorted orb in her hand that fluctuates from one size to another. A soft breeze blows her hair into her face, distracting her slightly. She glances at her nicely dressed companion as she tucks the stray locks behind her ear.

Aeserast reaches into thin air, his hand momentarily disappearing in a wave of distorted space. When he pulls it back, he holds a book. Amazed, Mara gapes, the globe dimming temporarily before shattering in her hand again. This time, though, it does not cut her.

"How did you do that?" she asks as he waves his hand without looking up. The faint purple mist pieces together the orb again.

"Teleportation hole," he murmurs almost absently, picking up the orb. "It can be used to relocate oneself, such as how we went from Earth to Blazhreia, or as a way of retrieving things if you know exactly where the item is and what it looks like."

Teleportation hole, she repeats in her mind, frowning slightly. *That is a long phrase. Teleporting hole... no. Porting hole?* "Portal," she whispers as he deposits the egg in her hand. Before it even strikes her palm, it is bigger than a softball.

"Yes." He smiles at her. "Teleportation hole is the official name of portals, although over the centuries, slang has made it shorter and shorter."

"Next they'll just be calling them holes or ports," Mara jokes lightly, refocusing on the orb. She thinks of the writhing black ball surrounded by the silver sparks and takes several deep breaths. In her mind, the ball stops thrashing as much. Peeking at the orb, she fights to keep from jumping in joy.

The orb is finally a stable size; still much bigger than all of the other orbs, but at least it didn't break. Only two thin black cracks run just underneath the surface.

Aeserast glances over and nods. "Good. Try to reduce the size."

"... I did."

Frowning, Aeserast closes the book and leans forward. "Mara, you are still putting out a lot. You need to pull it in."

Mara stares at him quizzically, careful to keep her emotions in check since she is still holding the orb. "That's what I did."

"Your Source did recede somewhat, but..." Suddenly, his eyes widen. He cups Mara's face with his hands, staring into her eyes. She feels an odd sensation of something at the edge of her mind, foreign and unfamiliar. Startled, Mara tries to pull away from him, but he does not let her go.

The Source globe between them explodes.

Wincing, Aeserast drops his hands to pick at his now tattered silky shirt. Mara clenches her jaw as she carefully pulls out the piece of glass lodged deep in her palm.

"What was that about?" Mara asks, still a little rattled at how close he had gotten.

Aeserast lifts the hem of his shirt to expose small shards of glass lodged in a well-toned abdomen. Taking a deep breath, he pulls them out. A bluish-purple liquid seeps from the wounds. "I thought your eyes had changed colors."

"That's the worst lie ever," Mara says flatly as he does his best to heal himself. Apparently, he is only good at very minor healing 'spells,' as the bigger cuts remain.

Aeserast grits his teeth as he finishes healing himself the best he can. "It's not a lie, Mara. It happens to individuals with high amounts of Source. For example, my eyes sometimes turn a darker or lighter shade of purple." He notices her guarded expression, and his eyes widen. "Ah. I would never do anything like that, Mara; you are like a niece to me."

"Good," she mutters, "because you're like my uncle. Why are your eyes purple, anyway?"

He chuckles. "It is because of my Quanaret blood – fey blood. Their Source permeates their physical form, so their body may take on the hue of their Source. I'm only part Quanaret, though, so it is just my hair and eyes. My Alkinian blood helps regulate the Source distribution."

"Mine's silver…" *and black*, she finishes, wondering if she should say that. She has only ever seen one working physically, though. *Maybe the other one is broken*, she tries to theorize and almost laughs at the thought. "An Alkinian is an elf, right?" she asks, curious. She had read the physical description of them just last night.

Aeserast gives her an odd look. "Has Ezra not told you yet, Mara?" She tilts her head to the side quizzically. "You're Alkinian."

She immediately touches her ears. They are long, but definitely not pointed. "Are you sure?"

He shakes his head. "When an elf fully matures, their ears grow pointed. Typically, this is between eighteen and twenty-four years old. Elves live for several hundred years, so this gap is nothing to them."

Mara fingers the tip of her ear, feeling the round curve that would someday turn into a point. She shakes her head. "Then what about my sixteenth birthday? What's that about?"

Aeserast smirks. "That has been around in some form or another for centuries. The Blazhreians – especially those from Garnesh – believe a child is an adult once they turn sixteen. Many children go into their profession and begin training at this age, giving them ample time to work up the ranks. Even Cerlail Academy, the hub of Source research and education, has adopted this practice. You must be sixteen to attend."

"It's pretty new, right?" she asks. Codi had been gushing over the Academy's smooth operation despite being relatively young when compared to other practices.

Aeserast nods. "Just a few years older than you, in fact. Your father designed the infrastructure it is built around. He thought the Highlord's robes were so amazing he wanted other mages, sorcerers, and medics to wear them, too," Aeserast adds, grinning.

Mara gasps. "Dad?" Her head spins.

CHAPTER 4
THE BIRTHDAY PARTY

Not even a moment later, Ezra enters their little secluded area. She bites her lip slightly as she glances between Mara and Aeserast as if afraid she is interrupting them. "How is it going?"

"Mom, did Dad really build Cerlail Academy?" Mara demands, turning towards her mother.

Aeserast chuckles. "Perfect timing; Mara shattered the Source globe again. Do you mind checking our injuries?"

Eyes widening, Ezra hurries over. A soft butterscotch-colored mist cascades from her fingers and envelops their injuries, taking away both the pain and the cuts. "You need to be more careful," she murmurs halfheartedly, knowing Mara would most likely do it again.

Mara smiles sheepishly. "Sorry, Mom. I'm trying."

Ezra sighs, glancing at Aeserast. "How is she doing with the exercises?"

Aeserast's lips tilt upwards. "She is improving. It's slow work since she is only learning of it now, but hopefully by her sixteenth birthday, she will have some basic control over it."

"I apologize for asking you to tutor her for so long." Ezra pats Mara's hands, her smile wavering. "I just worry about her."

Aeserast pats Ezra's shoulder reassuringly. "You know it is not a problem; even Timian would help out if he could. You're our friend, Ezra, which makes

Mara just as important to us as she is to you."

Mara glances between the lavender-haired fey-elf and her mother, a bit confused on why she would be important to more than just Aeserast and Ezra. "So how do you know each other?"

"We met when your father and I traveled to the capital for the first time," Ezra says, smirking. "We asked Aeserast and Timian to be your guardians if anything ever happened to us."

Mara frowns slightly, finally sitting up. "Wait, Aeserast is my guardian? Like... a godfather or something?"

Ezra chuckles. "Yes. He has been a good friend of your father and I for... decades, really."

Mara stares at Aeserast. *Well, that explains why he was around so much.* "How come you haven't aged?"

Aeserast smiles almost mischievously. "I am a Highlord, Mara."

Mara glances at her mother, confused.

"They are..." Ezra chews on her lip, struggling to explain. "To an extent, they are the police of all the realms. Anything involving multiple realms or the travel between realms has to be passed through the Highlord Council."

"I am the Creation'Lord, but most call me the Dream'Lord since I am located in Carni, the corridor realm between all other realms," Aeserast explains. "My duties comprise of watching the Tower of Discord and monitoring Carni as a whole, as well as assisting anyone who needs my abilities as an instructor or sorcerer."

"Oh, that's neat." Mara doesn't fully understand, but by what she had managed to gather from that explanation, his job sounds pretty interesting. She glances around. "Shaniel isn't a Highlord, right? What is he, anyway?"

"He *is* a Highlord," Aeserast chuckles. "As for his species, he is a laig'hius, a highly impressionable creature. His ancestors had taken the forms of a feline and a bipedal. However, his Alkinian and Blazhreian blood dilutes him enough to where he can only take on a bipedal form."

She takes a deep breath, processing the information slowly. *That would explain the cat ears and eyes, as well as the way he moves,* Mara thinks, staring at the shattered globe. "I keep messing up…"

Aeserast shrugs, fixing the globe yet again. "Are you learning from it?" Mara nods. "Then that is all that matters."

Mara gazes at the Source globe, wondering if she could go to Cerlail Academy after she turns sixteen. It would be neat if the academy from her father's and Aeserast's stories is Cerlail Academy. She slightly smiles to herself. *I wonder what else Daddy has done.*

"I actually need you to come with me, Mara," Ezra requests, standing up again. "Surana needs you to try on the dress."

Mara sighs. The day to torture her has arrived.

They wander through the mansion. Curious, Mara glances around as they pass by several casually-dressed servants preparing the mansion for the festivities later that month. The celebrations are not going to be too lavish or over-the-top, which makes her feel a little bit better about the event.

They step into a large, homely room filled with fabric rolls, thread, and other crafting essentials. Surana rests in a light blue loveseat by the window, adding a few final touches on a blue, green, and brown dress.

Kimala stands off to the side, fiddling with an ornate rectangular box a little bigger and thicker than a book. She is in a pleated crème skirt and a silky blue blouse that matches her eyes. Mara glances disinterestedly at the pretty girl who has tried several times these past few weeks to humiliate Mara during her studies – and failing.

Surana glances up and beams at Mara and Ezra. "Ah, you made it just in time."

"Hello, Surana." Ezra leans over and gives the woman a hug and a peck on the cheek.

Surana shakes out the beautiful earthen-toned dress. "Mara, could you try this on?"

Mara flicks her gaze to the dress and then to the door. Ezra subtly shifts to block her exit route, giving her daughter a knowing look.

Mara glances at her hands in time to see a silver bolt skitter across her knuckles. "I... I won't hurt you with this, will I?" Mara raises her hand, showing them the silvery sparks.

Surana's lips stretch into a reassuring smile. "Do not worry about me, Mara. I have already grown accustomed to your Source." She beckons Mara towards her. "Come; we need to make sure the size is correct."

Mara nods, although she doesn't quite understand what the woman meant about her Source. She hesitates outside the screened changing area.

Ezra takes the dress from Surana and pushes Mara behind it. "You can't avoid this one, Mara."

Mara sighs. She knows her mother is secretly ecstatic that she will be wearing a dress; ever since she was little, Ezra had found any opportunity she could to put her daughter into something frilly. One time, she had even threatened to replace all her clothes with dresses and skirts if Mara cut her hair too short. Thinking her mother was joking, she had chopped off her hair by herself one day only to scream the next morning to find all of her clothes had been replaced in her closet. She now kept her hair at shoulder-length as a compromise between them.

It should be all right just this once, she thinks as her mother laces the back of the dress. *I'll just pretend it's Mom's birthday, instead.*

Mara steps out in the exquisitely embroidered sweetheart A-line dress. Bright blue stones are sewn like flowers into the softly pleated green and brown skirt and short poufy blue sleeves. Silky brown gloves cover her skin all the way to her elbows. Catching a glimpse of it in the mirror, Mara sees the forest hues and loves the dress, but she still hates the way it tickles the top of her feet and ankles as she reluctantly spins at her mother's twirling finger.

"Can I at least wear flats?" she asks, hopeful. Ezra holds up a pair of brown heels with green accents. "Guess not, then…"

Surana adjusts the hem of Mara's skirt. "It looks like the right length. You don't have to keep it on anymore, although the party lasts for about half a day."

Kimala shoves the ornate box into Mara's hands. She avoids eye contact. "If you don't like it, tough. This was hard to get."

Mara stares at Kimala as she opens the box. Inside, a beautiful mask made out of flattened black wire lies on a bed of satin. Silver ribbons trail behind it.

"She specifically wanted a masquerade party,"

Surana whispers to Ezra excitedly. "She has this gorgeous silver-accented blue mask she has been dying to wear."

"It's beautiful," Mara breathes, gently lifting the mask out of the box; it is definitely prettier than some silver-lined blue one.

"You really think so?" Kimala asks, surprised.

Mara nods and turns to the mirror, fumbling with the mask. Kimala grabs the silver ribbons and ties the mask into place. Mara brushes her fingers over the surface, feeling the overlapping wires. The metal accents her cheekbones, making her look much older than sixteen.

Ezra smiles at Mara. "You look beautiful, sweetie."

Mara smiles back. "Thanks. I look forward to wearing it."

Ezra winks at Surana. *I told you so*, she mouths.

< * >

The day before the party, Mara hides in the deep recesses of the garden, keeping out of the way of the servants preparing both the field and the mansion for tomorrow's guests. Kimala's words from that morning bounce around her head, nagging her incessantly as she tries to study. Sure, she's a tein'stra, but surely no one would expect her to know how to dance since she had just arrived a month ago - right?

Ezra peeks around the corner and glares at Mara. "You had a lesson," she chastises her daughter, "and you didn't show up."

"I don't want him feeling me up," Mara grumbles her lame excuse, hunching behind her book. She and Shaniel had been getting along recently, but sparring and dancing are two different things. Even though he has promised never to do anything without her permission, she is still a bit wary.

Ezra snatches the book and tucks it under her arm. "He won't 'feel you up.' You need to know at least one dance, Mara, and Shaniel is a good instructor despite everything else."

She grabs Mara's wrist and drags her out of the garden. A huge flat platform had been set up in the yard, smoothing out the area for the ease of dancing.

Shaniel stands in the middle, flirting with one of the servants. Her cheeks are a bright red as she stares up at the handsome man through her eyelashes. However, as soon as she sees Ezra approaching with Mara in tow, the young woman quickly bows to Shaniel and excuses herself.

Shaniel turns around, confused, and rolls his eyes at them. "Did you have to ruin the fun, Ezra?"

Ezra raises an eyebrow at him. "And here I thought you've been having fun with Mara," she says, not releasing her hand from the girl's arm. "Sparring and playing games with my daughter is no longer fun? How about trying to teach her how to dance?"

Aeserast glides across the platform, having finished his conversation with Jonan about the lighting. "Ezra, aren't you being a little cruel? You know how these two have been recently."

"Perverted cat," Mara insults him, fighting the grin off her face to keep up the ruse.

"Danarko brat," Shaniel calls back, sticking his tongue out at her. He doesn't hold back his smirk.

Ezra sighs. "Quit the act. You two are as thick as thieves. I swear, if we had raised Mara here, she would have grown up stealing her way across Saheir with all the things you're teaching her." She narrows her eyes at Shaniel. "Don't you dare teach her any of *those* dances, got it?"

"Sera, sera," Shaniel waves off Ezra's concern, speaking the Xharos phrase for 'of course, of course.' He has been teaching Mara a few phrases during their Siege games. He splays his fingers towards her. "Well, little Danarko, shall we begin?"

Mara shrugs off her mother's hand and locks her grip around his wrist. "Don't you dare try anything," she warns as he takes her other hand.

He grins. "And why would I do that?" He asks innocently, guiding her hands into place and bumping her right foot with his toe. "Move that one back. This is the five-step dance – one of the simpler ones."

Mara follows his lead, noticing how he is keeping a large distance between them. She glances at Aeserast and Ezra who are conversing to one another now. "So what are the dances she doesn't want me to learn?" she asks him, suddenly wanting to know just to spite her mother for having her learn these cursed moves.

Shaniel shakes his head, his red-spiked black hair whipping around his face. "Nope, not telling."

"Oh, come on," she pesters him. "What's so bad about them?"

Shaniel raises an eyebrow at her. "I believe you would kill me faster than your mother would."

Mara's cheeks flush a faint pink. "... Ah." She stares over his shoulder and narrows her eyes as an idea comes to mind. "What other steps are in this dance?"

"There's a spin, a backwards step, as well as a dip." He eyes her warily. "What do you have planned?"

She grins at him. "Nothing in particular."

"Hmm." He holds their hands up. "Spin."

She does. After a few more minutes of the simple steps, he says, "When you step back, that's the best time to do a dip. Are you ready?"

Mara shrugs. "Sure." She steps back just as his right hand slips out of her grip and wraps around her waist, using their still joined hands to bend her backwards.

Mara subtly pushes on her heel, knowing he is not prepared for her upwards momentum. His eyes widen as she uses his bent position to her advantage, pulling herself around him with their still joined hands. He tumbles to the ground, barely twisting in time to avoid landing on his face. She laughs as he thuds on the grass just at the edge of the platform, rubbing his rump.

He bares his teeth at her, exposing his sharp canines. "You got me this time, Danarko."

Mara smirks down at him but squeaks as someone grabs her arm and spins her around, pulling her into a faster version of the five-step dance she had just been doing with Shaniel.

Aeserast smiles slightly at Mara's wide eyes. "I see you are getting lazy, Shaniel," he calls over to the laig'hius still on the grass. "I never would have imagined Mara would outwit you."

"Even she has some tricks up her sleeve," Shaniel tries to defend himself, his cheeks reddening. He rubs the back of his neck.

"Your footwork needs improvement, but you have the basics down," Aeserast compliments her, sending her into a spin that causes her tied-up hair to bump against her earlobe.

"I thought this dance was slower," she says,

struggling to keep up with the fast steps. She accidentally misses a move and steps on Aeserast's foot. "Sorry..."

"Shaniel was going easy on you," Aeserast informs her, brushing off her apology with a shrug. "This dance is usually performed to fast-paced music."

"Ah..." Mara tries to break away, but all Aeserast does is spin her again. "Is there... a slower one?"

Aeserast chuckles. "Knowing you, you won't want to dance any of the slower ones, as they involve the participants being much closer to one another."

Mara's eyes widen as she assesses the distance between them. "Wait, this is how far away you're supposed be?"

Aeserast nods. Suddenly, his hand is around her back and she is dipped down. Taken off guard, she stares at him, her eyes wide. "Please take it easy on Shaniel during the festivities," he requests quietly as he straightens her and resumes the regular steps. "He can get carried away at times."

Mara sighs, glancing at the sulking cat-eared man as he rubs the back of his head. "As long as he doesn't do anything stupid," she finally mumbles to Aeserast.

He smiles knowingly. "Knowing him, he probably will."

< * >

After her morning training, her mother and aunt drag her into her room, not even allowing her to go to the library for the first half of the day. By the time midafternoon rolls around and the guests are arriving in the prepared area, Mara's nerves are already frazzled.

As the sun sets, a huge crowd of about a hundred or so individuals fills the garden and entrances into the mansion. People with an assortment of lavish clothes from the gaudy to absolutely hideous to intricately beautiful mill around, their masks hiding their true features.

They clap as Mara and Kimala pause beside Jonan on a raised dais. Kimala looks comfortable in a shimmering blue masterpiece that sweeps around her legs in a mermaid style skirt, her straightened hair pulled out of her face via the braids wrapping around her head like a crown and meeting in the back.

Mara tries her best not to run away in her earth-toned A-line dress, a bit overwhelmed with how many people are here for Kimala's birthday. Her shoulder-length hair is in an elegant bun with her wavy hazelnut locks cascading around her face, accenting her angled jaw and cheekbones.

She knows her uncle is a tein'fu and in charge of Veera, but this is a bit much for his daughter's sixteenth birthday, isn't it?

I guess turning sixteen is a bigger deal on Saheir than turning twenty-one on Earth, Mara thinks to herself, a smile plastered on her face as she stares at the twin moons Narein and Naros in the sky, taking slow, deep breaths. The silver sparks of her Source occasionally flit across the fine, silky brown gloves covering her skin to her elbows; at least she has learned how to calm it somewhat during Aeserast's exercises.

Jonan places his hands on Mara's and Kimala's shoulders, squeezing them lightly.

"It is wonderful the things that can happen within a few days," he starts off his speech, gesturing to Ezra and Surana who are standing to the side. "My sister,

Ezra, came home last month. Who would have ever guessed Mara, her daughter, would share the same birthday as our precious Kimala?" A big grin stretches across his face. "Now, they turn sixteen in the same night. Welcome them to their silver years!"

The crowd claps, and a few people cheer. Mara spots Shaniel and Aeserast in nice formal attire near the back of the crowd, their distinct hair colors making them stick out like scimitars on a gun rack.

Mara leans towards Kimala and whispers, "Why silver?"

"It stands for the purity of the Four Ancient Sisters," Kimala murmurs abstractly, smiling and waving to the crowd.

I shouldn't have asked her, Mara grumbles to herself. *She's the one who gave me that book, after all.*

They walk towards the cake in the middle of the banquet table. It is an extravagant multicolored eight-layer cake that supposedly represents the "simple elements" within this world: fire and water, earth and air, light and shadow, Voyana and Source. Voyana looks like a soft gold that reminds Mara of sunlight while Source is a shimmery blue with grey-white lightning bolt-shaped decorations around the edges, representing Mara's and Kimala's Source.

Mara frowns, thinking of the black core underneath the silver sparks inside her mind. That is a part of her Source, too, isn't it?

Jonan hands the girls each a giant knife. Kimala daintily punctures the top of the fondant, pressing down with a practiced move. Mara, not trained in the kitchen, holds the knife like she would a dagger and chops a lightning bolt in half.

Kimala shoots Mara a glare before turning to the

clapping crowd. Kimala grins while Mara nervously smiles.

As the cake is passed around, Mara recedes into a corner and quietly nibbles on her small slice of "Shadow" which tastes like chocolate. The mask feels almost like a safety wall between her and the crowd – secretly, she is happy about it.

"Can't you socialize? You look like a gloomy dark spot," Kimala asks as she is whisked away by someone in a white and blue outfit that reminds Mara of a creepy prince from a Disney movie. She shakes her head, dispelling that ridiculous image.

Mara carefully sneaks across the cobbled garden in her high heels, heading for a table laden with finger-foods such as cheese, fruit, and vegetables. She doesn't want anyone to talk to her; what is she supposed to say? She knows almost nothing about the world, thus eliminating majority of conversations unless she wants to sound like an uneducated bimbo.

Grabbing a plate, she plucks a square cheese from the tray and immediately bites into it, frustrated she can't study right now. Screw manners. She doesn't even want to be here.

"How is it? I've been contemplating getting some for myself," Shaniel suddenly appears, leaning against the table where no one had been just a second before. His mask is solid black and covers his forehead down to his cheekbones, a red ribbon holding it in place. He is in a black velvet suit that shimmers like panther fur in the globe-light.

Mara jumps, startled by his sudden appearance. "Do you not know how to walk? Freaking cat. Quit popping in and out."

"It's called phasing, not popping. I could teach you

how to do it," he suggests, winking one of his gold cat-eyes at her. "It involves using your Source to give your legs a boost of speed."

Mara glances at him, a little curious. "Maybe one day," she finally caves.

"Will you have your first glass of liquor now that you are an adult?" he prods, grinning. "Might help loosen up those tense face muscles. You may even smile!"

Mara stabs another piece of cheese, irritated. "I refuse to get intoxicated at social events."

Wearing a silver wire facemask that covers three-fourths of his face, Aeserast chuckles. He looks almost like an elven prince in the silver-embroidered light blue tunic with a white belt crossing over the middle, a pair of white tights on underneath. His dark blue boots complete the birthday theme's colors. "Be nice, Shaniel. It's Tein'stra Danarko's birthday."

Shaniel flourishes his wrist and bows deeply from his waist, his lynx ears twitching in mischief. "My apologies. I wish you a very pleasant birthday, milady. May I have this dance?"

Mara giggles, unable to help herself. "I still don't know how to dance well," she admits.

"Perfect!" Shaniel grins, flashing a wide grin. He grabs her hands and spins her around.

Startled, Mara grabs his arms for support as they near the edge of the dancing area. "Shaniel – " she starts, her fingers digging into his arm. Silver sparks race along her knuckles, reflecting her agitation.

"Don't worry," Shaniel soothes her, his lips tilting up in a small smile. For once, it is not flirtatious. "Just follow my lead. Trust me, Mara; you'll need to know at least a few dance moves in your lifetime."

Mara stares at him, confused as Shaniel's mood flips like a coin. He leads her through some simple steps, keeping his hands on her arms and never going for her shoulder or waist. *One minute, he's the biggest flirt and playboy I've ever seen. The next, he acts like... like a brother.*

Suddenly, his hand slides to the middle of her back and he dips her backwards. Smirking, he stares into her eyes with a look like he knows what she is thinking. "Just so you know, Codi does not know the dance I am teaching you."

"Do you read minds, too?" she gasps as he pulls her back up.

"Didn't need to," he passes off, taking her hand again and twirling her. "It's written all over your face."

"Ah..."

"Don't worry about it," Shaniel says, giving her a lopsided grin. He glances off to the side. "Let's sit down," he suddenly suggests, leading her off to the side of the main garden area.

"Where are you taking me?" Mara asks, narrowing her eyes at him in suspicion.

He winks at her and presses a finger against his lip. "It's a secret!" he whispers, taking her hand and guiding her under the arch into a private seating area.

"Surprise!"

Aeserast, Codi, Ezra, Jonan, Surana, and even Kimala stand on either side of a small table that has about five presents on it. Shaniel leans over, giving her a big smile. "Happy birthday!"

Flustered, Mara backs up a few steps. "I-I told you guys no presents," she rebukes weakly.

"Oh, just open them," Kimala orders, shoving a

long, thin wrapped box into her hands.

Mara sighs and opens the gift. She pulls out a thin silver rod set with blue stones and black engravings. Testing the tip carelessly, she accidentally pricks her finger.

"Aunt Ezra said you really like different weapons," Kimala rambles nervously, "but I wanted to get you something cute. It's a hairpiece that also serves as a... a throwing spike that can channel Source for accuracy and speed."

Mara grins at Kimala, her opinion of the girl improving a bit. *Maybe she's not such a prick after all.* "Thanks. It's really pretty." She carefully puts it in her hair.

"Open mine next!" Shaniel exclaims with a big grin, handing her a bigger box.

Mara shakes it side to side, judging the weight. A small smile forms on her face as she narrows her eyes at Shaniel. "What did you get me?"

A small, strained chuckle forces its way out of Shaniel before he breaks down into loud laughter. "Just open it, Danarko! I want to see your face."

"Your gift is not befitting of a coming-of-age ceremony, Shaniel," Aeserast chastises him.

"I asked Ezra what she would like."

Aeserast opens his mouth and then shuts it, embarrassed. Shaniel smugly puffs out his chest.

Mara chuckles and pulls off the lid. Her eyes widen at the sight of two short, thin daggers in leg harnesses. She yanks them out and drops the box, pulling the daggers out of their sheaths and examining the blades. They shimmer, a deadly edge on them.

She props her foot onto a chair and pulls up her skirt, exposing her bare leg. "Mara, don't do that here!" Kimala squeaks, her face flushing a bright cherry red.

Mara ignores her and straps on one of the daggers. She beams. "It fits! Oh, my gosh. I've always wanted one of these." She stares at the matching one. "Now I have two!" she squeals, bouncing slightly on the balls of her feet. She wants to play with them, to test the edges and see how balanced they are. She wonders if Shaniel or Codi would duel her.

Shaniel grins. "So you like?"

Mara wraps her arms around him, hugging him tightly. "Thank you!"

Startled, Shaniel pats her back gingerly as if afraid she would flip him again. He chuckles. "You're welcome!"

She quickly straps on the second dagger, admiring it before dropping her skirt hem over the two weapons. Feeling deadly with the concealed weapons, she grins deviously at them.

Ezra chuckles, knowing Mara is currently thinking of all the trouble she could get into with these two daggers. She now regrets ever giving Shaniel the idea of the custom-made weapons.

Surana smiles softly. "I made these for you. They are from Jonan and I."

Again, Mara is stunned by Surana's needlework as she pulls the three tightly-packed earthen toned outfits from the box. "Wow..." Mara breathes, rubbing her fingers over the cloth. "It's so soft... I wish I could try them on now."

Surana chuckles. "There is always the morning; they are meant for training."

Aeserast rubs the back of his head, looking embarrassed. "I guess mine isn't as great as I thought it would be," he admits as his cheeks turn a faint bluish-purple in a blush. "But... it *is* functional."

He hands her a small paper-wrapped object. She tears it open and discovers a beautiful teardrop-shaped pendant on a leather string. The colors swirling inside the glass pendant match the colors that had been on the sandstone she had broken last month. "Um... thanks," she says awkwardly. "It's pretty, but I... don't wear jewelry."

"Whaaaat?" Shaniel whines, startling Mara. "Why didn't I think of that?"

"Mara, that's a summoning pendant!" Kimala lectures, grabbing Mara's hand and staring at the glass pendant. "If you focus your Source on it, it will alert that specific Highlord you're in trouble. Highlords only give these to people important to them."

Mara glances at Aeserast, frowning slightly. "So... what would I use it for?"

Everyone stares at her. Ezra is the only one who chuckles. "Remember what I said earlier? If you run into trouble, the best person to have by your side is a Highlord."

"Oh!" Mara looks down at the pendant. "So it's like dialing 9-1-1 without all the hassle." She stares into the blue and purple swirls, amazed as they shift slightly.

Aeserast smiles, trying not to laugh. "Yes, exactly." He takes the pendant from her and wraps the leather band around her neck. As soon as it touches her skin, a silver spark races across the odd gem.

"Thanks," she says, readjusting her hair.

She glances at the table; one present left. Codi picks it up and shoves it into Mara's hands. Mara glances at him before looking down at the suspiciously shaped object.

"This feels like a really big book, Codi..." she comments, raising an eyebrow at him – and then remembering he probably couldn't see it underneath the folded wire of the mask.

He twiddles his thumbs, nervous. "Just open it."

Mara rips the thin paper off and stares at the title. *The Science of all the Realms, Vol 34.* Her eyes widen and she flips to the index. "What the..." *How could anyone be this meticulous?* she cries inside her mind. *This thing has got to be at least four thousand pages.*

Codi holds his breath as she skims the five-page long index. *Alkina, Blazhreia, Carni... Even Earth is in here.* So many different names stretch down the page, full of sub-headings and indents for the different sections. *This would take me ages to get through... Wait. Are all of those names worlds?!*

She finally looks up to see everyone's expectant faces. She stares at Codi with wide eyes. "How many realms are there?"

"Fourteen documented," Aeserast answers, smiling. "That is, if you count Hariana separate from Eleth and Carni as its own realm, which most do."

Mara closes her eyes briefly to let that sink in. She smirks at Codi, her lips pressed tightly together. "Thanks for breaking it to me lightly, brother." *Not.*

Codi frowns. Realization dawns on his face and he slaps his palm against his forehead. "Agh... I totally wasn't thinking about that. Sorry, Mara."

Mara shakes her head. Sometimes, her brother can be oblivious. *Fourteen... that's amazing,* she thinks, sitting down in one of the chairs and examining the book.

"There is one more, sweetie," Ezra says as she

pulls a small container out of her pocket. Mara recognizes the steel box from their house. "This is from your father," she admits, her smile wavering slightly. "He wanted you to have it when you turned sixteen."

Mara takes a quick breath and opens the lid of the broken music box. However, the mechanisms within it kick into motion, and a beautiful familiar lullaby echoes among the little group.

Mara's eyes water. She had grown up with this lullaby being hummed to her at bedtime, her father's soft voice carrying her into wonderful dreams of labyrinth cities and huge glass towers.

Inside the box, only a single ring rests on a blue cushion. The sparkling goldstone refracts light onto the engraved symbols surrounding it.

"Daddy's ring," she whispers, smiling. She sniffles, carefully dabbing at her eyes through the mask. "I... I think this is what Bryce wanted."

Ezra frowns slightly, confused. "Perhaps... It is valuable. The Highlords made it for your father when he finished building Cerlail Academy."

"He always wore it on his pinky, but it's way too big for me." Nostalgic, she slides the ring onto her right pinky finger. Her eyes widen as silvery lightning bolts – her Source – dance around the ring. It shrinks to fit her finger. "Whoa..."

Aeserast smirks. "It resizes to fit the wearer."

Mara strokes the stone. "Thank you." Her voice cracks.

Ezra kisses her forehead. "He would have loved to teach you everything about this world."

Mara sniffles again, a tear escaping to race down her cheek. "I would've liked that," she whispers.

CHAPTER 5
PREPARATIONS

Mara nearly sprints to the field near the garden, excited to try out the new weapons. The new shirt and pants fit loosely around her joints yet snugly on her limbs, allowing for ample movement without getting in the way. Her new daggers are strapped onto her calves comfortably, conforming to the shape of her legs and not impeding her stride in the slightest. It makes her wonder if Shaniel had them custom-made.

She fingers the new hairpiece, still surprised Kimala had gotten her a gift. She now feels bad at not getting the girl anything, but at the same time, Kimala doesn't seem upset about it. Her hand migrates to the new pendant around her neck, and she wonders if Aeserast is all right; shortly after the festivities, he had said something about an emergency and had created one of those air-warping ovals – portals – and left.

Mara does a few stretches underneath one of the broad-leaf trees, too eager to practice with her daggers to do her usual t'ai chi routine. She flicks one of them out, flipping the blade and catching it. The hilt slaps against her palm, perfectly balanced. She grins.

"I'm glad you like them," Shaniel comments behind her.

Startled, Mara whirls around and stares at Shaniel. He hangs upside down from a low-lying branch, his arms crossed over his chest. It doesn't keep his shirt from falling a little bit, exposing part of his well-toned stomach. He grins at her, baring his teeth and tilting his head to the side. He is nearly on perfect eye-level with her.

"Good morning," she greets, watching him closely in case he does that weird phase-step thing again.

"Are you going to Cerlail Academy?" he asks. He reminds her of the Cheshire cat from Alice in Wonderland. Something shifts behind him, but before she could see what it is, he moves slightly and it disappears.

"I'd like to," she admits, flicking out the other dagger and practicing a few slashes. "I want to get this power under control; it affects a lot of people around me." A silver bolt races across her knuckles, and she frowns slightly.

Jumping from the branch and landing with a cat's grace, Shaniel asks, "Are you therakare or runkare?"

"Theh-ra-ka-reh?" Mara repeats slowly. "What's that?"

"You can use Source separate from Voyana. Runkare is the opposite; you use Source mixed with Voyana as an amplifier." Shaniel pulls a dagger from... somewhere on him. Mara doesn't even see where his hand had gone. He holds up his weapon and sinks into a fighting posture.

Mara shakes her head while smiling slightly. "I don't know what therakare is," she admits, taking a step forward. "But this looks more fun."

"Ohh," Shaniel purrs, his eyes narrowing into dangerous slits. "A fighter after my own heart."

They spar for a good fifteen or so minutes, eventually dropping the weapons and fighting with their fists and feet. Suddenly, Mara hears a faint buzzing sound coming from Shaniel's pocket. "Ah, give me a moment," he says and… disappears.

Remembering the last time he had done this, Mara glances behind her, but he isn't there.

"Ah, carc'ra," Shaniel says above her, and she glances into the tree limbs. He is sitting on the same branch as before, holding a strange transparent crystal-like device in his hand that glows a soft aventurine.

He tilts backwards, falling upside down again. His legs hold him on the branch as he sighs, disappointed in something. "The Academy calls. If you're ever in Quasala, just give a shout."

He winks as he drops headfirst to the ground.

Eyes wide, Mara sees one of those space-bending portals open up beneath him, swallowing him whole. The warped air shrinks again, turning back into a normal piece of space.

Curious now, she waves her foot where it had appeared. Nothing.

"Huh." Sheathing her new daggers, she heads into the mansion, looking for Codi. She had already hinted at her interest in attending Cerlail Academy with Codi and Kimala to her mother, but no one had mentioned her in the upcoming travel plans. *I'm definitely going, whether I have to sneak after them or not,* she thinks to herself, glancing down at her sparking hand. *It's the best place for me to learn how to control this, anyway. They shouldn't be complaining much.*

She finds her brother flipping through what looks like a scientific book on matter in the library. Something resembling the periodical chart is on a piece of paper in front of him, and he references the different materials.

"Hey," she greets, melting into a chair and staring

at him. "Are you going to Cerlail Academy?"

"Good morning to you," he murmurs absently. He blinks, registering her words. "Yeah. We're heading out either the first or the second – depending on how fast Kimala can pack," Codi grumbles.

It takes a moment for Mara to remember the calendar system. *Today's the twenty-eighth, which makes tomorrow the first of... Eona.* "Tomorrow? That's soon. What do I have to do to go with you?"

Codi stares at her, stunned. "Mara, you barely know anything about this world. Sure, you've been having a crash-course ever since you got here, but that's not enough. You need to learn of the dangers before traveling anywhere quite yet."

Mara raises her eyebrows. She holds up her hand, showing him the silver sparks flitting around her fingers – the physical representation of her irritation. "I do believe it is in the best interest of everyone that I control this," she points out.

Codi stares at the silver sparks, looking slightly uncomfortable. "I... guess so." Sighing, he closes the book and stands up. "Come on, then. We need to talk to Uncle Jonan and the others."

By the time they had gathered everyone – Kimala included – it is lunchtime. They occupy a corner of the dining room's huge table that can seat twenty or so people. Ezra sits next to Mara as Kimala and Codi sit across from them. Surana and Jonan are both at the head of the table.

The servants place the food in front of them as Jonan voices the same concern Codi had. "Mara, I urge you to reconsider. Right now is not the best time for you to leave Veera; Codi and Kimala will be traveling on foot because our portal engineer is at the

Academy studying."

Ezra frowns slightly. "What about the kranluk? Trading is over, isn't it?"

Jonan shakes his head. "Last year's Heakalius storm was mild, so we're predicting a stronger one this year. All the kranluk have been sent out to gather as many supplies as possible before this year's storm."

"How's Veera's barrier?" Ezra asks, concerned.

Mara quietly listens to the conversation as she eats, curious but slightly confused. *What is a kranluk? What is so terrible about a storm? Are there tornadoes? What do portal engineers do? What type of barrier are they talking about?* Again, her mind is flooded with questions.

Jonan shakes his head. "It needs to be reinforced. I worry our barrier specialist and portal engineer are not going to be back before the storm."

"When is the storm supposed to hit?" Ezra finally takes a bite of her food. "The admissions deadline is the eighth, right?"

Jonan and Surana glance at one another. "Late Eona to early Vuva," Surana murmurs. "Our specialist and technician are nearing their graduation dates, but they are close to the time the storm will hit."

That's... late next month and the following month, Mara realizes, glancing at Kimala and Codi. *No wonder they're heading out now.*

Ezra rubs her chin. "I see... this is a tight spot you're in, Jonan. I can help with the barrier, but portal engineering is out of my expertise. Have you thought of asking Adul'ne Roanoak for assistance?"

Mara's eyes widen slightly. She has learned a little bit about the social ranks, and the title her mother had just casually thrown out was that of a *king*.

Jonan shakes his head. "I have asked too much of His Majesty these past few months, and they are going through hard times, as well. Paro'ki Shasta has been antagonizing them recently." Mara recognizes the word for tyrant. "I worry there will be another battle between the two."

"I apologize for interrupting..." Mara cuts into the awkward pause, her voice quiet. "But... what's going on?"

Ezra's smile is strained. "Ah, I apologize. You're probably very confused. Politics and tein'fu duties, dear. I'll try to explain them later."

Mara rolls her eyes. "Mom, I meant with the trip. How does all of this impact whether or not I should go to Cerlail Academy?"

Everyone stares at her, stunned. It is as if she had just said something she should know the answer to. Irritated, she sets her fork down, not even paying attention to the crackling lightning bolts around her fingers anymore.

"It sounds like you have a lot of problems right now, Uncle Jonan," Mara directs her words to the tein'fu. "However, *this* problem – " she holds up her hand, showing off the silver fireworks, " – doesn't need to be one of them. Cerlail Academy is the best place for me to get this under control, and by me leaving, it will free you up so you can deal with what's going on here."

Surana, Jonan, and Ezra glance at one another, concern written all over their faces. "You're traveling on foot, Mara," Ezra explains carefully, as if picking the best words to convince her otherwise. "You will be going either through or around the Heramus, which is a very dangerous area between here and Quasala. It could take a good four to five days' travel —"

"Mom." Mara stares straight at her mother. "I know three different types of self defense, as well as how to use bladed, blunt, and ranged weapons. I also know how to camp. I'll be fine."

Ezra strokes Mara's hair. "I just want you to be safe," she argues weakly, knowing she is losing this conversation.

Jonan rubs his jaw, conflicted. "You do have a point, though... Cerlail Academy is the best place for you to control your Source. The Dream'Lord has been doing a fantastic job tutoring you, but we cannot depend on him nor the Common'Lord to teach you everything; after all, their position as Highlords comes before this."

Mara frowns slightly. She recognizes Aeserast's title, Dream'Lord, but who is the Common'Lord? Shaniel? They are very odd titles for such an important position as a Highlord.

He continues. "Three of my best guards will be accompanying them: Don, Beral, and Rick. Since the portal is not an option at the time, they are going to skirt the Heramus to avoid unwanted attention." He glances at Ezra. "One more addition to the party should not be a big deal; plus, Mara did bring up a good point. She has a better chance at the Academy."

Ezra slumps back in her seat, sighing. "I guess I can't stop you, then..." She eyes her daughter's grin. "Knowing you, you would have snuck after them even if we said no."

Mara's sheepish smile confirms her mother's suspicion.

After lunch, Mara nearly sprints to her room to pack for the trip. She carefully rolls up her clothes and packs them tightly in the new bag Surana had crafted just for her. She figures she can pack everything she had gotten for her birthday – well, except for the book Codi had given her.

Ezra comes in with an armful of clothes – one being Mara's birthday dress. "Mom, I don't have room for something like that," Mara tries to dissuade her mother as she balls up the extra clothes and the dress.

"You are going to the capital," Ezra explains simply, helping her daughter finish packing her bag. "You need at least one nice dress just in case you go to a formal event."

That's some excuse, Mara grumbles to herself, dropping the bag by the door. "Anything else you want to put in it?"

Ezra shakes her head. "I did want to show you something, though. Come with me. How far in your exercises did you get with Aeserast?"

Mara follows Ezra through the mansion towards the yard where the training dummies are. "I haven't broken a Source globe in almost a week," she announces proudly, grinning.

Ezra sighs heavily. "So not very far, then."

Mara frowns. "I haven't cracked a Source globe in four days," she adds, grumbling.

Ezra smiles as they stop several yards away from the training dummies. "You have to start somewhere. However, I want to teach you something useful."

She examines her daughter, trying to figure out how best to explain. "Hold your hands like this," she finally says, positioning her hands in front of her as if

85

she is holding a volleyball. "Focus in the middle between your palms. Imagine your Source – the little silver sparks – collecting there."

A butterscotch-colored orb slowly coalesces between Ezra's hands. Mara's eyes widen and she stares at it.

Ezra flings the ball at the nearby dummy; a few chips fly in every direction. She sighs. "Combat is not my field. Your turn, Mara."

Mara stares at her hands. *I… I can do that?* she thinks, and miniature silver lightning bolts dance across her fingertips in response to her emotions.

She closes her eyes, imagining the silver sparks coming together into a ball of lightning bolts. Peeking at her hands, she is instantly disappointed. There is no sparking orb there.

"Try again," Ezra encourages. "Imagine all of your emotions gathering on that one spot."

Gritting her teeth, Mara holds her hands apart and focuses again. She puts all of her anger, frustration, and confusion into that space, imagining all of those tiny silver sparks coalescing into a huge ball. If this doesn't work, nothing will.

A dark sphere surrounded by silver streaks of light grows between her hands. It looks like shooting stars in the night sky.

Mara grins, ecstatic. She didn't believe it would work; yet here it is, right in front of her.

Ezra's eyes also widen as she stares at the dark sphere with the silver flitting bolts. "Two…" she murmurs out loud just as the volatile orb of raw power starts to wobble, losing form. "Don't lose focus, Mara. Throw it!"

Mara glances at the training dummy. A spear of

doubt pierces her concentration.

Boom.

Mara flies backwards from the shockwave.

Ezra runs after her. "Mara, are you all right?" she asks, panic raising her voice up an octave.

Mara coughs. "Yeah," she rasps. "What was that?"

"Energy isn't a stable element," Ezra explains shakily, examining Mara for injuries. "If focus isn't maintained, it will react violently and possibly explode."

"Makes sense," Mara coughs. She hobbles to her feet and brushes off her pants. "Lemme try again."

"Are you sure…?"

Mara nods. "No better time than now. Might be useful later."

Having a better idea of how the orb is created, she holds her hands apart and focuses. This time, she imagines the sphere inside her mind taking form between her hands. The dark ball and sparking light appears again, more stable than before. This time, Mara maintains her focus on it and shoves her hands – and the ball – towards the dummy.

The ball fizzles out of existence as it floats to the ground, utterly harmless.

"Heh…" Ezra tries to smother her laughter to no avail. "You… you have to focus on what you want it to do, as well."

"Oh…" Mara stares at her fingers. Was she really doing this? A sense of exhilaration races through her, encouraging her to lift her hands and form that strange lightning storm between her palms.

Mara tries again and again. And again. And… again. Each time, she grows more frustrated and the ball of sparks gets livelier.

Ezra watches Mara closely, concerned. "Sweetie, you should take a break."

Mara wipes away sweat from her eyes. "I *will* get this!" she growls, adamant. She feels as if she has to prove something to the training apparatus – maybe to herself, even. Either way, she is planning to finish what she started.

She jabs her fingers forward, her palms facing one another. The black sphere emits ominous crackles as the silvery lightning storm plays around it. She tosses it towards the dummy, suddenly having a good feeling about this one.

The ball fizzles to the ground and disappears with a puff of dissipating black energy.

Mara grits her teeth, irritated and frustrated at the failures. *Why won't it work?* she demands silently, staring at the erratic silver bolts flitting across her hands and arms.

"Stop, Mara. Just rest for now. We can try again later," Ezra placates her, feeling her daughter's agitation through her uncontrolled Source's pressure weighing down the surroundings. She turns to the mansion, thinking Mara will follow her.

Mara glares at the untouched wood. "I will finish this," she says firmly. *If only it was a sword,* she thinks wistfully. *I've always been better with close-range weapons than projectiles.*

Something clicks in her mind. If she can mentally create the sphere in her mind and duplicate it in her palm, wouldn't the same work for the image of a sword?

Staring at her hand, Mara imagines the silver sparks and black blob coalescing in her palm and elongating into a familiar shape. She nearly loses focus when the katana flickers into existence. It isn't perfect, but it is obviously supposed to be a sword of some sort.

An excited smile creeps onto her face as she grips the hilt tightly, feeling an odd sensation of a solid and a liquid at the same time. She swings the sword at the dummy, knowing it is too far away to hit.

Boom.

Mara flies backwards as her Source-created sword blows up. Wheezing from the impact, she staggers to her feet. Hundreds of tiny silver lightning bolts play across her skin, and her body tingles as if energized.

Mara stares at the destruction of the yard. The ground between her and the low-lying wall is scored and scorched as if a giant burning blade had sliced through the dirt. One of the two trees next to the low-lying wall is gone, a few scraggly roots peeking out from the churned dirt. The wall behind it is completely blown out, rubble littering the street on the other side.

The dummy is nowhere to be seen.

Mara slowly turns to her mother. Ezra had turned as white as a sheet. She stares at the wall with wide eyes, her hand slowly creeping up to cover her mouth. "That was the tree your father proposed to me under…"

Mara glances back at the seared roots, appalled. She had just destroyed something that important? *Why did it have to be that tree?* she cries mentally, her hand matting in her hair as she glares at the untouched tree that had been right next to it.

A wave of dizziness washes over Mara, and she sways on her feet. Her head throbs.

Ezra quickly catches her and helps her into the

garden area. Mara rubs her temple, fighting to keep her headache from getting any worse.

Ezra kneels in front of Mara and grasps her hands. The headache abates. "Don't ever create something like that until you learn the mechanics behind it," she lectures her daughter. Mara can see the concern and anger warring on her mother's face. "Source-created blades and Source-created projectiles are two different things entirely, and many people have to go through months or even years of training before they can master the bladed version because it takes extreme concentration and a delicate balance of Source and your own skills."

Mara glances at the ruined yard, wincing at the destruction she had caused. "I... noticed."

Ezra takes a shaky breath and hugs her. "You could have gotten seriously injured," she breathes, her voice cracking. Grabbing Mara's shoulders, she pushes back and stares into her daughter's eyes, desperately trying to convey the importance of her next words. "Until you learn more at the Academy, try not to use your Source too much; it's in an extremely volatile state right now. It could blow up like today, and I am sure Kimala won't be of much help if you get seriously injured."

"Okay..." Mara leans against the chair's back. Now that she had experienced first-hand at controlling her Source, she feels like it would be a dangerous endeavor for everyone – including herself – if she did not gain more control over it.

Ezra's eyes twinkle with unshed tears. "I love you." Ezra pulls Mara into a tight hug. "I wish I could go with you, but I need to fix the barrier around Veera first. I'll try to come to Cerlail as soon as I can, okay?"

Mara nods and pats Ezra on the back. She stares up at the twin moons Narein and Naros, again reminded that this world is very different from Earth.

< * >

The next morning, Mara pulls her hair into a tight bun. She spears it diagonally with the hairpin Kimala had given her and checks out her new clothes, marveling at the flexible fabric Surana had used. She is in a green tunic and brown pants, her new daggers strapped to the outside of the snug material. Aeserast's trinket rests underneath her shirt, unseen and out of the way.

Ezra, helping her pack the last essentials, closes the top of the travel bag. "I want a letter when you arrive and when you're accepted into the Academy," Ezra demands. "Ask Kimala or Codi if you need help sending them. Remember all of your lessons. Make sure not to lose your father's ring."

Mara glances down at her right hand's smallest finger. The goldstone sparkles at her as if encouraging her forward. "Sure thing, Mom."

"One last thing," Ezra says, handing Mara the packed bag. "If you ever need help or you're in trouble, just call for Highlord Aeserast."

Mara's eyes narrow. "You seem to be really close to him. Did there used to be something between you two?"

Ezra shakes her head, chuckling. "Highlords, no. That man is too innocent for his own good; it still baffles me how he and Shaniel became such good friends, seeing as they are polar opposites of one another. Let's go; no need to keep the others waiting."

Mara has a hard time wrapping her mind around this casually mentioned information as they walk through the hallway towards the front entrance of the mansion. She hears Codi and Kimala arguing about their bags as Jonan tries to play mediator between them. Three guards stand off to the side, wearing a mix of what looks like leather and plate armor. One is significantly shorter than the other two, but all three look to be middle-aged and well-trained.

"Wait." Ezra grabs Mara's arm and stops her before she can follow them into the street. "Be safe. Stay on guard. Don't strangle your cousin."

Mara grins lopsidedly at her mother. "I love you, too, Mom."

Ezra taps the pendant around Mara's neck. "You can contact Aeserast through – "

Mara grabs Ezra's hand, squeezing it tightly as she smiles. "It's okay, Mom. It's only a few nights of camping, and then we'll be there." She kisses Ezra on the cheek. "I love you, Mom. I'll see you when you get there."

Ezra strokes Mara's hair, her smile wavering. "I love you, too, Mara. Just... try to keep an open mind. And no matter what, know that your father would be proud of you."

Mara's eyes sting at the thought of her father's praise. "Really?" she asks softly.

Her mother nods, stroking her hair one more time.

"Mara! Are you coming?" Codi yells from the road, in a simple tunic with breeches and boots. His backpack is nearly the same size as his torso, and an odd sword with a two-handed hilt bumps against his waist.

Mara waves. "Yeah!"

Kimala cocks her hip off to the side and flicks her hair behind her. She is in a nice-looking shirt with skin-tight pants and thin shoes. Surprisingly enough, her small backpack looks light and easy to carry. "Great. This is going to be a fun trip."

"You sure you have everything you need, Kimala? That's a really small bag..." Mara comments, staring at the tan satchel.

Kimala huffs. "It has a translocation spell anchored to the inside, so the outer appearance does not matter."

"What about those shoes? They might fall apart," Mara comments, now examining the girl's slippers.

Kimala crosses her arms. "These shoes are meant to be walked in."

"She's going to snap if she steps in a mud puddle," Codi mumbles.

"I'm not that oblivious, Codi," Kimala snaps. The three guards behind Mara chuckle softly.

They walk down the road. Mara turns and waves, grinning at her mother one last time before disappearing around a corner.

Several hours later, they are meandering on a dirt-packed road that trails through the woods. Codi whistles as he strolls ahead, following behind the guard, Rick, in front. Kimala walks in the middle like the little princess she thinks she is. Mara hangs behind, glancing around in curiosity. "So we're going through the forest?" she asks, noticing the nearing tree line.

Kimala trips on another rock. "Ow! Yes. This is

the fastest way." The two guards behind Mara, Beral and Don, sigh. Mara wonders if Kimala will be complaining every hour of the trip.

"Enrollment ends on the eighth, so if the portal engineer had been here, we could have left this weekend," Codi informs Mara.

Mara does a quick calculation in her head. "So we have a week to get there."

Codi nods. "It only takes about four to five days to get to Quasala by foot, but it's always good to take precautions."

"Owww!" Kimala yelps, stopping in the middle of the road.

They watch the duke's daughter clean out her flimsy shoe for the fifth time since they had started their journey.

"Do we need to turn around?" Mara asks.

"No." Kimala jams her shoe back on.

"You sure? The road could get worse."

"I'm fine!" Kimala snaps.

Splock.

They all glance down to see one of Kimala's shoes completely submerged in filthy stagnant water. Kimala squeals in horror and disgust.

"Told you so," Codi mumbles. The guards turn away, but Mara could tell by their quivering shoulders that they are all fighting their laughter.

Mara sighs and takes off her travel bag. She digs through it and pulls out her hiking toe shoes that had been in her original duffel bag when they had arrived in Veera. Tugging off her boots, she tosses them at Kimala. Hopefully, they will fit; she looks about the same size. "Put those on."

Kimala wrinkles her nose up at the notion of

sticking her feet in the worn boots. "I refuse to – "

"Either we turn around – thus wasting a whole day – or you wear my boots for the rest of the trip." Mara takes off her socks and fits her toes into the slots. She rubs her ankles, wishing she had something to protect them in case she ran into bramble. Her pants leg ended two inches above her ankle, leaving the area between her anklebone and the cloth bare.

Kimala wrinkles her nose as she tightly laces the boots. She storms ahead of Codi and Mara. The other guard, Rick, hurries after her as the others take their time.

"You're welcome," Mara mutters to Kimala's retreating back.

"This is her first time outside of Veera," Codi informs her.

Mara glances at him, surprised. They follow after Kimala through the forest. "How could you be worried about *me*?" Mara hisses. "She won't last twenty-four hours out here."

Codi rolls his eyes. "There's twenty-six hours in a day here, just so you know. Also, she's been trained."

"At what? Fashion?" Mara raises her eyebrows at Codi, and he sighs. They catch up to Kimala and Rick.

Codi's eyes widen as he stares ahead. "Is that…"

Kimala covers her mouth. "It's spread since the last Heakalius storm…"

Mara stares ahead, confused. A few hundred yards in front of them, a grey border separates the healthy green trees from the dead, warped woods. Even the grass suddenly ends. It reminds her of some Halloween movie.

"We've made it this far. What difference is there if

we have to go through the creepy woods?" Mara asks.

Kimala shuffles her feet. "If the Heramus is bigger, that means the next storm might just send the borders closer to Veera."

Rick gestures to the right. "But this is just the edge. We should be able to avoid the Hemius easily, as the puddles are smaller on the outskirts. If we turn around now, we will just have wasted that much more time."

Kimala nods. "He's right. The bigger puddles don't form until deeper into the forest, so we should be fine as long as we're careful."

"Let's go, then." Mara takes the lead with one of the guards, continuing down the worn trail. *Sounds like there's some special puddles called...* she pauses, mentally sounding out the Xharos word to help herself memorize it, *Hee-mee-us. I wonder what's so important about them.*

As they approach the grey border, a chill runs up her spine. It is as if someone had drawn a monochromatic grey line between the two different sections; one can clearly see where the grass and dirt had turned a dark greyish color.

Before the indescribable line between the two regions – the lush green forest and the warped grey woods – Mara's foot stops. Something feels... wrong. She feels like she shouldn't go any farther or something terrible will happen. Her fingers itch, wanting to reach for the blades on her legs.

She shakes her head, dispelling the feeling. *There isn't anything wrong with walking through some creepy woods. We'll be fine.*

"You okay, Mara?" Codi asks, pausing beside her.

"Yeah." Mara steps forward.

They cross the line between the forest and the Heramus.

CHAPTER 6
THE HERAMUS

Mara's eyes flit around, a tingling sensation sliding down her spine. She clenches her fists, recognizing the feeling.

Someone – something – is watching them.

The guards move closer to Mara, Codi, and Kimala, circling them in a triangular fashion with two guards bringing up the back and one leading. "Is something wrong, Rick?" Kimala asks the one in front.

"We're being watched," Mara responds in a hushed voice, and Kimala raises an eyebrow at her.

"You have a good intuition, Tein'stra Danarko," Rick acknowledges, not taking his eyes off the pathway.

Mara scans the forest. The twisted trees and branches droop in a distinct pattern as if something heavy had been thrown on them, bending them out of shape... but not breaking them. A dark, inky puddle stands out against the pale bark of a gnarly tree.

Mara's gaze sharpens, catching movement in the corner of her eye. *There's nothing there...*

"What?" Codi asks, glancing in the direction Mara is looking.

"... Just my imagination."

"We need to be out of the Heramus before nightfall," Beral, one of the guards behind them, rumbles quietly. Mara and Codi nod, agreeing with the guard.

As they continue deeper in, more inky puddles appear. Kimala keeps acting like Miss Know-It-All who cannot be touched, striding along the path with her head held high while Codi walks alongside Rick in the front. Mara keeps catching movement in her peripheral vision; finally, she turns to look directly at a puddle not even six feet away.

Ripples spread across the plate-sized inky spot.

A chill runs up her spine, colder than all the other ones. It wasn't her imagination. "Mister Beral."

The short, stocky man pauses next to her. "Yes, tein'stra?"

"The puddle – something moved in it."

Beral glances at it. "That is a Hemius puddle."

Mara frowns as they continue walking. *Is it normal for things to move in the Hemius puddles?*

Unnoticed by the group, little finger-like nodes rise out of the murky liquid, bobbing and swaying. They watch the group continue down the pathway.

Hours pass by. They take a break for lunch, sitting in the middle of the path and munching on the sandwiches the kitchen staff had provided. Mara glances around and notices a puddle slightly bigger than the other ones – nearly the size of her backpack, ironically enough.

"What's so significant about running across a big puddle?" Mara asks, balling up the paper from her sandwich.

Codi's face is grim. "The bigger the puddle, the braver it is."

"It may even reach out and grab you," Kimala informs her while putting up the rest of the food. "Especially if you're too close to it."

"What are these, children's bed stories to keep you from wandering into the forest?" Mara sniggers, unable to keep a straight face. This sounds more like a made-up story to keep kids from playing in the woods than actual facts. "Seriously, what's so terrible about this place?"

Codi, Kimala, and the guards stare at Mara. "The Hemius," they chorus.

Just a few puddles in a dead swamp? It's hard to believe something so inconspicuous could be so feared... "What's so dangerous about this Hemius stuff?" she asks, twisting the sandwich paper in her hand.

"This area stretches for miles," Kimala berates, her blue eyes flashing with a strange anger. "Those 'puddles' contain a liquid that slowly kills you from inside. It has been around for a thousand and seven hundred years, yet we still don't know how to cure it."

Mara's hands drop to her sides. *I've never seen her this angry. What happened for her to react this way over it?* "I... didn't know that."

Codi's jaw clenches; his voice is unusually low and quiet. "Don't take this world lightly, Mara. It's not like Earth; there are plenty of things here that would have fun torturing or killing you. Hemius is alive – it can come out of its puddle and latch onto you like a leech. But as soon as it touches you, it spreads like water. It will infect every cell of your body until you die." Codi takes the balled-up paper out of Mara's hand and tosses it at one of the puddles. The ball makes an indent on the thick surface. "It's not something to brush off."

The surrounding liquid rises up like fingers and encases the paper, dragging it down.

Mara stares at the puddle, her face pale as the thick

liquid shifts and churns over its meal. An air pocket breaks the surface, almost like a quiet burp. "I'm sorry... You're right."

"We just don't want you to get killed out here," Codi says as he stands up and swings his bag over his shoulder.

Mara keeps a closer eye on the deadly puddles as they walk down the rock-strewn dirt pathway. It is hard to believe those innocuous puddles can be so deadly, but after seeing one of them eat her paper wrapping, she determines it would be best to avoid testing that theory.

She catches more movement as they head deeper into the woods. As they walk around a bend with a particularly thick section of trees, Mara glances to the side. Concerned, she says, "It's getting more act – "

Beral clamps his hand over her mouth, pulling her head around to face forward.

A huge puddle of the thick, viscous liquid lies ahead. Purples and reds swirl on top of the black surface, giving it an oily sheen. The colors shift in gentle arcs, although nothing stirs the shallow-looking liquid. It spans just a little over five feet in length and three feet in width – and it is perfectly perpendicular to the right of the trail.

Kimala stands just behind Rick, looking tall and regal – but her balled fists tremble slightly. *She's putting on an act,* Mara realizes, narrowing her eyes as she stares at the pond-sized amount of Hemius. *She must be really scared for that thing to affect her this much.*

"How did a big puddle like that end up at the border?" Kimala's voice is steady and assertive, not revealing a hint of her fear.

"I don't know, but we need to figure out a way

around without alerting it," Rick says quietly, eyeing the pathway suspiciously strewn with rocks and pebbles. "It has set a trap for its prey... let us hope it remains ignorant to our presence."

Mara frowns. "It doesn't know we're here?"

Kimala shakes her head. "It can't see; it hunts through sound and vibrations in the ground." She jerks her chin towards the calm swirls. "Nothing is coming out, so it must be inactive. We have a chance of slipping by it."

"Tein'stra Codi, shall we go first?" Rick volunteers, glancing at the black-haired youth. Codi nods.

Mara glances over and notices the two-yard gap between the farthest edge of the road and the puddle. "That's not enough space?"

"It can grab you," Kimala, Don, and Beral hiss.

"All right, I got it." Mara snatches Kimala's wrist, tugging the girl next to her. "Kimala, stay with me."

Kimala yanks her hand back, scowling at Mara. "Don't grab me like that."

Everyone's eyes are on the Hemius as Rick and Codi creep around it with as much distance between them and the pond. It doesn't move at all. They make it to the other side and ease away from the inky pool. Codi waves to Mara and Kimala.

They both glance across the twenty or so yards between them and Codi. *This is going to be tricky,* Mara grumbles to herself as she turns back to Kimala. "Roll your foot to reduce impact and noise," Mara advises.

Kimala rolls her eyes and stalks after Beral, her head held high. *If she doesn't lower that big head of hers, she's going to trip,* Mara thinks, exasperated. *She's not used to my boots.*

Kimala stumbles on a stray rock, falling to her

knees.

"Thought so," Mara mutters as Beral whirls around and helps Kimala up. Mara catches movement in the pond; eyebrows snapping together, she stares at the rippling surface. Something rises from it – no, that isn't right. The *liquid* rises in the shape of a node. A very large node.

Don darts towards Kimala and Beral, pulling out his sword and yelling, "Run! It's alert!"

Mara stares after her guard. The thing hadn't even moved much –

The node splits into four tentacles.

"Hey, over here!" Don yells, his voice quivering slightly. All four of the tentacles point towards him as Beral helps Kimala limp away.

Dread sinks into Mara, recognizing that type of limp. A twisted ankle. *They won't make it in time.* She rushes in, slipping her backpack off and holding it in her hand to prepare herself for a fight.

The tendrils focusing on Don streak in, almost too fast to see. One wraps around his sword arm, and he shrieks in agony. Another wraps around his throat.

His scream turns into a wet gurgle.

The two remaining tendrils take their time, turning into two sharp points and pressing gently into the man's torso. He jerks and thrashes, still alive.

Mara's hand claps over her mouth in horror, bile rising to the back of her throat.

Beral pushes the shocked Kimala towards Codi and Rick. He draws his sword, trembling. Seeing Mara, he jerks his head soundlessly towards Kimala.

Getting the idea, Mara quickly and silently sneaks by the now dead Don and yanks Kimala's right arm over her shoulder. Keeping herself between the pond and the injured girl, Mara does her best to help her cousin across the rock-strewn path as Beral shouts at the tendrils.

I guess it was done with its first meal, Mara thinks sickeningly. She doesn't want to look back, but she needs to know.

Don is now being dragged into the puddle, armor and all. Only two tendrils lazily slap at Beral's sword, toying with him as if it has all the time in the world.

"What happened to your ankle?" she asks Kimala in a low voice.

"Sprained it." Kimala grimaces, her eyes hazy. "I can heal it, but... need to be sitting."

Mara shifts her bag in her hand, bending over and flicking out one of her daggers. She transfers it into her empty left hand still wrapped around her cousin's small waist.

Plop.

Ahead of her, Rick and Codi cringe just as Beral shrieks. Whipping her head around, she sees him being lowered into the pond by several different strands. There is no sight of Don.

Swallowing bile, Mara drags Kimala noisily along the pathway.

"What are you doing?" Kimala hisses, staggering beside Mara. "You're making too much noise!"

"You need to get out of here." *Ten feet left,* Mara calculates, using Codi's and Rick's expressions to determine what is happening behind her. *Eight feet...*

Their eyes widen in horror.

Mara shoves her bag and Kimala towards them and whirls around, immediately blocking the tendril that would have grabbed her arm – just like with Don. Gritting her teeth, she shoves her blade against it, cutting deep.

The tentacle rears back as if in pain.

Mara grins. She had injured it! She switches hands, gripping the smooth metal in her right palm. Maybe she can fool it with her ambidexterity.

The next attack comes at lightning speed, not giving her time to draw the second dagger. The black whip bypasses her defenses in an entirely different set of moves. A hot, slimy substance slips around Mara's right wrist and bare ankle above the shoes, scorching her skin. A scream rips from her throat as her dagger tumbles from her hand, clanging against the stones on the pathway.

It tosses her into the air. Mara barely has time to regain her senses before the black cords wrap around the same ankle. It dangles her above the oily liquid, slowly lowering her. Her necklace falls out from underneath her shirt and hangs around her jaw.

Mara gasps for air, slowly gaining control of the burning pain. *I really ticked it off...* Codi, Rick, and Kimala stare at her in horror. Her father's vacant eyes flash through her mind. *I need to protect them.*

"Run." They only stare. "*Run!*" They scramble away, putting distance between themselves and the pond.

The Hemius writhes beneath her, and tendrils chase after Codi and Kimala. "Hey, up here, you giant oil spill," Mara croaks. "Up. Here!"

Mara grabs her hairpin with her right hand, ignoring the twinge in her burnt wrist, and the dagger from her left leg with her other hand. She slashes at the black vine holding her ankle.

It recoils as if injured, and she plummets towards the pond. It snatches her ankle again, dangling her only a foot or two above the oily surface.

Fighting through the white-hot burning pain, she stares down at the shallow-looking surface of the pool. More tendrils rise from the ground, reaching for her.

Mara's breathing speeds up as it draws closer and closer. She slashes out, but the Hemius cords wrap around the blade and yank it out of her one good hand. It grabs her already burning right wrist, and she shrieks in agony as the hairpin spike tumbles into the pond.

Belatedly, she remembers her new ability and tries to create that sparking ball from before. A churning black orb surrounded by silver lightning bolts forms at the tip of her fingertips and blasts away some of the Hemius, but the explosion knocks her across the pond. Her right shoulder strikes a tendril, and a burning kiss races along near the base of her neck where her shirt collar ends.

She screams.

A shockwave of power bursts from her, knocking Codi, Kimala, and Rick several feet away from the pond as her necklace glows a blinding silver before shattering into pieces. They turn around and stare at the unconscious Mara dangling not even a foot over the pond as her inky restraints slowly lower her to its surface.

Codi covers his mouth, horrified. "No... someone, help..."

A brown traveling cloak swirls by Codi. He glances up, startled, and is greeted with sharp, unfriendly blue eyes. "Stay back," the man says, his hand wrapping around a short curved blade at his side. Pointed ears peek from underneath his straw-blonde hair.

He throws the weapon at the Hemius and speaks a few words in Xharos. The Hemius recoils and flings Mara to the side.

The man phase-steps across the distance. He skids to a halt and catches Mara, nearly tumbling backwards from the momentum. Kneeling on the ground, he reaches into his pocket and pulls out a vial. Flicking the lid off, he tosses the vial and all of its contents into the puddle.

The Hemius tendrils jerk and writhe in agony, slowly receding into the inky pond.

He quickly catches his flying curved weapon and sheathes it. He phase-steps to the others, snatching Mara's dagger that had fallen outside of the pond on his way. He jerks his head down the pathway. "Can you walk?"

They nod. Rick, supporting Kimala, is instantly wary of the newcomer and narrows his eyes at him. They scramble to keep up with the blonde elf's fast pace.

After several yards, the man slows down. He gently lowers Mara to the ground, careful not to touch the bleeding wounds where the Hemius had touched her.

"Thank you for saving her." Codi kneels beside him. "But... who are you?"

"Ace," he quickly introduces himself, distracted as he assesses Mara's injuries. "Do either of you know any healing spells?"

"I-I do," Kimala stammers, still rattled by what had just happened. She takes a deep breath and leans over Mara, careful not to touch the wounds or the blood seeping from them.

"Can you close them?" he asks as he digs through

a small pouch on his hip.

Kimala nods. "Yes."

Kimala closes her eyes and hovers her hands over Mara's bleeding shoulder. A silvery sky blue light spills from her fingers and coats Mara's injuries, the skin slowly knitting itself back together. She does the same for her cousin's wrist and ankle. She scans Mara's vitals next, making sure her body is not going into shock. Her sky-colored Source does not pick up any abnormalities.

Finished, Kimala leans back and takes a deep breath. "Her pulse is regulated. There's no infection other than the Hemius," she says, her voice trembling ever so slightly as she subtly touches her ankle, quickly mending the torn ligaments the best she can. It would still hurt, but it would be better than before.

Ace hands her a cloth and some gloves. "Wipe away the blood."

Kimala nods, slipping on the tan-colored gloves and dabbing carefully at the black-tainted blood on Mara's shoulder. Underneath, only a blackish-purple bruise with horrible red undertones remains, looking worse than any normal bruise. It stretches over her shoulder, about the width and length of her thumb.

Her wrist isn't much better. As Kimala wipes away the blood, she finds herself lifting Mara's hand, having to go all the way around the girl's wrist to see the extent of the inch-wide bracelet that shifts and tightens underneath the skin as if alive.

Gritting her teeth, Kimala pats Mara's ankle, finding that the two inches of exposed skin between her shoe and her pants leg is completely infected. Wiping off as much blood as she can, Kimala says, "I need a knife."

Ace hands her Mara's dagger. Staring at it, Kimala wonders what had happened to the hairpin she had given her cousin. She carefully cuts away the cloth from Mara's ankle where it had come in contact with the Hemius creature, tossing the ruined fabric off to the side.

Tiny black veins trail up Mara's leg, fading away about three-quarters of an inch from where the solid anklet of Hemius ended. Kimala lets out her breath, relieved. "It hasn't hit a major artery," she announces, putting the knife aside.

Ace nods as he hands her a jar. "Rub this over the Hemius infected areas."

Kimala eyes it warily. "What is it?" she demands. She was not about to put a foreign substance on her cousin's wounds – no matter how much she disliked her.

"It's orica, Hemius ointment. It numbs the pain and slows down the Hemius," Ace explains quickly.

Kimala recognizes the name from her studies and takes the jar from him.

"Are you sure – " Rick begins, suspicious of the substance.

Kimala dips her fingers into the substance and sniffs it. Recognizing the concoction, she nods at the guard. "It's orica." She gently rubs her fingers over Mara's exposed shoulder, grimacing as Mara writhes slightly underneath the application. "Codi, Rick, hold her down."

Startled, the two move to Mara's left side, keeping the unconscious girl still as Kimala continues the application. The churning Hemius underneath her skin slows down and finally stills as Kimala meticulously coats each infected area.

Mara's breathing regulates as she sinks into a deeper slumber. "Thank you, Ace," Kimala says, carefully stripping off the biodegradable gloves and tossing them into a gnarly bush. She tugs off her bag. "I have some bandages we can use, too."

Ace nods. "Good idea."

"How did you know we were in trouble?" Rick demands as Kimala quickly wraps Mara's wrist and ankle in bandages. She uses a square piece of gauze and some medical tape to cover the area on the shoulder.

"I noticed a flash through the woods and felt the shockwave of power," he admits, his smile strained. "It's a good thing I let my curiosity get the best of me."

Codi and Kimala stare at the empty chain around Mara's neck. Her brow creasing, Kimala murmurs, "Her Source must have shattered it."

"Will he know we're in trouble?" Codi asks aloud, voicing their concerns.

Noticing the tense air, Ace changes the topic by asking, "What should I call you?"

"Codi," he introduces himself, leaving out his last name. "This is my sister, Mara." Ace glances at Mara's face as if committing her name to memory.

"Kimala," she instantly supplies, and then winces. Her name is commonly associated with her father.

Ace pauses, staring at her in surprise. "Tein'stra? Where's your guard?"

Kimala gives a weak smile. "Rick is the last one. The others were killed."

"That's terrible." He glances at Codi and Mara. "Are these your friends, then?"

"You sure do ask a lot of questions," Rick growls,

on edge. "Shouldn't we be leaving?"

"Ah, yes, you are right." Ace stands up and brushes off his tan pants.

Codi scoops Mara into his arms. "I'll carry her."

"We should be able to make it to Cerlail Academy before her Hemius spreads too much," Kimala says, striding ahead of them. She doesn't want to go back through the Heramus with that monster lurking around, and Cerlail Academy's medical facilities are the best option for Mara's survival. They cannot get rid of it entirely, but there are ways to sedate the Hemius.

"If she doesn't overexert herself beforehand, then yes." Ace follows their group. "I'm traveling that way, as well, so I will accompany you."

"It would be nice having an ally here," Codi admits. Ace seems accustomed to traveling.

Rick trails behind, staring at Ace's back with narrowed eyes. He cannot disagree with Codi's statement; one guard would be at a heavy disadvantage to take care of three nobles. He will just have to keep an eye on Ace.

Underneath the cloth covering Mara's wounds, three blemishes darker than bruises stain the skin where the Hemius had touched her. They writhe and taint her from the inside.

< * >

Mara coughs and claws her shoulder at the base of her neck. Gauze greets her fingers. She rolls onto her side and rubs her right wrist; bandages coat the skin. Hands shaking, she touches her right ankle. Same thing.

"Mara, don't take those off!" Kimala's voice snaps.

Mara's hand is yanked away from the bandages. Weak and disoriented, she collapses on her back, trying to keep from retching. *Why is my neck hurting so much?*

"How many fingers am I holding up?"

Mara opens her eyes again, her vision swimming slightly. Kimala's sky blue eyes and honey blonde hair come into focus. "Two," Mara croaks and clears her throat. "Where are we?"

"Camp," Kimala responds simply, rummaging in her bag. "Sit up and drink this."

Wincing, Mara boosts herself onto her left elbow, cradling her right arm against her stomach. She glances around the clearing in the midst of healthy-looking trees. A colorful sunset stains the sky with color.

Kimala shoves a drink in Mara's hand just as she catches sight of Codi, Rick, and a stranger at the campfire. She downs the vile liquid, forcing herself to swallow it. "Awful," she coughs, handing it back to Kimala.

"That's what you get for throwing yourself in front of Hemius," Kimala half-heartedly chastises. "What would I have told your mother if you had died?"

Knowing this is the closest she is going to get to anything resembling sympathy from her cousin, Mara smirks at her. "Aww, you do care."

"Don't push it," Kimala grumbles, shoving the latches closed on her bag. "I need to doctor your infection. Come closer to the fire; it's getting too dark over here."

Mara slowly rises to her feet, testing her ankle. It twinges as she uses it, but it is tolerable. Limping to the campfire, she carefully sits down next to Kimala and nods to the blonde-haired stranger. "Hello. Um... did you help us?"

He smiles at her, his blue eyes amused. "Yes. My name is Ace. How are you feeling?"

Mara returns the smile, feeling comfortable around this man for some odd reason. "Better than I thought I would after getting tossed around like a ragdoll. I'm Mara."

Kimala yanks off the bandage on her shoulder a little harder than she could have. Mara winces. "You're infected with Hemius in three places," she begins as she pulls out a jar and glove. "Your ankle, wrist, and shoulder. All on the right side."

The cold cream stings as it goes over the mark on Mara's shoulder. She jerks partially away, startled at the pain. "Well, there goes my plans to live to a hundred years old," she tries to joke.

Ace chuckles. "It's possible you may do just that, Mara. Every Hemius patient is different."

"Knowing her, she'll probably not even make it to eighteen," Kimala grumbles, but Mara hears a tone of guilt underneath the snarky comment. She reapplies the adhesive bandage and gestures for Mara's wrist. "The more you strain your body, the faster it will spread. You need to take it easy until we get to Cerlail Academy, Mara. Once there, they will be able to more effectively sedate the Hemius from spreading so easily."

"All right," Mara sighs, watching Kimala unwind the bandage. A nasty bruise rings her wrist. Mara jumps when it shifts underneath her skin, twisting almost like a snake. "It moved."

"Of course it did. It's Hemius." Kimala slathers the stinging ointment over the infected area. The

Hemius slows down and finally stops; she wraps the bandage around it again. "Are you going to keep making stupid comments?"

Ace watches the interaction between them, a small amused smile on his face. "I assume you have not seen a Hemius infection before," he comments.

Mara glances at him and notices two pointed ears sticking out from his straight hair. *Elf,* she thinks, remembering Aeserast's brief lesson on them. *Which means he's at least eighteen.* "Not before today," she admits as Kimala works on her ankle. She frowns, examining her leg. "What happened to my pants?"

Kimala huffs. "I had to cut part of it off because they were searing into your flesh from the Hemius's touch. It probably hurt me more than you, since it *is* my mother's handiwork."

Mara sighs as Kimala finishes up and tosses the wasted glove into the fire. It disintegrates in a blackish-purplish plume. "I'm just glad you're okay, Tein'stra Kimala."

Kimala stares at the dissipating purple plume. "Don't do that. It sounds weird coming from you."

Mara watches Codi and Rick prepare dinner. "Yeah, it does."

Kimala hesitates. "Hemius sometimes creates new injuries from within. If you feel lightheaded or suddenly have sharp pains, let me know immediately."

Mara glances out of the corner of her eye at the stoic girl. *I guess she can care.* "Sure thing."

"That's a medic's traveling satchel, isn't it?" Ace queries, pointing to Kimala's tan bag.

Kimala is unable to decide whether she should be flirtatiously embarrassed or wary of the cute elf's curiosity. She picks the latter. "It's not much of a secret if everyone knows about it."

He grins. "Nah, I have a medic friend who loves those things. She shows them off anytime she has a chance."

Codi and Rick prepare supper as Kimala and Ace chat over the different types of medical bags. Mara stares into the Source-created fire; she could barely make out the flat object in the middle of the stones that was emitting the heat and flame-shaped designs into the air above it. The artificial flames dance, reminding her of the Hemius's burning tendrils wrapping around her limbs and tossing her through the air.

Shivering from the memory, Mara crosses her arms and places her head on her knees, blocking the view of the flames and hiding her sparking hands. Tuning out her companions, she focuses on the surroundings, trying to calm down.

The sun had set several minutes ago, so the nighttime animals are stirring. Mara listens to the odd hoots and screeches, remembering Codi's comment that this is a dangerous world. *We'll have to assign guard*, she thinks, listening to the noises and ignoring the dull ache in her injuries. *I probably won't sleep well tonight. I wonder if I can get the first shift…*

A strange hollering noise drifts on the gentle summer night breeze. Focusing on it, Mara jerks her head towards the right where she can faintly see the trees thinning towards the pathway. "There are people coming."

Everyone stops and stares at her. A distinctive nasal voice shouts in a foreign language.

"Slavers," Ace breathes, his eyes going wide. He waves his hand over the Source fire; it dims before being snuffed out. "Stay quiet."

Rick slowly unsheathes his sword and walks to the edge of the clearing closest to the road. Ace follows suit, holding his rounded blade.

Mara glances around, searching for her weapons. Codi reaches behind him and holds up one of her dagger sheaths. He tosses it her way, and she catches it.

The voices grow closer. Mara slinks towards Ace and Rick, staring through the trees; Narein and Naros illuminate the pathway several hundred yards away.

A caravan rumbles down the north road. Oddly enough, there are no animals pulling it. Instead, four people trail alongside it, their hands touching the wooden panels of the large enclosed wagon.

Mara pauses next to Ace. "Do you think they'll come this way?" she breathes.

Ace glares at the caravan, his blue eyes dark and frightening in the night's shadows. "It is well-known that travelers rest here," he murmurs back. "They may try sending a small group to thieve or even kidnap us."

Mara grips her sheath, touching the thread around her neck. Startled at the lack of a pendant, she glances down.

Ace notices and smiles bitterly. "Tein'stra Kimala said it broke."

Mara groans inwardly. She wonders if Aeserast will be angry. Clutching her single dagger, she mourns over the losses in the Hemius pond. She hopes Shaniel hadn't paid too much for the daggers...

"Get ready," Rick whispers as the caravan of people approach. The big wagon-like box stops just a few hundred yards away, and several men hop out of the back and work their way towards the clearing with weapons drawn. The four people walking alongside the wagon sit down, leaning against the box in exhaustion.

"Those are the mages," Ace comments in a low voice. "We have to do this quietly; we don't need them involved."

Mara nods and swallows hard. It feels wrong to ambush these people, but when she glances at Codi and Kimala, even they look determined. Kimala has a small knife – probably Codi's – while Codi wields his two-handed short sword.

As soon as the first two walk between Rick and Ace, they leap out and slash at the unsuspecting intruders. They collapse to the ground, not moving. The remaining four slavers charge in, and the scuffle begins.

Mara's fingers strike the nearest man in the jugular as her other palm collides with his face. *Crack.* The man chokes and falls, his nose broken. Mara snaps her dagger's pommel against the big man's temple and he collapses, unconscious.

Ace and Rick efficiently take care of the other three intruders while Mara incapacitates the fourth one. *That went smoother than I thought it would,* she thinks, kneeling next to the unconscious man and emptying his pockets.

Ace raises an eyebrow. "What do you think you'll find?" he murmurs.

"Nothing," she murmurs, pulling out knickknacks. "But we don't need him pulling out a hidden weapon while we're interrogating him on how to get by without being noticed by any other scouts." Feeling a round object, she pulls her hand out. A bright orangish-red stone glows softly like an ember in her palm. She frowns.

Ace kneels beside her and snatches the stone, staring at it in shock. "This is a dragon stone," he whispers, his hand shaking slightly. He stares at Mara. "This means…"

"They have the missing dragon duir'ne," Rick finishes, his expression grim.

CHAPTER 7
THE DRAGON DUIR'NE

"Here should be good," Rick says. He and Ace release the restrained slaver, and he collapses on the ground. He groans, shifting uncomfortably.

Mara sinks against a tree and rubs her ankle, still shocked that the stone she had found belongs to a dragon prince. Kimala drops her satchel next to Mara and pulls out bandages, swabs, a glove, and the stinging ointment. Mara winces, knowing what her cousin is about to do.

Rick yanks the slaver into a seated position as Ace paces. The guard slaps the big man awake.

Ace stalks towards the slaver and grabs his collar, growling, "Where is the dragon duir'ne?" He uses the Xharos term for prince.

He avoids Ace's icy gaze. "I donno wha' yer talkin' abou'," he slurs. Stunned, Mara stares at the man, recognizing the accent from when she was little; her father's murderers had had the same accent.

Codi helps Kimala with Mara's treatment. Mara winces as her shoulder twinges underneath the stinging application of the ointment. She blocks out the pain the best she can.

Ace grins, baring his teeth. His blue eyes darken visibly as his thumb barely touches the slaver's collarbone underneath the shirt. "Barrew, is it? Tell me where you're keeping the dragon duir'ne and I'll let you off easy."

Everyone's eyes widen as Ace speaks. "Mind-weaver," Rick breathes, paling significantly.

Barrew gulps, unable to look away from Ace's terrifying gaze. "I-I won't say," he forces out.

Ace releases the slaver, his facial features oddly smooth. "So be it." He grins, something bright flashing through his eyes. "Tell me, which do you prefer? Being trapped inside your own mind, or experiencing your fears in the world?"

The blonde elf's palm covers the man's forehead before he could respond. Ace closes his eyes as Barrew's face slackens. Ace removes his hand and wipes it on his tunic, glaring at the man in disgust.

Rick levels his sword at Ace. The tip trembles. "Who are you?"

Shocked, Ace stares at the tip of the sword. "Someone could get hurt if you point with that…"

"Answer me, mind-weaver!" Rick demands, gritting his teeth.

Ace looks the guard directly in the eyes. "Ace Narweun, spy for the Quasalan Council," he finally admits, slowly easing a smooth medallion out of his pocket. A gold tree on a green background is etched on the surface. "I was sent to investigate this year's black market in hopes of finding the missing dragon duir'ne."

He's a spy? Mara thinks, in awe. *How do you even get a position like that so young?*

Rick holds out his hand for the crest, and Ace tosses it to him. The guard examines it closely, narrowing his eyes as he inspects the sigil. Satisfied with whatever he found, he lowers his sword and hands the sigil back to Ace. He bows deeply from the waist. "I apologize for doubting you, sir."

Ace shakes his head. "There are too many of the

royal guard I can fool just by flashing this around. To see you inspect it…" He eyes Rick, smiling slightly. "It is good to know there are still some who check the facts before taking them at face value."

Startled by the compliment, Rick straightens. "Thank you, sir." He glances at the glassy-eyed Barrew. "What… did you do to him?"

Ace smiles innocently. "Oh, just found what his worst fear is and locked him inside his mind with it."

Mara's blood chills at these words. She hisses as her wrist throbs painfully under the application of the orica. Kimala and Codi seem surprised by Ace's identity, but act as though his ability to mess with someone's mind is not unusual.

Ace touches Barrew's forehead lightly. The man heaves in large gulps of air, his face breaking out in a cold sweat as he hunches over and trembles at Ace's feet. His eyes are filled with terror.

Ace squats in front of the man, his arms resting on his knees. "If you do not tell me everything you know on the dragon duir'ne, I will retrieve the information myself – and you will definitely not like that."

The skin around Barrew's lips turns a little green. He looks as if he is going to hurl. "I-I'll tell ye," he rushes, swallowing hard. "Just… please. No more."

Ace beams at the man. "Great! Where is the duir'ne?"

The slaver takes a deep breath. "The wagon has a holdin' cell. Boss put some necklace on 'im when we first got 'im."

Ace closes his eyes and pinches the bridge of his nose. "A forced morphing charm…"

Kimala accidentally yanks the bandage around Mara's wrist a little hard. Mara glances at her in time to see her lips tremble. "What's wrong?" Mara asks, suddenly worried.

Kimala jerks her head from side to side. "A morphing charm is... illegal."

At Mara's confused expression, Codi explains quietly, "It forcefully condenses the creature into a bipedal form, making it an unnatural transformation. Kidnappers and slavers use morphing charms to make the individual... transportable." He spits out the last word in disgust.

Mara pales. She could imagine the bones shifting, aching as they are crammed against one another. They chafe and cut into muscle as they shrink... She takes a deep breath, casting the odd imagery out of her mind. Where had *that* come from?

Rick frowns, all of his focus on Ace's conversation with Barrew. "That means the duir'ne's power has been restrained, as well. It explains why he has not escaped yet."

Ace nods. "It also explains why he is able to fit into the wagon."

Kimala finishes bandaging Mara's ankle. "Help me up," she asks her brother. Confused, he clasps her hand and pulls her to her feet, helping her towards the others. "Do you mind if I ask a few questions?" she directs at Ace and Rick.

Ace shrugs. "I see no harm in it."

Mara gestures at the big man. "The others like you. How many are there total, not including those in the attack earlier? How many are mages? What are your formations?"

Rick and Ace appraise Mara, recognizing her natural talent for the tactical field. Ace bumps the toe of his boot against the silent Barrew. "Answer her."

Barrew fidgets, glancing between his interrogators. He opens his mouth, spilling the secrets of his comrades.

Within minutes, they learn there are twenty-five slavers in all: one leader, four mages, and twenty regular fighters. The leader is a creature native to Quanaris, but no one stops to explain to Mara what exactly a tav'luk is. Five slavers are on guard around the caravan at all times, and another five act as scouts in the woods ahead and behind the caravan. Shifts are five hours except for the last shift of the night, which is six hours long.

Two guards watch the entrance of the enclosed wagon at all times with the strongest shift on watch during the nighttime and the weakest shift at mealtime. Only the two on the last shift know combative Source techniques; the mages only know translocation and movement spells.

Ace claps his hands together, looking almost excited. "I do believe we have all the information we need. Thank you."

"What if he is lying to try to deceive us?" Mara asks.

Ace gives the slaver a nasty grin. "If he's lying, I'll find out – and our little bargain is off."

The slaver gulps, terror flashing through his eyes.

Ace rubs his hands together and glances at Rick. "Could you help me out?"

Rick warily examines Ace's innocent expression. "What do you need me for?"

"Oh, just carrying him." Ace's fist flies to the slaver's face, knocking him out in one blow. "That felt good."

Sighing, Rick helps Ace drag the unconscious man

into the woods. Kimala, Codi, and Mara glance at one another, none of them quite sure how to take what had just happened.

Finally, Codi clears his throat. "You should try to get some sleep, Mara."

Mara shakes her head. Her ankle had started throbbing several minutes ago, but she doesn't want to ask Kimala for help. "I'm not tired," she fibs, subtly shifting her weight onto her left foot to relieve the pressure on her infected limb. "Anyway, when they get back, we need to figure out a plan to get the-the duir'ne." She stammers over the new word, still unused to it.

Kimala ruffles through her satchel, her hand reaching deeper into it than possible. "You should at least try to rest." She pulls out a vial of blue-green liquid and offers it to Mara. "Drink this."

Mara takes it, examining the swirling liquid. "What is it?"

"It will help you," Kimala states simply as she reorganizes some of the items within her bag.

Mara knocks the potion back in one gulp. The liquid slides down her throat, making her tongue and esophagus tingle slightly. She hands the vial back to Kimala.

"So how long does it take to work?" Mara asks just as Ace and Rick walk back into the clearing. She leans against the tree, taking more weight off of her foot as the throbbing in her ankle lessens.

"A minute or two. Codi, could you keep an eye on her?" Kimala asks as she takes Mara's sleeping mat and spreads it out.

"I can do… that…" Mara's head swims as soon as she starts to move. Clutching her head, she falls against the tree and sinks to the ground with Codi's help. "Cheater," she mumbles, her eyes slipping closed as she recognizes the feeling of strong painkillers taking a hold of her consciousness. She passes out, falling against Codi.

Ace frowns as Codi carries his sister to the mat. "What did you give her?"

Kimala sets up her own mat. "Anesthetic."

Codi, tucking Mara in, glances at Kimala. "Why did she pass out, though?"

Kimala shakes her head. "Pain was keeping her up; despite the ointment, I could tell the infection was still hurting her."

Codi stares at Mara's face, noticing in the dim moonlight that she looks relaxed. "At least she's finally resting. What did you do with the slaver?"

Ace drops his bag next to a tree, taking first shift on guard duty. He cheerily answers, "Wiped his memory, planted fake ones, and sent him on his way."

They stare at the humming elf in stunned silence.

< * >

Mara stands in front of a silver engraved door fading into the surrounding darkness as if it barely exists. Oddly, she feels lightweight as if gravity has no influence on her. She could tell she is dreaming, but it feels oddly real.

The engraved door creaks open and a slender hand beckons to her.

"Come here…"

The voice is unfamiliar, but melodic and beautiful. Mara creeps closer and peers into the darkness. Someone stands on the other side, reaching towards her. Is it… herself?

"Let me help you…"

This time, the voice is a young girl's, hauntingly eerie in its innocence as the hand points at Mara's Hemius. She feels as though the little girl is not really there.

Mara peers around the door to get a better look.

Shokain leans forward, reaching for her hand just like he used to do when she was little. "Let's go home," he says, his burnt golden eyes warm and inviting.

Mara jolts upright, breathing heavily. Her heart pounds in her ears. Despite it being a dream, she has a nagging feeling she would not have been the same if she had taken that hand.

She glances around, noticing the stars are still out although the moons had set. Three other sleeping mats rise and fall gently as her companions sleep.

"Nightmare?" Ace asks softly, leaning against a tree with his head back, gazing at the sky.

Mara creeps towards him and sits against a neighboring tree, rubbing her ankle. It doesn't hurt as much as before, although the throbbing is starting up again. "Something like that."

Ace closes his eyes. "Never fun."

A comfortable silence falls between them. After a while, Mara finally asks the question that has been nagging her for a while. "Where are you from?"

Ace glances at her, his lips quirking up. "Alkina. You?"

She sighs. "Complicated. So are you really a spy? What's it like?"

Ace chuckles, turning his head towards her. "Interested in being one?"

Mara stares at her bandaged wrist; she still can't

believe this... thing is going to kill her eventually. "By the sounds of it, I won't live much longer for it to matter."

Ace reaches over and takes Mara's left hand, squeezing her fingers gently. Startled by the unexpected touch, she glances into his eyes. Are they... glowing? "Please don't think that way," he pleads, his voice soft.

Mara nods mutely.

He pats her left hand, smiling slightly. "Are you planning to study at Cerlail Academy? What do you want to study?"

Mara's eyelids grow heavier. The pain in her ankle, wrist, and shoulder fade into the background, easily ignorable. She draws her legs up and places her head on them, staring at his fingers still on her hand. "I dunno."

Ace chuckles. "Getting sleepy?"

Mara closes her eyes, suddenly exhausted. "Yeah..."

"Do you need help back to your mat?" he asks, glancing across the small camp at her sleeping mat not even ten feet away.

The weird dream from earlier flashes through her mind. She shakes her head rapidly, sitting upright and blinking away the tiredness. "I'll just stay up for a bit."

"You need to rest, Mara." He lets go of her hand to grab the long brown coat on top of his bag. He puts the folded material on his leg, patting it invitingly. "Here."

Mara stares at it. Not fully registering what she is doing, she curls up next to him, resting her head on his cushioned leg. Her eyes are closed before she even mumbles her appreciation.

Mara jolts awake at the clatter, momentarily disoriented by the sunlight streaming through the leaves and the serene atmosphere. Glancing around dizzily, she sees Kimala and Codi cleaning up from breakfast. *When did I fall asleep?*

"Sorry!" Codi apologizes in a low voice next to Kimala. He winces as the utensils clash together again.

"They might just hear you if you keep that up," Kimala grumbles. She notices Mara sitting upright. "See? You woke up Mara."

Relaxing, Mara takes a better look around. Her head had been on Ace's coat, but the elf is on the other side of camp with his back to them, sleeping. Rick is leisurely putting up the sleeping mats.

Kimala sits down in front of Mara, beckoning for her hand. "Did you sleep well?"

Mara nods, giving the girl access to the infected limbs. "What about the slavers?"

Rick sets the last sleeping mat off to the side, now packing the clean utensils. "They set up camp and are scouring the woods."

Codi plops down in front of Mara. "Probably looking for their missing scouts – or their ambushers."

Kimala finishes Mara's wrist and immediately checks her shoulder. "It hasn't moved much, which is good."

Mara glances at Ace, wondering when he had went to sleep. She hadn't even noticed he had moved, and usually that sort of thing wakes her up. Rick notices and says, "The mind-weaver passed out about thirty or so minutes ago. He spent the whole night on watch."

Mara frowns. "What's a mind-weaver?"

Codi glances at Ace uneasily. "It's someone able to manipulate memories and dreams." He examines her face closely. "You don't think you know him, right? Because we don't."

Mara quickly shakes her head. "Of course not."

"You were sleeping in his lap," Kimala points out, one eyebrow raised daintily.

Mara shrugs, but cannot hide the red creeping in around her ears. "I fell asleep next to him."

Codi glares at Ace's back. "I think he's messing with your head, making you like him."

Overprotective brother, Mara mutters to herself. She doesn't think of Ace in that way. She glances at Rick, who is strapping on his sword belt and making sure his armor is fastened correctly. "Where are you going?"

"To see where the wagon is. If I am not back by the time the sun peaks, move to the west."

They nod, watching him leave. Kimala finishes redressing and treating Mara's infections, patting her cousin's ankle before ruffling in her satchel. Codi whittles away at a piece of wood with his knife, occupying himself for the time being.

Mara limps over to Ace, leaning against a tree and sinking to the ground. She frowns, staring at his face. She had told Codi she doesn't know him, but she cannot deny the nagging sense of familiarity. She wonders if he really is messing with her mind.

Ace peers at her with one blue eye, smirking slightly. "Like what you see?"

"Hmph." Mara watches Kimala pull out clean clothes and tell Codi not to peek as she disappears around a bush to change. "You look familiar. Did you do something to me?"

Ace raises an eyebrow, surprised. "I don't tamper with my comrades' memories." He props himself on an elbow. "I just have one of those faces. It is an annoying coincidence."

A name hovers just out of reach in Mara's mind as Ace glances around the camp with a relaxed, almost serene expression. Leaning her head back against the tree, she closes her eyes briefly. She wonders if Kimala would be mad if she did a few t'ai chi patterns.

Rick jogs into the camp, panting. He slings his bag onto his shoulders as he nods to Ace. "They are packing. If we want to catch them, we should head out now."

Ace nods and grabs his pack. Codi and Kimala don't move from their positions, still lounging in the small camp. "Let's hurry, then. The sooner we free the duir'ne, the sooner we can get to Quasala."

Mara quickly stands up, snagging her bag off the ground. "I'm coming with you."

Rick shakes his head. "No. You will stay here with Kimala and Codi and move to the west when the sun reaches its peak." He nods to Codi. "Do you still feel comfortable with the plan?"

Codi nods confidently. "Yes, sir."

"Good." Rick starts through the trees after Ace. "We will meet you by the lake, then. Thana baro."

Mara grits her teeth. She may not know what the Xharos words mean, but she has a brain and can guess it is some form of 'see you later.' She rushes past Kimala and Codi.

Codi's brows snap together. "Mara, you need to stay – "

"I'm going with them." She slips through the trees, easily catching up to the two men. Startled, they whirl around and stare at Mara.

"You need to return to the others," Rick orders, gesturing behind her.

Mara shakes her head. "You'll need all the help you can get to save that prince." She ignores the odd look he gives her at the unfamiliar terminology from Earth. "I know how to fight; I can help."

Ace sighs in resignation. "I believe the only way we can make her stay is to tie her down," he mutters.

Mara raises an eyebrow. "Try me."

Rick steps between them, holding a placating hand towards Mara. "You may accompany us, but please understand you should try to keep all your movements to a minimum. Your Hemius – "

Mara steps around Rick and Ace, continuing along the narrow path through the woods. "Kimala has lectured me enough on it." She glances over her shoulder. "Are you coming?"

They sigh and start to follow when the other two teens stomp through the forest after Mara. Gritting his teeth, Rick turns to them. "Follow the plan!"

Codi glances at Mara, confused. "But Mara – "

"She's coming with us since she won't listen," Ace says in a deadpan voice, shrugging.

Kimala crosses her arms, glaring at Mara. "If she's going, then so am I. Who knows what she will get herself into; plus, I am training to be a field medic."

Codi rises to his full height of five and a half feet – only an inch taller than Mara. "An extra sword won't hurt, right?"

Rick slaps his palm against his face as Ace shakes his head. "That failed…" the mind-weaver mumbles, placing a slender hand on his hip.

The small group heads west, following the slavers while carefully avoiding the scouts. The wagon is forced to travel along the path at the base of the gently rolling forested hills while Mara and her companions skirt along the ridgeline.

When the caravan stops for lunch, the seven-foot tav'luk leader with greyish-black skin climbs out of the wagon. Mara cannot help but stare; the man almost looks like he is made of some type of metal, and he has extra joints in his arms and legs.

Munching on some jerky, she watches as some of the slavers carry food into the wagon and then exit empty-handed. She assumes they are feeding the prince. She mulls over how they can get close enough to rescue the duir'ne.

"The time to attack would be during mealtime," Ace plots, examining the way the slavers collect around the front of the wagon – leaving the back unsupervised except for the two guards standing by the door. "During the evening would be best because of the darkness. We should avoid the final night shift."

Rick nods. "If we go in from the back, we should only have to deal with one or two scouts until we reach the guards."

"The challenge is, then, getting in and out without someone noticing the dead scouts," Ace says, grim. He narrows his eyes as the dark-skinned tav'luk climbs into the rear of the caravan and closes the door behind himself.

Mara glances at him, seeing an idea spark in his eyes. *What isn't he telling us?* she wonders, frowning slightly.

He gives her a small smile as if saying, *Wait and see.*

They use the darkness to slip between the trees, nearing the estimated location of the first scout. Mara frowns as she glimpses a flash of purple through the trees. Rubbing her eyes, she wonders if Hemius gives a person hallucinations. She hopes not.

Ace, walking ahead of the others, pauses next to a tree and peers around it. He beckons the others over. "Look," he whispers, gesturing ahead.

Mara strains her eyes. A man is slumped against a tree, snoring slightly. *Not a very reliable scout,* she criticizes as they slip around him. However, it does give them a little bit more time to rescue the duir'ne.

They sneak to the rear of the caravan where two guys play a strange game with the pebbles strewn around. The other slavers laugh around a campfire several yards away, not paying any attention to the enclosed wagon.

"I call the left," Ace murmurs.

Rick nods. "I shall take the right, then."

"I can help – "

Rick shakes his head, cutting off Mara. "We can take care of this. Please stay back for now."

Ace moves forward. As Rick prepares to navigate to the right, Mara yanks Rick behind her and stalks past him, leaving the guard no choice but to stay by Kimala and Codi. *What if a scout had snuck up on those two?* Mara grumbles inwardly. *They need a* real *guard to protect them. At least I know how to do this much.*

She brushes her fingers over her dagger, contemplating whether or not she should use it for this fight. She decides to stick to her familiar methods.

Ace pauses only briefly when he sees that Mara is

on the other side and not Rick. He glares at her as they close in on their respective targets. She and Ace strike at the same time, taking out the slavers simultaneously. Mara knocks out her target with one blow as Ace quickly wipes his blade clean and plucks the key off the dead man's waist.

"You should be with the others," he hisses, carefully fitting the key into the lock.

She clenches her jaw tightly. "Did you have to kill him?"

Ace glances at her. "He would have alerted the camp." He quietly unfastens the bolts as Kimala, Codi, and Rick join them.

The door opens onto two anchored chairs and a small table. Deeper in the wagon, two glowing orange-gold reptilian eyes stare out from within a barred section.

A young man looking to be only a year or two older than Mara huddles in a corner of the cell, his skin patterned like scales and glinting at the slightest bit of light. The ember-colored pendant around his neck nearly matches the color of his oily reddish-orange hair. His curved, elongated ears are nearly hidden underneath the limp locks. Filth and mud cake his gold-embroidered flame-red clothes.

A long, scaly golden-edged red tail flicks about in agitation, twining around his pants and thudding against the wood. He stares at them, wary and afraid.

Mara snatches the key from Ace and hops into the wagon before he could stop her, ignoring the painful jolt in her ankle. She holds her hands where the dragon-boy can see them, unable to resist marveling at the scale-like pattern over his skin. Slowly creeping towards the door, she explains in a low voice, "We're here to get you out."

"Be more respectful, Mara! That's a dragon duir'ne!" Kimala hisses. Ace hushes her, peeking around the side of the wagon to make sure no one had heard the girl.

The dragon-boy narrows his eyes, the fiery orbs drilling into Mara. "Who are you?" he asks, his voice hoarse and wispy.

Ace climbs into the wagon, padding to the bars as Mara reaches the door of the cell. She unlocks it as Ace quickly whispers, "I apologize, Your Grace, but introductions will have to wait. We need to get you out of here."

Mara opens the door. He shuffles forward on his hands and knees, taking her outstretched hand. She helps him stand, noticing how he wobbles on his feet.

"Are you injured?" she asks, pulling him out of the cell and allowing him to use her as balance. He smells of cinders and campfires. Ace quickly takes the duir'ne's other arm to help support him.

He shakes his head as he leans on them heavily. Mara can't believe how much he weighs; he looks to be around her size but is easily two or even three times heavier than what she had anticipated. "I am not used to a bipedal form," he articulates oddly, wincing and flexing his jaw. "Especially... this one."

Mara's face pales. Again, the odd memory-like sensation of having her bones jammed together and condensed rushes through her senses, causing her to shiver in sympathy.

"We'll get you somewhere safe," she promises, surprised at the amount of emotion in her voice at that statement.

Ace and Rick help the dragon duir'ne out of the

wagon as Codi offers his arms to Mara so she can break her impact. She winces as her shoulder and wrist twinge.

"Kimala, Mara, take the duir'ne and run into the woods," Ace instructs.

Mara nods, tucking herself underneath the dragon-boy's arm again. "Kim, grab the other side," she grunts, wincing as the Hemius on her shoulder and ankle pull.

"Don't call me that," Kimala says half-heartedly, giving Mara a worried glance as she takes the prince's other arm. "Pardon me, Your Grace." Her eyes widen as she shoulders some of the weight.

The guard Mara had knocked out stirs. Before they can stop him, he shouts, "Intruders! They're taking the dragon!"

Rick and Ace stab him at the same time, but it is too late. Ace spins in a tight circle, one of his hands gripping the hair on top of his head. Mara stares, suddenly certain she had seen someone else do the exact same thing once.

"Get out of here!" he hisses at Mara and Kimala as footsteps rapidly approach.

CHAPTER 8
STUBBORNNESS

Mara ignores the pain in her infected limbs as she tugs the duir'ne and Kimala along. She glances back at the clash of weapons, wishing she could help them against the attackers. Gritting her teeth, she focuses ahead – but stops at the sight of the ebony-skinned tav'luk leader ambling towards them from around the front of the wagon.

He sneers, flexing his extra-jointed limbs. "You think you can escape me, little dragonling?" he rumbles in a gravelly voice. He has many of the same features as a regular person, and Mara wonders if the pressure points are similar, too.

"How strong are you?" she asks the 'dragonling,' a plan formulating in her head.

Kimala shakes her head. "You shouldn't fight – "

"What do you require of me?" the dragon duir'ne asks, shifting on his feet slightly to remove his weight off Mara's shoulders.

"Throw me at him feet-first."

"Prepare yourself." Hands wrap around her waist and catapult her towards the dark-skinned tav'luk. She aims with her bad foot, already calculating the damage the impact would do to it. She cannot afford to hurt her only good ankle on top of her current injuries.

The tav'luk is definitely not slow. He catches her bad foot in mid-air, causing the bones to grate against one another. Mara grimaces as pain shoots through her ankle.

She performs a swift kick to the nape of his neck with her one good foot. As gravity kicks in, she uses her entire body's momentum behind her arm and slams her elbow between his legs, hoping it is a weakness like most male bipedals.

He grunts in pain, dropping her. She catches herself with her hands, rolling away and getting back to her feet. She favors her right leg, testing her balance on her twisted ankle as the tav'luk recovers. Whipping out her dagger, she flourishes it in her left hand, unsure if her right one would be able to hold it because of the impact with the ground.

"No honor," he growls, straightening. He steps forward, and the impact trembles the ground slightly. "You will pay for that, little girl."

Mara grins recklessly, masking her fear of the giant man. "And kidnapping a prince – a duir'ne – is honorable?" She holds up her knife, sinking into a crouch. Behind her, the dragon-boy sucks in his breath and mutters something in a strangely familiar guttural language.

Hatred flashes through the tav'luk's eyes. Using incredible speed despite his size, he swings his fist down.

Mara dodges, wrapping her arms around the limb and guesstimating a pressure point. She jams her fingers into the tender patch of skin as she stabs his arm.

He howls in agony, bringing his other fist around. Again, Mara dodges, but her ankle gives out on her.

She stumbles.

He catches her by her throat, slowly crushing it as he raises her off the ground. The dagger slips from her fingers.

Gasping for air, Mara rakes her nails across his arm, but it doesn't faze him. Red spots splash across her vision. She holds her hand out, reaching for the tav'luk.

The ebony creature's laugh sounds like a rumbling thundercloud. "Puny child," he chastises, smirking. "Do you wish to beg for mercy?"

"As… if." Mara spits in the tav'luk's face. He closes his eyes and wipes away the spittle – giving her an opening.

Silver sparks gather at her fingertips, shooting outwards with a wave of black fog barely in the form of a sphere. It explodes in his face.

The tav'luk howls and falls backwards as Mara catapults across the ground from the mini explosion. She slams into someone; his arms encircle her, protecting her as they ram into the side of the wagon.

The dragon prince winces as he sits upright. "Take off the pendant," he orders. Mara stares at him, stunned by the demand. The tav'luk struggles to stand up, clutching his bleeding face. "Now!"

Mara fumbles with the charm, flinching as the stone's heat bites into her fingers. Finally, she figures out the latch and unclasps it, pulling it off his neck. The stone turns black.

His body stretches and morphs.

His neck elongates and his hair hardens together into flaming red scales. His face pushes out into a muzzle ridged with spikes and bumps. Mara slides to the ground as he grows, his arms turning into scaly claws that flatten the grass on either side of her. Two beautiful orange-red wings stretch out and scrape the trees on either side of them.

The dragon crouches over Mara protectively. He

shakes his head and roars.

The tav'luk grins manically, his dark eyes shining with bloodlust. A deep-throated snarl rumbles through the dragon's chest, and Mara's eyes widen as she stares at the scales vibrating in front of her face. She tilts her head back, watching upside-down as the tav'luk charges at them.

The dragon swipes his extended claws at the tav'luk, sending the creature crashing into the wagon. Whirling around, he roars at the other slavers, rising onto his forelegs to tower over everyone. Codi, Rick, and Ace scramble out of the way as the scaled beast lunges at the slavers, swiping his huge claws at the attackers. His tail swings around, sweeping several off their feet.

Kimala helps her cousin up. Mara winces as her ankle twinges painfully.

"Are you all right?" Ace asks worriedly. He glances behind the two girls and his eyes widen. "Carc'ra."

The tav'luk staggers to his feet, rage contorting his face. He roars and charges at them.

Ace quickly grabs Mara's right arm while Codi takes Kimala's place, supporting Mara as they dart into the forest.

Rick widens his stance, gripping his sword as he waits for the charging tav'luk.

"That idiot," Ace mutters, releasing Mara and racing towards Rick. Mara watches in dread, wondering who will reach the soldier first.

The tav'luk does.

The guard leaps out of the way at the last second, slashing at the tav'luk's unprotected back. Howling, the extra-jointed creature whirls around with his fingers curled into claws, slashing across Rick's armored torso.

The armor falls apart like ribbons. He staggers back, clutching his chest in pain.

Mara's eyes widen as Kimala covers her mouth. Ace stabs at the tav'luk, but the blade chips as it glances off the skin. *It hardened its exterior*, Mara thinks, unable to see this creature as a man anymore.

The tav'luk swings his curled fingers at Ace; he barely dodges it, and the claws scrape against his arm. Rick lunges, defending Ace's back as the tav'luk tries to land another hit.

Mara steps forward to help them, but her right ankle caves underneath her and she collapses on the ground. Kimala and Codi quickly help her up and support her.

The dragon, finished with wiping out the slavers, pounces on the tav'luk before it could turn Ace into flank steak. Claws glinting, the dragon slashes at the ebony creature, opening deep gashes into its torso. The tav'luk howls in pain and lashes out at the dragon.

Ace grabs Rick's arm and scrambles towards the others. They collapse in front of the teens. Four shallow claw marks ruin Rick's shirt and bite into his skin; Ace has a nasty gouge on his arm where the tav'luk had caught him. It is too dark to see the blood against their dark-toned clothes.

Mara leans forward and examines Rick's injuries. "It-it needs to be treated," she says numbly, swallowing hard as she glances at Kimala. "Can you help him?"

"Not now," Ace growls, grabbing Mara's arm and pulling her with him. He nods his head towards the darkness of the woods. "We need to head out."

"What about – " Codi starts, turning to the dragon.

The red-scaled reptile gracefully glides across the ground, pausing beside them. The tav'luk lies against the wagon, either knocked out or dead.

"Follow me."

Mara's eyes widen as she hears the dragon's voice inside her mind.

Letting go of Ace, Mara stumbles alongside the dragon. She ignores her screaming ankle and cradles her wrist, wishing the pain would abate just for a bit. Codi supports Rick as Kimala struggles to close his wounds while they walk.

Hoping for a distraction, she asks the dragon, "What's your name?"

"Mara, that's no way to – " Kimala starts.

"Ryutaro," the dragon cuts off the girl, releasing a rumble that Mara quickly identifies as a chuckle. *"Thank you for rescuing me."*

"We should be the ones thanking you," Ace quickly bows while walking alongside Mara. "Ace Narweun, Your Grace. This is Mara and Codi, as well as Tein'stra Kimala Brunet."

Ryutaro bobs his giant head in a nod. *"It is a pleasure to make your acquaintance."*

Mara examines the dragon's fiery scales, still blocking out her screaming ankle and wrist. "How are you speaking like that? It's like... telepathy."

Ryutaro chuckles. *"To an extent, it is. I am using my Source to communicate directly to yours."* He stares at her with a fiery eye. *"Tell me, how can you have so much power yet still be infected by Hemius? Usually, that poison avoids those with power."*

Mara stares at him. "How could you tell?"

"I can sense people's minds and Source like how you can see

the trees grow. *Your mind is pure logic despite the amount of Source coursing through your body. Tell me, why are you holding yourself back?"*

"Pardon me, Your Grace," Codi cuts in, still supporting Rick on the dragon's other side with Kimala. "Mara has had an inhibitor on her up until recently. I think the Hemius could tell she didn't know how to use it."

"Most likely." Ryutaro swings his head around to Mara, his fiery reptilian eye gazing into her. *"What do you wish to ask of me, Mara?"*

Startled, Mara blurts out the question burning in her mind. "Where do dragons come from?"

Kimala rolls her eyes as the others chuckle. *"I assume you are not from here?"* Ryutaro queries, and Mara shakes her head. A deep, rumbling laugh emanates from his throat. *"Dragonkin originate from Saronis, although different nests have relocated to various worlds. My nest is here, in the Gwynhavo Mountains."* His nostrils flare as he catches a scent. *"Do you have my stones?"*

Ace digs in his pocket, pulling out the fiery stone. "It's how we knew you were captured, Your Grace. However, the man we acquired them from only had one; probably nabbed it for himself."

Ryutaro pauses and sniffs the stone delicately. *"I would use it now, but I am not eager to return to a bipedal form quite yet. I hope this form does not inconvenience you too much."*

Ace quickly shakes his head. "Not at all, Your Grace. I will keep it safe in the meantime." He tucks the stone back into his pocket.

Ryutaro starts forward again. *"Please do not bother with formalities. You may call me Ryutaro."*

They walk alongside the dragon for several hours.

Multiple times, Ace catches Mara as she trips over roots or her ankle tries to cave. Her wrist and shoulder burn as if a white-hot poker rests against them, and her ankle doesn't feel much better. She suspects she had pulled something major in it during her fight, but clamps her mouth shut; she knows Kimala would lecture her for being so reckless and she doesn't know if she can handle her cousin's sharp words right then.

After watching Mara's pained expression for the last five minutes in the dawning light, Ace suggests, "Let's take a break."

Tired, Codi pulls out a firestone and sets it on the ground, surrounding it with rocks. His brows wrinkle together as he waves his hand over it, and the stone emits small smokeless flames. He pulls out some dried food, passing some to Ace. Ryutaro curls up on the ground behind them and closes his eyes.

Kimala sits next to Mara, eyeing the circles underneath her injured cousin's eyes. She forces a smile as she unwinds the bandage from around Mara's ankle. "We should be able to rest here for – " She gasps in shock, her eyes widening as she stares at Mara's ankle.

"What's wrong?" Mara asks, worried at Kimala's reaction.

Her fingers trembling, Kimala tugs off Mara's shoe and carefully rolls up the already-ripped pants leg. Mara peers around her knee and pales at the sight of the Hemius. Originally, it had been a two-inch band over her ankle; now, it reaches to the middle of her foot's arch and halfway up her calf, looking like a giant, massive bruise. Black veins trace their way up her knee and down to her toes.

"Why didn't you say anything, Mara?" Kimala demands, her voice quavering. She puts a glove on both of her hands, nearly breaking them. "You *must* have felt it moving. Why didn't you have us stop?"

Mara shakes her head. "We needed to get away, Kimala. We didn't have time to – "

"The longer this goes untreated during its active state, the sooner you will die!" Kimala yells. Mara stares at her, stunned. "If you don't let me help you, Mara, you won't even make it to Cerlail Academy."

Ace examines Mara's Hemius and frowns, thinking. "Ryutaro, you said Mara has a huge amount of Source, correct?"

Ryutaro bobs his head up and down in the semblance of a nod. "*Yes.*"

Ace turns to Kimala. "What if she uses it to heal herself?"

"It doesn't work," Kimala shoots the idea down as her fingers glow a soft blue, healing the sprain. She scoops out a big glob of the ointment and massages it into Mara's foot and leg. Mara winces, clenching her teeth to keep from making noise. "It is impossible to completely drive out the Hemius through healing spells; portions of it move all over the body, entering the bloodstream. It's how infections can relocate. Also, it can hide within an individual's Source, and there's currently no way to purify someone's Source if it's tainted with Hemius."

Ace rubs his face as Ryutaro rumbles in thought. Kimala finishes Mara's ankle and checks her wrist, her lips tightly pressed together as she examines the rapid spread on Mara's hand, as well. It stretches to the middle of her palm, black veins tracing her fingers. One-third of her forearm is covered in the black bruise while her veins are outlined all the way to her elbow.

"What of stopping her biological processes? Would that halt it?" Ryutaro murmurs.

A chill slides down Mara's spine. Stop her biological processes? What does that mean?

Kimala shakes her head, though. "Even Highlords can die of an infection," she points out, applying the ointment. "The Hemius moves on its own, so even putting her in stasis wouldn't work."

Mara watches Kimala bandage her wrist with shaking fingers. "What is Hemius made of?" Mara asks, her mind mulling over chemical compounds. What would make this reaction inside her body? Is it biologically based, or man-made?

"It is the physical representation of an enraged Sister's Source and her anger upon the Highlords," Ace explains softly, his eyelids hooding his eyes briefly in a terrifying expression. "During the second Ecalain War two thousand years ago, the Dark Warrior had called the elements together and infused them with her corrupted Source. She made it rain, and whatever that black rain touched became infected with the embodiment of her hatred for living creatures."

"The Heakalius Storm," Codi breathes.

Ace nods, closing his eyes briefly as if recalling something painful. Kimala works on Mara's shoulder, not commenting on the thumb-sized oval that had spread to be almost as big as her palm.

"The area the rain had fallen became known as the Heramus, the rain and puddles as Hemius, and the storm as Heakalius," Rick breaks down the terminology for Mara. "Hemius means 'living curse,' and that is essentially what it is — a curse the Dark Warrior had cast upon this land just under two thousand years ago."

"A universal cure still hasn't been found despite all that time, though," Kimala whispers, finished with Mara's shoulder. She moves to help Ace and Rick. "Hemius just consumes the body, taking it over from the inside…"

Mara's mind whirls through ideas. "So… Hemius is Source based." Ace and Kimala nod. "Does that mean someone can use their Source to invade others?"

Ace's eyebrows snap together and Kimala gasps, covering her mouth. Codi and Rick pale. Even Ryutaro narrows his eyes slightly at the question. Mara glances between them, confused. "What?"

"That… is what the Dark Warrior does," Ace admits, not looking directly at Mara now.

Mara frowns. The person they are talking about is dead, right? After all, it had happened two thousand years ago. "If Source can invade a body, can't Source also drive it out?"

Kimala opens her mouth but pauses, thinking. "I think someone tried that. It took all of their Source to negate the Hemius, though, and it didn't get rid of the blemishes." She glances at Mara. "It could work. But… how did you come up with that? You barely know anything about it."

Mara shrugs. "If it does one thing, then I assume it can do the opposite, as well. Driving out attackers is the opposite of laying siege, and both are a part of war. Why would Hemius and Source be any different?"

"When put that way, it sounds quite logical," Rick

comments, concern creasing his brow. "However, what if you do not have enough to negate the Hemius?"

Mara groans as she stands up. "I don't have many options. I can either die or try to save myself." She smirks. "At least I'd be able to do something other than make things explode with this."

Ryutaro lifts his head. *"You should not walk, Mara. Your Hemius is in a volatile state; until it is regulated at the Academy, you should refrain from straining yourself."*

Mara shakes her head, picking up her bag and walking past them. Her ankle hurts, but not near as bad as earlier. "I can go a little farther."

Kimala huffs, packing her satchel. "This is what I was talking about, Mara! You're going to push yourself and – "

Irritated, Mara snaps, "Maybe *you* should rest, Kimala. You've been tripping over those boots for the past few hours." She stalks into the woods, still limping despite her ankle being healed.

Kimala stumbles to catch up to the injured girl. "You're going to flare up the – "

"I'll be fine." Silver sparks flit over Mara's body in reaction to the ball of rage uncurling inside her.

"Why won't you *listen* to me?"

Mara whirls around and faces her cousin. Startled, Kimala takes a step back, but Mara follows her. "I think I can say the same thing. I told you to roll your foot and watch where you were going, but you had to do it your way – and you tripped. Now, two men are dead because of it, and I'm next."

Kimala's eyes tear up. She avoids eye contact, looking guilty for the first time since the incident.

Mara turns back to the pathway. "Let's just keep

moving," she advises, her voice softer. "The faster we get to Cerlail Academy, the sooner I can get this treated. There's a way to slow it down, correct?"

Kimala nods. Mara glances back to see Ryutaro lagging behind, turning his giant head around to look behind him. His nostrils flare and the ridges and spikes along his spine flex, almost as if he is agitated.

"Is something wrong?" Mara asks, frowning slightly.

A snarl emanates from deep within the dragon's chest. *"The slavers caught up."*

"Carc'ra," Rick curses and whirls around while drawing his weapons. "Get out of here," he orders the others, standing next to Ryutaro and Ace. "We'll take care of them."

Mara hesitates, but Codi and Kimala take either side of her and tug her down the pathway. "Wait! I can help!"

"Mara, you're injured," Codi tries to convince her.

"I'm fine!" Mara argues, glancing behind them. "I can – eeh!" she squeaks as Ace picks her up and slings her over his shoulder.

"Change of plans," he breathes, running with Mara. Ryutaro and the others follow close behind.

Mara blushes slightly as she feels Ace's hands on her thighs. "Let me down." The ground rushes by underneath her as his long legs dart over the forest floor. "Let me run on my own, Ace!"

Startled by the increase in silvery bolts, Ace sets Mara down, finally seeing her red face. Embarrassed, he quickly glances away, not looking at her. "I apologize, but we needed to get moving."

Mara jogs lightly with him. "I get that, but I don't need to be carried."

Kimala starts griping about Mara being on her feet again, but quickly shuts up when she realizes *she* is the one about to get left behind. Mara nearly laughs as Kimala stares intently at the ground, trying her hardest not to trip on the relatively even ground.

Suddenly, Mara's ankle spasms. Crying out, she collapses on the dirt, the air hissing in and out between her clenched teeth. She grabs at the bandages, feeling her muscles twitching underneath the layers.

Kimala kneels next to Mara, eyes wide. "What happened?"

"It's... spasming," Mara gasps, closing her eyes against the pain. "I-I think it twisted on something." *Though the ground was flat...*

Kimala's hand hovers over the ankle. Her face pales. "The Hemius locked up the joint. Carc'ra, we don't have time for this! We need to – "

Ryutaro sinks to the ground next to Mara. *"Get on. You as well, Kimala."*

Kimala hesitates for only a moment. "Thank you," she murmurs as she and Codi help Mara onto Ryutaro's back between two spikes. Mara ignores the twinge in her hand as she grips the bone-like protrusion. The dragon's scales are cool to the touch despite his fiery color.

Kimala settles herself behind Mara, wrapping her arms around her cousin's waist. Ryutaro pads along the ground with Codi, Rick, and Ace as they dart through the woods. Mara leans against the spike, a wave of nausea rolling through her.

"Are you all right?" Kimala asks, her tone sharp. Ryutaro's head swivels around, and he blinks one orange-gold eye at them.

Mara swallows hard and nods, clutching her shoulder. "Yeah," she tries to brush it off, but her voice sounds slightly hoarse. "Hurting," she admits reluctantly.

A soothing coolness seeps into Mara from where Kimala's hands keep her upright. Mara takes a deep breath, blinking as the nausea abates.

"Better?" Kimala asks, her voice not as harsh.

Mara nods. "What did you do?"

Kimala lets go of Mara briefly to swing her satchel forward. She digs through it. "The Hemius is in your bloodstream, so it may start affecting other areas. The run could have made you sick as it went through your bloodstream faster than before. Here; drink this."

Mara eyes the vial held by the slender fingers. The odd dream flashes through her mind again. "I don't want to sleep," she rejects.

"It's not for sleep," Kimala assures her, "although that would be good for you, too. This one is for pain and nausea."

Mara takes the vial and knocks back the contents, coughing slightly as it burns on the way down. "Is it supposed to burn?"

Alarmed, Kimala pulls Mara's shirt away from her neck, examining the bandage in the growing light of dawn. The Hemius writhes, stretching out from around the bandage. Gritting her teeth, she hooks her satchel around Ryutaro's knobs. "Sorry," she mutters to both the dragon and Mara, slipping on a glove and quickly applying some ointment to the infection.

Mara winces as Kimala rubs in the ointment, her fingers feeling like tiny teeth biting into her skin.

Once done, Kimala ruffles in her bag again, pulling out another vial and handing it to Mara. Mara examines the sparkling red liquid, wondering what concoction Kimala was trying to create inside her stomach. "What's this one?"

"Just… drink it." Kimala says grudgingly.

Mara narrows her eyes and twists around to stare at Kimala, wary at the girl's tone. "I'm not drinking anything else until you tell me what you're giving me."

Kimala exhales and leans back, glaring at Mara. "It's a tincture I made for Hemius patients, all right? I wanted to take it to Cerlail Academy to see if there was a cheaper way to reproduce it for the general population. It drastically slows down and often stops rampaging Hemius for a day or two – long enough to seek medical treatment."

Stunned, Mara stares at Kimala. *She's giving it to me? But why?* "This is your only one, though," Mara argues, handing it back.

Kimala pushes it towards her. "I have the recipe! This is the best opportunity to see if it works."

Mara narrows her eyes. "I am not your guinea pig."

"Just drink it, Mara!"

"Has this even been tested?"

"Yes!" Her cheeks flushed in anger, Kimala reaches over and yanks the lid off, shoving the small bottle against Mara's lips. "Now just drink it already!"

Glaring at Kimala the entire time, Mara upends the bottle into her mouth. She swallows the oddly sweet-tasting liquid and hands the vial back to the girl. "How long should it take to kick in?"

"I don't know." Kimala pops the lid back on and drops the vial into the satchel.

"What are the side effects?"

"I don't know."

"Do you know anything about it?"

Kimala shoots Mara a deadly glare. "Yes. It stops the Hemius from eating you alive within a day."

Mara blinks rapidly, her vision blurring. "You can add drowsiness to your list of side effects..." she mumbles, leaning heavily against Ryutaro's back.

"It's not supposed to make you sleepy," Kimala informs her, frowning slightly as she pulls out a long band of cloth from the satchel and wraps it around hers and Mara's waists, keeping her cousin from falling off. "How's the Hemius? Is it hurting as badly?"

Mara slowly shakes her head, finding a surprisingly comfortable position on the dragon's scaly spine. "I wish you... would stop... drugging... me..."

< * >

About six years old, she wanders through the woods with a blanket and a basket of food. Her curly silver hair bounces around her round face, matching the color of her eyes. Her ears stick out from her head and curve upwards like a dragon's, yet the tips are forked like a pixie's. Her tail whips around her in excitement, the silver scales tipped with a light blue the farther down the tail they went. Her off-white dress looks sun-kissed against her pale, silvery-scaled skin.

Tiny wispy wings extend from her shoulders, dainty yet utterly useless with her mixed dragon and fey blood; the tips brush her lower back as the top joints barely reach to the nape of her neck. The wings and bone structure are a faint blue color, but the swirling patterns and veins are silver.

She dumps the small picnic next to an unconscious elf with platinum blonde, almost white hair. His clothes are made of a simple fabric that matches the color of the grass on which he rests on. His chest slowly rises and falls, indicating his coma-like state.

"I brought you some food, mister elf!" she says cheerily. Her smile slowly fades away as she stares at the elf's beautifully sculpted face. "Are you going to wake up today?"

He doesn't answer.

She munches on a sandwich as she sits next to the elf, still rambling. "It would be nice if you woke up today, mister. Sleeping all the time is really bad for you."

She sighs heavily and sips at a canteen of water. Biting her lip, she slowly reaches forward and touches the elf's long, pointed ears. A silver flash lights up the already-bright clearing, and she yanks her hand back, startled.

The young man stirs and groans.

"You woke up!" she gasps excitedly.

The man opens his eyes and blinks at her. "What are you doing here, little dragonling?" he murmurs sleepily, yawning. When he speaks, it sounds almost as if he is humming a soft lullaby in an unfamiliar accent. "It is dangerous to wander alone."

"I found you while I was playing last week," she says, beaming at him. "Here; want some sandwiches? I made them."

The man blinks and stares at her. "What are you, six, seven? Where are your parents?" he asks, baffled. His voice had lost some of the musical quality, but it is still mesmerizing to listen to.

"They left and never came home," she says cheerily, pouring him some water. "Everyone else won't talk or play with me, but they give me food if I do stuff for them. Here."

The man takes the sandwich and water from her. His smile is soft and warm. "Thank you, ah... What's your name?"

She shrugs. "I don't know. My parents just called me 'thing,' and the villagers just say, 'hey you.'" She peers at him, curious. "Are names important?"

The man stares at her, his eyes wide. "Why are you so happy?" he blurts out.

She smiles cheerily. "I was hoping you would wake up, and you did!"

This startles a laugh out of him. "I'll call you Hope, then."

Hope hums, closing her eyes slightly as she listens to his voice. "I'll call you Lyrik! That was the name of this one man who had a pretty voice like yours."

He laughs and pats her head. "I'm... Lyrik, then. Thank you for waiting for me, Hope."

CHAPTER 9
DRAGONIR

Rick and Codi carefully pull Mara off of Ryutaro's back. Codi frowns in concern. "Kimala, are you sure what you gave her wasn't a sedative? She should have woken up by now."

Kimala shakes her head. "I made sure not to mix a drowsy formula into that potion. People need to be able to travel on it. However, I did give her some painkillers earlier." She bows to Ryutaro. "Thank you so much for carrying us, Your Grace. I apologize for inconveniencing you this way."

Ryutaro shakes his head from side to side. *"Please do not apologize. It is the least I could do for one of my kin."*

Everyone stares at Ryutaro in confusion. "Your kin?" Codi repeats, the first to recover. "Mara is an Alkinian elf, not dragonkin."

Ryutaro's head tilts slightly as if in confusion. *"When I saw her fight earlier, she was using similar methods to a dragon's bipedal fighting style."*

Codi slowly shakes his head. "Maybe Dad taught us some of the styles. He did know a lot of the different species, after all."

"Perhaps." Ryutaro watches Kimala kneel next to Mara, unwrapping her ankle.

Mara emits a strange guttural sound in her sleep, almost like a snore. Codi bites his lip, trying to keep himself from laughing. "I never thought she was a snorer," he chuckles, glancing at Ace. The amusement flees from him as he notices Ace's shocked expression. "What's wrong?"

"That… was Dragonir," Ace breathes, staring at Mara. He turns to Ryutaro. "Wasn't it?"

Ryutaro nods, his eyes narrowing in suspicion. Codi shakes his head slowly.

Kimala glances at Mara's face, frowning slightly. "She barely knows any Xharos. How would she know *Dragonir*?"

"Maybe her father taught it to her?" Rick theorizes.

Codi shakes his head. "If that's the case, then he would have taught me, too."

Kimala shakes Mara's shoulder lightly. "Mara, I need to treat your Hemius." When the girl does not stir, Kimala tries again, shaking her cousin's shoulder a little harder. "Mara, wake up."

Ace kneels next to her, pulling the bandage away from Mara's neck as Kimala checks Mara's wrist. "It hasn't spread since the last time I checked it," Kimala says, biting her lip, "so it's not the Hemius. What's going on?"

"Let me try," Ace suggests, shaking Mara's shoulder slightly. "Mara, you need to wake up."

She doesn't respond.

Kimala rolls her eyes. "I just tried that, Ace. If it had worked, she would already be awake."

Ace ignores her, placing his fingertips on Mara's temples and closing his eyes. Kimala slaps his hands away as Rick steps forward, drawing his sword. "What are you doing, mind-weaver?" the guard demands.

Exasperated, Ace explains in a rush, "If she's trapped in some mind-prison, I can get her out."

Rick's sword tip bumps against the ground as a look of horror crosses his face. "The mages."

Ace nods as he touches Mara's temples again. He

closes his eyes and focuses, sinking out of his body and into the one beneath his fingertips. He makes sure to ease in from the side so her mind and her Source do not feel as if they are being attacked.

A sparking silver barrier blocks his way.

Frowning, Ace tries to find a way around this barrier. He is pretty sure it is Mara's – it looks like her silver lightning bolts – but he knows she does not have the control nor the knowledge of such an ability. He tries peering through the barrier, but he cannot see whatever Mara is dreaming about. Alarmed, he withdraws.

"Something is keeping her asleep," he announces.

"It wasn't the potions – "

Ace quickly shakes his head. "No, not that. Her Source is protecting her mind, as if she does not want to wake up or have anyone interfering with her."

Kimala and Codi stare at Ace, baffled. "But... she can't control it like that," Codi points out.

Ace says grimly. "That is what concerns me."

Kimala stares at Mara's face. "What is her Source doing?"

Ace shakes his head. "It's shielding her mind. I don't want to force my way through it; that could injure her."

Mara frowns slightly, stirring. Everyone watches her closely, hoping she is waking up. Instead, she mutters something in the strange guttural Dragonir language.

Ace glances at Ryutaro pointedly. Ryutaro lowers his head, staring at Mara intently. "*She had said, 'I would rather play*,'" the dragon-prince repeats.

Alarmed, Codi glances between Ryutaro and Mara. "Forget the Dragonir. That doesn't sound like her at all."

"No kidding." Kimala dresses Mara's Hemius. The unconscious girl doesn't flinch at the application of the cream. "I can't imagine her choosing to play over her training or books."

"We should continue on to Cerlail Academy. Ryutaro, do you mind carrying her again?" Ace asks, feeling guilty to be using the duir'ne in such a way.

"*I do not mind,*" he says, stretching out on the ground again. "*Do not worry about me; let us hurry and arrive to Cerlail Academy before anything drastic happens.*"

< * >

Vivid colors splash across the sky as they reach Quasala's walls. Exhausted and hungry, they stumble to a halt, staring at the stone in front of them.

"We made it," Rick gasps, leaning against a tree.

Ryutaro sinks to the ground, allowing Codi to slide off with Mara in his arms. "*Ace, would you give me my stone?*" the dragon requests.

Ace nods wearily, digging into his pocket and pulling out the glowing stone. Ryutaro tilts his jaw up, exposing the soft scales on his throat. Ace gently presses the stone into the scales, watching it sink into the thick skin.

Ryutaro's eyes close as his form slowly shrinks, smoothly transitioning from the four-legged reptile to a two-legged boy with a scaly tail and fiery hair. He shakes his arms, glancing over his fiery clothed body; this time, he looks more comfortable in the form, albeit still unfamiliar with it. The glowing dragon stone rests in the hollow of his collarbone.

Walking to Codi, Ryutaro holds out his arms. "I can carry her."

Ace smiles tiredly at the dragon duir'ne, shaking his head. "You have been carrying her this whole time, Your Grace."

Codi struggles to stand up with Mara. He falls to his knees with a grunt, nearly dropping his sister as he winces at the impact.

Ace quickly takes the unconscious girl. "Are you all right, Codi?"

He nods and turns to Kimala who is leaning against a tree. "How are you doing?" Codi asks as she straightens.

"We made it. That's all that matters," Kimala mumbles, stumbling after Ace through the gate. The others follow.

They pass by beautifully crafted buildings with curves and angles in the Alkinian's advanced style as well as the upturned roof gardens and ledges in the Blazhreian's traditional style. Trees and bushes populate the large spaces between the houses and shops.

Mara opens her eyes, blearily looking around. She feels like she had slept for days; maybe she had. She barely registers they are in a town. Three tall glass towers stretch into the sky ahead of them, glinting tunnels stretching between them every five or so floors. They are built in the Alkinian's sweeping curved design with limited edges and highest functionality while still looking beautiful and exquisite. They look slightly out of place among the more traditional Blazhreian style of angles and edges.

Turning her head up to the person carrying her, Mara finally pinpoints why Ace looks so familiar. She has seen that exact same expression on Aeserast when she had been bleeding against the vehicle on Earth:

160

concern, worry, and contained panic.

"Ace..." she mumbles out loud, clenching his shirt.

Ace glances down, surprised. A light purple flashes across his blue eyes briefly. "Mara, what happened? You fell asleep and we couldn't wake you."

"Ah... nice dream... No nightmares this time..." Her eyelids slide shut.

"Mara, you need to stay awake!"

Her eyes snap open. Glancing around, she notices that robed and casually clothed people are staring at them. Fighting to stay alert, she asks, "Where are we?"

"Quasala. We're almost to the Academy." Ace stares ahead at the three interconnected glass towers.

"How long was I asleep?" she asks, her consciousness trying to slip away again. "I'm so tired..."

"Over a day. Just hang on." He glances down to find she had fallen back asleep. "Carc'ra."

"Get her to the Academy," Rick says as Codi and Kimala lean on one another for support. "We will meet you there."

Ace nods and phase-steps the rest of the way to the three buildings despite his exhaustion. He heads straight for the milky-white opaque glass building, zooming by a white-robed medic. He stops in front of the emergency ward counter, gasping.

"Admit her," he orders the startled medics in white robes with colored bands along the edges denoting their rank.

"I apologize, but we can't without proper paperwork and identification. You will have to – "

"Her name is Mara Danarko," he rushes, fumbling

with his right index finger. A ring materializes as he pulls it off; his blonde hair turns lavender and his blue eyes a deep purple. His skin pales significantly. "And I am Creation'Lord Aeserast Corymth, her guardian. Admit her now."

< * >

Cracking open her eyes, Mara stares at the smooth walls and closed sliding door across the room from her. To the right of the sliding door, the suspicious-looking seams in the wall suggest the sections can be pulled out or opened. The wall perpendicular to her feet is made completely out of glass and overlooks a city with an array of beautiful houses, roof gardens, and odd trees.

Shifting her throbbing right hand, she looks down to see Aeserast's lavender hair brushing over her bandaged fingers. He looks uncomfortable resting on the rail between the bed and him. A small circular glass panel dangles from around his neck and rests on the bed, the words "GUEST: Guardian" etched in white letters.

Absently, she touches his arm, wondering if she is dreaming. She hadn't thought she would see him again so soon. She notices the tears in his clothes, her brows furrowing in recognition. Aren't these the clothes Ace had been wearing?

Aeserast's eyes pop open and stare at Mara, shock and relief playing across his face. "Mara!" he gasps, straightening and leaning forward in his chair. "How are you feeling? Are you in pain?" He glances at the door and, noticing it is closed, stands up. "Let me get a — "

Mara grabs his sleeve, staring at the stained and

ripped material. "You... you were Ace," she realizes.

Aeserast slowly sits back down, giving her a wobbly smile as he gingerly takes Mara's bandaged hand. "Yes," he says simply.

"Why didn't you tell me?" Mara whispers, her throat dry. Her infected limbs ache sharply, reminding her of her ordeal. She feels as though he has lied to her, betrayed her, even. Why hadn't he been honest about his identity?

"I apologize..." He hangs his head, chagrined. "Highlords have to wear a disguise whenever they are doing things outside of their duties." He laughs nervously. "I'm... probably in trouble for what I did."

Anger, confusion, sadness, and concern turn into a jumbled mess inside her mind. She stares at him, barely comprehending his words. "You're... in trouble? Because of me?"

Aeserast winces at the memory. "I... dropped my disguise at the front desk to get you admitted immediately instead of following protocol."

She takes a deep breath and looks up at the ceiling, still getting her bearings. She is in Cerlail Academy, then. "What happened?"

He stares at the bandaged hand he holds. "They regulated your Hemius and healed the lacerations it had caused inside of you."

She clenches his fingers tightly at the word 'Hemius,' ignoring the throb the motion sends through her entire hand and wrist. She remembers the odd dreams she has been having, wondering if they are brought on by the infection. She stares at his torn sleeve; she had put his life in danger.

Swallowing hard, she feels the dull ache throughout her leg, arm, and shoulder. She knows without looking that the Hemius had spread exponentially. *I probably don't have much time left,* she thinks solemnly. "Aeserast..."

"What is it? Do you need something?" he asks.

Ever the doting guardian, she thinks, finding it harder and harder to keep her eyes from tearing up. "Tell... tell Mom I love her."

Aeserast's breath sucks in. "Don't talk like that."

"Let Codi know he will be a great guard if he trains hard and learns after Rick," she continues, her eyes watering. She tries to blink them away.

"Mara, stop it."

"Tell Kimala that I'm sorry for yelling at her about the attack in the Heramus." Mara squeezes her eyes shut to keep the tears from spilling. "She'll be a good medic one day, despite her bedside manners."

"Stop!"

Heat drips through her bandages. Startled, she opens her eyes. Aeserast hunches over her hand, hot tears falling from his shadowed cheeks onto the back of her hand.

"H-hey – "

"It's my fault," he whispers, his face hidden behind his lavender hair. "I... I should have noticed the steady increase in your Source. I had been around you long enough to tell the difference, but by the time I got there, it was... too late." He squeezes her hand a bit too tightly. She winces. "I never wanted you to get hurt..."

Mara shakes her head. "Don't blame your – "

"I'm your guardian!" he sobs, gently touching his forehead against the back of her hand. "Shokain entrusted your safety to me, and I – I failed."

She reaches over and pats his head with her left

hand, brushing the fine strands away from his forehead. He finally looks at her as another tear slides down his cheek.

"You didn't fail," Mara whispers softly, patting his hands with her good one. "I'm here, aren't I?"

"If I had been sooner, you – "

"It's okay, Star." She smiles. "I'm the one who decided to take a shot at the scary carnivorous paint."

Aeserast chokes on a laugh, wiping at his face. Mara carefully pulls her right hand out of his. His eyes widen and he quickly lets go. "Was I hurting you?"

Mara catches one of his hands in her left one. "It's fine," she reassures him. Her eyes drift around the room and her expression turns gloomy. "I wonder what I should do now…"

"Don't give up."

Mara glances at him quizzically. His amethyst eyes pierce into hers, pleading. "Don't give up on what you originally came here to do. Don't – "

Understanding what he is trying to say, she smiles at him. "I won't, Star."

"Good." He stands up and leans forward, firmly pressing a teardrop-shaped object into her hand. He ruffles her hair and plants a kiss on top of her head. "I'll let the others know you are awake."

Stunned, Mara watches him walk across the room and wave his hand along the side of the door. It opens, and he immediately turns to the left.

She looks down at the small pendant in her hand as the door closes; it looks like the one he had given her on her birthday. The purples and blues swirl within the odd stone as she touches her forehead with the back of her bandaged hand. She takes a deep breath and clutches the Highlord's pendant in her hand tightly. *I won't give up,* she promises. *No matter what.*

Someone knocks gently at the door. "Come in," Mara calls out, her voice cracking. She rubs her throat, wincing.

"Hello." An old man with grey-streaked black hair enters the room, his white robe and silver shoulder bands making him look important. His ears are slightly pointed and curved, looking more wolf-like than elven. She wonders if he is part laig'hius like Shaniel.

"I am Medic Advisor Robert Kiravon," he introduces himself as he sits on the edge of the chair. This time, the door into the room does not close. "How are you feeling?"

"Hurting," Mara admits, knowing better than to lie to a doctor. She glances at the open door to see Aeserast peering in. He waves slightly before disappearing around the corner again.

The medic advisor's hand hovers over her right arm. The pain abates as he moves the railing out of the way.

"You have been here for two days," he explains. "While you were unconscious, we regulated the Hemius and have been administering direct infusion three to four times a day. However, now that you are awake, you have the option to switch to tablet form."

Mara crosses her arms, subtly checking her elbows for needle bruises as she holds down her bile. It wasn't so much the pain but the cold sensation of something foreign shifting underneath her skin. "Direct... infusion?"

Kiravon nods, reaching into an inner pocket. Mara mentally prepares herself for a syringe but finds herself staring at the blunt, flat-ended tube. "It sends the medication straight into your bloodstream and the surrounding area for instant relief. It is applied over the affected areas." Gesturing to her shoulder, he admits, "It is time for the infusion, in fact. It does not hurt, I assure you."

Mara warily allows him to pull back the bandaging on her shoulder. She feels the cold end of the tube press against her skin and tenses as his thumb moves over the trigger. However, instead of a sharp prick, she feels coolness seep into her muscles and relax them. The pain ebbs away.

Mara stares at the tube with wide eyes as he pats the gauze into place. "That's amazing," she murmurs as he unwinds the bandage around her arm. The bruise-like infection covers over half of her forearm and her entire hand. He presses the application on the inside of her wrist, and coolness spreads throughout the limb. She sighs, flexing her fingers as the pain abates.

"We can continue using the infusion, although it can only be administered inside the medical ward. The pills are best if you know you will not be in the ward all day since you can take them with you outside of the medical wing," he informs her as he pushes the covers to the side. Her leg isn't bandaged, exposing the nasty reddish-purple Hemius infection tainting the skin over halfway up her calf. He presses the tube into the soft spot by her anklebone and then tosses the blankets over her leg when done.

"Both the pill and the infusion are essentially the same thing; the biggest difference is your lifestyle." Kiravon slips the tube into his pocket again. "Being only sixteen, I would imagine you would want to leave the medical wing as soon as possible."

Mara glances out the window. "What are my restrictions?"

"No heavy exercise; you are very athletic, so I am sure you know your limits." He gives her a trustworthy smile. "I heard from your friends and family that you practice self defense and train with weapons; give the medication another day or two to take full effect, and you can return to your normal routine."

Mara eyes him dubiously. "I thought Hemius couldn't be stopped."

Kiravon shakes his head. "Not yet. However, we have derived different ways to drastically slow it down. We are still trying to mass-produce the pill form so more areas can have a supply on hand."

"Are their side effects?" She asks, her mind mulling over possibilities. Maybe she really could go back to her normal life.

Kiravon chuckles. "We are still documenting them. So far, there is a small risk of drowsiness since this is a form of sedative. However, all patients have reported they can function through it. It can potentially reduce your appetite a little, as well." He reaches inside his robe again and pulls out a glass container full of blue pills. "Two with each meal should do for now. We need you to stay in the medical wing for a few more nights to make sure the Hemius isn't playing games with us, but you are more than welcome to wander the halls of the Academy or visit Quasala during the day so long as someone accompanies you."

Mara gingerly takes the pills from him. She stares into the old man's face, suddenly hopeful. "So... I'll live?"

He shifts uncomfortably, glancing at her shoulder. "I will not lie to you, Mara. The one on your shoulder is extremely close to your heart, lungs, and brain. I would prefer if you kept your heart rate below one-sixty."

Mara nods, understanding. "Makes sense. So... is it still infectious?"

He nods. "If you are cut or injured in any way, it will transfer on whatever surface it touches. This includes clothes. I will have one of the medics bring in a skin glove for you; it will fit snugly over your arm, and you will be able to feel through it as if you are not even wearing anything." He smiles at the light in Mara's eyes. "It will be toned to your skin, so it will look no different than your good hand."

"Thank you," she whispers, suddenly overwhelmed. She had thought for sure she would have been stuck in bed for the remainder of her life.

"I do recommend telling your friends and family, though," he murmurs solemnly. Mara glances at him, startled; he looks at her in sympathy. "Hemius is quite unpredictable even when sedated. There is a possibility you could die sooner rather than later."

"I understand." She glances at the door again and jerks in surprise, her eyes widening. "Mom?"

Ezra, who had been hovering at the entrance and listening in on their conversation, rushes in and hugs Mara tightly. Her eyes glisten with barely contained tears. "Oh, sweetie, I'm so glad you're safe."

"H-how did you get here?" Mara demands, glancing over her shoulder to see Shaniel fidgeting in the doorway. "Did Shaniel bring you?"

Ezra pulls back and sits on the edge of the bed,

stroking Mara's hair out of her face. She gives her daughter a wavering smile. "He showed up yesterday and told me you were in the emergency patient ward. He brought me back with him through the portal." A tear spills over and races down Ezra's cheek as she hugs Mara again.

Suddenly worried about her uncovered hand, Mara tries gently pushing her mother away, but she only squeezes tighter. "Mom, be careful – "

"Don't you dare pull away from me!" Ezra chastises, her voice breaking. "Losing your father was too much. I can't lose my baby, too."

Medic Advisor Kiravon slips out of the room, murmuring something to the Common'Lord before he disappears down the hallway. Shaniel slowly approaches, staring at Mara with wide eyes.

"I'm glad you're all right, Danarko," he says, easing into the vacated chair. His face falls as he glances towards the door. "Before he passed out earlier, Aeserast did tell us he was traveling with you, but I didn't think it was that bad."

"Where did he go?" Mara asks. "Where are the others?"

"They were all sleeping in the waiting area when Aeserast came and got us." Ezra bites her lip. "They were exhausted after the trip and refuse to leave to get proper rest... even the duir'ne hasn't left yet, poor thing. As for Aeserast, he was escorted out of the waiting room by Highlord Timian's assistant."

Mara hangs her head. "I... I thought I would be able to say bye before he left."

Ezra strokes her hair. "I'm sure you will see him soon. Timian is not unreasonable." She glances at the doorway. "Where did Robert go?"

Shaniel jerks his thumb to the door. "Escaped before you could drill him for information. He said Mara is good to go as long as she comes back this evening."

Ezra sighs. "I'll speak with him, then. Do you mind..."

Shaniel shakes his head. "Not at all. Go on."

Ezra kisses Mara's cheek and gives her one more hug. "If you need anything, just ask Shaniel." She gives her daughter a worried smile. "I'll see you later."

"Okay..." Mara says, watching her leave. She turns to Shaniel.

Shaniel stands up and stretches his arms. "You need to see something other than these boring walls."

Mara snorts at Shaniel's obvious attempt to distract her. "If you haven't noticed, I'm not really dressed to wander around."

"I'll fix that." He darts out the door. Within a minute, he is back with plain black clothes and a thin clear glove. "They said you get this, too..."

Mara picks up the glove, confused. It is definitely not skin-colored. She carefully pulls it on, surprised at its resilience. Once it is in place, the material shimmers briefly before turning the color of her natural skin tone, completely hiding the Hemius. "Whoa," she breathes. "That's cool..."

Shaniel smirks as he sets the clothes on the side of the bed. "I'll be in the hallway." He steps outside, waving his hand along the outer edge of the door. It silently glides shut.

Mara eyes the window, finally noticing how high up she is. *I must be on at least the fifth floor,* she thinks, slowly swinging her long legs over the edge of the bed and gingerly touching the floor with her left foot. She is surprised to find it warm. She slowly puts weight on her right foot, expecting a twinge or sharp jab of pain. However, it only mildly aches like an old sprain.

She picks at the hospital clothes. The thin cloth shirt nearly tears under her gentle tug; her simple pants are made of the same material. The material is cleanly ripped a couple inches above her right knee, allowing for easy access to the Hemius while preserving her modesty. The same goes for her right arm.

Shaking out the black turtleneck, she marvels at the soft material. The pants, made of a thicker fabric, are the same. Luckily, they have a pocket for her small container of medicine. She quickly changes, finding the simple black shoes at the bottom of the pile and slipping them on. Staring down at herself, she wishes there is a mirror in her room – as well as a ponytail.

Walking towards the windowed wall, she marvels at the city before her. Some of the odd buildings stretch above five stories while others hug the ground. There is much more room between the houses and stores here than back in Veera; colorful trees dapple the ground, looking natural beside the upturned roof-gardens and gently curving buildings. If she had seen a picture of this place in a book, she would have believed it was an elven city - although now she knows that is far from the truth. Blazhreian architecture is known for its natural look and how the houses can blend into a forest or the plains; the upturned roof-gardens, squat houses, and soft angles prove this. However, the gentle curves and tall buildings that ooze sophistication and elegance are of the Alkinian style.

As Mara heads for the door, she mulls over the

differences between the two cities. Veera is cramped within its walls, its roads a hodgepodge of grid lines and shortcuts. The buildings are a delightful mix of the Blazhreian and Alkinian style, showing how the two species had melded together over the millennia. However, Quasala shows more of the ancient traditions of Blazhreia with its serene groves, nature-inspired houses, and lazy roads meandering through the cobbled streets not yet smoothed out by flattening tools. By how she understood it from the history and culture books she had poured over in Veera, Quasala is the hub of Saheian customs and culture; it accepts the Alkinian way, but will not allow the Blazhreian traditions to fade.

She smiles to herself. The Alkinian ruling system had integrated itself into Blazhreian customs, although the younger world still clings to its kings and queens - adul'ne - and merely has the royals act as spokespeople. The citizens still listen to those charismatic royals, though, even if they are only one part of the council.

She examines the door next, waving her hand next to it like how Aeserast and Shaniel had done. A faint blue light pulses as her hand glides over a certain section, and the sliding door disappears into the wall next to the entryway. Jumping a little, she stares at Shaniel's back.

He turns around, his lynx ears twitching. He is now wearing a long robe that brushes the top of his ankles, the collar stiff and sticking straight up around his neck as if protecting it. Nestled between his shoulder blades, a magenta lock and key is silhouetted against the smoky grey material. Magenta tribal-like designs twist and stretch across the material, originating from the bottom of the robe's thick magenta border.

"What are you wearing?" Mara asks, biting her lip to keep from bursting into laughter.

Shaniel's cat-pupils turn into thin lines, and his gold eyes are almost deadly – if it wasn't for his indignant, embarrassed look. "My student chased me down and forced me to put it back on. Dratted robes – I hate them, you know. Never good for sneaking around."

Mara smirks as she walks with him down the hallway. "So that's the fabled Highlord's robe you kept complaining about?"

Shaniel's head droops as he sulks. "It was so nice not having to wear it in Veera... These things get so hot and stuffy, and I feel more like a noble than a commoner." He wrinkles his nose at the words as if he is truly offended at the thought of being considered in the higher social ranking.

"By what I understand of Highlords, you're actually a bit higher-ranked than a noble, aren't you?" Mara asks, frowning. After all, Shaniel and Aeserast did not grovel at Jonan's or Surana's feet during the entire time they had been in Veera.

Shaniel's lips quirk into a grimace. "Don't remind me."

CHAPTER 10
VIAL OF LIFE

They walk down the opaque glass corridors that have a warm, off-white glow to them. The hall gently curves to the right, opening onto a large area filled with over fifty couches, chairs, and stools. Tables and desks are sprinkled amongst them with games and books on them, giving the guests somewhere to set down their possessions or entertain themselves while they wait. The ceiling glows a soft color, giving the room a natural lighting that does not strain the eyes.

Mara nearly laughs at her companions. Codi is sprawled on one of the couches, fast asleep with his arm bent at an awkward angle underneath his head, his fingers brushing the carpeted floor as he breathes heavily. Kimala had obviously tried to be prim and proper in the plush red chair, but her attempts had turned to dust when she had passed out, her feet still on the floor and her head bent uncomfortably as she snoozes. Ryutaro, still in his bipedal form, rests in a chair across from Kimala, his left elbow on the armrest as he supports his head with his hand. His tail is curled over his lap, his fingers fitting perfectly between the ridges.

They are all going to regret not sleeping in proper beds after waking up from those positions.

Creeping next to Codi, Mara carefully pinches his nose. After a few seconds, he sucks in a breath through his lips and stares at her groggily. His moss-colored eyes widen and he sits up on the couch, staring at her as if she is a ghost. "What – How – "

"Medic Advisor Kiravon cleared me," she informs him with a chuckle. "They still want to monitor me to make sure the Hemius is under control, but I'm free to roam during the day."

Kimala and Ryutaro stir at the sound of her voice. As soon as Kimala sees her cousin, she leaps from her chair and jabs a finger at her. "What are you doing up? You should be resting! Your Hemius – "

"Is regulated," Mara cut in before the girl could launch into one of her lectures. "Have you guys gotten any proper sleep since you got here?"

Ryutaro yawns, exposing an abnormally sharp row of teeth. "We were too worried about you, Tein'stra Danarko," he murmurs, blinking at her sleepily. "I am glad you are feeling better."

Mara shifts uncomfortably at hearing the dragon prince call her by her title and last name. "Please, just call me Mara."

Ryutaro gives her a small smile. "It was a shock to discover both you and Codi are the children of Goindun Danarko." At Mara's quizzical look, he explains, "It is an honorary title given to those who are not dragonkin, yet we consider them one of our own."

Mara's head spins slightly at this new information. *The next thing I'll learn about Dad is he was considered a prince,* she thinks as the dragon duir'ne stands up and stretches, his tail twining around his leg languidly.

"Kimala." They turn to see Ezra glaring at the blonde girl. "Care to explain to me what you had my daughter drink while on your way here?"

Kimala's hands tremble, but she squares her shoulders and holds her head high. "It's a brew I made under Medic Surv's supervision. It is meant to stop the Hemius for a day or two, giving them time to — "

"Need I remind you." Ezra gives a chilling smile as she continues to glare at Kimala with eyes as cold as a glacier's heart. Her voice is as quiet and slick as ice. "You are a *trainee*, not a medic. Do *not* use my daughter as your guinea pig ever again."

Kimala shrinks under Ezra's chilling gaze. "Yes, ma'am," she squeaks, barely audible.

Medic Advisor Robert Kiravon peers around the slender woman, eyeing the encounter worriedly. "Ezra, please go easy on the poor girl. If it wasn't for that potion, Mara would have died."

Kimala, trapped by Ezra's frightful wrath, doesn't respond to the man's compliment. Ezra glances at him briefly, giving him the exact same glare. "And what if she had mixed in too much Rexillano? Or worse, Loscrun? She was playing with dangerous tinctures, any of which could have possibly had the *opposite* effect on the Hemius."

Mara frowns. Kimala did something so reckless? No... she is too smart for that. "Mom, I think you're being too harsh on her." Ezra switches targets for her deadly glare. Mara gazes back, unaffected; she had grown up with that look. "I don't think she would have given it to me it if she had doubted if it would work or not; she's too proud to risk losing any chance of becoming a medic."

They gape as Mara defends her cousin. "Also, Kimala had told me she had been working on the tincture for quite a while and was bringing it to Quasala to try to see if it could be produced into a cost-effective form. She wouldn't have put that much confidence in a prototype that hasn't even been tested; who knows, she may have even tested it on herself to make sure it didn't have negative side effects before administering it to her first patient."

Kimala's face flushes bright red, proving Mara's assumptions are correct. Ezra slowly turns to Kimala, her expression not as harsh. "How many Hemius patients had you treated with this before Mara?"

Kimala winces. "... One." At the fire raging in Ezra's eyes, she quickly explains, "H-he was going on patrol and asked for the prototype to take with him just in case anything happened on the border of the Heramus; we both never actually expected he would have to take it!"

Codi's breath whooshes out in recognition. "Kael," he murmurs, his eyes wide. "So... it was because of you that he made it back alive?"

Kimala nods, tears glistening in her eyes. "However, I-I had used all of the materials to make that one tincture perfectly, and we had ran out of the direct infusion cylinders. After the potion wore off, the Hemius came back full-force, and even the maximum dose of pills didn't..." She buries her head in her hands, her shoulders shaking slightly. "He didn't..."

Codi pushes by Mara and hugs Kimala tightly. Ezra, stunned, slowly sits down on the armrest of the nearest chair. "Kael... died? That's why he wasn't at the mansion?"

Codi nods.

Mara stares at Codi and Kimala, realization dawning on her. Kimala had been acting so oddly ever since Mara had been infected, and Codi had shot worried glances at her *and* Kimala. He seemed to always support Kimala's pursuit in the medical field despite her insufferable personality. The same type of personality, now that she knows what is behind it, that Mara could relate to: shutting off the world and building a wall around oneself to block off the pain of losing someone you looked up to and loved.

Mara rakes her fingers through her hair, exhaling sharply. She had experienced loss before. How had she not seen it?

Kimala pushes Codi away, her jaw clamped tightly shut. "It gave him a few extra days he wouldn't have had," she forces out. Mara stares at her cousin as she replaces her grief with anger – not at them, at herself. "He got to say goodbye to Mom and Dad, as well as all his friends and his fiancé. Most people in his state don't even get that much."

"Where was it?" Ezra asks softly, grief saddening her eyes. Mara's heart clenches; her mother always has this look whenever it is close to the anniversary of Shokain's death.

Kimala's voice is barely audible. "Here." She touches the area beneath her right collarbone. "He... he had two extra days. Two extra days to live."

She's trying to convince herself, Mara realizes, glancing down at her hand. *Telling herself it wasn't all pointless and that it wasn't her fault.*

Striding forward, Mara takes Kimala's hand and clutches it tightly. Startled blue eyes meet a stubborn set of burnt gold orbs. "If I was given a choice to take it again, I would in a heartbeat. I'm pretty sure I would have died without your help, Kimala. Thank you."

Kimala's eyes water as she grits her teeth. "I told you not to push yourself," she lectures. This time,

Mara doesn't interrupt her. "I warned you: If you didn't tell me when it started hurting, you weren't even going to make it to Cerlail Academy, and you didn't listen to me! I didn't want to use the Vial of Life. I knew there was a possibility of the Hemius speeding up after it wore off, but you – you – " She makes an unladylike sound, stamping her foot in frustration.

Mara laughs, patting Kimala's head. Her blonde hair is a mess. "Vial of Life? I like it." Smirking at Kimala, she admits, "I don't like asking for help."

"I'll just sit on you next time," Kimala grumbles, avoiding Mara's gaze as her cheeks flame a bright red.

Mara's grin flashes her stubborn personality. "If you can knock me to the ground first!"

Ezra watches the exchange, her eyes soft. "You win this time, Surana," she whispers, unheard by the two girls.

< * >

"Mara, don't touch anything!" Kimala snaps, her face flushed in barely contained rage and embarrassment.

Mara's hand hovers over the surface of the table. She had only wanted to rest her hand on it so she didn't accidentally lose her balance while leaning over and examining the glistening bowl inside the hollow table. "But it's just – "

"Did you miss the sign at the entrance, or did you forget how to read?" she lectures her cousin. "This is the Voyana experimental area! You're not supposed to touch *anything!*"

Shaniel rubs his temple, pressing his lips together in irritation as the lab medic next to him glances between the two girls nervously.

Insatiably curious, Mara asks the most irritating, annoying, and redundant question of all: "Why?"

Kimala throws her hands up into the air, exasperated. "They're coating the objects with a high concentration of Voyana, Mara!"

Mara tilts her head to the side. Her still-unbound hair shifts, the waves sliding along her neck. "Why is that dangerous?"

Kimala, near her patience level, rolls her eyes. "Did you forget that Voyana is a *biochemical*? It's Voyana that chemically altered several species to begin with! They are trying to see what will happen to objects over days, months, or years of exposure to concentrated Voyana. Everything has to go through this test before it is released to the public."

Mara glances at the glistening ceramic in the glass and metal table. "But... it's just a bowl."

Kimala stares at Mara, her mouth hanging open. "You... you..."

Shaniel's pocket buzzes. He desperately digs out his calling stone and stares at the soft golden glow emanating from the crystal, listening to the message attached to it. He narrows his eyes, baring his teeth as if he hears something unpleasant. "Now, of all times?"

He glances at his three charges. Ryutaro had requested to be taken to the palace to greet the royals and get settled in until an escort could be sent to take him home to the northern mountain range, so they had parted ways in the hospital waiting room. It was probably a good thing; dragons do not fair well in emotional environments such as these.

Kimala is still lecturing Mara, who nonchalantly

asks questions just to irritate her cousin. Codi tries to get them to stop, saying they are drawing too much attention.

"Heh." A spiteful smirk curls on the Common'Lord's lips. "So be it. I'm on my way."

He tucks the communication device into his pocket. "Brats, settle down before you knock into something." All three of them look at him: one in relief, one in disinterest, and the other in annoyance.

Shaniel points at Kimala's irate expression. "You might want to fix that. Lilly doesn't like it when people walk into her office angry."

Kimala's expression switches to one of excitement and adoration. "Life'Lord Lilly Mirana, Executive Medic Advisor of Cerlail Academy?"

"Pretty sure there's no other Lilly," Shaniel mumbles, strolling to the lift. The three teens follow after the Highlord, leaving the lab medics to sigh in relief. He mouths an apology to the head researcher who shrugs as if saying, 'How else would they have acted?'

Sighing, Shaniel swipes his hand over the entrance into the small circular space. The sliding door closes and Shaniel flattens his palm on the smooth, milky orb resting at hip-height on top of a thin stem of metal. His magenta Source barely flickers across the surface of the orb. The platform slowly rises, gaining speed.

Mara stands as far away from the orb as she can, her fingers itching to disassemble it to figure out how it works. The last time she had come close to one, the elevator-like platform had jerked up and down, nearly making Kimala and Codi sick. Shaniel had warned her that she is still expelling too much Source and would need to get it under some semblance of control before she can properly operate Cerlail Academy's floating platforms and hovering boards.

As they emerge from one of the thirteen underground research and storage floors, the opaque walls around two-thirds of the platform abruptly switch to clear crystal, exposing the breathtaking view of the inner triangle of Cerlail Academy. Comprised of three hulking buildings called wings, the enormous structures pierce the sky at thirty floors high from the ground level. Crystal walkways and platforms create an intricate weave between the three spiraling buildings, allowing for their inhabitants to go from one wing to another with ease. People in safety vests and sky shoes skate along the air, trailing streaks of Source from the mini jets.

However, that is not enough for the sole research facility on Source, technology, and medical advancement; each of the buildings stretch deep into the ground, the sorceral wing holding the knowledge of the realms within twenty floors of library and restricted sections. However, the tactical wing is no laughing matter; the deepest floor within it stretches even farther down than the library, housing dangerous and forbidden artifacts from all over the realms. Monstrous real-environment simulated stadiums are below ground to both train students and deter a curious mind from finding out how to enter the banned areas.

Mara stares at the field in the middle between the three buildings. There are only a handful of trees to offer shade in the summer heat to those lounging on the grassy expanse almost big enough to host a football game. Some black-robed mages and grey-robed sorcerers chat over an object in the middle of their group, comparing notes and tweaking the mechanics.

She touches the transparent wall between her and the dizzying drop with her right hand. She feels the cool, smooth crystal underneath her fingers, still amazed at the preciseness engineered into these gloves. They had visited the section where they test the gloves and she had gotten an invigorating lesson on it by an excited intern eager to show her how her glove works; both the medics and sorcerers create the gloves by putting thousands of miniscule feelers into the material that activate when they touch biological skin, lining up with the nerves in the limb and giving the wearer full sensation without exposing their real skin to the environment. It is used for patients with burns, Hemius infections, and other skin-based problems; some can even feel better with the glove on because the gloves also act as a conduit through scar tissue and calluses, making it possible for people who had damaged the nerves along the surface of their skin — such as frostbitten or burned individuals — to feel again.

Dad did it, she thinks, flexing her right fingers against the glass and looking up at the central teleportation platform suspended between the three buildings by several walkways. *His dream to create a place where people come together to share with and learn from one another came true.*

Their platform comes to a stop on the top floor. Mara stares across at the teleportation platform, amazed that a mere six transparent tunnels hold up such a fragile-looking structure. Realizing she is being left behind, she rushes out of the lift after Shaniel and the others.

"So how come there's a teleportation platform if you can just pop in and out whenever you want?" Mara starts her next round of questions.

Shaniel heaves a great sigh, glancing at Mara in incredulity. "You sure like asking a lot of questions, don't you, Danarko?" She shrugs. "The Academy has anti-porting charms all over it. Unless someone has an access stone corresponding with a specific anti-port area, no one can enter that area via portal." He jabs his thumb over his shoulder at the teleportation platform. "Anyone who gets here through portal has to go either there or, if they're coming through their own portal, outside the ring of buildings."

Mara mulls over this. "So... there are areas you can't teleport to?"

Shaniel shrugs. "Plenty, actually. Some are natural-formed locations while others are created. There are also some areas you can anchor a portal but cannot create an emergency portal, and vice versa."

Fascinating, Mara thinks, a grin splayed across her face. *So there's no way someone will just randomly show up in my room! Good!*

Shaniel pauses in front of a door made entirely out of a glimmering white opal with a detailed gold carving of a bandage and scissors on it. He raises his hand to knock on the stone, but the door swings inwards before he can touch it.

"I apologize, Ezra, but not today," a baritone voice says in a thick accent. Shaniel leaps out of the way as a bronze-haired young man with sun-kissed skin rushes by. Mara glimpses sharply pointed ears and a lean build underneath simple grey pants and black tunic. He nearly runs down the hallway as if escaping from the room.

Mara stares after him, her eyes wide. He had spoken in the same thick accent that Bryce had spoken in. *Xharos*, she remembers the language's name, *the Alkinian language*.

"Darion!" Ezra peers down the corridor after the elf before mournfully turning to Mara. "I wanted to introduce him to you…"

Mara knows that look. She sighs. "Forget it, Mom."

Mara examines her. Something seems… different about her, but she can't place her finger on it. She has on a robe like Medic Advisor Kiravon – most likely her old rank from when she had lived here. Her hair is braided oddly, too. As her mother looks down the hallway again, Mara realizes her ears are pointed like those of an elf's and her features are much smoother than what they had been before. Mara wonders if her mother had had some sort of illusion on her while they lived on Earth.

A beautiful woman joins Ezra in the entrance, wearing a simple white turtleneck with gold bordering the hems and seams. Her silky straight blond hair is tied in a large loop, a few strands loose around her face and pointed elven ears. Her grey-blue eyes examine the visitors curiously. She links arms with Ezra as if they are best friends even though the woman looks to be in her mid-twenties.

"Is this your daughter?" she murmurs quietly, eyeing Mara with a calculated look. Mara is instantly on guard, not liking the woman one bit. "She looks like Shokain."

Ezra turns to the woman, beaming. "Doesn't she? It's like having a mini him running around the house

– well, without all the theatrics and drama, anyway."

"Mom!" Mara exclaims, her cheeks reddening.

The woman's lips quirk up slightly. "It is good to finally meet you, Ariela," the woman greets her, holding out her hand. "I am Lilly. Your mother and I have been close friends since before you were born."

Stunned, Mara stares at the woman in confusion. How does she know her middle name? She slowly takes her hand, shaking it firmly. "Nice to meet you…"

Lilly frowns at Mara's reaction and quickly turns to Ezra. "You *did* name her Ariela, right?"

Ezra huffs, looking disgruntled. "Shokain and I had the biggest fight over that, believe it or not! Her name is Mara Ariela."

"The audacity!" Lilly pivots on her heels and they click on the marbled floor. Glancing at one another, the group hesitantly follows. "To think he would go against us!"

"He did it to spite you," Ezra murmurs, too low for Lilly to hear but loud enough for the others. She raises her voice. "It was either Mara Ariela, or Ariela Riley."

Lilly whirls around, her fingers splayed across her gold and silver edged white marble desk. "Riley?" Her face twists up in disgust. "That beast of a War'Lord?"

Ezra shrugs. "What could I say? They were good friends. At least I convinced him quickly out of Ariela Conrev."

Lilly shivers violently as if at an unpleasant memory. "Riley would have been better than that airhead Conrev. Thank the Council she retired."

Mara looks anywhere but at her companions, thoroughly embarrassed by the odd looks they are now giving her. She examines the two robes hanging on opposite walls in display cases. On the right, a silvery robe shimmers in the soft glowing light of the room, making the dark grey diagonal lines along the main body and grey borders around the hem, stiff collar, and cuffs stand out. Two bands of cloth with grey parallel lines on them are flush with the fabric on the shoulders, reminding Mara of the shoulder boards that run parallel to the seam on the shoulder used with military uniforms on Earth.

On the left, a white robe with silver borders glistens brightly. A silvery dust covers the back, looking like a cloud of stars rising from the bottom hem. The shoulder bands have the same design on them as the back of the robe.

Mara wonders if the designs indicate a specialty in a field. She knows the white robes are medics, grey robes are sorcerers, and black robes are mages. Lilly must have a specialty in both the medical and the sorceral fields; Mara is now curious to know what they are.

While she was distracted, Ezra had finally introduced Lilly to the rest of the group. Kimala obviously idolizes the older woman; she does not shut up about reading "all the publicly released medical reports and findings" Lilly had published. Lilly drills the girl on the information – which, surprisingly, she manages to answer everything correctly. Even Ezra looks impressed.

Shaniel, perching on the edge of the marble desk, cuts in with a sly smile, "Lilly, she was the one who made that tincture in the report."

Kimala flinches, immediately waiting for another lecture. However, Lilly's eyes spark with interest.

"Yes, Ezra was saying something of it earlier. Do you have the recipe with you? I would like to see how you made it. It could be extremely useful in advancing in the Hemius treatment field if we could replicate it."

"Y-yes." A bit stunned, Kimala reaches into her side pouch deeper than possible and pulls out a notebook. She flips somewhere in the middle and hands it to the woman.

Lilly's eyes widen. Ezra leans over her friend's shoulder and peers at the pages, curious. Her jaw drops open. Lilly turns the page slowly, staring at the neatly written words as if they are the key to some mystery.

"Do you know what you have done, girl?" The Life'Lord's voice trembles in awe, barely audible.

"Ah…" Kimala fidgets, unable to look the two women in the face.

"'Vial of Life' indeed," Ezra murmurs in amazement. "I never would have thought of drying out that one, or of mixing that volatile element with its opposite. It just sounds so unstable. However, to produce that kind of outcome…"

"How many times did you fail? Were there any casualties? Injuries?" Lilly demands, still staring at the pages.

"Um… I… I failed fifty-six times," Kimala whispers quietly. "The medic in Veera taught me, and he was often out of the room when I was working on it, so… only I got injured. No-no casualties caused directly by it."

Lilly's stormy eyes shift their intense gaze from the pages to Kimala's downcast face. "What do you mean?"

Ezra rests her hand on her friend's shoulder. She

whispers in Lilly's ear, although they can all guess she is telling the Life'Lord about Kimala's deceased brother by the amazed look shining in Lilly's eyes.

Lilly slowly lowers the notebook, staring at Kimala solemnly. "My condolences," she says softly, handing the book back. Kimala bows slightly, accepting it without looking the woman in the face. Lilly's eyes flick to Mara, calculating, before returning to Kimala. "Why did you make this potion?"

Kimala peeks up at the two women in front of her. Seeing no anger or condemnation in the Life'Lord's gaze, she straightens and states in a firm voice, "I refuse to stand by and watch people perish from something that has haunted this world for too long. I live next to the Heramus, so travelers and soldiers are constantly infected and tend to die without proper treatment. A dear friend of mine was infected through a cleaning cloth that hadn't been washed properly; she had died at nine years old." Kimala's hands clench around the booklet as she holds her head high. "I don't want that to happen to anyone else."

She's like me, Mara thinks, remembering the promise she had told herself long, long ago over her father's grave.

Lilly assesses Kimala's determined expression and nods. "You came here to be a medic? What specialty did you want to intern under?" she asks as she walks around her desk and ruffles through a drawer.

Puzzled, Kimala watches the Life'Lord pull out a small packet of papers. "I plan to intern under two, actually. Field and Unique Ailments."

A faint smile hints at the corners of Lilly's mouth as she presses her fingers against the pile. "How would you like to intern under Ezra and I, then,

Kimala? One of my specialties is Unique Ailments, and Ezra is still of the best out in the field. Your 'Vial of Life' is still a bit rough, and I would enjoy working with you to make it better so we can put it to use here in this very facility."

Kimala gasps, glancing between Ezra and Lilly. "I would love to! But what-what about the aptitude tests?"

The Life'Lord smiles, and the room feels more welcoming at her tranquil expression. "Aeserast traveled with you, did he not? I will review his report and visit him in Carni to gather information about your performance on the trip. However, based on what I have heard so far, you have far exceeded any 'test' the Academy can provide. Right now, though, I need you to fill this out."

Ezra silently walks to the others, ushering them out the door. Shaniel smiles slightly. "She's excited. This is the closest she's gotten to finding a cure to that dratted curse."

Mara glances into the office, watching Lilly answer Kimala's questions as she fills out the paperwork. "She kept looking at me oddly..."

Ezra rubs Mara's arm reassuringly. "You really do look like your father when dressed like that," Ezra admits, biting her lip slightly.

Mara glances down at herself, seeing her black garb. "Sure, but..."

"It's more than that, Danarko," Shaniel adds. "Shokain had this nari about him; we all felt it. Even though it is unstable because of your Source, we can tell you have the same nari. Do not be surprised if more Highlords want to meet you after today."

"Nari?" Mara repeats.

"It's similar to charisma, but it's related to the feeling your Source gives others. It is based off the theory that your Source reflects the ideals and goals of an individual." Shaniel stares at her with his gold cat eyes. "He always wanted to protect those he cared for, right to the end. You have the same nari as him."

CHAPTER 11
A CAT'S TAIL

Mara never thought she could be so lost in a building. At this point, she doesn't know if she is walking on the ceiling, walls, or the floor; nor does she know if the next door will lead to another bizarre room or a dizzying drop.

The sorceral wing is a labyrinthian funhouse.

Ahead, Shaniel whistles as he transverses from floor to wall easily. Codi and Mara hurry after him, feeling the odd gentle shift in gravity as they do so. "This is really confusing," Mara mutters, trying to look out the window to see if they are upside down or not.

Codi has a huge grin on his face. "What, you don't like it? It's like a giant puzzle!"

He's always loved mind puzzles more than me, she grumbles to herself as Shaniel grabs one of the stems of metal holding a Source globe. He pulls it down like a lever, and a panel recedes into the wall. "After you," he encourages, bowing slightly as he floats in the zero gravity somehow seeping into their area from the room beyond the entryway.

Codi literally dives through the doorway and hoots in excitement. Mara tugs herself through and gasps as she enters the craziest and most spectacular planetarium she has ever seen.

Entire worlds glide by, hulking over her. Detailed landscapes cover the planets as the clouds swirl above in a beautiful blanket. No two worlds are alike. With a start, Mara recognizes Earth in the mix.

"Are these all of the known planets?" she breathes, amazed. Close to two dozen float in the open space, some of them looking more like moons – they are even drastically smaller than the others.

"Yup." Shaniel leaps after her, his robe floating around his shoulders. Mara could swear she had seen a tail flicker behind him, too. "Not all of them are inhabitable, but these are all the worlds we have visited. Go ahead and explore them. This room is filled with sensors to tell angle and velocity; it's fun once you get the hang of it."

"Woohoo!" Codi rockets by, heading straight for one of the worlds. Mara gasps as he suddenly flips around and lands softly on top of an invisible surface just above the churning red cloud layer. He crouches down and taps on the surface of the planet, and a control panel appears at his fingertips. He starts fiddling with it, and the world's surface changes.

Shaniel chuckles. He does a lazy flip over Mara's head. "Looks like Codi has the hang of it. If you tap on a planet, a control panel will appear. Some mechanics aren't perfect, but it helps in educating students about geography, tectonic plates – hey!"

Mara takes an experimental leap, discovering that she goes about three times as far as a normal jump – without the downward pull of gravity. *This is fun!* She grins, twisting her body into a spin and feeling the gentle pushes as the invisible sensors respond.

A hidden world in the back of the room catches her attention. Most of its landscape looks as though meteorites had destroyed the surface quite a while ago. The cities are so large and expansive that they are visible as gleaming tall elven spirals and huge layered floors. As she draws closer, she gasps; this one is much, much bigger than the rest of the planets. If she had to compare, she would say this one is Jupiter compared to a bunch of Earths and Neptunes.

"Careful." Shaniel grabs her arm, keeping her from getting too close to the world. "Alkina is fully interactive."

Mara sucks in her breath. "Alkina? It looks so…" Desolate. Dead. Uninhabitable. There is no plant life, the brackish water doesn't form currents like the other worlds, and the clouds look more like smog over a polluted city.

"Hmm." Shaniel slowly floats towards the replica of Alkina. As he passes into the atmosphere, a couple curved screens appear around him in a circular fashion. Mara gapes, staring at all of the control windows that had just appeared around him. "Looks like someone had set it back four thousand years." He tweaks the controls.

The planet before her gradually changes. The ocean grows and turns an odd purplish blue; the land gains a blue-green vegetation; the clouds turn a faint gold color. The spiral cities expand across the surface, and one sprouts in the middle of the vast mass of water, taking up one-fifth of the entire area.

Mara kicks back some so she can see the entire world. In the north and south poles, a soft blue glimmers at the top of the mountain peaks. With a start, she realizes it is snow. She circles the world, investigating the dark side now.

Glowing forests take her breath away; they light the land with a gentle gold light, much like how the clouds had reflected that color. The cities on this side are a beautiful twirling expanse of cool, gentle colors:

greens, blue, purples, and silvers.

Shaniel exits the atmosphere and lounges near Mara. "Alkina rotates extremely slowly around its blue star, so one side is always dark. That side – " he nods to the dark landscape illuminated by the trees and cities, " – is moon elf territory. The other side is sun elf. The section that is in between is the twilight elf region. Of course, these are the names in the Common language and are only of the general areas, but – "

"How do you go back?"

Shaniel blinks, surprised at her question. "You have to enter at least the thermosphere to activate the panels. Then you can reduce the – "

"Thanks." Mara barely applies pressure to her heel and enters the outermost atmospheric layers of the gigantic Alkina replica, ignoring Shaniel's grumbling comments. Panels encircle her, filling her vision with charts, swivels, diagrams, and buttons; all of it is in Common, so she can easily decipher it.

What a pity, she thinks, disappointed as she easily finds the year and dials it back before Voyana's explosion and tweaks a few other elements, such as making sure the surface is visible through the smog she has read about. *A child could do this. I guess that's to be expected, though; this is for educational purposes.*

She glances up at the bright city just as it fades into a bleak landscape. She hears both Codi and Shaniel gasp behind her as she takes in the dead world in front of her.

She had toned down the smog levels so she could see the surface, but even that does not help much. Alkina's surface had been utterly destroyed by centuries of a species that did not care for its well-being, after all. Enormous factories billow smoke, which fades out once it hits the filter Mara had placed on the planet. The cities are not the spiraling towers and elegant layers; instead, they are full of grinding gears, oily mechanisms, and harsh lights. Where the glowing forest had been, there is a red bubbling field inside a deep crater sinking into the heart of the world.

Frowning, Mara launches herself sideways, remaining in the thermosphere as she circles the planet. She wants to see the sunlit side. Kicking out a foot to stop her momentum, she stares stoically at the dry expanse of surface where an ocean should be. Again, there are those monstrosities of mechanic, smog-covered cities, but something seems off about these ones. Tapping the dial to speed up time, she pinpoints the difference: the cities move.

Searching for water, she thinks as she watches one find a lake and stop. The lake visibly decreases in size before the city moves away, and after several achingly long seconds, the lake slowly swells. Rain clouds are few and far in between.

Mara changes the time back to current day and compares the structure of the landscape, noticing that the gaping crater that had been in the past version is definitely not in the present-day version; if anything, the ground is raised. The lava fields must have cooled and spilled over for thousands of years, creating the hills and a nutrient-rich ground for plant life to grow there. Excited, she turned to Shaniel with a huge grin on her face. "Who came up with this? Can I talk to them?"

Shaniel stares at her, stunned. "Mara… do you realize…"

She frowns. "What?"

"That... past version of Alkina. It was before the explosion."

Nodding, she floats out of the world's atmosphere. The panels fall away from her. "I read about the Fall of Alkina in some history books back in Veera. The engineering of this project is spectacular; I'd love to see the mechanics behind it. So who made it?"

Shaniel stares at her as if seeing a ghost. "Shokain did."

Mara blinks, momentarily confused. Glancing at the world over her shoulder, several emotions war within her. *The spectacular engineer who had created the best academy ever...* she mulls, sadness temporarily winning the war as silver bolts flick around her arms. *You were telling stories about yourself, weren't you, Daddy?*

"Now, now, Shaniel. He wasn't the *only* hand behind the design of this masterpiece." Mara whips her head around to see a man with long bluish-white hair in a careless bun, his extremely pale hands tucked into the pockets of his pants. His blue-white eyes bore into Shaniel with a disgruntled look. A silver robe with grey borders and element-based designs is slung unceremoniously over one of his shoulders. "Who are your little friends?"

Shaniel gives the man a baffled look. "What are you doing in the planetarium? I thought it was about time for you to be teaching another class!"

The man sulks, glaring at Shaniel. "I have to fill in for Chief. I've taken on all of her duties again, which leaves me no time for lessons."

Shaniel sighs heavily. "If you keep doing that, you're going to *get* her job. Where is that elusive woman, anyway?"

"Probably traipsing around the silver forest again."
The man turns to Mara and the others. "My apologies
for being so discourteous. I am Wizard Narbundel."

Codi's eyes widen as Mara's narrow. Something
seems off about the tall man.

Her brother excitedly pushes himself a little closer,
grinning. "It's an honor to meet you, Wizard
Narbundel! My name is Codi Danarko. I've read all of
your work on blending elements together into
weapons."

So that's what all his studying was on, Mara realizes,
nearly chuckling.

She watches Narbundel shake Codi's hand,
rubbing the back of his head in embarrassment.
However, his cheeks do not change color from the
odd pallor of his skin. "To think one of Shokain's
kids is a fan; I don't know what to do with myself!"
He laughs, and oddly, his voice tinkles like crystals in
the large space. "I have something in my office you
might be interested in, then."

Shaniel and Codi immediately set off after
Narbundel, but Mara lags behind, wishing she could
stay longer. Shaniel pauses, glancing back. "Come on,
Danarko."

"Now, now, Shaniel. Be more polite." Narbundel
smiles at her. "What is your name?"

"Mara," she introduces herself, leaping to catch up
quickly. The motion stabilizers in the area quickly
slow her down as she had predicted. "It's a pleasure
to meet you."

He examines her face with eerie intensity. "It won't
do to lie to me, Mara. Tell me, why are you wary of
me?"

He's like Ryutaro, she thinks, allowing her frown to

crease her brows. *But... not. There's just something off about him.* "Are you... fey?"

He stares at her with a blank look before bursting out into loud laughter. Mara stares in shock as little light particles expel off of him, and her silver bolts flicker to life as if in defense.

He eyes the inadvertent display of her Source in amusement. "Have you not met an elemental before, Mara?"

Mara slowly shakes her head.

He chuckles again. "I am a light elemental," he explains simply, holding up his hand. It disintegrates into a cloud of light particles that is nearly the size of his current body. She squints against the light, startled. "I consist of ti-ny particles that create light when they are not squeezed into a solid form, like this bipedal one."

Mara cautiously reaches out and touches the glowing cloud. They sting. "Ouch..."

Narbundel chuckles. "Yes, I will hurt you if you touch me in this form." The light condenses back into a hand.

"So what exactly are elementals?" Mara asks, a little bit less wary. It would explain why she felt like he moves weird.

"We are spirit creatures from Gaia. Think of it like the elements being conscious of their surroundings, some even developing speech and thought process. The more advanced elementals – like me – tend to condense their form into a bipedal shape. Most try to mimic the different species more precisely, but I see no need for that. As long as I can speak to those of the different realms, my form does not matter."

"Are you..." Mara's cheeks flush. "Are you really

male, or just taking on the form of a male?"

Narbundel burst into laughter. His form partially disintegrates, little blue-silver light surrounding the group. Mara's eyes widen in shock, and her silver Source sparks around her defensively. "It is not often I am so surprised that I lose my form," Narbundel chortles, smirking. "I merely created a form that would be easy for me to communicate with your kind; it just happens to look like a male. Tell me, what do you want to study here?" Narbundel asks, glancing between Codi and Mara.

Codi blushes slightly. "I would like to work under your field, Wizard Narbundel. I've always wanted to create an elements-based gauntlet."

Startled, Narbundel eyes Codi up and down. "Hand-to-hand combat?" The green-eyed teenager nods. "Hmm. I have a prototype, but no one to try it... instead of my office, would you like to accompany me to the testing site?"

Shaniel rolls his eyes as Codi nods eagerly. "We'll see you two later, then," Shaniel waves them off. "Enjoy your toys."

Mara stares after them, curious. "Testing site? What's that?"

Shaniel taps a rhythm with his foot, floating in circles around Mara. "They're gonna go into a room with a lot of newly created gadgets and tinker with them with Source or screwdrivers." At the glint in Mara's eyes, Shaniel sighs. "And when it comes to Source-based weapons, the less people, the better. They're dangerous in their unstable form, and nearly all prototypes are unstable."

"Hmm." Mara kicks off and does a backflip, catching a glimpse of the tail again. A red streak races down the middle. "Is that a real tail?"

Shaniel's face turns nearly the color of a pomegranate. He slaps his hands down his robe, flattening it along his body and subsequently covering his tail. "None of your business!" he yelps, kicking off towards one of the various entrances into the large planetarium. "Let's go to the tactical wing!"

Mara narrows her eyes and chases after him, kicking down to keep her speed as she catches up. Seeing the nervously flickering tip from underneath the robe, Mara curiously reaches forwards and grabs it.

The cat's startled yelp echoes through the chamber.

< * >

People in grey robes stare at the Highlord and black-clad girl walking down the crooked hallway. Mara's hands are shoved firmly in her pockets while Shaniel's robe is fastened tightly shut, protecting his throbbing tail.

"I said I'm sorry. Will you stop sulking?" Mara says, exasperated.

"When the tail disappears," he grumbles, tucking his chin underneath the stiff collar of the robe and hiding his still-red cheeks.

"Why is it so embarrassing to you? Haven't you always had it?" she prods, keeping her voice low for his sake.

He glances at her, evaluating. Finally, he shakes his head, not speaking a word.

Mara's eyes widen. "If not, then how?"

Shaniel winces at the memory. "It was the biggest mistake of my life. Never trust a Wizard who knows how to mix potions. Never." He pauses. "Unless it's Aeserast. But even then, be wary with the tinctures he gives you."

Mara raises an eyebrow. There is a story behind that, but he doesn't seem too eager to share it with her right then. They wander the funhouse corridors of the sorceral wing as they head for one of the intersections connecting the buildings together.

A commotion ahead draws their attention. Arriving in the intersection, they find a young rookie with a flat grey robe – the lowest rank in the sorceral wing – bowing and apologizing repeatedly as he scrambles to help pick up the scattered books. The tall man waves his hand dismissively, a soft, reassuring smile on his lips.

Mara's breath nearly stops. She watches the man reassure the boy as he piles the books together. His medium-length dark hazelnut hair is pulled back into a ponytail, accentuating his smooth, tanned cheekbones and gold eyes. His soft, reassuring voice rocks through Mara.

"It is quite all right. What is your name?"

The heavy Xharos accent jars her out of her shock. This man is not her father; Shokain had not pronounced his vowels so clearly, nor had he slurred the consonants. She stares at the dark brown robe; the borders as well as the silhouetted scroll and pen are in the same colors as the parchment the man is picking up. The shoulder bands reflect the emblem of the Time'Lord – the record-keeper and historian of the Highlords.

"Hey, Gramps," Shaniel greets informally, picking up a stack of books.

The man, looking to be in his early forties, turns

his kind, patient smile to the Common'Lord. "Shaniel, what a pleasant surprise. How may I assist you?"

"More like you need the assistance," Shaniel comments, handing the books to Mara and picking up some more. "Need some help?"

"I would hate to inconvenience you…" His eyes land on Mara. They aren't the same as her father's; they twinkle like lapis lazuli, the gold more prominent on the outer ring of his iris. She wonders how she had missed the sharp, pointed elven ears the moment she had seen him. "Might you be Mara Danarko?"

Stunned yet again, Mara merely nods.

He chuckles lightly at her silence as he picks up the last of the books and begins walking. "How fortuitous. I am Timian, record-keeper and Time'Lord."

Mara blinks, finally breaking her silence. "You're my guardian?" she asks, her mind flashing back to when her mother had told her that both Aeserast and Timian are her guardians.

Timian gives her a charming smile. "Indeed, I am. I apologize for never visiting when you were younger; it is always so hectic around here I barely have time for a stroll, let alone a visit to my niece."

Mara's cheeks flush. "Are you Dad's brother?" pops out of her mouth before she could stop it. *Stupid me! Dad was adopted! Of course he didn't know any blood relatives!*

Timian chuckles again, his eyes twinkling. "Many have wondered that. I do not know if he truly is related to me, but I am one of those who helped raise him. If it was not for his Xhavio appearing so soon, I may have retired and allowed him to become the next Time'Lord."

Mara's brows scrunch together. "Sha – sha-vee-oh?" She repeats the word slowly, unable to remember if she had seen it in the brief time she had poured over the Xharos book in Veera.

Shaniel glances at Timian with an odd look. "Kind of like soul mate. It's an old, forgotten term. So where are you taking these, Gramps?"

"Gerard requested them," he responds. *He has such a mellow temperament,* Mara thinks, slightly awed. "He wished to give a few to his current intern."

They step into one of the lifts. Timian shifts his stack and tilts his hand, not touching the directional orb. The platform slowly rises.

Mara's eyes widen. She wonders how much control and Source it takes to operate the lift like that. She is curious if it would be easier to operate it by just hovering her hand over the control unit.

They stop on the tenth floor and enter one of the crystal walkways connecting two of the buildings together. Mara stares through the crystal, marveling at the level above her that has an entire forest growing on it. Tree branches stretch out from the building as if reaching for the sun.

Careful not to look down at the semi-opaque floor, Mara asks nervously, "Um... Highlord Timian, what should I call you?" Unlike all the other Highlords and officials she had met, she feels nervous calling this man just by his first name.

Timian glances at her. "Anything you wish. Shaniel and the others call me grandfather or ruicov because of my age, although a few call me uncle." His smile is slightly lopsided at a memory.

Timian looks to be about the age her father would be now; she couldn't imagine calling him a grandfather in Xharos or Common. "Th-then, Uncle Timian?"

"Yes?"

"What do you do all day?" she asks, curious. Surely, he doesn't just sit around and record *all* the time.

Shaniel sniggers as Timian gives her his easygoing smile. "I manage the Highlord records and reports, log the history, make sure timesheets are kept in order, keep the contracts updated, and other menial yet time-consuming tasks. You could say I am the secretary and recorder of anything related to the Highlords and most of the realms."

Mara stares at him in awe. "That must take forever!"

Timian laughs softly. "It sometimes feels that way." They finally reach the other side and head down the middle corridor in the grey-walled tactical wing. "What are you studying?"

Mara blushes. "Not... much. I would like to learn here, though..."

"The tactical wing?" he queries, and she nods. "Ah, Shokain loved studying the different strategic movements and choices throughout history. If you would like, I can show you those books." He furrows his brows. "I apologize. I suddenly assumed you liked what he does..."

"Oh, no, I would love that!" Mara quickly shakes her head, smiling excitedly. "Dad and I made this game together when I was little. It was called Siege. He drew out this really elaborate city and made all the pieces for it. I loved playing that game."

Shaniel tilts his head to the side. His ears twitch. "Wait, is it that game I played with you and Codi in

Veera?" Mara nods. He turns to Timian with a smirk. "It was a vague replica of Danarkana. She beat me at it every time."

Mara stares at Shaniel. "Danarkana? Dad called the city Lunesh'kun."

Timian raises an eyebrow and smirks at Shaniel. "Its official name is still Lunesh'kun, but everyone calls it Danarkana as a show of respect to your father," the Time'Lord explains as they pass some black-robed mages.

Mara examines the plain walls of the tactical wing, mildly surprised they do not curve like the medical wing. "Why after my father?"

"He built it."

She stares at the Time'Lord. Again, her father's stories flash through her head.

"This is the city, Mara," he gently says to the little seven-year-old girl. "An engineer had built it with his friends, layering the streets so it became a city beneath a city."

"Is this the same engineer who made the big school?" Mara asks, leaning over her father's lap to get a better look at the city's layout.

Shokain's gold eyes glint in amusement. "Yes, it is."

Mara laughs weakly. "Of course he did…" They arrive at an elaborate door with engravings of a map on it. The ridges and grooves imitate mountains, hills, lakes, ravines, and valleys. It looks as though it had taken a long time to make it.

Timian doesn't even knock. Nudging the door with his foot, it swings open silently. He strides into the room, Mara and Shaniel close behind him.

Mara stares around in amazement. Maps of all kinds cover the walls: topographical, political, physical, climatic, road, and other unfamiliar types.

On some of them, such as the climate map, she could see the clouds moving, a storm brewing over the ocean in the southeastern corner. Hip-height bookshelves line the walls of the slightly rectangular office. On either side of the bookshelf along the back wall, two bay windows open onto a narrow balcony. The wooden desk rests near the back of the room.

A large portrait of Shokain hangs on the back wall, centered between the balcony windows. His brown hair is long enough to curl against his head, although his pointed ears still peek through. His gold eyes and big smile reveal his friendliness. He carries a book labeled Tactician Strategies in one hand and a katana in the other. He is dressed in a simple blue tunic with black pants underneath a grey-accented black robe with silver bordering the edges and decorating the shoulders. She has to avert her eyes quickly, afraid she may start tearing up in front of the others.

Different objects cover the space on top of the bookshelves: weapons of all types, jars of sparkling clouds, and a myriad of miniature three-dimensional city models. There is even one that looks oddly like the drawings Shokain had shown her of Lunesh'kun — which, she realizes with a start, must have been built before she was even born.

Mara marvels over the detail in the city's design. She knows elves can live to be hundreds of years old, but the timeline with everything her father had done is just not adding up. He had to have been at least in his forties by the time everything was completed, but her mother is only just now looking to be in her late... thirties...

Elves don't age the same as humans.

Suddenly, Mara's mouth goes dry as she wonders

exactly how old her parents really are.

Her thoughts are interrupted as a tall man takes the books from her. His barely pointed ears peek out from underneath the mop of black curls. He gives her a wide grin, his white teeth flashing against his dark skin. His cheekbones look too wide and his shoulders too bulky to be of full Alkinian descent.

"Hello there," he greets her as he sets the books on his paper-strewn desk. A silver scale is etched into the dark wood facing the room, perfectly level. A small scale rests on the desk, wobbling slightly back and forth as if something keeps influencing it.

"H-hello," Mara responds, a bit taken aback by the room. She wants to explore the shelves and examine the 3-D models.

Timian introduces them to one another. "Mara, this is Headmaster Gerard Folion of the tactical wing. Gerard, this is Mara Danarko, Shokain's daughter."

Headmaster Folion's dark eyes widen; he holds his hand out to Mara. "A pleasure to meet you. Your father and I worked together quite often; we were good friends, despite me being his junior."

Mara shakes his hand, noticing the calluses on his palms. "Junior?" she repeats, startled. "But you don't look much older than Uncle Timian."

The three men laugh as if at an inside joke. Gerard walks around his desk, opening a drawer. "Your father was in his fifties when he disappeared sixteen years ago," he explains with a grin, pulling out a book and two letters. "Your mother, too. Elves age much slower than Blazhreians. Let me guess, Ezra still looks to be in her thirties?" he directs at Shaniel and Timian.

Shaniel chuckles. "Barely older than the last time I

saw her!"

Timian sighs. "I have yet to see her since she has returned…" he admits dejectedly, hanging his head.

Gerard carries the book and letters over to Mara. "I don't know where he went, but it was quite odd receiving this almost a decade ago. The messenger didn't even know where Shokain was." He hands the three objects to Mara, his expression quizzical and curious. "However, they are for you. He said in the letter to me that he planned to give them to you himself, but then I heard about his untimely demise. My condolences."

Mara's fingers quiver as she takes the book and letters from the headmaster. The envelopes are addressed to her and Codi. She gazes at the title, scared to flip open the heavy cover.

The Spectacular Engineer and Other Crazy Stories by Shokain Danarko.

She flips open the book, the world fading away as her heart pounds in her chest. Her breath nearly catches in her throat at the dedications page.

This is for Mara and Codi, my two brilliant children who have the craziest imaginations in all the realms. I cannot wait to play the Siege game I had specially made at the Academy. I am so proud of both of you.

"Mara, are you all right?" Timian asks, touching her shoulder lightly.

Mara blinks rapidly, snapping the book closed before she loses her composure. "I-I'm sorry. I'll take a look at it later. Thank you for giving me these." She bows slightly to the headmaster, mentally cursing the silver sparks lighting up her wrists.

Gerard glances at the letters. "I did notice one is addressed to someone else…"

Mara smiles, grateful that it doesn't waver. "My brother. He was adopted shortly after I was born. He's currently speaking with Wizard Narbundel; he wants to study in the sorceral wing."

"And what about you?" the headmaster asks. "Have you decided yet?"

Mara nods firmly. She tucks the book and letters underneath her arm, allowing her to reach up her long-sleeved shirt and carefully peel away the glove. She shows them the Hemius.

Before they can express any sort of pity, she declares, "I'm going to get rid of this, but not through the healing arts. The tactical wing is known for its implementation of Source in normally impossible situations; creating barriers and dampeners solely through the implementation of Source, as well as traceless weapons such as bombs and aerial weapons. If one Source can eradicate another Source through forceful means, why can't it be possible to drive out the Hemius in the same way?"

They stare at her in stunned silence. Shaniel is the first to speak up, his eyes and twitching ears revealing his concern. "Danarko, what you're saying will take extreme concentration and precision. With your amount of Source, the slightest miscalculation could rip you to shreds."

"Only one other man has successfully done that," Timian murmurs grimly, his jaw tight. "It was a Nature'Lord who had died over fifty years ago. It took nearly all of his power to hold off the infection, and in the end, he had compensated too much when renewing the anchored spell and his body exploded. Are you sure about this, Mara?"

Mara swallows the lump in her throat, willing her

heart to settle down. Despite her medication, her Hemius is beginning to ache from the excitement from the day. *If I don't do this, it might as well be considered suicide,* she thinks, hardening her resolve. *I won't give up just because people tell me it's hard or impossible.*

She glances at the book under her arm. She knows the first story by heart, especially the ending.

Never give up, because if you give up, then you will never find out what you are truly capable of.

"I won't give up."

Timian examines Mara's expression: determination, stubbornness, and a little bit of fear. "Your father said those words to me once," he murmurs. "So many people were against Cerlail Academy, but he just stood like you are and said those words. Now the three wings pierce the sky, defiantly showing those in doubt that anything is possible."

Shaniel snorts, crossing his arms as the challenge of the situation reflects in his narrowed eyes and smirk. "I can assure you she's inherited his stubbornness."

Gerard bows slightly, his eyes twinkling in excitement. "Then the tactical wing welcomes you with open arms, Mara Danarko."

CHAPTER 12
THE SPECTACULAR ENGINEER

Mara sinks onto her bed in the medical wing, exhausted. She flexes her shoulder gingerly, worried the ache would return despite the medics' treatment; however, as she rolls and stretches the joint, the smooth, painless motion reassures her.

She plucks at the letter addressed to her. Just minutes before, she had handed the other letter to Codi and watched him hurry away, his eyes glued to the parchment.

Taking a deep breath, she pulls out the folded paper.

> *Dear Mara,*
> *You are the best daughter I could have ever asked for. You listen to your father's crazy stories and ask all sorts of questions, taking so much interest in everything I teach you. By now, you know all of those stories aren't just fictional tales - they are real. However, I thought you would still like to revisit those old stories with me some day, so I wrote them all down with the old illustrations I used with them.*
> *I look forward to seeing your face when I hand you this book. Oh, the surprise and shock! Hopefully delight, too. I know how much you and your brother loved these stories — especially you. I hope you like my present for getting into the Academy.*

No matter which wing you go into, know I will always support you – though I secretly hope you join the tactical wing. I want you to find your passion and go after it. That's why I built the Academy; I wanted to give you your best chance in your chosen field. Hopefully, by the time you are sixteen, Cerlail Academy will have attracted many more great minds and be a hub for technology and knowledge. I hope you love it here just as much as I loved building it.

I love you.

– "The Spectacular Engineer," Your Father

P.S. As soon as you find the hidden Siege game in the book, we'll play the most intense strategy game you have ever known!

A soft sob slips between her lips. Tears slip down her cheeks as she carefully holds the letter away from her, not wanting to ruin her father's curved handwriting. She curls around the thick book, fingering the spine. A small, folded board rests in the seam between the leather and the binding.

"What about the Siege game, Daddy?" she asks softly, her fingers tightening on the book's spine. Her tears fall in an endless stream, finally released after years of holding in the grief.

$< * >$

Shaniel catches her yawning in front of Headmaster Folion's office the next morning. "You're pretty pale today. You feeling all right, Danarko?"

Mara shoots him an icy glare. "I didn't sleep well last night." He doesn't need to know she had spent half the night flipping through the book, alternating between laughing and crying. She rubs her face, feeling lucky that her features don't remain splotchy after crying. Codi, on the other hand, wasn't as fortunate. That morning, his eyes had been bloodshot and his cheeks still red.

They open the door. Timian and an unfamiliar man in his thirties talk with Gerard at the desk. The man's shock of carrot orange hair compliments his red, grey, and yellow robe with harsh angled designs over the main body. The pattern of a fiery colored sword and axe cross in an X shape on his back.

"Ah, good morning, Mara," Timian greets her, his usual kind smile lighting his face.

"Good morning, Uncle Timian." She bows slightly to the headmaster. "You requested me?"

Gerard nods. "Yes. I would like you to try on the magelet – "

"This is Shokain's kid?" the middle-aged man booms in a Scottish brogue, interrupting Gerard. "She's a wee bit taller than I thought."

Shaniel bares his teeth at the man. "What are you doing here, Riley? Didn't you have a job in Danarkana?"

Mara stares at the man, curious. He must be the War'Lord, another close companion to her father and one of the Highlords that had helped design Lunesh'kun and Cerlail Academy.

Riley grins at Shaniel, challenging the laig'hius with his eyes. "They can live without me fer a few days. I'm not 'bout te let Shokain's daughter be taught by some incompetent idiot."

A hiss escapes Shaniel's gritted teeth as his pupils constrict, nearly disappearing completely in the gold iris. His ears tilt back, displaying his anger at the insult.

Timian sighs and crosses his arms, raising his eyebrow at Riley. "You know I cannot allow that, Riley. You still have a task to complete in Lunesh'kun before continuing to Aihalia."

Riley wrinkles his nose. "Who will teach her, then?"

"Most likely, Shaniel and I," Gerard says coolly, glancing at Mara. "If that is acceptable."

Mara slowly nods, eyeing the War'Lord's reddening face. She hopes he doesn't attack Shaniel right there. However, after glancing to her left, she nearly leaps away from her friend at the scary snarl he is giving Riley.

"And why should the cat be allowed to mentor Mara?" Riley snaps, looking as if he wants to punch the laig'hius.

"Perhaps because I'm not a barbarian like you?" Shaniel leers at the big man.

Riley curls his hands like paws and holds them underneath his jaw while swinging his hips from side to side, giving the best cute kitten imitation a burly man like himself could do. "But the cute kitten won't be able te play," he taunts in a high octave.

Shaniel's ears flatten against his head. He flicks the top of his robe open, freeing his neck for movement. "You're going to regret that, halfbreed."

Riley sneers. "Yer blood is too mixed to be even a halfbreed, mutt."

"Don't call me a dog!" Shaniel charges Riley, and they move almost too fast for Mara to make out their punches.

She gasps, suddenly on the other side of the room and out of harm's way. Timian releases her arms, staring at the two fighting men in disapproval; however, he does not try to stop them. Mara glances at Gerard, wondering if he would do something about it, but he just has an exasperated expression on his face as he buries his head in his hands.

They're used to this, she realizes, appalled. She stalks forward, but Timian catches her arm and stops her.

"Don't," he whispers. "They will stop soon enough."

Mara yanks her arm free. "They need to stop *now*." She watches their movements for a moment, calculating.

Leaping in between punches, she grabs Shaniel's collar and yanks him aside just as Riley's punch flies towards her shoulder. She sees his eyes widen slightly as he realizes he can't stop it in time, but then even more as she catches his fist in midair and rocks backwards to absorb the impact.

"Stop fighting like bucks during mating season. Highlord Riley," she addresses the Scotsman first, "I understand your desire to mentor me, but you have a job to do; you should not shirk that just because I am the daughter of your friend."

"And you," she hisses, drawing Shaniel within inches of her face. She glares with a vicious snarl, silver lightning bolts zipping around her. "If you do not teach me everything you know on Source, I will give you to Kimala as a guinea pig – and I bet she's worse than a wizard who knows how to mix potions."

Shaniel's eyes fill with pure terror. Even Riley seems unsettled by her words.

Timian watches the Source-induced lightning storm crackle around Mara's body, his lips pressing together as the weight of it washes over him. He has a feeling that things are about to get interesting.

< * >

"I can't do this!"

The twig smacks into the cliff-styled walls and tumbles to moss-covered rocks and boulders. The ceiling of the stadium looks like an open sky with a few clouds, although a breeze does not stir the central pond's surface. A fold in the rock walls hides the door to the stadium.

Mara sits cross-legged on a large, flat stone a few feet away from the pond. She huffs, exasperated. "I can take being thrown around by carnivorous paint. I can endure said paint eating me alive. I can fight against a steel inkpot. But this. Is. Ridiculous!"

"You've only been trying for a tock!" Shaniel exclaims, exasperated. He uses the Alkinian term for an hour. "Just focus your Source around the stick."

Mara glares at the Common'Lord. His grey and magenta robe is tossed in the corner near the hidden door while she is forced to wear hers. She tugs on the charcoal grey material with green patterns, still uncomfortable in it. *It's so stuffy, the sleeves get into everything, and the bottom tangles with my legs on a daily basis,* she whines inwardly, her nerves frazzled. She had gotten the robe yesterday after the fiasco with the War'Lord, but she already wanted to burn the thing.

Shaniel sighs. "Didn't Aeserast have you doing Source molding exercises?"

"What's that?"

Shaniel hangs his head. "So we found the problem... did you at least learn how to materialize your Source?"

Mara mulls over this one before holding out her

218

hands and concentrating. A writhing ball of black and silver forms between her palms.

Shaniel's eyes widen. He quickly claps the sphere flat between his magenta-flamed hands, dissipating it. "Don't make a bomb!"

"You asked if I knew how to materialize it..."

"Sure, but I didn't tell you to make a bomb! Where did you learn to do that?!"

"Mom taught me," she states simply.

Shaniel rubs his face, looking exhausted even though it is early morning. "We need to start from the beginning. Do you know how to examine your Source?"

Mara nods. "I think so."

"Give it a shot, then."

She expels all of her breath in a whoosh. "I'll try," she breathes, turning her focus inwards.

Her mind bounces between several thoughts. What will her mother do if she does die? Is there truly an 'afterworld' – Eleth? What about this 'incredible Source' everyone tells her she has? Why can't she control it? How come it is so hard to do anything with it?

Mara takes a deep breath. *Stop*, she orders her thoughts. She focuses on one fact: Voyana is not magic. It is a measurable, free-flowing substance in the atmosphere, interacting and connecting everything through the energy people are born with in their bodies. It is like radiation exposure; some people are affected more than others, and they contain the symptoms within their body.

She pushes past her thoughts and scours her mind for her emotions – something she had compartmentalized a long time ago. She nearly makes a face at her self-evaluation. She is agitated, of course, but not because of energy or Source. She is worried that she won't be able to learn enough before she dies.

Mara squashes this worry with a black blade, thus ending her agitation. Her mind slowly calms down and she sees it – a ball of silver sparks.

She examines it more closely. Something dark hides underneath the layers of silver. She nudges aside the pretty silver bolts and examines the black tendrils, recognizing them from Veera and anytime she makes the Source bombs.

She frowns. It looks similar to Hemius, but she knows she has had this one since waking up on this world. The tendrils and silver sparks rise up and attack one another. The silver sparks attempt to bury themselves into the black tendrils, but the vine-like knot whips out and smacks the silver sparks just like the Hemius had done to her. Despite having a higher quantity over the black tendrils, the silver sparks wilt and submit to the dark knot.

Mara gasps. Her eyes pop open. "Whoa..."

Shaniel kneels in front of her. "What happened?"

Mara's mind races. "Is it possible that Hemius can infect Source?"

Shaniel's eyes widen and his jaw slackens. "Yes, but... only in the final stages." He holds his hands close to her neck. "May I?"

Mara raises an eyebrow. "Don't go trying anything."

He wrinkles his nose as if detecting an unpleasant smell. "As if. It was a mistake the first time."

She allows him to pull down her turtleneck, ready to jerk away if he made any move towards her. She watches him grimace at the sight of the slowly pulsating bruise-like mark. "Did you take the medication this morning?" She nods. "Do you mind if I check your Source?"

"You can do that?" Mara asks, startled.

He nods. "Most Highlords have the ability. It... might feel a bit intrusive, though. Are you sure?"

Mara nods. Shaniel places his fingers on her temples; he closes his eyes, and she follows suit. His fingers feel so warm...

Suddenly, she feels something foreign prying inside her mind. Her mind blanks, and she shoves against the foreign presence.

"Mara, you have to let me in," Shaniel says straight into her mind. She is startled by this, but slowly relaxes. She feels the odd pressure against her mind again. *"I'm not as skilled as Aeserast; you need to open up."*

Experimentally, Mara mentally reaches towards the pressure, accepting it; the strange sensation of feeling crowded inside her own head nearly causes her to shove him back out as she tries to direct him to the core of her abilities. She can almost see him rubbing his jaw while staring at her Source.

"This is not Hemius," he slowly informs her, still communicating directly to her mind. *"It's as if you have two Sources vying for control. It is odd; the only time I have seen this is in possessions, but you are obviously not possessed. Both of these are yours."*

"How do I control them?" Mara directs this thought towards him, and she senses his surprise like a shock of cold water in her mind. He had not expected her to catch on to the telepathy so quickly.

"What you need to do is make both of them bend to your will. It looks like the black one is already under your control;

it's just the silver rebelling. How is your mind structured?" he asks, curious. *"Sometimes, problems with Source can originate from there."*

Hesitating for only a second, she opens up to him even more. Long ago, her father had taught her the 'door method' to help her organize her mind; any event or piece of knowledge went into a neat little spot and had a single door to represent that section, helping her think clearly and efficiently by giving her a way to trigger certain things. Now, she imagines an ornate wooden door with a gold torii gate engraved on it; her mind is flooded with her self-defense and meditative techniques, all categorized under style, type, and intensity. Even Shaniel's lessons from Veera are loosely organized in the mix.

She senses his amazement at the control she has over her mind. *"How old were you when you started this?"* he asks.

"Daddy was big into meditative techniques." A big oak door is next. Behind this one, the memories of her father's lessons wait to be revisited. *"He told me to find something I liked and try to associate it with certain memories. I finally picked doors."*

She feels her secret interest in doors slip by her guard at this. When she was younger and listening to her father's stories, she had imagined every door was a portal and would leap through it, pretending the room or area on the other side of the doorway was a different world. She had always held a fascination for them even after her childish beliefs had sunk deep into her mind.

She feels Shaniel's amusement like a teasing breeze. *"It's cute."* His confusion washes through her, and she shifts uncomfortably underneath his fingers. She doesn't like being able to sense his emotions. *"So what is the problem? Why are you having trouble?"*

"It's hard finding something to relate to it. I keep reading about Source, but none of it is helping me because I don't know exactly what I should be doing."

"I'll show you, then," he says, and Mara has the odd sensation of moving without moving. Suddenly, she is in Shaniel's mind.

He shows her his Source, a reddish magenta smoke that twists and spreads through his entire mind. It is a part of him just as much as his memories and thoughts are. He shows her how he settles it by calming his own mind and how he can gather it into one central location.

"Source is malleable," he tells Mara as he crafts it into a smoky magenta horse inside his mind. *"It's a part of you, so you can control it just like any of your other limbs. The way your mind is compartmentalized reflects your sense of control, but the only way you can use your Source is if you allow it to have access to your mind just as much as you have access to it. It's the only way your Source will be able to work properly."*

Shaniel pushes her back into her own mind and breaks the connection. He leans back. "Do you get it now?"

"Yes." Mara tilts her head to the side, curious. "But how do you get it so... accurate?"

"Do you remember how I gathered and formed it in my mind?" Shaniel asks. Mara nods. "I do that, and then I focus on where I want it." He looks at the palm of his hand. His Source swirls around his hand like smoke; the magenta horse appears, bouncing on his fingers. "Your turn. Try to do it with at least the uncooperative Source, though both would be best."

Mara closes her eyes. She focuses inwards and

instantly finds the ball of Source, mentally grabbing the silver sparks. A shockwave rips through her body and her hair stands on end. She gasps and opens her eyes.

Shaniel wheezes, flat on his back several feet away. He stares at Mara with wide eyes.

"I'm so sorry," she apologizes, shocked at herself. "All I did was touch it."

"Maybe touch it... a little gentler," he advises, wincing as he sits up.

Mara nods and tries again, hesitantly brushing her consciousness against the sparking ball. The black tendrils slowly entwine with the silver, albeit reluctantly.

"They're no longer attacking one another..." Mara murmurs, her eyes half-closed.

"Good. Now envision something in the palm of your hand," Shaniel guides her.

Mara imagines a beautiful silver rose with black-tipped petals. Squinting, she tries to imagine the delicate glass-like flower materializing in her hand. A lumpy mass forms.

Shaniel frowns, staring at it. "Is that what you had imagined?"

"No," Mara growls.

"Oh." He bites back a smile. "Think of the energy dissipating into the air to dispel it, then."

Mara closes her eyes this time and mentally breaks down the energy, watching it dissolve. Peeking at her palm, she sees the last few sparks blinking out of existence.

"Good. Try again."

Having a better idea of what she should be doing, she closes her eyes again and imagines the rose's construction one thread and spark at a time. It slowly forms in her mind, the partially transparent petals rising from the bottom-up in a beautiful full bloom. Opening her eyes, she discovers the exact replica of her imagination resting in her hand, only it felt as light as a piece of paper. Mara frowns; it should not be so lightweight...

"That is a beautiful rose," Shaniel compliments, smiling. "Brilliant control. The construction is perfect, and you blended the two Sources together excellently. Now, try to hit that target."

Mara looks in the direction of his pointing finger and sees a bulls-eye target near the end of the room. "When did you – "

"That's not important," Shaniel interrupts. "Just hit the target with your Source and we will conclude today's lesson."

Mara focuses on the target. *It has to go a certain speed at a certain angle to strike the middle. It's too light, though.* Mara frowns and looks down at her delicate rose. *Wait, what am I thinking? My mind controls it, right? I should be able to vault it over a distance like that.*

Mara imagines the silver and black rose streaking across the distance and smacking dead center in the bulls-eye. She squashes her disbelief and throws out her hand.

The rose floats to the ground like a delicate petal and shatters into a million tiny sparks as soon as it touches the moss and stone.

Mara stares at it, mute.

Shaniel guffaws. "You have to see how it's going to do it *and* believe in it, Mara. Your mind is too physics-oriented for Earth. The physics behind Voyana are not the same."

"I get that," Mara mutters, creating another rose in her hand. This one is significantly heavier than the last, and the colors look more opaque. It will definitely hit.

Shaniel's eyes widen. "Don't – "

Mara throws the rose at the target. It explodes on impact, blowing a huge hole into the rock wall and tossing Shaniel and Mara against the entrance. They cough, choking on the smoke and dust filling the room.

"How much Source did you pack into that thing?!" The Common'Lord screeches as they crawl out of the smoking room. People in black and charcoal grey robes stare at them.

"I don't know," Mara gasps. "I had to make it heavier."

"Don't make it heavier with *Source*! This is why you're blowing up things, you know!"

"So how am I supposed to tell if I'm using enough Source?" Mara demands.

Shaniel gingerly rubs his throbbing head. "You're impossible, Danarko."

< * >

Mara limps next to Codi down the busy shopping district in her green-patterned dark grey robe. He is in his own light grey robe with light blue bands around the edges, the intern band on his right arm displaying Narbundel's personal symbol. Kimala and Rick had already split from their group, heading into the clothing district; the guard had looked a little disgruntled to be pulled away from his new job as a guard in the palace – courtesy of "Ace Narweun" – to babysit Tein'stra Kimala on her outing.

Mara fingers the cloth bag hidden underneath the edge of her new tunic, still stunned at the gifts from her guardian. Timian had spent nearly an hour arguing with Ezra, who claimed they were fine on her brother's allotment; however, Timian would have none of it and gave her, Mara, and Codi each a monthly allowance of money as well as a place to stay for as long as they needed it. Kimala, of course, stayed with them, although Mara – still under medical surveillance because of her Hemius – hasn't had a chance yet to check out their new home halfway between the Academy and the palace. When Codi and Ezra had explained the monetary system, her head had swum at the amount the Time'Lord is so freely giving them.

"I'm surprised you took a day off." Codi pauses at a stall to admire a small dagger.

"Shaniel ordered me to," Mara says, shrugging. "He said I nearly took out a whole floor of the tactical wing again."

"What did you do, make another bomb?" Codi hisses, alarmed.

Mara winces. "Yeah."

"Yeesh." Codi stares down the road. "So... how's the training coming along?" Codi asks as they meander down the street.

"Great." Mara grins, admiring what looks like a rapier. "My only problem is I don't know how much is too much. They stuck me on the roof stadium for safety reasons. I think they should have done that five days ago when I had blown up the first room."

"How can you not tell?" he asks as he looks at a matching set of fist weapons.

"It feels as if it will shatter when there's only a

227

little," she admits.

"You're probably desensitized from your own Source." Codi shakes his head as they move on. "How's the Hemius treatment?"

She grins. "Great! It hasn't spread at all yet since we got here. The medics said that what movement there is is normal." Wrinkling her nose, she grumbles, "The pills taste awful, though."

"So when can you spar again?" he asks.

She shrugs. "Today if I wanted to. The only condition is if I feel any movement or twinge whatsoever, I have to return immediately to have the Hemius checked."

He nods. "Makes sense."

Walking down the market street, Mara marvels over the array of strange weapons. Even now, she is surprised that such an advanced society would still use bladed weapons; something about the ability to use Source disappearing if someone killed another with it. She hadn't quite understood it when it was explained to her; there had been weird rules and exceptions to that law.

Some of the weapons are similar to the ones in history books on Earth, but others are more sleek and crafted of a strange metal. She knows now that Alkina and Blazhreia had influenced Earth's history several times, but she never expected it went all the way down to the types of weapons created.

Most of the vendors have either temporary or semi-permanent stalls ranging from cloth to sheets of welded metal. However, the more prominent businesses actually have their own buildings – and the prices on the weapons are outrageous.

Codi tugs on Mara's left wrist excitedly, pointing to

one such store. "Let's go in there!"

The sign over the door reads *Wester's Armory*. It is in the traditional Blazhreian style of a flat roof with upturned edges to capture rainwater for the garden growing on top of the building. Surprisingly, the smooth reddish-orange stone is unpainted, and the storefront has a large glass window overlooking the cobblestone street. Mara can see rows and rows of all sorts of weapons, neatly lined up in their appropriate sections.

"We won't be able to buy anything, though," Mara points out, trying to pull out of her brother's grip.

He stares at her with wide moss-green eyes, pleading, "That's where Gamerog, the Foreboding Blade, is kept! It's one of the most important swords in history, and it only appears here!"

Mara frowns at his wording. 'Appears here'? What does he mean by that? "All right, but no buying anything," she says firmly. He had already purchased a rather expensive set of bladed fist weapons.

He grins, tugging her inside the store.

She can't help it; her burnt-gold eyes light up in excitement as she takes in the myriad of weapons: dirks, katanas, maces, rapiers, axes, sabers, staves, scimitars, and many more. She knows most of them have their own Xharos names, such as scio'thi for the katana and salev'i for scimitar.

The heavy, harsh sounds of a hammer hitting an anvil in the back are muffled through the building's walls. Mara takes a deep breath, feeling oddly calm and relaxed as she takes in the smell of heated metal, warm leather, and cold stone.

She strokes the cool, smooth blade of a scio'thi on display. The blade sings under her light touch, and she exhales as she lifts the weapon off the stand. She feels a thrill go through her as the weapon nearly melds with her hand. Her heart hammers in her chest as she reluctantly puts it back onto the stand. She doesn't dare look at the price tag.

As they continue through the store, she is drawn to the dagger section. Shaniel didn't seem angry that she had lost his dagger during the incident in the Heramus; however, she couldn't help but wonder if she could get a new dagger to fit the leg harness.

Codi stares at one of the sets, his lips parting in bewildered surprise. "Mara, come look at this."

She hurries over. There, displayed for all to see, is a set of daggers that look exactly like hers. Beneath it reads, "For Display Only. Custom-Order Leg Dagger, 10 Danlar. 17 Danlar for set."

"Seventeen – " Mara chokes on the ridiculous number. *That's seventeen hundred dollars!* she cries inside her mind. *And I had... dropped it.* She hangs her head, thoroughly ashamed of herself.

Codi pats her back comfortingly. "Come on," he distracts her, "Gamerog should be in the back."

As they approach the rear wall, she notices a tall display case that could hold three swords side-by-side and not seem crowded. The lone scimitar glints a dull copper and blue-grey as if splattered blood had stained the steely surface. Its metal guard is made of a pointed rod between two sharp-tipped crescents, all of it a deep, dark blue-grey. The hilt is wrapped in a black sheet of tiny scales, the pommel glistening yellow-orange like a dark citrine stone.

Mara feels as if an ice spear is touching her spine. She stares at the bloodstained blade, trying to understand the sudden terror racing through her veins.

Codi's fingers brush over a metal plaque, and he reads it aloud in awe. "'Gamerog, The Foreboding Blade. May its presence in its chosen resting place constitute the absence of the Dark Warrior from the living realms.' The Dark Warrior had taken it from her sister and killed her with it. It's stained with her blood."

Mara steps forward and rests her hand against the silver wood bordering the glass case. She stares at the salev'i, entranced by the blue-grey metallic clouds churning under the dried blood staining the elegant blade. *There's something moving underneath the surface... Symbols, maybe?*

Someone grunts by the door leading into the forge. Mara glances over to see a stocky middle-aged man with rounded ears and short-cropped hair gazing at them. "Nice to know the young are takin' an interest in the cursed blade," he rumbles warily in a southern Blazhreian accent much like the one the slavers had had. "You better not be up to no good."

Codi's eyes widen in recognition. "Are-are you Blacksmith William Wester?"

"That I am," he confirms, eyeing them. "An' who are you?"

Codi bows deeply. Mara quickly follows suit. "Codi Danarko, sir. This is my sister, Mara. It's an honor to meet you!"

William's bushy eyebrows raise into his forehead. "Well, isn't this a fine day. You two better not get into trouble like your father. Tried takin' the sword outta the case, he did, an' nearly got touched with fire. He's lucky the sword liked 'im an' didn't infect 'im."

Mara tilts her head to the side, her gaze flicking

towards Gamerog. "Why would the sword infect him?"

At William's baffled look, Codi quickly explains, "My sister just recently arrived here. She's not from Alkina or Blazhreia."

"Ah." William leans his heavy frame against the glass; it doesn't budge. "Gamerog is made of livin' metal called kareia that feeds off of Source to survive. It usually picks its owners; kareia don't like weak owners that can die easily just as much as people don't like dyin'. However, Gamerog here – " he taps the glass with a knuckle, and Mara hears a distinct hum like ringing metal come from within the glass prison, " – has the unfortunate fate of bein' under the Dark Warrior's control. Bein' that as it may, it can pick 'favorites,' you could say, so it doesn' accidentally burn someone with the Dark Warrior's vile Source still leakin' from it."

Mara stares at the sword, her mind racing through information. She remembers Ace – Aeserast in disguise – explaining how the Hemius had been a side effect of a war. "So... it can infect people with Hemius?" William nods. "Why isn't it underneath the tactical wing in the dangerous artifacts section, then? I would imagine having a sword like that in the open wouldn't be safe."

William's deep laugh rumbles through Mara. "You really aren't from around here, are you? Gamerog doesn' like to be locked away. It isn't named the Foreboding Sword for nothin', either; by it bein' in the open, we know immediately when it disappears, which gives us an estimate on when the Dark Warrior will be comin' back to the land of the livin'."

Mara's eyes slowly widen. "Come... back?" she

repeats, appalled. "But... I heard that two thousand years ago – "

Codi blushes slightly, as if embarrassed at her ignorance. "Mara, this sword is almost six thousand years old. The same with the Dark Warrior."

Mara turns to her brother, stunned. "That's impossible," she breathes. She couldn't imagine anything that could survive for six thousand years.

"It is possible, magelet," William says, unlocking the side of the glass panel's myriad of safety mechanisms. He reaches in and grabs the sword bare-handed. "I'm one of the few it doesn' burn," he explains to her dubious expression, winking at Codi who had known. "That makes me its caretaker. I clean the blade the best I can with Source stones, but no one has been able to fully purify Gamerog before the Dark Warrior reclaims it."

The sword vibrates softly in his hands, emitting a long, slowly fluctuating sound. Mara could only think of it as singing or humming. "Ah, its worked up over somethin'," William says, looking at the sword apologetically.

He lets go of it.

CHAPTER 13
ROSE BOMB

Why would he do that?! Mara screams in her head, leaping forward instinctively and catching the hilt in her right hand. A sharp jolt races up her arm that takes her breath away.

"Carc'ra!" William exclaims, hurriedly snatching the salev'i out of her hand. "You foolish girl!" He examines her palm, his eyebrows jabbing together in puzzlement. "Yer not..."

"Ah." Mara raises her hand and flexes her fingers. The strange jolt is gone, although she feels a bit strange, as if something had been drained away. Doing a quick mental assessment of herself, she passes it off as her imagination. "I'm wearing a skin glove from the Academy's facility. Maybe that's why it didn't do anything..."

William frowns. "Why do you have on a skin glove?"

Mara grins lopsidedly at him. "Ironically, a Hemius infection."

William's eyes soften as he shakes his head. "The glove would not have stopped it from burnin' you. Gamerog tends to not further injure those already cursed." Glancing down at the sword, he says, "It's a bit clearer than before... do you feel a diff'ence in your Source?"

Again, Mara does a mental evaluation. She sees nothing wrong with the sparking ball of black tendrils. "No..."

"Mara has a lot of Source, Master William," Codi quickly chimes in. "It's why she came to Cerlail Academy; to control it."

He snorts, eyeing her magelet robe and the sparring clothes underneath. "I suppose it won't hurt – at least for a few ticks." He offers the sword to her.

Mara accepts it reverently. Grasping the hilt, she feels that odd jolt through her arm again; this time, a bolt of silvery lightning races down her arm and wraps around the blade. It sinks into the sword as if absorbed by the metal.

She gingerly touches the flat of the blade, finally noticing the odd symbols rising to the surface only to sink back into the churning metallic swirls. The reddish hue lightens ever so slightly.

She carefully tests the weight of the sword, barely restraining the urge to go through a few moves with it. The hilt fits perfectly in her hand as if made for her. *It doesn't look or feel like a six thousand year old sword*, she thinks, now examining the deep grey-blue guard. She notices a small nick in the dark metal, as if it had stopped a hard blow. *It's worn, but not so much it hasn't lost its shine… which means it's well taken care of.*

William examines her face. "Do you feel a diff'ence in your Source?" he asks again.

Just like before, Mara checks the writhing ball of power. It does seem calmer than before, but not much else. "Not… much," she admits, unnerved by the intensity of the Blazhreian man's stare. "Maybe a bit calmer?"

Codi stares at his sister. "Mara, this is the calmest I've ever felt your Source," he tells her quietly.

Mara frowns. "I don't feel that different…" As she stares at the sword, she admits, "Maybe a little tired,

235

but that could be from all the training earlier."

William holds his hand out for the sword. "Mos' likely it's the sword."

She reluctantly gives it back. As her hand pulls away from it, a single strand of silver extends between the sword and her before snapping with a loud crackle. Everyone jumps a little, though William doesn't say anything. He frowns slightly, deep in thought as he carefully places Gamerog back on the crystal pedestal inside the case and locks it again.

"It's a beautiful sword," Mara finally breaks the silence, staring at the salev'i within its glass cage.

William glances at her, seeing the look of awe and respect on her face. "That's because you don' know about it," he grunts, although he looks a little pleased at the compliment. "Would you like t'see the forge?"

Mara and Codi glance at one another, both startled at the sudden offer. "Yes, please!" Codi says, excited again.

"We wouldn't want to be a bother..." Mara interjects, glancing at her brother.

William chuckles. "After what Gamerog pulled on you, it is the least I can do."

They follow him through the open doorway into the hot forge room. Mara glances around, taking in the different tools for welding, cutting, hammering, and more. *I guess Source isn't used for everything*, she muses before asking, "What do you mean?"

William chuckles as he picks up an incomplete short sword with an odd curve to the middle. "Gamerog does not fall to the ground like a normal sword. That salev'i has a mind of its own and offen plays tricks on the gullible." He blinks, and then gestures behind Mara and Codi. "Jus' like that."

The nape of Mara's neck tingles. Slowly, she glances over her shoulder – and leaps away as Gamerog hovers behind her and Codi. It turns slightly towards her as if to follow her.

Codi backs away slowly, unnerved. "Uh... I've never heard of it doing this."

William shakes his head. "Every now and then, Gamerog takes an interest in someone with a high amount of Source; the last one it took a liking to was Master Mage Shokain Danarko. The moment he walked through that door, Gamerog would greet him, and he would speak to the sword like an old friend." William shakes his head. "Crazy elf. One would think he an' the sword knew one another longer than jus' a few days when he first showed up." He gives Mara an odd look. "Figures it would take up with one of you."

Still unsettled by the floating sword, Mara glances at William. "So it... isn't dangerous like this?"

William shrugs. "You seem to do fine with it. However, I wouldn' test your luck, boy; Gamerog has a strange way of picking who can touch it. Just leave it be; it likes watching."

At this, Mara forces down her uneasiness and strides towards William at the forge. The salev'i floats forward about a foot before stopping a good distance away from them, keeping out of the way. Codi stares at it, his eyes wide; it truly is as if the sword is watching them. The hairs on the back of his neck stand up on end.

"Uh, Mara, I think I'm going to continue looking around a bit," Codi blurts as he edges towards the door. The salev'i hovers, perfectly still as it faces William and Mara. "Thank you so much, William. It was an honor meeting you." He bobs his head in a quick bow as he rushes out of the forge.

Mara gazes after him, frowning slightly. *I guess he wasn't interested...*

William smiles slightly, knowing the real reason behind the rookie's nervousness. Turning to Mara, he asks, "Would you like to learn how to make a sword?"

She quickly shakes her head. "I wouldn't want to take up your time like that."

He waves away her excuse. "I feel bad for the prank Gamerog pulled on you. Plus, you helped feed it today; since I'm only a Blazhreian, I have to use Source stones, and normally, those who can tolerate the drain of a kareia cannot touch the blade. I must pay you back for the inconvenience some way or another, and I assume you were in the shop for more than just a little history visit." He grins at her embarrassed face.

"I-I received a gift from a friend of mine for my birthday," she admits, nudging aside her robe to expose the remaining dagger strapped over the cloth on her left leg. "However, when I was protecting my cousin from the Hemius, I... dropped one of them in the pond. I-is there any way I could – "

Her cheeks turn a vibrant red. She couldn't continue; she feels selfish and foolish for asking such a request. *I should have just kept my mouth shut,* she mourns.

"Let me see that one there." She unfastens the straps holding the knife and sheath, handing them over. He examines it, fingering the creator's signature on the inside of the harness – his signature. "Do you know why my weapons are so expensive?"

"No, sir," Mara whispers, embarrassed.

He smiles at her, his eyes warm. "Handmade

swords are hard to come by nowadays, especially those on the same level as Source-created weapons. My own Source is nearly nonexistent, so I learned to forge with my own two hands. There's just somethin' relaxin' about the repetitive motions."

"It's like your mind is given a break from the daily problems," Mara whispers, her lips quirking up. "You can finally relax."

William's eyes spark. "Ah, so you have your own hobby?"

"Self-defense." She glances down at her hands. "If I sit still, I think too much. I have to be moving."

"Take off your glove an' robe; you can set them over there." He jerks his chin towards a bench along the wall as he ambles to a box of precut weapons, pulling a short-guarded dagger from the chaos. "I'll make sure you don' sit idle."

Mara takes off her robe and glove, rolling up her sleeve as she stares at the Hemius covering her hand and forearm. It still hasn't spread since she had woken up in the medical wing, although she does occasionally see it moving underneath her skin.

William eyes the bandage stretching across the base of her neck and disappearing underneath her tunic's collar. His eyebrow raises at seeing her Hemius-covered hand. "I have seen many like me with the scars of entering the Heramus, but you, lass, must have put up one good fight to be so burned."

Mara stops next to the anvil. "You're infected, too?"

He nods, lifting the hem of his left pants leg just enough to see the ugly bruise. "Has only moved two handspans in the past twenty years, thank the Highlords. As soon as the Life'Lord developed those miracle pills, the movement slowed down to the point I could resume workin' again. I owe her my life."

Mara nods. "If it wasn't for my cousin, I would have been dead by now." She examines the knife, missing William's curious look. "So what are we doing first?"

"We're goin' to hammer it." He hands a huge hammer to Mara. "An' you're doin' the hard work."

The rest of that afternoon consists of pounding the metal flat, reheating it, and pounding it again. After about an hour or so, Codi pops his head in to let Mara know he is walking down the street a ways; he refuses to stick around with Gamerog still eerily 'watching' the two of them work. They take brief breaks to rest or drink some water; otherwise, they work together over the anvil, slowly flattening the metal into their desired shape.

By the time Codi returns to drag Mara to dinner, Mara's arms are sore and she is exhausted. William invites her to come back whenever she has a chance in her studies to work on the dagger; he claims she is a naturalist with the blacksmithing tools, despite how she had missed several times and nearly walloped herself in the collarbone or chin from the subsequent rebound effect.

That night, she ignores her exhausted muscles and checks out the blacksmithing section of the library beneath the sorceral wing, taking a book back to her room in the medical ward. She falls asleep while studying about different techniques one would use at the anvil, and she has strange dreams about working a forge.

That morning after exercising in one of the upper stadiums, she finds out from Headmaster Folion that students do not typically have classes on Xhenuni, the last day of the week. She races into the market district, wondering if she can work on the dagger with William today.

She is relieved to see the marketplace is open and bustling with more customers than yesterday. Hurrying through the throng of people, she slips into Wester's Armory. A few customers browse the shelves.

She pauses for a moment, unsure if she should go straight to the back door leading to the forge or ask the young man working the sales counter. Choosing the latter, she approaches to the plain looking man flipping through a book. "Is Mister William here today?"

The man glances at her, and he straightens up as he examines her robe. "Are you Mara Danarko?" he asks, and at her nod, he smiles apologetically. "I apologize, but Master William takes Xhenuni off; only the assistants are here today. He will be back tomorrow, though."

"Ah, okay. Thank you." She turns away before she could see his confused look at the English word. Drawn to the back, she works her way slowly through the rows, examining all of the weapons. She fingers a particularly beautiful axe.

The rhythmic pounding of a hammer echoes weakly from the back room. She tilts her head, wondering if the 'assistants' the man had spoken of make their own weapons to put on the shelf.

She cautiously peeks into the room and sees two people – one a big woman, another a buff man – working together over a long sword. She quickly closes the door before they notice her.

Glancing to her left, she sees Gamerog sitting quietly in its case. She touches the silver wood, staring at the sword. An idea races through her mind; she hurries back to her room in Cerlail Academy, grabs her father's sketchbook and some drawing supplies, and returns to the shop. The man at the counter doesn't say anything as she strolls to the back of the room and leans against one of the sturdy shelves, flipping open the sketchbook to the back where there are still several blank pages.

She pauses, biting her lip. *Dad would like it if I use his sketchbook,* she tells herself, setting the pencil onto the paper. Her right hand flows across the parchment in shaky lines as she loosely sketches out the shape of Gamerog. She knows she isn't the best artist, but she wants to at least try to draw it.

By the time Shaniel finds her next to the case, she is curled up between the sword's display and the nearest rack of weapons with her head against the glass, as out of the way as she could be. She jerks awake at Shaniel's light touch on her shoulder.

"Hey." His brows crease in worry. "Are you feeling all right?"

Mara straightens up, yawning. "Yeah." She glances down at her drawing and wrinkles her nose. *It's awful.*

Before she could stop him, Shaniel takes the sketchbook from her. His lips quirk up as he glances at Gamerog. "I see you've taken a fancy to the Salev'i of Foreboding. Any particular reason why you decided to draw it?"

Mara blushes slightly, embarrassed. "Yesterday, Codi and I came here, and I met William. He offered to teach me how to make a new dagger to replace the one I had dropped for helping him out yesterday."

Shaniel raises an eyebrow at her. "Oh? And what did you help with?"

Mara gestures up at the bloodstained blade. "Something about my Source and the salev'i. I don't feel any different, though, so I don't quite understand it." *If it really did... eat... my Source, I would feel it, right?*

Shaniel's eyes widen as he says in a higher pitch than normal, "You touched the sword?"

Mara nods, unsure why he is upset. "It's just a sword..."

Shaniel helps her to her feet. "That is no ordinary sword, Danarko. The fact that you could touch it just means it likes you. That you don't feel the drain..." He stares into her eyes. "How much sleep did you get last night?"

Mara rubs her face, still tired. "It doesn't feel like much, although I slept throughout the night. I was reading a blacksmithing book and ended up dreaming about the methods." She sighs.

He shakes his head. "I think the sword drained a lot more than normal from you yesterday, and you're not used to that much being depleted from you so fast. You should rest." He leads her down the row of weapons, glancing back only once to see Gamerog hovering just at the edge of the glass, angled towards them as if watching Mara leave.

Shaniel hurriedly faces forward again, unsettled. "Creepy sword."

"Huh?"

"Nothing."

< * >

Mara sprints through the crowd. Both Shaniel and Folion had laughed at the distracted twinkle in her eyes; her dagger is almost complete, so she had had trouble focusing on their lessons because of her excitement. She and William are on the final stages of sharpening and polishing the blade today, and then she will have her very own dagger – a dagger she made.

As soon as she opens the door, she is greeted by Gamerog floating in front of her. "It's rude to block the door like that," she mutters to it, and it slowly glides out of the way. It follows her, gently emitting a long, drawn-out ring as if it had been drawn from its sheath.

William steps out of the forge just as Mara passes through the middle row. He stares into the case, alarmed, until he catches sight of Gamerog floating behind Mara. "Dratted sword will give me a heart attack some day," he mutters, smiling at Mara. "It's like a puppy, eh?"

Mara laughs as she – and the salev'i – enter the forging room. She immediately strips off her robe and glove, tossing them unceremoniously onto the bench. She finally turns around at a particularly loud metallic ring. "Why is it doing that?"

William slowly closes the door, a deep frown creasing his forehead. "I don' know. Come; I have your – "

Mara yelps as Gamerog suddenly floats closer. It nudges her left hand with its hilt. "Wh-what should I do?" she asks the weaponsmith.

Baffled, William shakes his head. "It looks like it wants you to grab it."

Mara hesitantly wraps her hand around the hilt, feeling the odd jolt in her arm. Just the other day, she had finally placed the sensation; it is as if the Source 'leaking out' of her is suddenly pulled into the salev'i, giving her the odd sensation of something tugging on her arm. She remembers Shaniel's comment that her Source isn't as rampant as it had been when she had first arrived.

Maybe it's a good thing I can touch it, then, she thinks to herself, examining the blade. It still has bloodstained splotches on it, but it looks significantly clearer than when she had first seen it. Squinting at the blade, she wonders if the darker color of the metal is just her imagination.

She pats the pommel with her right hand and lets go of the salev'i. It hovers in place, no longer ringing quite as loudly. "I need to finish my dagger," she tells it.

It nudges her hand again.

William guffaws, realizing the sword's problem. "I do believe it's jealous," he says, grinning. "To think! The ancient harbinger, jealous of a puny hand-crafted blade!"

Gamerog rings as if in indignation, startling a chuckle out of Mara. She pats the pommel again. "If you were my sword, it wouldn't replace you," she says to the sulking kareia. "But this is to replace a gift that I had lost. No worries; I'll visit you." She catches William's odd look and suddenly feels self-conscious. After all, she is talking to a sword. "What?"

He shakes his head. "If it were possible, it would be nice if Gamerog could imprint on a new owner." He glances at the stained blade. "The Dark Warrior's hold on it is strong, though, I'm afraid." He turns to the sharpening wheel, ending the conversation.

The concept of time fades away as Mara flattens the remaining ridges, wraps the handle in simple leather, and sharpens the blade while William works on one of his swords. By the time she is done, she has sweat pouring down her back from the heat of the nearby forge and Gamerog is nowhere to be seen. She slips the new dagger into her leg harness; it fits perfectly.

She takes it to William. "It's done!"

He examines the blade and nods, beaming at her. "If you weren't a magelet, I would want to hire you as my apprentice. You have a talent for the forge, Mara." He hands it back to her.

Mara's cheeks redden. Before she could respond, a shriek outside alerts them of trouble.

Mara bursts through the door connecting the forge and the shop, on high alert. She nearly falls back into the workroom as she takes in the figure in front of her, her breath catching in her throat.

A purplish-red mist in a vaguely humanoid shape rolls like coiled smoke. Tendrils drift off of it, floating for a moment before dissipating. It holds Gamerog in a semblance of a hand; the blade is a vibrant red like freshly spilled blood.

The creature turns towards Mara, emitting a wind-like shriek from its dark maw. Gamerog releases a high-pitched ring in response.

Terror and anger war inside of Mara. She can feel the hatred and malice rolling off the creature, but the sight of the salev'i in its grip sends white-hot rage through her body.

"Let Gamerog go!" Mara orders as the store attendants and customers escape through the entrance.

"*And why should I listen to you?*" a slimy, raspy voice hisses in her mind.

She adjusts her grip on her new dagger, fighting down the terror at seeing the creature and hoping William had escaped through the back door of the forge. "Because that sword doesn't belong to you," she says firmly, ashamed of the fear tingeing her voice.

The creature cackles, raising Gamerog high. "*Insolent girl.*" The red salev'i falls, moving sluggishly as the creature strains to swing the reluctant blade.

Mara sidesteps around it, tucking her new dagger into her boot and grabbing a scio'thi — a katana — off the nearest rack. *Sorry, William,* she quickly apologizes, promising to somehow pay him back for the sword.

The next swing is a little faster, but she blocks it with ease. Metal sings against metal as she slides up the blade and against the guard. She grits her teeth, surprised at the strength of the creature.

Suddenly, the pressure lets up and Mara breaks free. Gamerog rings indignantly.

"*You* dare *defy me?*" The creature's misty body stretches over the blade, and it chirps like metal striking against metal — a brief scream of pain. Mara shakes her head, wincing.

The mist slowly digs into the sword and disappears. *It's forcing its Source into Gamerog,* she realizes, feeling a little sick as she watches it. Rage and anger fill her with reckless courage.

"Leave Gamerog alone!" Mara yells, swinging the scio'thi at the creature.

It passes through, utterly harmless.

Mara drops the white-hot sword, her hands aching from the extreme heat. She glances up just in time to defensively throw her arms in front of her face as the mist slams into her.

She cries out in pain as she shoots across the room, ramming against the spear rack. Gasping for breath, she cradles her right arm as the Hemius writhes viciously underneath her skin.

She struggles to her feet and grabs one of the staves in her left hand while trying to block out the pain of her fractured arm. She braces herself as the mist slowly approaches as if any more speed would cause it to disintegrate.

That's it! Mara realizes, a crazy plan coming to mind. *Maybe I can break up its form —*

The mist expands.

It forms a crescent, trying to trap her against the staves rack. Gritting her teeth, she knocks the staves to the side and vaults over the stand just as the mist engulfs the area she had just been in.

"*You,*" it whispers, unsure about something. "*Who are you?*"

"I think I can ask the same thing," Mara says as she backs up. Her hip bumps into another sword rack – the one near the display window. Outside, people stand in a circle, distancing themselves from the shop as they look on in fear.

Mara grits her teeth together. Why aren't they farther away? Focusing on the mist, she goes on the offensive, performing a couple swipes. The staff merely passes through the creature, and a blackish-red rot corrodes the wooden section. Mara drops the staff, horrified.

It laughs, an awful, grating sound. Again, the mist encircles her. As she grabs another sword behind her, the creature mocks, "*It won't protect you.*"

Panic finally sets in. She cannot escape, and she cannot defeat it.

She charges, holding the sword level with her shoulder. The misty tendrils encompass her, trapping her as she tries to knock Gamerog out of its grip.

It shrieks in rage, swinging at her viciously.

Clang.

Mara stares into the red mist, terror and determination warring within her. She gasps as the mist touches her broken arm, making the Hemius writhe and burn. It creeps up her skin, and the Hemius moves with it, scorching a path over her body.

She screams, both in defiance and in pain. Dropping her sword, she allows Gamerog to cut into her right shoulder as she grabs the back of the blade.

This time, she feels the sword guzzling at her power, almost as if it is starved. Silver lightning bolts crackle across the sword as the red seeps away to be replaced with a greyish tinge.

"*No!*" The creature recoils from the sword as if Mara's Source had shocked it. "*You cannot have it! It is mine!*"

"Not... anymore," Mara pants, her right arm hanging loosely at her side as she pulls Gamerog out of her shoulder, clutching it tightly in her hand. She fights to breath; she feels as if there is liquid in her lungs. The viscous poison crawls through her body, scorching its way across her right side. Her jaw and ear ache as it creeps up her face, and her leg tries to cave underneath her weight as it burns.

The creature reaches forward with the tendrils. She slashes wildly at them, satisfied when the creature shrieks breathlessly in pain. Gamerog can injure it.

Suddenly, an unexpected punch in her abdomen sends her sailing past the last rack and crashing through the window. The glass sparkles around her as she collapses in a heap on the cobblestones, her fingers constricting around Gamerog. "R-run," she urges the crowd surrounding the shop. "Run!"

The Hemius mist rolls out of the broken window, sniggering as civilians scramble away in terror. "*So gallivant,*" it mocks, a tendril wrapping around Mara's neck. She chokes, gasping for breath as the Hemius crawls over her skin, burning like a stream of lava.

Last chance, Mara thinks grimly, holding out her right arm. She nearly passes out from the shooting pain brought on just by lifting the broken limb.

"*Begging, are we?*" It pauses choking her, and she gasps for breath. "*I will listen to your pathetic —* "

Mara slashes it diagonally with the salev'i as a Source-created rose surges from her right fingertips, the black twining with the silver. It expands rapidly, shoving against the creature. It shrieks as her Source pushes it away from her.

In a flash, everything in a five-yard radius is destroyed.

Mara sways on her feet inside the mini-crater in the road. Her breath rattles in and out; her skin feels as if it is being flayed off her entire right side while being burned at the same time. Her right eye blurs, the colors distorting into purple and red swirls.

Her legs give out from underneath her.

Please… let it end soon… she begs, unable to speak. The vision in her left eye wavers from the pain racking her body.

"*Mara!*" Someone screams, collapsing beside her. A silver-banded white robe barely comes into focus. "Mara, can you hear me?!"

"Mom…" Mara rasps, finally getting a word out.

"I... love you."

"No, no, no, no, no," Ezra repeats over and over. Mara's vision blurs again, although she catches sight of a black robe with gold borders fluttering next to Ezra.

Mara feels as if she is drowning. She coughs and feels something warm drip down the left side of her face. "Is... it gone?" she asks, more blackish blood trickling out of her mouth.

"Yes, it's gone," Ezra sobs, stroking Mara's hair.

"Careful," an unfamiliar strange voice warns her. "She is bleeding."

"I know." Someone lifts Mara out of Ezra's arms. "Sweetie, how many... how many fingers am I holding up?"

Mara chokes up more blood. "Can't... see," she forces out, her face twisting in agony as her body shifts in the stranger's arms. "Make... it end. Please."

Mara feels the Hemius writhing within her, trying to take over. She feels her black Source weakening, but the silver Source rears up and attacks the Hemius directly, trying to push it back.

Kill me. Get it over with.

She tries to speak, but nothing comes out.

Her consciousness hangs on by a thread, making her painfully aware of everything happening inside of her and nothing else. The Hemius and her Source war over her body, but the Hemius slips by her Source's attempts to protect her.

Mara does not know if her screams are out loud or in her head.

Her entire body convulses in uncontrollable seizures; people try to restrain her flailing limbs. She catches snippets of panicked words around her, but she does not process them in her mind.

Finally, Mara sinks into her subconscious, escaping the pain.

Mara stands in front of the silver door that blends into the darkness surrounding it. The door creaks open just like before, but this time, a hand does not appear. A soft silvery glow emanates from within.

"Come here..."

Mara steps back and her surroundings change. She stands in front of a mirror, wearing only a tank top and shorts. In her left hand, Gamerog's blade is black with runes racing across the surface. Silver bolts flit over the surface as if charging the salev'i.

She watches in fascinated horror as Hemius crawls over her skin. It infects her entire right leg and arm; stretches across her collarbone and down into her torso; and creeps over her face, discoloring her right eye. Her head throbs.

"I want to live..." Mara sobs, covering her face with the back of her left hand still clutching Gamerog; her right one is in too much pain to move.

"Then live." The voice changes, as if it is piecing together words and phrases to make sentences. Mara finds herself back in the darkness with the silver door. *"Come inside – and live."*

Mara shakes her head slowly. "No."

"You – will perish." The door creaks softly, urging Mara to open it. The voice pleads with her, worried. *"Join with me, and – you will not – suffer."*

Mara hesitantly touches the door, opening it a little bit wider and peering inside. Her breath hitches as she sees the sleeping man – Lyrik – from one of her first dreams. The scenery slowly fades and the forge from the blacksmithing dream comes into focus.

She closes the door, leaning against it heavily. "Who... who are you?" she asks. She closes her eyes, refusing to look again.

"*I am – a part of – you,*" the presence says disjointedly in that odd way of snatching phrases spoken by other people and stringing them together. "*You do not – accept me. I am trying to help you.*"

This last sentence is complete and sounds like Aeserast's voice, although she had never heard him say that to her before. Mara sinks to her knees, torn; should she accept the strange offer and hope she lives, or...

A reddish-black liquid seeps through the wall of darkness, silhouetting the black tendrils encasing Mara and the door.

"*Let me help you.*" Another complete phrase, although this voice is unfamiliar and sounds more desperate.

She feels the door press against her back, encouraging her. Taking a deep breath, she stands up and opens the silver-etched wood, staring into the meadow where her father had died. She squares her shoulders and walks in.

The silver door swings shut.

CHAPTER 14
GIFTS

Mara sucks in a huge breath of air.

A shockwave of power bursts from her, tossing the unprepared medics against the wall. Silver lightning bolts fill the room, crackling ominously. Suddenly, they zoom towards the unconscious girl, coating her skin. Her body absorbs the Source.

Everyone stares at Mara, wondering what just happened.

Ezra's hand covers her mouth. Her eyes water. "Is... is she..."

Life'Lord Lilly slowly approaches the cot. Her robe has blackish bloodstains on it, and her originally white gloves are now a deep, dark red. She carefully places one of her hands on Mara's shoulder and then shakes her head.

"She is alive," Lilly informs everyone.

Ezra exhales, slumping beside Kiravon against the wall in relief.

"She needs to be monitored for a few days, though." Lilly looks pointedly at a young handsome elf with bronze hair and leaf-green eyes. "Darion, could you keep an eye on her?"

He dips his head, eyeing Mara's still form. "Of course."

Kiravon and Lilly direct the lesser-ranked medics as Darion and Ezra approach the bed. Mara's breathing, which had been wet and forced, is now clear and even; despite the Hemius now covering half of her face, she does not look as if she is in pain. Her skin shimmers slightly, her veins glowing a soft silver.

Ezra strokes Mara's hair. "Sweetie, can you hear me?"

Mara's eyelids flutter. "Mom?" she rasps, her voice rough. "I had these strange dreams…"

A tear slips down Ezra's cheek as her voice cracks. "You were having seizures. The Hemius moved into your heart and your brain at the same time."

Mara finally opens her eyes, revealing that the whites of her right eye are a slowly swirling reddish-black color with tiny silver veins stretching like lace over her eye. Dark colors swirl in her vision as she looks first at her mother and then at the elf standing next to her.

"Tein'stra Mara, it is a pleasure to see you are doing well," Darion begins, "My name is Darion, and I…" his words fade out as Mara's head aches and her vision hazes over.

Mara frowns slightly. She is pretty sure he is talking about checking something, but the increasing roar in her ear is drowning out the handsome elf's slow Xharos accent. "I'm sorry, Darion. What did you say?"

Ezra gently touches Mara's left cheek. Mara sighs in relief as the headache abates. "Sweetie, he needs to look into your mind and make sure you're still… you."

Confused, Mara just nods, guessing it is just another step in the process of leaving. "Is it like what Shaniel did during training?"

"What did Shaniel do?" Darion asks as Ezra moves back a little.

Mara slowly raises her left hand and touches her

temple. "He... put his fingers here and looked into my mind at my Source. It was weird."

Darion chuckles. "This is indeed similar to that."

Her eyes slide closed; she is so tired. She feels his callused fingers brush against her forehead, pushing aside her bangs as they trail down to her temple. She barely feels a presence at the edge of her mind, peering in. Suddenly, it is gone, and he pulls away his hand.

Mara opens her eyes and stares at him sleepily. "That's it?"

His lips quirk up. "It is a part of my job to be able to check someone's Source without being intrusive on the mind."

"Hmm." Mara's eyes feel heavy. *I guess... he's like a psychiatrist, but without having to ask questions.* She closes them again, drifting off to sleep.

Darion and Ezra step away a little, allowing her to rest. Lilly and Kiravon return to the room, an advanced medic in a silver-banded robe assisting them. Several hours pass by as they check the movement and activity of the Hemius.

By the time Mara wakes up, the sun had set and the city's nightlife had already died down. The room glows with a soft blue light, nearly making her fall back asleep. Turning her head, she sees her mother stretched out on two chairs, a blanket tossed over her. Darion stands by the window, his hands behind his back.

He glances at her as she struggles to sit up. "It would do you best to remain lying down," he advises.

She ignores him and, finally upright, examines herself. The hospital's soft uniform covers her shoulder and her arm down to her elbow despite the

256

Hemius that now covers her entire right side. She marvels at the pulsing silver veins and touches the thin yet rigid sleeve covering her wrist and arm. "Is this a... cast?"

He nods, his footsteps nearly silent despite his large black boots as he takes an extra chair from just outside the door and places it by her bed. "How do you feel?" he asks quietly as he sits down. Ezra doesn't even stir.

Mara slowly flexes her right fingers. "It doesn't hurt at all..."

"It should be fully healed by morning," he informs her, pointing at the brace. "That is a rapid-heal brace. It stimulates and encourages the muscles, tissue, and bone to heal at a faster rate than normal."

She sets her hand down, staring at the opaque glass wall beside her. A soft silvery light reflects back, obviously coming from her since the lighting in the room is blue. "I glow," she breathes, appalled.

Darion chuckles. "Indeed, tein'stra. Do you know how you did it?"

"Please, call me Mara," she insists. Holding up her hand again, she shakes her head. "As for this... I'm not quite sure. I-I think it's doing it by itself, but that just sounds crazy..."

Darion's lips tilt up in a mysterious smile. "Sometimes, an individual's Source can do more than what the person knows how to do. To an extent, our Source is a part of us, but it is also a part of Voyana, which has its own will." He gazes at the thin veins stretching over her right cheek like a tree branch. "It is rare, but if a person has a strong connection with their Source, the Source will protect itself and the body whenever possible – with or without the mind's need to control it."

Mara thinks back to several instances when her silver Source had reared up, uncalled for, and had sparked protectively around her. She gazes at her fingers thoughtfully. "I thought... all those times..."

Darion leans forward to catch her words. "Your Source has acted on its own before?"

Mara slowly nods. "Yes." She raises her left hand, inspecting the faint silver veins pulsing in rhythm to her heartbeat.

He watches her for a moment longer. "You have done what only one other person has achieved; driving back the infection with high amounts of Source. As long as your Hemius continues to be restrained by your Source, it should not give you any more trouble. I would not complain about your Source acting on its own this time; it saved your life."

"I'm glad it isn't too weird." Taking a deep breath, she glances at Ezra. "How is everyone... taking this?"

Darion glances over his shoulder at the sleeping woman. "They are worried. Ezra is the only one who refuses to leave, and no one can force her since she *is* a medic advisor." His green eyes glint in the soft light of the room. "Try to rest a little longer. Your friends will most likely be here at the start of visiting hours." He stands up, taking the chair with him.

"Thank you," Mara whispers.

Confused, he pauses. "Whatever for?"

She waves her hand around, the dim light of the room hiding her blush. "For all that you did. You don't know me, yet you..."

He smiles softly. "I help many people, Mara. Most of them I had never met before and will never meet again." Mara watches him take the chair to the window and sit down, gazing over the city.

He looks so... Mara mulls over his silhouetted frame as sleep pulls her back onto the pillow. She doesn't finish her thought, sinking into her dreams.

The next morning after Mara's arm brace is taken off, she explains what had happened in the shop in as much detail as possible. It is visiting hours by the time she finishes, and she is surprised that Kimala is the first to enter. She storms to Mara's bedside, anger, worry, and relief warring on her face.

"What were you *thinking*?" Kimala demands, her voice harsh. "You're ignorant, reckless, and stubborn as always! You could have died, Mara. Even the *Death'Lord* was pulled in on the situation. Why couldn't you have run away like everyone else?"

Ezra, eyebrows raised, stares at Kimala from her seat against the wall. "He would have been pulled in on it anyway, and by the sounds of it, Mara didn't have the opportunity to run."

"It is a miracle in and of itself that she fended off the Dark Warrior so efficiently," Darion adds in, leaning against the wall between Ezra and the large window. "You should be more grateful your cousin is not possessed or stabbed to death."

Kimala whirls around. Her eyes widen at the sight of Ezra and Darion, and her cheeks flame a bright red. "You – ah – I apologize for my – "

Darion chuckles and Ezra laughs at Kimala's sudden humiliation. Codi hesitantly enters, his face pale as he stares at Mara. "Are you..."

Mara smiles at her brother, flexing her Hemius-covered right arm and shoulder. "All healed," she reassures both him and Kimala, "although Gamerog left a bit of a scar on my shoulder. Kiravon and Lilly said it's not infectious as long as my Source – ah." Startled by her brother's unexpected hug, she pats his arm.

"Don't do something like that again," he whispers, letting her go. His eyes glisten brightly as he wrings his hands. "You really scared us all. We-we thought – " His teeth grind together as he takes a shaky breath.

Kimala gestures to Codi. "See? This is why you shouldn't do crazy stuff like that again. Codi would be depressed for *years*." Mara can't help but notice that Kimala's eyes are watery, too, but she doesn't say anything.

Suddenly, she is swept into a tight hug as lavender hair tickles her face. Aeserast pulls back and stares at her, touching her right cheek lightly. "What happened?"

Mara pats his hand, smirking at him. "I decided to be reckless and stubborn. Again."

Darion frowns. "Aeserast? I thought you were on realm lockdown."

Aeserast glances around, his entire body sagging in relief as soon as he sees the bronze-haired elf. "Darion. So you were there? What happened? How's Mara's condition?"

"We can all speak of it later," Timian says from the doorway, holding a plain white box in one hand. "I am giving Aeserast the morning to visit before he has to return to his realm."

Shaniel saunters in after him, holding something behind his back. He flourishes a bouquet of strange red flowers. They look like roses, but the petals are more pointed and curved, forming teardrop shapes at the tips of the petals before folding down like morning bells.

Mara accepts the odd roses, startled as he, too, gives her a hug. He rests his chin on top of her head. "I'm glad you're recovering, Mara."

"I think that's the first time you've ever called me by my first name," she jokes, smirking at him as he rubs his nose and backs away.

Timian sets the white box in her lap, patting her head affectionately. She lifts the lid and gasps. A beautiful flower shaped like the strange roses in the bouquet is nestled in black satin, the petals silver with black accents. "It's beautiful..." she murmurs, amazed.

The Time'Lord smiles slightly. "I hope you like it. It is Garneian silver chocolate in the shape of a per'lusa flower."

"Thank you," Mara whispers. She stares at the flower, trying to swallow the lump in her throat.

"Uh..." Everyone turns to see William peeking in, looking slightly intimidated by the group of people in her room.

"William!" Mara greets, happy to see him. Suddenly, she remembers what had happened to the shop and grimaces. "I'm sorry... I'll pay you back for the damages."

He shakes his head as he eases into the room hesitantly. "I'm jus' glad to see you're alive, and to bring you your stuff. I figured you'd be missin' it about now."

Shaniel holds out his hands, and William gives him Mara's neatly folded robe, skin glove, and pendant. Aeserast finally leaves Mara's side to inspect the trinket.

William bows slightly to Timian. "Haven't seen your 'Lordship around in several years. How fares the evula I made you?"

"Thankfully, I have not had to use it much," Timian admits, glancing at the long, thin object swaddled in cloth underneath William's arm. "A gift for Mara?"

Mara finally notices the object and quickly shakes her head, recognizing the shape. She couldn't possibly accept it – not after what had happened to his shop. "William – "

"It wouldn' quit whinin' until I brought it with me," he cuts her off, exasperated. He sets the swaddled weapon in her lap. "Sulkin' the entire night, keepin' me up. Take it before I go insane."

Mara gasps as she uncovers the familiar black-scaled hilt and citrine pommel. "Gamerog…"

Timian frowns. "William, you know it is against – "

"I know," William huffs. "But you haven' seen these two. They're inseparable as soon as Mara enters the shop. A few minutes shouldn' hurt anything."

Mara uncovers the rest of the sword, gasping at the ornate, elegant sheath. The pointed guard is cupped in a brilliant blue, reminding her of a budding flower. The main portion of the scabbard is silver with a blue band along the edge. A slit runs down the length of the blade, exposing the still tainted metal underneath. Resting in the middle of the scabbard's elegant design is a glistening silver dragon with black onyx talons on a vivid blue background.

Mara strokes the scabbard. She cannot help but imagine how the sword must have looked before tainted with that awful red… whatever it was. *You must have been worried, too,* she thinks, smiling slightly when the sword hums softly underneath her hand as if in confirmation.

Headmaster Gerard Folion, looking as though he had pulled an all-nighter, clears his throat. "So many people," he comments, smiling tiredly at Mara. "It looks as though you are doing better than I heard, Mara."

Mara beams at Folion, patting Gamerog's sheath. "Look at what William brought!"

Folion frowns at the sword. He glances at the Highlords surrounding her before returning her smile. "I guess you weren't joking when you said you could touch it. Here; Narbundel and I made you something."

Mara takes the small package from him. Opening it, she discovers a dull, transparent band. She gives Folion a questioning look.

"Put it on your right wrist."

She slips the band over her hand; it settles comfortably on her wrist. Her skin ripples, and suddenly, she is staring at clear skin. She gasps, flipping her hand over in amazement.

"It is designed to hide Hemius. That band can fit over your wrist or your ankle; it's stretchy and durable. However, if you put too much force on it, it *will* snap," he warns her. She nods attentively, fingering the strap. "Also, please drop by my office as soon as you're released. I have your magelet intermediate robe ready for you."

Mara starts to nod again before his words register. She gasps. "You mean – "

Folion grins. "I believe driving out your Hemius and defending yourself against the Dark Warrior merits a graduation. Congratulations, Mara."

< * >

Mara tugs nervously at her new red-accented robe as she walks between Ezra and Darion. "Mom, are you sure what I'm wearing is okay?"

Ezra snorts. "When have you cared about that?"

Since you told me we're going to meet the royal family, Mara thinks, crossing her arms over her chest in her attempt to hide her comfortable training clothes. She loves Surana's gifts, but even she knows they are not meant to be worn to meet nobility.

Darion's lips quirk up. "Do not fret, Mara. The summons was sudden, so they will not be expecting us in our finest."

So says the handsome elf who looks good in whatever he's wearing, Mara grumbles to herself. He is in a simple black tunic and dark red pants that look soft and comfortable. Her mother is in her white medic advisor robe, and underneath, she has on a blue shirt and tan pants.

Mara peeks once again at her snug training garb. The cloth hugs her legs, various pockets strategically placed to maximize efficiency as well as maneuverability.

It definitely screams commoner.

She sighs. *For once, I should have listened to Kimala and went shopping for nicer clothes.*

The huge fountain in the middle of the plaza creates beautiful, arching designs in the air as people mill about the old-styled area in front of the palace. Mara follows Ezra up the wide stairs as the guards open the palace doors.

They walk through the hallways of the grand palace. Mara cannot help but marvel at the tapestries dangling from the ceiling, the green cloth swaying slightly as the gold tree glistens in the sunlight streaming through the windows and skylights. Portraits of the royal families throughout the centuries line the corridor.

More guards stand alert beside a gate-like set of doors. They turn and open them wide, silently admitting the guests. It opens into a large throne room sparsely decorated with the green and gold livery; at the other end of the room, three people occupy all but one of the masterfully crafted wood and metal chairs.

Mara's eyes are drawn to the beautiful queen sitting between her husband and son; her long, straight amber hair nearly burns against her tanned skin in the filtered sunlight, her freckles standing out against her ocean blue eyes. The king's tight blonde curls nearly disappear against his fair complexion, hinting at some ancient descendancy to one of the moon elf covens. Their son has his mother's straight hair and ocean eyes but his father's complexion and hair color, looking about eighteen or so. He is a perfect combination of the two adul'ne.

The man stands up, beaming at them. "Ezra, how wonderful to see you again." To Mara's surprise, he steps forward and gives Ezra a brief hug and a peck on her cheek. "Is this your daughter?"

"It's so nice to see you, too, Edgard." Ezra wraps her arm around Mara's tense shoulders. "And yes, this is Mara."

Edgard and the woman give Ezra an odd look. Mara barely hears the duir'ne mumble, "Such an odd name."

Finally, Edgard clears his throat and says bluntly, "Ezra, I – *we* would like you to accept voi status and move into the palace."

Mara stares at the king, stunned. She doesn't know what 'voi status' is, but moving into the palace seems to be a bit much. She keeps quiet, hoping to catch on to the rest.

Ezra shakes her head. "Edgard – "

The red-haired woman grabs Ezra's hands, pleading, "Please, Ezra? You know you are just as much family to us as Shokain was."

"I know, Cleo, but Mara – "

"Would receive voi'duir'stra status," Edgard interrupts Ezra.

Mara's eyes widen, finally catching on to the topic. *Voi... is that like an honorary position title?*

Ezra bites her lip. "I would hate to impose..."

"You would not be imposing. Quite the opposite!" Edgard says.

The fair-haired prince leans towards his mother and whispers in her ear. She shakes her head, tugging the boy forward. "Mara, you're studying in the tactical wing under Headmaster Folion, correct?"

Startled at being addressed directly, Mara stammers, "Yes, ma'am."

"Alec, our son, is under Headmaster Folion's care, as well. Perhaps he can give you a tour while we speak to your mother."

Mara glances at Ezra, who gives her daughter a wavering smile. "Go on, sweetie. You don't have to stay."

Mara steps after Alec who is already striding out of the room. Darion moves to follow them, but Edgard requests, "Darion, do you mind staying? I have something to ask of you."

"Of course, Your Majesty." The green-eyed elf

bows slightly to the king, shooting Mara a concerned glance. She shrugs at him.

Alec offers his arm to Mara, and she hesitantly takes it. "Which field do you wish to study in?" he asks as they turn down a long corridor.

"I'm not quite sure yet." Mara gazes out the large bay windows as they pass by. "There are so many options... I wish I could learn them all."

Alec chuckles, relaxing a little. "You could certainly try. You know Tein'stra Kimala Brunet, the Life'Lord's most recent intern, correct?"

Surprised, Mara glances at him. "Yes. She's my cousin." She catches his thoughtful expression and refrains from smiling. "Would you like to meet her?"

Alec's cheeks turn a faint pink. "Ah... it would be nice, but she always seems so busy."

"I'm sure she won't mind," Mara assures him. *In fact, I think she would* love *the opportunity to speak with a prince.*

He leaves her briefly in the main hall so he can change, returning in a black mage robe with green curving designs along the main portion of the cloak. Rick, trailing after the duir'ne, silently follows them down the roads leading to the Academy as Alec advises her on what she needs to study to advance out of the magelet robes and she gives him some pointers on a move his combat instructor had given him. Mara even offers to spar with him on the roof stadium sometime later in the week. By the time they make it to the medical wing's fifteenth floor, both of them are much more comfortable and relaxed around the other.

In the study lobby, Mara approaches Kimala. She is sitting down at a desk, her white intern medic robe with gold, green, and red bands around the borders fitting comfortably on her frame. A crème band with the symbol of a bandage – Highlord Lilly's sign – marks her as the prestigious Life'Lord's intern. Underneath her robe, she is wearing a simple pleated pastel skirt with a silky white top. She looks extremely professional – nothing like the girl Mara had known in Veera.

Tapping the intern's shoulder, Mara says, "Kimala, there's someone I want you to meet."

Kimala sighs, turning around. "You pick the most inconvenient ti – " She stops as soon as she sees Alec standing slightly behind Mara. Leaping to her feet, Kimala bows deeply, shocked. "Your Grace! To what do I owe the pleasure?"

Alec's eyebrows mesh together in concern. "I apologize for the inconvenience, tein'stra. I merely wished to speak with you."

Kimala quickly shakes her head. "It is no inconvenience, Your Grace."

He flashes a relieved smile. "That is good to hear. How are your studies?"

Mara takes a step back, giving them an opportunity to talk. Hearing a commotion by the lift, she turns around to see Darion and Ezra rush off the platform. They stare at her, both wearing matching expressions of relief and exasperation.

"You should have notified us you were leaving," Darion lectures her before Ezra could catch her breath, "especially with the duir'ne."

Rick chuckles behind his hand as he watches them from the side. Mara crosses her arms, glaring at Darion. "What was I supposed to say? 'Give me a sec as I tell my overprotective guardian and mom that we're leaving'? Alec wanted to come straight here."

Ezra rests a hand on Darion's arm, stopping his next words. She walks towards the chatting nobles and pulls Alec off to the side, speaking to him quietly.

Seeing an opening, Kimala rushes to Mara, her face flushed. "Mara, how do you know the duir'ne?"

Mara shrugs. "We went to the palace, and I met him."

"You just *happened* to meet him and then dragged him all the way here?" the medic intern asks, disbelieving.

"I did *not* drag him here. He wanted to meet you." Mara smiles as Ezra and Alec approach.

"Kimala, I need you to accompany us back to the palace," Ezra says, not even pausing next to the two teenagers as she strides towards the lift.

"I apologize, but I can't. Lilly wanted my report on today's morning surgery." Kimala truly looks regretful as she turns towards her desk again.

Ezra doesn't turn around. "It wasn't a request. If Lilly throws a fit, direct her to the Roanoak family. We're moving to the palace."

Kimala stares after Ezra, flabbergasted. "The palace?"

Ezra nods, pausing by the lift as Kimala hurriedly packs her books and follows them onto the lift. "I managed to convince Edgard to let you stay with us since you don't have your own place yet."

Alec leans towards Darion. "Darion, are you sure it is all right for you to..."

Mara rubs her head, missing part of the conversation. *Maybe I should have Mom check it out,* she thinks, concerned. However, the nagging headache disappears just as quickly as it had appeared.

"... is currently handling things," Darion is explaining to Alec with a smile. "If he needs me, he can contact me easily enough."

"So how long will you be at the palace?" the duir'ne asks as the platform lowers.

Darion shrugs. "A few more days, at most."

"Are you visiting the tactical wing?" Alec looks at Darion, hopeful.

He shakes his head. "Lilly asked for my assistance."

Mara stares out the window. "I don't see why you need to babysit me. I'm perfectly fine."

Suddenly, a wave of dizziness slams into her. She clutches her head and falls against the glass wall, trying to fight it off; however, it is as if she had been drugged. The last thing she sees is Darion's alarmed expression and Kimala's wide, shocked eyes.

Her vision goes black.

A wooden door blows inward, showering snow and splinters over Mara. She screams and throws her hands over her face.

"Oh Essence, where are you?" a female voice singsongs as someone steps inside.

Mara trembles, peeking from underneath the table. Someone grabs her by the hair and pulls her out. She screams and kicks, but the person doesn't let go.

"It is not nice to ignore a guest," the strange girl snarls. She looks no older than sixteen or seventeen with wavy dark brown hair and pale skin. Her eyes shine a reddish color. She brandishes a salev'i with a dripping red blade and a bloody stone on the hilt.

Mara cries. "Please... have mercy..."

"Mercy?" The girl throws her head back and cackles. "This body will be mine, Essence. Kneel before me."

The girl throws her to the floor. Mara grovels. "Please. I do not know who you think I am, but you are mistaken. My name is Lori – "

"Shut up, Essence." The girl's sword nicks Mara's – no, Lori's neck. The girl squats in front of her, examining Lori's eyes. Disappointment fills the glowing red orbs. "You are not strong enough. Pity."

Lori freezes, terrified.

The sword swings. Excruciating pain, and then blackness so complete and endless that it swallows her consciousness.

Mara jolts straight up in the bed, screaming hysterically. She claws at her neck, not fully comprehending that it is still attached. She fights against the multiple hands that pry her fingers away from her throat.

Several people yell something – is it at her? About her? She doesn't know. All she knows is the utter blackness that had spit her out.

She had died. There is no other explanation for it.

Arms wrap around her and hold her still, restraining her thrashing. She fights against the vice grip but it doesn't loosen at all. After a moment, a steady sound breaks through her terror.

Thu-thump. Thu-thump.

Mara sucks in a deep breath, entranced by the steady, calming sound.

Thu-thump. Thu-thump.

Another deep breath, and another. She becomes aware of her surroundings.

Thu-thump. Thu-thump.

A heady scent of the chill that comes only from eternally dark places infuses the shirt she is pressed against. A steady voice murmurs calming words over her head.

"No one will hurt you, Mara. We will protect you."

271

Thu-thump. Thu-thump.

Mara takes a big breath. She tries to yank back, reminded of the darkness from her dream, but the arms lock her against his chest.

"You are safe," the voice repeats. *Thu-thump-thu-thump.* The heartbeat increases a little bit. "We will protect you."

"Mmnn," Mara moans, leaning into the form and taking another deep breath. She listens to the steady heartbeat and dozes off with her fist clenching his shirt.

She looks in the mirror and sees a young girl with long, dark blonde hair. Her eyes are a pretty sky blue and her skin is pale as if she doesn't get out much.

She picks up a beautiful ribbon with an emblem of a silver dragon on a blue background. Her guardian had given it to her and told her to never take it off while walking around, and she intended to follow his instructions. She ties her hair with it and leaves the little cottage with a basket of dirty linens on her arm.

Her new friends swarm her and tell her how she glows with the fresh look of a young woman in love. She blushes, unused to all of the attention; she had moved to the small little village only recently. Two days ago, though, Tris had made their courtship public.

Someone grabs the ribbon and yanks it out of her hair, examining it closely.

"Give that back!" she exclaims, a jolt of panic shooting through her. Not even her lover knows why she is really in this tiny village. She doesn't want to put any of them in danger.

Their eyes widen when they recognize the crest.

"It is the Alamir family's crest! Where did you get this, Anabel?" one of them asks.

Horrible at lying, she admits, "It... was a gift."

They throw it on the ground and bury it. Anabel tries to

stop them, but they warn her, "If the queen sees this, she will kill you for treason!"

She watches them, tears streaming down her face. "It was supposed to protect me from her," she argues.

Her friends look at her, startled, and then quickly back away with horrified expressions.

"Weak," a voice rasps behind her. "Too weak. I should kill you all."

A sword protrudes from her ribs. Anabel looks down and sees the bloodstained metal of the salev'i.

As her consciousness slips away, she turns around and sees the girl with wavy dark brown hair, pale skin, red eyes. "Who... are you?"

The girl blinks, surprised for some reason. "You... were the Essence?" she asks, horrified. She grabs her hair, suddenly enraged. "You are too weak to be the Essence!"

CHAPTER 15
DUELING THE BEST

Mara jerks awake again, though this time she does not scream. She takes jagged breaths and clings to the same shirt as before. The steady heartbeat brings her back to reality.

Mara takes one last deep, steady breath and opens her eyes. She stares at a black silk shirt. "I'm okay," she tells the person.

The arms release her and Mara pulls back to discover it was Darion. Her face flushes bright red.

"I'm sorry," she immediately apologizes, letting go of his shirt and scooting away from him. Glancing around, she stares at the ornate bedroom. "Where are we?"

"A guest room in the palace," He informs her, straightening out the fine material of his shirt. "We brought you here when you collapsed. You refused to let go." His lips quirk up.

"I'm sorry," Mara repeats, scanning the room for people. She feels a little bit better after discovering she is still in her magelet robe and casual clothes. "Where is everyone?"

"Shaniel is helping my assistant while the others are dining in the great hall." He stands up. "I will let you rest."

Mara nods, drawing her legs up to her chest. As he walks away, she shivers as the dreams haunt her. She buries her head in her knees, remembering the cold darkness that had swallowed her at the end of each.

"N-no..."

"Mara?" Darion is at the edge of the bed again. Mara's head jerks up and she stares at him. His eyes widen at her pale face. "What is it?"

"I-I had these dreams," she breathes, her breath whooshing in and out. "Nightmares. They felt so real."

He touches her hand. She jerks, surprised. "I apologize," he says, pulling his hand back. "I did not mean to startle you."

She shakes her head. "No, it's okay."

Darion digs something out of his pocket. "Take this. It is a protective amulet, but it may also help with the dreams."

Mara unfolds the small cloth and lifts a ribbon. Attached to the middle of it is a crest of a silver dragon with onyx nails on a lapis blue background.

Mara gasps, recognizing the amulet.

Anabel, one of the girls from her dreams, had been given an amulet *exactly* like this one by a Highlord before she had been taken to a remote village where she had fallen in love with one of the locals. As long as she had worn it, no one could track her, not even the Highlords. Mara runs her fingers over the exquisite dragon embellishment.

"How did you get this?" Mara asks, amazed.

Darion shrugs, watching her closely. "I collect powerful trinkets as a hobby. Why?"

Mara shakes her head, taking a deep breath. "I was just curious." She flips it over, noticing a scratch on the back. She fingers it, remembering the detail from her dream. *It's the exact same one,* she realizes, a chill sliding down her spine. She grips the pendant tightly.

"You will be safe, Mara." He reaches across and

touches the pendant in her hand. A silvery spark shocks him, and he jerks away.

She rubs her palm. "I'm so sorry. I've been doing that recently. I just want to be normal for one day…"

Darion brushes his fingers over the pendant, touching her hand again. The stinging silver bolt hits him again, but he does not pull away this time. "I am fine. See?"

Mara nods at Darion, biting her lip. The nightmare still haunts her, taunting her in the back of her mind. She squeezes his fingers, desperately needing the reassurance right then. *I'm alive,* she reassures herself. *I'm alive, and that person is gone.*

The door bangs open.

Mara jumps, dropping Darion's hand. Shaniel storms in, his freckled face pale and ears flat against his head. "Never," he whispers, shoving a finger in Darion's direction, "am I filling in for you again. Some creep thought he could sneak past me! He – he – "

His face is a bright red as he tucks his magenta and grey Highlord robe around himself.

"Grabbed your tail?" Darion finishes calmly as Mara straightens, slightly embarrassed that she had just grabbed Darion's hand. "Maybe you should learn to tuck it better."

Shaniel shivers. "Just… stop making me fill in for you, Darion. You know Aeserast is better at that than me."

"But Aeserast is on realm lockdown," Darion points out, "and Lilly was unavailable. I certainly couldn't send Ezra, either."

Shaniel wrinkles his nose. "Good point." He eyes Mara. "How are you feeling?"

"Better," Mara admits, smiling ruefully. "I've been meaning to tell Mom I've been getting dizzy spells."

Shaniel sighs, shaking his head. "You're going to collapse one day – and it won't be for a simple nap, either."

< * >

The next day, Mara resumes her daily routine of training with Shaniel in the morning and Headmaster Folion in the early afternoon. Darion shadows her, making sure she does not pass out. However, his presence is quite distracting to the young magelet; she fumbles in the classes only for him to give her advice in his smooth, Xharos-accented baritone voice. She is happy the following day is Senuni – Saturday – and she will not have lessons other than her midday spar with Shaniel.

Mara kicks at Shaniel's side; he easily blocks it, grabs her ankle, and knocks her off balance. She tumbles to the ground, her breath whooshing out of her.

Shaniel steps on either side of her hips and looks down at her, frowning. "Your movements are delayed, Danarko. Something on your mind?"

"She *is* still recovering from the other day," Kimala says matter-of-factly from her position on a large cloth underneath a tree. She daintily sips at her tea as Alec munches on some fruit. Codi lounges on the grass, reading a book assigned to him by Narbundel.

Mara scowls at the laig'hius hovering above her and aims a kick between his legs, but he quickly leaps out of the way, unfazed. "It's hard keeping the spell going while you're beating me up."

"You have to try." Shaniel flicks off a piece of

grass from his shirt. "If you can learn how to maintain this while doing other things, imagine how much faster you can get it done when you're focusing completely on it."

Mara glares at the stick in her hand. Shape manipulation is supposedly one of the basic skills of a mage, but she is unable to hold it very well when her mind is distracted. "Why can't I just make it *look* like a knife?"

Shaniel rolls his eyes. "Because then that would be an *illusion*. You need to learn object manipulation before you can learn light manipulation."

"Fine," she grumbles, focusing on the particles within the stick. She shifts them around with her Source, and the wood turns into a vague semblance of a knife.

Shaniel nods. "Good! Let's continue."

Mara glares at the makeshift dagger. "Is this even possible?"

Shaniel rolls his eyes. "Of course it is, Danarko." He holds out his hand and she grasps it firmly. He tugs her to her feet.

"It just doesn't feel like it..." Mara mutters.

"Let's practice the laig'hius style again," Shaniel says, sinking into the now-familiar stance. He has been teaching Mara different fighting styles for a while now; laig'hius is just one of many.

They duel for several minutes, not noticing the silent arrival of Darion. He watches as Shaniel grabs Mara's arm, flings her over his shoulder, and pins her to the ground.

"It's failing again," he informs her, releasing her arm and straightening. She glances at her stick, which wavers back and forth between a knife and its original shape. He grins at Darion. "Yo! Ya need something, Darion?" Darion shakes his head and sits next to Codi on the grass.

"I just don't understand why it needs to be a knife," she huffs, tossing the stick down as Shaniel picks up his water canteen.

"If you'd rather turn it into a pencil, then go for it," he says, raising the canteen to his lips.

Mara subtly reaches forward and brushes her fingers along the smooth metal canister, making it turn green and have the vague semblance of a turtle. Shaniel yelps, dropping it and spilling water on his shoes. He glares at her.

She shrugs. "What? Just practicing."

Shaniel grins wickedly, turning to Darion. "You should try dueling her, Darion!"

Darion languidly rises to his feet and walks towards them, stretching his arms. "If I duel her, then you must take responsibility for what happens, Thief'Lord."

Shaniel pouts. "Quit calling me that! I'm the Common'Lord!"

"Only if you quit stealing my books." Darion takes off his outer shirt, exposing a simple black shirt underneath.

"Oho, you're serious." Shaniel grins as he leaps to his feet. "Good luck, Mara!"

Kimala rolls her eyes as Codi and Alec chuckle, waving to Mara for luck.

"Are you going to make me do crazy spells while fighting you?" Mara smirks, a thrill going through her. She hasn't sparred with anyone new in a while, and by the others' reactions, Darion will be a hard opponent.

A faint smile tilts the corner of Darion's lips

upward. Mara senses his muscles coil in preparation. "I want to know what you are capable of," he murmurs, widening his stance. "I will not set limitations on you."

Mara bounces on the balls of her feet, excited. "Let's get started, then."

They size each other up, attempting to guess what the other's strengths and weaknesses are. The others sit silently, sensing the tension between the two combatants. Even Kimala watches with anticipation.

Darion makes the first move. He leaps forward and tries a simple yet fast combo, testing Mara's capabilities. She blocks and dodges all of them, executing her own moves next.

Their movements blur. Mara's fast reflexes are on par with Shaniel's natural movements, but Darion has obviously honed his body to react even faster. Mara struggles to keep up with his abilities, not willing to lose any ground in the duel.

"Amazing," Alec murmurs, his eyes wide as he watches the fight. "Mara is pushing him to his physical limits."

Shaniel nods, impressed. "I haven't seen him fight this hard since Wayne left."

Alec shakes his head. "It is phenomenal. Mara is quite skilled to be able to keep up with Darion of all people."

Codi smiles secretively, his arms crossed over his chest. "No, she's losing."

They stare at him.

He points at her left foot. "You see how she has nearly completely stopped kicking since the last time he threw her? She knows she has a disadvantage. She's pouring all of her skills into her arms and speed instead."

"You truly were raised with her," Alec comments.

Shaniel mutters, "I've been sparring with her regularly, but I never noticed that."

Codi shakes his head. "I've only seen her do it a few times before with Dad. It's her 'last resort' stage."

A loud thud draws their attention back to the dueling pair.

Mara gasps for air, grinning wildly up at a faintly smiling Darion. She is flat on her back, his hand on her shoulder from where he had flipped her.

He helps her up. "You fight well," he comments, shoving his hair out of his face. His pointed ears peek past the bronze locks.

Mara leans over and grabs her knees, her breath whooshing in and out. "I should say that to you! I was the highest in all three of my classes."

"Aikido, Taekwondo, and Shotokan, I assume?" he asks.

Mara shakes her head, a little surprised that he knows the Earth self defense arts. "Not Taekwondo. Judo."

"Not bad, not bad," Shaniel congratulates, clapping. "Now, let's try that barrier spell again."

Darion and Mara exchange glances. They tackle Shaniel, grabbing his arms and tossing him to the ground.

Shaniel laughs and sweeps his foot out to catch one of them; however, both of them dodge the Common'Lord's favorite attack. Shaniel grabs Mara's leg, knocking her off balance, and Darion suddenly turns to her and initiates a couple close-range strikes.

She gracefully dodges and blocks as Shaniel stands up and strikes at the back of Darion's neck. The magelet and laig'hius team up, performing short, fast strikes against the elf.

Darion steps back, having difficulty holding his ground against the two fighters who are in perfect sync with one another.

"It is quite amazing," Alec notes. "Darion is considered the best in all the realms at hand-to-hand with Shaniel following close behind."

"She's pretty good with unarmed skills," Codi boasts as Mara knocks Shaniel onto his back. He quickly hops to his feet again, defending against her blows.

Kimala sighs. "I need to learn how to do that..." she murmurs to herself. Alec hears her.

"I can teach you," Alec offers, smiling at her.

Kimala's face reddens. "R-really?"

Darion knocks Mara onto her back, knocking the wind out of her. She groans and doesn't move this time. He frowns, concerned. "Are you all right, Mara? Did I hurt you?"

Mara grimaces. "I feel like tenderized meat." She takes his offered hand, pulling herself up. "But it was fun," she admits, grinning at him. He returns it with a smile.

Early morning rays brush against the field as a light breeze sways the tree limbs. She replays Shaniel's lessons from yesterday in her head as she commits the movements to muscle memory.

I wonder if I can defend my mind like she did, Mara thinks to herself as she cuts through the air. *There are mind weavers, after all. What if one tries to get into my head? Maybe that's what I was dreaming about; a mind-weaver messing with my head. It does seem like something I would be worried about.*

"May I join you?" Darion asks, but she doesn't notice. "Mara," he calls out, trying to get her attention.

She performs an uppercut. Her fingers spark mildly, reflecting her calm mood.

"Mara." He steps closer, his hand reaching for her shoulder.

Mara senses the presence of another and swings around. Her fingers stop a hairsbreadth away from his neck. He fights the urge to swallow.

"I'm so sorry," Mara gasps, quickly lowering her hands. "How... how long have you been there?"

"A minute or so. Are you feeling well?" he asks, staring at her.

Mara nods. "I-I remember reading somewhere that mind-weavers can get into your head and really mess you up, but there's a way to shield your mind," she fibs, not looking him in the eye. She couldn't bring herself to tell him it was her dream of Aliyah – the girl who had had her mind ripped apart – that had given her the idea. She stretches her arms, flexing her wrists. "I don't know if I'm doing it right, though."

"I can help." He gestures to a tree. "Sit down."

"You're a mind-weaver?" she asks as she sits cross-legged in front of him.

He nods, confirming her suspicion. She had guessed since she had met him; it makes sense, really, seeing as he has been monitoring her mood since she had woken up from that incident in the market.

Darion stares at her neck with an odd expression. She reflexively touches the pendant that rests there and discovers that both the Alamiran crest and

Aeserast's pendant had fallen out of her tunic.

"Annoying things…" she grumbles, tucking them back under her tunic self-consciously.

"It is good you are wearing them, though," he says.

Mara blushes. "Y-yeah. Though I feel bad… I've already broken one of Aeserast's charms."

Darion shrugs. "It is what they are meant for, so do not feel terrible if you must use them. Keep me from looking into your mind," he suddenly orders.

Mara doesn't have enough time to ask him what he means when she feels that creeping sensation of someone entering the same private space of her own consciousness. She immediately throws up walls, creating a smooth glass casing around her and the presence.

"*Not enough,*" Darion murmurs into her mind. He shatters it with a finger, a prod of mental capability. He is definitely better at this than Shaniel. "*You have to believe in your defenses.*"

She throws up a titanium wall fortified with folded magnesium-based alloy and steel. *This will definitely keep him out,* she thinks. She encases her mind with it, creating a seamless sphere around her entire being. No cracks, no crevasses. Completely smooth like glass, but tougher than any diamond. The hardest, most impenetrable wall possible.

Something pushes into it, creating a dent. Mara watches in fascinated horror as her defenses crumble like a blanket fort underneath Darion's pressure. He withdrawals, sensing her panic.

"Mara, calm down," he murmurs, grabbing her hands and bringing her back to the physical world. "Focus on me."

Mara takes a deep breath and stares into his gold-flecked leaf green eyes, trying to squash the terror of someone else invading her mind's space. "It felt so crowded," she admits quietly. "How did you break it so easily? I thought I had built the strongest wall."

Darion gives her a lopsided grin. "If it had been a physical wall, then yes." Darion holds up his hand and a leaf-green sphere with gold flecks materializes, perfectly matching his eyes. "However, this is Source we are working with. If Source is breaking into your mind, you need Source to defend yourself." He examines her face. "Do you want to try again?"

Mara nods. "Give me a moment." She takes several deep breaths and closes her eyes. "I'm ready."

Mara throws up the same solid fortification as before, but this time, she infuses her Source into it. The wall accepts the black like a sponge, but the silver sparks refuse to meld with the metal. After a nanosecond, they bond and strengthen the sphere. As Darion presses in on her mind, Mara fuses more and more of her Source with the wall.

Mara loses track of time as she constantly feeds her Source into her mental barrier. She feels Darion straining against it, not even making a dent. He pushes all of his power into one single spot in a last attempt to break through.

Mara reinforces that area, creating a slight crescent moon shape extending outwards from her barrier to diffuse the damage. His power rebounds off the bowl and hits him. The pressure disappears.

Mara opens her eyes, wondering what had happened to him. He lies a couple yards away, flat on his back. His bronze hair looks as if he had stuck his finger into a light bulb, and a little bit of blood drips from his nose.

"Darion!" Mara dashes over and collapses next to him. *Did I do this?* "Darion, can you hear me? Darion!"

His eyes do not open and his breathing is ragged and uneven. She stands up, needing to find Kimala. She feels a tug on her pant leg.

Darion's hand drops. He stares up at her, his eyes dazed. "I am all right."

Mara collapses to her knees. "I am so sorry," she apologizes, grabbing his arm. "I didn't know that would happen."

Darion winces. "Talk... lower," he mumbles, his other hand covering an ear. "You are pretty strong," he comments, grinning at her. "I was not expecting that much Source to be integrated into it. How much did you use?"

"I just kept feeding it," Mara rambles. "I didn't know how much it would need."

"Le... fora cauna..." Darion trails off, smiling faintly at her. He had said 'You are spectacular' in an old version of Xharos. Mara understands it, although she knows intuitively she shouldn't have known. His eyes slide closed as his head nods off to the side.

Mara's breath hitches.

"*Kimala!*" she screams, knowing the girl can't hear her but still shouting. "*Kimala! Help!*"

Shockingly enough, Kimala appears five minutes later, out of breath and with Shaniel trailing after her. She stares at Mara, stunned. "Did you seriously just call for me with Source?"

"You heard me," Mara breathes, relieved. She lets go of Darion's arm. "Please, help him."

Kimala kneels beside Darion. Her eyes widen as she analyzes him. "He has a severe concussion and heavy damage to his torso. What did you do? Beat each other up?"

"He was teaching me how to shield my mind," Mara explains. She wipes away the tears cascading down her face and sniffles. "It rebounded when he attacked. When I opened my eyes, he was a few yards away."

Shaniel stares at her, amazed. "You managed to keep him out of your mind?"

Mara nods. "If I knew it would do this, I never would have done it, though," she moans, squeezing her eyes shut. "I didn't want to hurt him. I was just doing as he instructed me to."

"Then it's his own fault," Kimala says, her hands glowing a silvery sky blue. "Shut up so I can focus."

Mara's jaw snaps closed, and Shaniel pats her shoulder reassuringly.

Darion groans under Kimala's hands. His breathing picks up pace and his eyes open into narrow slits. He glances at Mara before closing his eyes again. "Do not cry, Mara. I told you to do this."

"I'm so sorry," she moans, a fresh wave of tears spilling out. "I didn't want to hurt you..."

Darion grabs her hand. She squeezes his fingers. "Do not worry about it," he reassures her, grinning. "I have a good medic."

Shaniel glances between Darion and Mara, his eyebrows raising ever so slightly.

Kimala taps Darion's shoulder. "This medic won't stay if you keep talking. Hold still. I'm almost done."

A few long minutes later, the soft silvery-blue glow dissipates from Kimala's hands and she leans back, exhausted. She rubs her face and smiles tiredly at Mara and Shaniel. "He's good now, just needs to rest." She turns to Darion. "No more mind wars."

"Yes, ma'am," he concedes, still lying on the ground.

"Shaniel, could you help me to my room?" Kimala requests, wobbling to her feet. "I... I need to lie down for a bit." Shaniel quickly steps over and grabs her arm. They walk towards the palace.

Darion glances at their hands. "I cannot feel my fingers."

Mara loosens her grip and glances down. "I'm so sorry!"

Darion flexes his fingers and examines them. "I have never seen them this color before." He glances at Mara and his eyes widen at her tear-filled gaze. "I was joking, Mara. I am fine."

"No, it's not," she argues, shaking her head. "I nearly killed you."

"I am hard to kill." Darion sits up and pats the top of her head. "See? All is well."

"No more mind wars," she sniffles.

He smiles softly at her. "No more mind wars."

They enter the palace, leisurely working their way to the great hall where the townsfolk had the opportunity to dine with the adul'ne. They don't speak of what had happened, and Mara is grateful; she doesn't quite know what to say to the handsome elf she had almost killed by accident.

She admires the paintings. Strange flowers and sceneries capture her attention, and she wonders if she should study about this world's geography and plant life.

Darion walks alongside Mara, glancing at her from the corner of his eyes. "Are you feeling better?"

Mara remembers the feeling of his hand patting

her head and struggles not to blush. "Yeah. I'm sorry for worrying you."

He quickly shakes his head. "It is not your fault, Mara. I miscalculated how strong you are; I should have asked your instructor before beginning such a task."

Shaniel lopes down the hallway, grinning at the two of them as if he knows some secret they don't know about. "Hey. Everything all good? So what really happened?"

"You are her regular instructor, correct?" Darion asks, and the laig'hius nods. Darion sighs. "You could have warned me about her Source."

Shaniel raises an eyebrow. "You seriously couldn't tell?"

"I knew she has a large amount, but you could have told me she does not know how to moderate it well." Darion gives Shaniel a reprimanding look.

Mara avoids looking at them. "I've been getting better..." she mumbles.

They are almost to the great hall when Darion pauses and pulls out a flat crystal device that glows softly. Mara watches him as he 'listens' to it, remembering when Folion had pulled out a similar device during their lesson and had to run off to an emergency in a lower section of the tactical wing. *Seems like it isn't just Highlords that get the cool stuff,* she thinks as he sighs and returns the cellphone-like contraption to his pocket.

"Gotta go?" Shaniel asks as if he already knows the answer, tucking his hands into his pocket.

Darion nods, raking his hand through his hair in irritation. "How hard is it to console someone? I take a few days off, and everything goes to Eleth..."

Mara purses her lips together, fighting her giggle. "I-I'm sorry. That's just funny." *Much better than the Earth version,* she thinks as Darion clasps Shaniel's hand in parting.

"I'm going on ahead," Shaniel tells Mara. Before she can say anything, he is gone.

Mara slowly turns to Darion, finally daring to look into his sun-dappled green eyes. "So... will you be back?"

Darion shakes his head. "I might as well return. I have stressed my assistant enough as is." He reaches forward and tucks a strand of hair behind her ear absently.

Mara's breathing stops.

He blinks, realizing what he had done. "Ah, I apologize. I was not thinking."

Mara blushes, not looking at him. "I'll see you around, then," she mumbles, backing up and heading in the direction Shaniel had taken.

Darion stares after her for a moment before walking in the opposite direction. Mara glances back once, and an image of a man flashes through her mind. He was walking away, just as Darion is now, but the man had held a giant two-handed blade nearly as big as himself and wore an odd gold-edged black robe.

Mara pauses and rubs her temple. What is wrong with her? She glances at Darion again and frowns. Suddenly, she feels a sense of déjà vu. Her eyes widen. *Impossible. He can't be the same guy.*

Darion turns down the next hallway, out of sight of Mara. He glances at the hand that had tucked her hair behind her ear. A small silver spark flits across his skin, making it tingle. A fine, silvery dust coats his fingers.

< * >

The door to Wester's Armory swings shut as Mara stares at Gamerog floating in front of her. Her head tilts to the side as she examines the blade intensely. Did it... look *darker* than the last time she had seen it?

"Mara? Is that you?" William calls from the back.

Mara pushes her robe away from her legs and sidles around the salev'i, frowning slightly. She wonders why the old blacksmith isn't at his forge; it is already late afternoon. Despite Folion keeping her in his office longer than usual, she knows William would normally still be hammering away at some new weapon.

"Hi, William," she calls out as she rounds the corner only to stare at Gamerog's exquisite sheath in his hands. "Why do you have Gamerog's scabbard?"

William fidgets, nervous and excited at the same time. "Well, ye'see, I spoke with the Highlords about it and..."

Mara's brow creases in concern as Gamerog butts against her elbow. She absentmindedly lifts her hand and rests it on Gamerog's pommel. "They're not going to put more constraints on it, are they?"

William shakes his head and holds the sheath out to her. "They want you to have it for now. Y'just gotta give Timian weekly reports on when you use it an' where."

Mara's fingers tremble as she takes the sheath from him. The salev'i slides itself into its home, humming from inside its scabbard before suddenly disappearing. Mara, used to its random vanishing acts inside the store, thinks nothing of it. "But... why me?"

William gives her an odd look of awe and respect. "I'm sorry, Mara. I'm not allowed to say."

Mara looks at him – *really* looks – when he says this. He does not seem afraid, just...

"I'm not special," she mumbles, disconcerted by the look in the old man's eyes. "Gamerog just likes me because I have a lot of Source." She pats the scabbard affectionately despite her blunt words.

William chuckles. "So you like to say. Visit whenever you like; you know I enjoy your company."

"D-don't I need to hide it?" Mara asks, remembering how William had covered the kareia weapon when he visited her in her hospital room.

William shakes his head. "Jus' stick your hand out an' think of Gamerog. Some of its seals have been released, so it can move around freely now – as long as you hold the scabbard, that is. So don' lose that scabbard."

Mara bows her head in respect to William. "Th-thank you, William." She grins, marveling at the sword's sheath in her hands. "I will take good care of it."

William bows to her deeply, startling her. "It is an honor," he breathes, his eyes tearing up. "Go; I know that sword is just as eager as you to get out of here."

CHAPTER 16
TRAINING AND FESTIVITIES

Mara nearly sprints back to Cerlail Academy in her excitement, Gamerog's sheath tucked into her belt. She doesn't mull over William's strange behavior; she is eager to reach the roof training stadium that is set up like a park. She rushes into one of the lifts and holds her hand almost a foot away from the orb; it slowly ascends despite the distance. The closer her palm moves towards it, the faster the platform ascends. She is grateful Uncle Timian and Shaniel had taken the time to teach her how to operate it.

The platform slowly decelerates as she nears the top. Stepping out of it, she rushes through the park on the roof. Clusters of trees offer shade and privacy to visitors of the natural abode, and benches line the pathway. Wildflowers grow in random patches.

Mara crosses the expansive park, pausing briefly to gaze at the twenty-foot pond in the middle of the stadium. In the middle, a crystal fountain spouts water in pretty designs.

The south corner of the roof is usually abandoned because of the lack of elevators. After the little incident last week where she had blasted through an entire tree, Headmaster Folion deemed that corner to be the official training spot for Mara and alerted the whole Academy that the area is off limits unless escorted by a Highlord or professor.

Mara glances at one of the scorched trees as she passes into the tree line of the secluded area. She hesitantly reaches out as if to touch something, thinking of Gamerog just as William had told her to do.

The coppery salev'i materializes in front of her.

She examines the floating sword in the sunshine for the first time. The blade has a darker sheen than usual, and the bloodstained part is significantly more diminished than before. The Xharos symbols appear and disappear slowly as if telling a story.

She pokes the sword, and the hilt swings around as if to meet her hand. She pats it with a smile, running her fingers along the tiny scales of the grip.

"That is an interesting salev'i you have there," someone comments. Mara jumps and turns to see a handsome young man of about nineteen years old with pointed elven ears and platinum blonde, almost white hair. His ice blue eyes stand out against his pale skin. He leans against a tree, smirking at her.

Lyrik...? Mara wonders, momentarily shocked. This man looks exactly like the elf who had helped Hope, a young dragon-girl in the woods. *That had just been a dream – right?*

Mara realizes belatedly that he is talking about Gamerog. Her face pales, worried of his reaction to the supposed 'cursed blade.' "I-it's not what it looks like." Gamerog's pommel bumps into her left hand. *You're not helping,* she thinks towards it.

"It looks as though it wants to be held," the man suggests, smiling playfully at her. Mara is taken aback by his flirtation.

"Who are you? Are you a student?" Mara demands, widening her stance defensively. The sword hovers beside her, reacting to her agitation.

The silver-haired man chuckles. "I despise those

robes too much. No, I am not a student." He eyes the red designs on her grey magelet robe. "You are, though."

Mara narrows her eyes. "What do you want?"

The man squats, balancing on the balls of his feet while watching her. "I sensed your power nearly a week ago, so I wanted to meet you."

Taken aback by the comment, Mara's defensive stance loosens. "You... sensed it?" she repeats, suddenly concerned. *Nearly a week ago... the event with that ghost-thing, the Dark Warrior?*

The man shrugs as he leans against the tree. "I could teach you how to contain it more efficiently, but this isn't the best place for that kind of horseplay."

Mara's eyebrow shoots up in defiance. "Oh? Try me."

The elf's lips stretch into a wide grin, reminding her of a white Cheshire cat. "I will, then."

He vanishes.

Mara reflexively grabs the floating salev'i on her left and whirls around, her Source sparking defensively as the metal clangs against the man's long dagger. He bears down, several inches taller than her. He grins.

"Great job deflecting it!" he congratulates, breaking away from her and clapping.

Mara stares at him, stunned. She drops Gamerog and it vanishes. "Why did you attack me?"

"You asked me to teach you."

A faint blue glimmer is all the warning she is given. She throws up her hands defensively, suddenly wishing she had learned some defensive Source abilities. A giant blue ball slams against her, pushing her backwards before shattering harmlessly into tiny fragments.

He laughs merrily. "Do you like my light show?"

"Why are you attacking me?" Mara demands, silver bolts dancing over her body in reaction to her panicked emotions.

This person is nothing like the Lyrik I know. She pauses, startled by that thought. Lyrik was a figment of her imagination from some crazy dream she had had a while back. However, this man looks exactly like him. "Who are you?" she whispers.

He winks at her, pressing a finger against his lips. "And why should I tell you something like that, dan'te?"

"Dante?" she repeats, confused. "How am I like a Crusades man who goes to Hell and back for a woman he cheated on?"

He raises an eyebrow. "Wait, you really don't know?" At her blank look, he rubs his forehead. "In Xharos, danti means silver and ute blood. Dan'te is slang for 'silver-blood.'"

"Okay..." She examines him, frowning. "But... who are you?"

He examines his nails in a bored fashion. "How about a little bet? If you win, you can ask me anything you want and I have to answer truthfully. If I win, I can ask you anything and you have to answer truthfully." He looks her directly in the eyes, his expression serious. "Deal?"

"What will we be doing?" she asks warily.

"Dueling, of course." He holds up his hands, brandishing his fists in an unfamiliar style. "Just hand-to-hand. Does this sound good?"

Mara grins wickedly. "Sure, why not?"

Within three minutes, she regrets those three small words. He is faster and more varied in his attacks than Shaniel; his kicks and punches come in at a speed she nearly can't keep up with, and he doesn't even seem to be using Source to amplify his muscle coordination.

Huffing, she glares at the white-haired man pinning her down by her neck. She doesn't even know how she had ended up on the ground. "What's your question?" she spits out through gritted teeth.

The man releases her, allowing her to sit up. "You are a good fighter." He rubs his jaw thoughtfully. "Hmm. What's your favorite color?"

Stunned, she responds simply, "Black."

He tilts his head to the side. "How... interesting."

"Can you teach me how you did that?" Mara blurts, still unnerved that he had beaten her so easily. "I've never seen anyone move so fast before."

He blinks at her question and then laughs. "Sure, why not?" He grins at her. "What's your name?"

"Mara," she tells him, leaving off her last name. "And... you?"

"Thanos."

"Nice to meet you, Thanos," she greets, relieved when her voice doesn't tremble. *So... it's not him.*

"Good to know." He smirks, standing up and dusting off his light-colored clothes. "We will certainly meet again, Mara."

"Wait! What about training – " He vanishes. " – me?"

She huffs, glancing around the little grove of trees. "I guess... I'll just come back here."

After her lessons with Headmaster Folion the next day, she returns to the same spot to find Thanos napping in the branches of one of the trees. From then on, he trains her – not only in self-defense, but also in Source, showing her more ways to control and utilize it. He helps her comprehend her lessons with Shaniel and Folion better, and teaches her new tricks on top of it all.

As the days turn into weeks, she keeps her lessons with Thanos a secret. She knows exactly what everyone would say: she's pushing herself, she needs to take time to rest, she shouldn't be training hard, she would only burn herself out... However, it is like an addiction. Even on the weekends, she gets excited anytime she shows up in the grove with Thanos. He teaches her different fighting styles; he instructs her on how to pump Source into her legs to move faster without face planting; he guides her through the various methods of focusing one's mind to hold multiple spells at once.

Gerard and Shaniel see the improvement of Mara almost instantly, but do not say much. She blows through the magelet ranks, hitting intern in just over two months since first learning about Source in Veera. Her two instructors believe it is because of her inherent adaptability like her father, but Mara thinks it is all of her hard work with Thanos. She studies under a master optical illusionist and a master battlefield strategist for her intern robe, wishing to follow after her father in the two fields.

Almost seven weeks after she had started training with Thanos and only two weeks before Sonatheia, the autumn festival, Mara is preparing to head to the rooftop to train with Thanos that weekend when Kimala suddenly barges into her room, grabs her arm, and drags her into Quasala. Not wanting to give away her secret training and make the girl mad at her, Mara keeps her mouth shut about having plans – but soon regrets it as her cousin drags her around to every dress shop.

"I have a dress!" she complains to Thanos later that day, lying on the ground and staring at the fiery colors burning the sky as the sun sleepily dips below the horizon. "But no, that won't do. I need something new. Why does she care, anyway?"

Thanos chuckles as he whittles away at his wood project from against a tree. She always catches him doing something in his spare time; he has already given her several of his miniature figurines. So far, her favorite is the dragon. "For festivals, you do not wear the same outfit you wore earlier that year. Also, that was for your birthday, correct?"

Mara props up onto her elbow, glaring at him. "Quit siding with her."

He lowers his hands, smiling slightly. "I am merely telling you the truth."

Mara sits up and does a few stretches. "So what's today's lesson?"

"Festival etiquette," he says with a straight face as he puts his carving supplies in his small bag. "Seeing as you do not know much about it, it seems."

Mara groans, falling onto her back again. "Not you, too... I get enough of this from Kimala!"

He smirks at her. "Then how much will it impress or shock her if you already know it?"

Mara shoots upright, staring at Thanos with wide eyes. "You're right!"

Thanos laughs, tossing a stick at her. "Manipulate that to look like a cup while we talk."

He explains the different seasons and the festivals

that go with them; the Sonatheia is one of the four major festivals, even though it is not a huge event like the Toratheia or Aloratheia, the summer and winter festivals. After explaining to Mara the different types of festivals and the expectations for each, he surprises her one day with a new type of lesson: dancing.

"I don't see how this is relevant," she mutters, blushing as he leads her through the glade.

He pauses his humming, glancing down at her in surprise. "When it comes to festivals, dancing is an essential part. Some say it shows your respect to the festival and what it stands for." He pulls her back into motion. "The seven-step is the most common dance during the autumn festival; the movements themselves show how two people can move in harmony throughout all the tribulations of their lives."

Mara accidentally steps on his toes again.

"I-I'm sorry," she quickly says, clenching her jaw tightly. "I'm just not good at this…"

"I don't believe that." He pulls her closer, grinning mischievously. "You just need some more practice, then you will be dancing like a pro."

Mara glares at him. "Are we supposed to be this close?" she demands, trying to ignore his body heat; he is only a couple of inches from her.

"Closer, in fact, but I figured you would try to kill me if I tried to teach it to you properly the first time around." He winks at her.

Mara yanks her hand out of his and slaps her palm against his chest, pushing him away. He laughs, wrapping his fingers around hers. "Come now, Mara. It can't be that bad."

Mara cannot stop the heat creeping up her neck.

Thanos's hand is so warm in her own; her fingers constrict around his without her noticing. His eyes widen slightly. "I... I'm not used to being so close to other people," she admits, not looking at him.

He touches her chin lightly, and she looks up, startled. He moves in close, smirking. "My dear Mara, you need to get over that fear. In this world, physical touch is commonplace amongst friends."

Mara swallows hard and tries to move away, but Thanos does not let her. "Let go," she growls into his face, twisting her wrist in his hand.

His smile softens. "Not until you learn this dance move."

She stares at him, flabbergasted. "But – that could take all night!"

"Then I do hope you are prepared to spend the night up here. Shall we start from the beginning?"

Mara settles between Shaniel and Codi, ignoring the idle chatter in the great hall about the Sonatheia starting tomorrow. Adul'ne Edgard and Cleo make a rare appearance today and are chatting with two women in Highlord-styled robes – one water-themed, the other fire-themed – at the head of the noble's table.

Wanting to hurry up so she can train with Thanos, Mara chews the fruit, cuts her egg in half, and pours honey on her toast at the same time. She has grown addicted to his lessons; for some reason, she grasps his concepts better than others. Plus, he had said he would teach her a more complicated dance move tonight if she did well with the close combat. Because of his lessons, she has become more comfortable with dancing, though she is nervous about dancing with anyone other than him now.

"Are you a little hungry?" Codi asks, chuckling. She makes a face at him.

She raises the toast to take a bite just in time to see a light blonde haired man about eighteen or so walking up the middle aisle from the entry door, two strange guards in black and red armor flanking him. His slightly pointed ears look odd against the facial features that are obviously more Blazhreian than Alkinian; wide jaw, strong cheekbones, and stockier frame than the typical elf.

He has the air of someone who believes he is more important than everyone else in the room. As the young man saunters up the aisle, the usual chatter in the room full of permitted guests dies down.

"Who's that?" Mara asks Alec, keeping her voice low.

Alec frowns. "That's Evan Shasta, the eldest of Paro'ki Naiya's children."

Evan stops at the foot of the stairs. One of his guards steps forward and calls out in a ringing voice, "Duir'ne Evan Shasta from Alamirana." The guard returns to his original position.

The Highlords at the table with Adul'ne Edgard and Cleo stand up, shielding the royal couple. Edgard glares at Evan as if he wishes to run the prince through.

Mara watches the tense situation, wondering if the tyrant's son is really that dangerous.

"To what do we owe the pleasure, Duir'ne Shasta?" Edgard asks formally, his voice changing to bitterness over the title. His bow is stiff yet deep.

Mara's eyes widen. She knows Paro'ki Naiya had

taken over the Saheian continent, but she did not know that even Edgard would have to bow to the tyrant's son.

Evan smiles slightly. "I came to enjoy the festival." He waves his hand at his guards. "I brought gifts."

The guards upturn an empty-looking satchel. Jewelry, elaborate weapons, and fine clothes rain onto the floor and create a large pile.

Evan picks up an ornate glove and puts it on. "Nothing is poisoned; I am here in good will. You can even have your mages go over it."

Adul'ne Edgard's lips twitch.

Evan's head tilts forward in a small bow. "I am here on Adul'ne Naiya's orders; I do not recommend testing her patience, Your Majesty."

Mara glances at Alec, confused. He gives her a grim look. "The last time we went against her orders, she destroyed parts of the castle, reducing it to the palace it is now," he explains quietly, watching Evan.

"That's horrible," Mara whispers.

"Don't let him hear that," Alec warns. "Evan is like her eyes, ears, and mouth. Desdemona is her blade. If Evan is here, we have a chance. Pray that Desdemona does not show up."

Mara glances sideways at Alec, wondering who Desdemona is.

"I shall have the best room prepared immediately, Duir'ne Evan," Edgard stiffly announces, waving to the servants along the walls. Slipping on gloves, they place the valuable items in a bag. "In the meantime, feel free to dine with us and visit Cerlail Academy."

"Thank you." Evan bows slightly to the king and waves at his guards. They station themselves by the Quasalan guards, the black and red armor of the neighboring city starkly contrasting the brilliant green and gold Quasalan colors.

Evan approaches Alec, bowing slightly. "It is a pleasure seeing you again, Your Grace."

Alec stands up and glances at the others, willing them to remain seated with his eyes. "What are you doing here, Duir'ne Evan?"

Evan smiles. "I have always appreciated your curtness." He sighs. "Alas, my story is quite boring. I am here to participate in the festival and…" he pauses, glancing at Kimala. "Enjoy the company of your guests."

Alec steps between the prince and medic, shielding Kimala.

Mara slowly stands up, her robe shifting around her as sparks flit across the colorfully accented black cloth. "Tein'stra Kimala is Alec's guest to the festival." *So back off,* she finishes in her head.

Evan's eyes widen and he glances between Alec and Kimala. "Settling down already? So young." He clucks his tongue and smiles at Mara. "And who might you be?"

Mara feels a warning tug on her sleeve by Codi. She ignores it. "Mara Danarko."

"Oh, my." Evan covers his mouth with his hand. "Shokain's daughter? Amazing! Where is he? I have always wanted to meet him."

"He's dead." Mara's voice is flat and emotionless.

Evan's face falls. "You have my condolences. He truly was a great man. Just between you and me," he lowers his voice, "he did a number on my parents. Great diplomat."

Mara stares at him, unable to tell if he is making fun of her or not.

He grins at Shaniel. "Highlord Shaniel! It is a pleasure seeing you again. How are you?" He sits down in the empty chair next to the Common'Lord.

"I am quite well, Your Grace," Shaniel says slowly as Mara eases back into her seat.

"So, Voi'stra Mara," Evan begins as the servants set a plate laden with food in front of him. "Are you attending the festival with anyone in particular?"

Mara sees the others flinch under the shortened title. *I guess 'voi' always needs to be accompanied with the title, not the descendancy,* she deduces, *else it is too informal.* "I am accompanying Highlord Shaniel," she admits, glancing at Shaniel, who looks a little surprised.

Evan's eyes widen slightly. He glances between them. "Y-you're – "

"Huh?" Shaniel's lips twist up in disgust as he watches the visiting duir'ne's cheeks turn red. "Oh, Highlords, no. We're *not* together. She's like the annoying sister I never wanted."

Mara rolls her eyes. "Gee, thanks."

Shaniel smirks and rubs the top of Mara's head, making a few strands of hair come loose from her ponytail. "I'm just teasing, Danarko."

Evan chuckles, a strange tension draining out of him. "Would you mind if I accompany her to the festival, then? I will take extra good care of her."

Shaniel eyes Evan warily. "How do I know you will keep your word?"

Evan clasps his left hand over his heart, his expression serious. "You do not. The only thing I can give *is* my word, though." His eyes flick to Mara, and he gives her a rueful smile. "Would you accompany me?"

Mara's mind works on overdrive. The festival is

the last place she wants to be, but she already has to attend. Her friends will be with her all day – even during the ball – so she shouldn't have to worry about anything. Plus, if she refuses the tyrant's son's request, it could incite horrible repercussions on Alec and his family; she doesn't want to cause that kind of trouble to her mother's friends. *He holds a lot of power for just being the son of Queen Naiya,* Mara realizes, *and he knows it.*

Mara's smile is sickeningly sweet. "It would be my pleasure to accompany you, Your Grace."

As Mara finishes eating, Evan questions her about her internship. He then asks her for a tour of the Academy; she is relieved he asks Shaniel to accompany them, but at the same time, she is annoyed he has taken such a liking to her. After all, she should be training with Thanos in the grove right now.

He asks to see the tactical wing first. They walk around the different training stadiums; he comments on their design and beauty, complimenting the structure whenever he can. On the roof stadium, she catches sight of Thanos in one of the trees, watching them sleepily. She waves apologetically, and he smirks back. Neither the Highlord nor the visiting prince notices the white-haired young man.

They go through the sorceral wing next. Evan is fascinated by the planetarium but does not go in; however, he wanders the bookshelves in the library for nearly half an hour before they move on.

In the medical wing, he asks more questions and seems more involved in the conversations. Mara watches him closely, suspecting he is most interested in the medical field – although it doesn't quite make sense why he would want to be a medic, considering his status as a tyrant's son.

Finally, Mara finds an appropriate time to escape to the rooftop stadium, but Kimala catches her as she is leaving the medical wing. "You," her cousin hisses, "are coming with me."

They head back to the palace where Kimala drops Mara off in her room. She collapses face-first onto her bed, exhausted. *Maybe... maybe Thanos will be okay if I don't show up this time,* she thinks as she begins to doze. *He did see me walking around with the visiting duir'ne, after all...*

A few moments later, Kimala enters with a bag draped over her arm. Mara stares at the bag in horror. "What did I get myself into?" she cries, staying on her bed.

"You're playing politics. Get up; you need to try on the dress to make sure it fits."

Mara glares at her. "I can't go."

"You can," Kimala says, pulling open the bag. "And you will."

Kimala holds up a long piece of black cloth with lacy black patterns. Solid strips run up it vertically, keeping it straight. A silver ribbon holds together the middle and hooks are on either end.

Mara fervently shakes her head. "No. No! No way in all of the realms am I wearing one of *those*!"

Exhausted from the physical ordeals she had just been through, Mara staggers into the grove just as the sun dips below the horizon. "Thanos..."

Thanos drops out of the tree, his eyes wide. He leaps forward in time to support her, pulling out a dagger and analyzing the pathway she had just come from. "What happened? Is someone after you?"

Mara shakes her head, gasping for air. "I… I barely managed to get away from Evan… he was still at the Academy, and…"

She pauses, still trying to catch her breath. She slumps against Thanos, who frowns in confusion. "Paro'stra Evan? The one from earlier?"

Mara nods, easing to the ground. He kneels next to her, his hand on her upper arm.

"Why is he following you?" he asks defensively, glancing down the path again.

"He's here for the Sonatheia and wanted a tour of the Academy." Mara leans back, exhausted. "Then Kimala had me try on the dress for tomorrow and stuck me in a – a – "

Her cheeks turn a bright pink.

Thanos smirks, finally relaxing. "A corset?" he finishes casually.

"H-how did you know?" Mara doesn't look at him.

He shrugs. "Women often wear them to the festivals." He leans against the nearest tree. "So… Duir'ne Evan is following you around like a puppy?"

Mara groans. "He wants me to accompany him to the Sonatheia…"

Thanos shoots forward, grasping her shoulders tightly. "Please tell me you didn't accept."

Mara glances at him, confused. "I did. I knew if I rejected, it would only cause problems between the Roanoak family and the Alamiran adul'ne. I didn't want anything bad to happen to them."

Thanos's hands loosen their grip as he stares at her in wonder. "You thought that far ahead?" She nods. He sits back down and laughs slightly. "You amaze me, Mara."

Mara smirks, but then remembers what Evan had called her at the breakfast table earlier. *I didn't get a chance to ask anyone... maybe he will know.* "Hey, Thanos."

"Hmm?" He pulls out a wooden carving and starts whittling away at the small figurine.

"What does voi'stra mean?"

His gaze shoots up and meets hers. "Voi'stra by itself with no rank accompanying it is like calling someone the child of an invalid or orphan. It's like a polite, socially acceptable way of saying the person is the child of someone who is a nobody."

"So it's like son of a witch." She yawns, shaking out her tense muscles.

He chuckles, amused. "Yeah, something like that. You truly do not like cursing, do you?"

"Nope." She collapses on her back next to him. "I want to play a game of Siege with you sometime."

"Siege? What's that?"

Mara props her head on his leg, staring at his plain brown boots. "A strategy game."

Thanos chuckles. "Sounds like fun. Do you want to go get it?" She doesn't respond. "Mara?"

He leans forward to see her eyes closed and her breathing steady. He strokes her hair.

"I wish... you were coming..." Mara murmurs, half-asleep. She wraps her fingers around his and pulls his hand forward so she can hold it.

Thanos's eyes widen slightly. He gives her a soft smile, squeezing her fingers. "I think I can drop by for a bit," he murmurs.

< * >

Mara gloomily follows the lavishly dressed prince through the crowd. His flashy blue suit with orange and red needlework stand out against the autumn-based and plain colors of everyone else. Even his guards in the paro'ki's red and black colors blend in better with the crowd than the visiting duir'ne.

Mara, on the other hand, isn't much better. Her gold-embroidered jade green shirt and gold-embellished black pants had been a gift from the Roanoak family for today. On the right side of her belt, Gamerog's empty sheath rests on her hip. Adul'ne Edgard had wanted her to wear it while walking with the duir'ne just in case anything happens.

Shaniel and Codi, both dressed in red and brown colors, accompany Mara as they follow the excited duir'ne from one stall to the next. *It's as if he's never been to a festival,* she thinks to herself. Granted, she hasn't been to one either, but she had been to a handful of fairs on Earth. The Sonatheia festival seems quite similar: food vendors, souvenir and trinket stalls, game niches, and resting areas, to name a few.

Evan pauses by a jewelry stand and fingers a gold necklace with a red stone. He picks up the one with a green stone and shows it to her. "This would look lovely with – "

He freezes, his smile twitching when he sees Mara's thunderous look. Her hands are shoved deep into her pockets, and silver lightning bolts crackle around her wrists. Shaniel and Codi both seem unfazed but still keep a safe distance from the mild light show.

Evan quickly puts down the necklace and

continues down the street.

Shaniel walks alongside Mara. "Get rid of that frown," he whispers. "You're scaring him."

"I wanted to train, not walk around here. I have no intention on spending my money on any of this." She casts her glare to the ground. *I didn't even realize I was frowning.* She takes a deep breath.

Evan, having eavesdropped on the conversation, gives Mara a wavering smile. "Train for what?"

"Hand-to-hand combat." She catches a glimpse of white hair in the crowd and wonders if Thanos is here. Maybe she could slip away...

"Ah, would you like to duel sometime, then?"

Evan's question startles her. She eyes the duir'ne up and down, a lazy grin spreading across her face. "Sure. Let's go."

"N-Now?" Evan says, startled.

Shaniel and Codi sigh. "Now you've done it..." Codi mumbles.

"Prepare yourself, Your Grace," Shaniel advises the duir'ne.

He glances between the two men giving him pitiful looks and swallows hard.

They head to a secluded spot away from the majority of the crowd. Mara stretches as Evan talks to his guards briefly before rolling up his sleeves. She murmurs to Shaniel, "Bet you a danlar he won't last two minutes."

He stares at her, surprised. "You do remember the conversion, correct? That's about a hundred dollars."

Mara gives the Common'Lord a nasty grin. "Oh, yeah. I remember."

He raises an eyebrow, intrigued. "All right, then. I bet two danlar he'll last over two minutes."

"Two danlar it is." She clasps his hand, handing over Gamerog's sheath. "Take care of it for me?"

"Of course." He dips his head slightly, taking the scabbard from her.

Evan watches them, too far away to hear their conversation. Mara turns to him, bumping her fist into the palm of her hand. Evan is taken aback by the look in her eyes; she is fired up over something.

"Shall we begin? I'll give you the first move," she offers, a sly smile spreading across her lips. Even Codi and Shaniel are surprised at this.

Just as Mara had suspected, the visiting duir'ne knows nothing of true combative skills. She gives him a few seconds just to make sure, but in under a minute, she has him on his back. His guards step forward, ready to intervene if she tried doing anything further to harm their prince.

She holds out her hand. "Never been trained?"

Evan shakes his head, his cheeks slightly pink as he clasps her hand and pulls himself up. "No... I've only ever watched the guards and tried to imitate them."

Mara eyes him. "You need to watch your left side better. You're full of openings, but that side is worse than the others."

Startled, Evan stares at her. "Thank you. I... don't know much about all of this."

"I could tell," Mara snorts, turning back to Shaniel and snatching her sword sheath from him. She jams it into her belt loop. "You owe me two danlar, cat."

Shaniel rubs the back of his head as he digs in his purse with the other hand. "Ahh, I never should have bet with you."

Evan's eyes widen at the exchange of the silver coins.

After that, they wandered around the festival for about half an hour more before they parted ways to prepare for the masked ball later that evening. Mara escapes to her room, grateful for the reprieve; Kimala enters shortly after, her cheeks flushed a slight pink color as she shoves the dress into Mara's hands and orders her to change into it. Mara guesses she had been with Alec up until this point.

Mara steps out in the black dress. A silver lacey layer patterned like shattered glass begins right above her hips and flares out like a skirt. Kimala wraps a black lacy underbust around Mara's waist and fastens the hooks underneath Mara's breasts.

Mara glares in the mirror at her reflection as Kimala tightens the ribbons in the back. "Get this stupid thing off of me. I look ridiculous."

"Hold onto the dresser," Kimala orders.

"What?" Mara shrieks.

"Just do it!" Kimala growls through gritted teeth while tugging on the strings. Mara grabs the edge of the dresser, shocked.

"Wait, this is really how you put these things on?!" Mara asks, appalled. "How am I supposed to breathe in it?"

"Take a deep breath and hold it in." Mara turns her head towards Kimala, and the blue-eyed girl gives her a stern look. "Seriously, Mara."

Mara sucks in the biggest breath has ever taken. Kimala pulls on the strings, working all the way down Mara's spine. She quickly ties it off. "Okay."

Mara, feeling like she is being squeezed to death, releases the breath and sucks in more air. She relaxes, trying to breathe regularly despite the tightness. "Huh, not as bad as I – ugh." Mara sits down, holding her head.

Kimala sighs heavily. "Do we need to loosen it?"

"No, no, I'll be fine. Just... give me a moment. You *did* just try to squeeze me into three sizes smaller." Mara runs her hand through her hair.

"Stop messing with it." Kimala slaps Mara's hand away. "I'll get to it in a minute. Look in the mirror."

Mara glares at Kimala and stands up. She feels oddly straight and... regal. She glances down and all she sees is the black cloth covering her breasts. "Is this how it's supposed to look?"

"Just look in the mirror already!" Kimala snaps, rubbing her forehead.

Mara sways towards the mirror, unsure about the underbust and the dress. She freezes when she sees her reflection, though, and wonders if Kimala had cast an illusion spell on her.

The underbust blends in with the black cloth of her dress, making it look as though she has on an elegant black top with a silver-patterned skirt. The bottom edge of the corset is black, forming a border between it and the skirt's silver sparks. The black transparent sleeves drape over her arms, narrow near her shoulders, and widen the farther down her arm it is until it sweeps around her wrists in a fold of cloth. She looks like a sun-kissed elf – minus the ears, that is.

Mara gasps, covering her mouth. The willowy elf-girl in the mirror does the same. Disconcerted, she begins, "I..."

Kimala smiles hopefully.

"I really need to cut my hair..." is all Mara can get out, staring at her hair that falls in long layers past her shoulders.

Kimala slaps her forehead. "Really? That's what you have to say?"

"Did you cast an illusion spell?" Mara asks her, still disconcerted and unable to believe the girl in the mirror is her. "That doesn't look like me at all. She's too beautiful, like an elf or something."

Kimala stares at Mara. "Did you just say what I heard?"

"What? Beautiful?" Mara repeats, staring at herself in the mirror. "Well, whoever that is, she's definitely not me. Put me in something that reflects me, not... whoever that is."

"We can't do that." Kimala directs Mara back to her seat and pushes her down. "Now time for hair and makeup."

"Oh, no." Mara stands up.

"Oh-ho-ho, yes," Kimala argues, forcing her back down. "You're under my care now."

"Don't you need to get ready?"

"Don't turn this around on me, Mara. I already have everything planned out for mine. It won't take me but an hour to get ready."

"An hour?! Then what about me?"

"I'm estimating... two. Maybe more if your hair is uncooperative."

"That's too long..."

CHAPTER 17
KALEIDOSCOPE OF COLOR

"Please welcome Tein'stra Kimala Brunet and Duir'ne Alec Roanoak!" the announcer calls out, and everyone claps as Kimala and Alec link arms and walk down the stairs from the entrance into the large ballroom full of hundreds of guests.

Kimala is absolutely stunning in her sky blue dress accented with swirling silvery designs in her skirt and underbust – the separated colors of her silvery blue Source – with silver eye shadow accents to draw attention to her blue eyes and the silver-and-blue stones scattered in her honey-colored hair. Her new silver-wired mask only enhances her features and doesn't take away from her dress at all. She glows with joy and beauty.

"Thank you for attending this year's ball," Alec says to the guests, a charming smile on his face as Kimala beams happily. "As most of you know, I am also celebrating my eighteenth birthday on this wondrous day. Please, relax and enjoy the festivities."

The crowd politely claps as the couple meander their way across the ballroom.

"Stunning," Duir'ne Evan Shasta in a red and black suit with a red mask comments, glancing at Mara. "But not as much as you, my lady."

Mara's lips tilt in a small elegant smile as she claps for her cousin and the prince. Standing there in the four-inch heels that bring her to a whopping five feet and nine inches, she feels as if she is the attraction of

316

the night in the overly-tight underbust and the daringly slim silver and black dress that accents all of her features. Her tanned skin glows softly from nervousness against the contrasting black material; her illusion band is not designed to mask her Source-filled veins, after all.

Mara's chestnut locks accent her angled jawline and soft yet narrow cheekbones. Half of her hair is swept into a bun and fastened with a beautiful, swirling silver clasp, falling in a beautiful cascade around her long neck. Makeup smooths out her features, bringing out the gentle angles of her face and making her look older than sixteen. She has on the silver-ribboned black wire mask from her birthday; it is the only thing Kimala would allow her to wear from the birthday party.

She truly looks like an elven princess.

Unused to the added weight of the cuff links along the fold of her elongated yet rounded ears, Mara fiddles with the Alkinian charms dangling from the earpieces. She has never pierced her ears before; she is lucky Kimala let her get away with wearing only the cuffs.

Alec and Kimala work their way towards them. The Quasalan prince appraises her from head to toe, his eyes inadvertently lingering on her bust, waist, and hips. "You are quite beautiful in a dress, Lady Mara," he comments from behind his white mask, smiling. Wearing a frilly white shirt with a light blue vest and a darker blue jacket, Alec looks downright steamy – literally. She breaks out into a sweat just looking at him.

"Happy birthday, Your Grace," Mara says, curtsying the best she can.

"You look brilliant tonight, Tein'stra Kimala," Evan murmurs, kissing the back of Kimala's hand. She blushes.

"Kimala, so lovely to see you," Shaniel saunters into their little group, his arms outstretched. He is in a magenta and black velvet suit that nearly glistens like fur in the light of the banquet hall's bright Source globes. His red-tipped black hair is slicked back, making his cat ears more prominent and bringing out the sharp angles of his black mask.

He kisses Kimala's cheek, keeping a healthy distance between their bodies. Mara is impressed at his restraint – until he turns towards her.

"My little Danarko, you could melt my heart." He holds his clenched fist over his chest, looking heartbroken.

Mara rolls her eyes, recognizing his usual playful banter. "Forget it, Shaniel."

He couldn't have looked more heartbroken if his first love had slapped him. The others snigger as Evan gazes on with a small confused smile.

"Excuse me…" Someone with a shock of curly black hair pushes by Mara and approaches Kimala and Alec. "Wow, Kimala. You look amazing. Uh, have you seen Mara anywhere?"

Kimala chuckles and points behind him. He turns around and his eyes widen. "I've seen a vision…"

"Oh, stop it, Codi," Mara snaps but cannot stop the blush from forming at her cheeks. His eyes are locked on her face, searching. She checks him out at the same time, noticing the green vest over a purple tie and the green mask complimenting his mossy eyes. "Who are you, the Riddler?"

Codi frowns. "Who?"

Mara shakes her head. "Never mind. You never saw that movie." She rubs her stomach. "Can I eat in this thing, Kimala?"

"Of course." Kimala waves her hand dismissively. "Just keep it small."

"Got it." Mara hurries off to the banquet tables lining the edges of the huge ballroom, completely ignoring Evan. Alec shakes his head as Kimala rolls her eyes.

Evan stares after her, aghast. "Does she not like me? She has been this way since yesterday…"

Codi shakes his head. "Don't take it to heart. She hates events like this."

Shaniel sniggers. "You should've seen her for her birthday. She hid in the garden the majority of the time."

Mara returns, bearing a small plate with finger foods on it. "Kimala, I *can* sit in this, right? It just doesn't feel like it…"

"Highlords, you're ridiculous," Kimala exclaims, strutting to the banquet table and daintily plucking her choice of delicacies from the spread.

Evan offers his arm, giving her a charming smile. "Shall I accompany you to the table, Voi'duir'stra Danarko?"

Mara blinks, surprised. She glances at Shaniel and Codi as she takes Evan's arm, allowing him to guide her to the nearest vacant table. He pulls out the chair for her and, once she is seated, eases into the chair next to her.

He chuckles as she moodily chews her food. "I hear you dislike these events, as well."

Mara raises an eyebrow. "At least you had a choice."

Evan winces. "My mother ordered me to socialize this year; she said I have been pent up in my room reading too long."

Mara tilts her head, curious. "You don't like socializing?"

"I don't like conflict," he corrects. "There's a difference. It would be much better if my mother was nicer to people, then I could walk along the streets with no fear for my life."

Mara chews her food. "Why don't you just run away?"

"You really think running is an option?" Evan snorts. "My sister can open portals. It is not easy to escape when she can catch you and drag you back to the castle."

"Danarko, would you care to dance?" Shaniel interrupts their conversation, holding out his hand.

Mara smirks at him. "Aren't you afraid of me dropping you again?"

A suspiciously innocent smile spreads across his lips. "I am only offering because I know how much Aeserast had wanted to be here for your first festival."

Mara tilts her head to the side. "Wait, so because Aeserast isn't here, you're willing to dance with me in his stead? You're so brave for him."

Evan watches the banter with amused curiosity. His eyes widen in surprise when Mara takes Shaniel's hand. "You know how to dance?" he asks.

Mara, feeling bold behind her mask, gives him a wink. "Only if I feel like it."

Shaniel sets her straight to the seven-step dance, probably hoping to trip her up since he hadn't taught her this one. However, Thanos has been making her practice, and he is ruthless. She keeps up with Shaniel, enjoying the shock and surprise flitting across her friend's face.

"You've gotten better," Shaniel murmurs as he sends her into a spin. The silver layer of her dress flares out, looking like a lightning storm around her.

"I've been practicing," she admits, smirking at him.

Evan clears his throat, holding his hand out. Behind his simple mask, Mara can see the awe and desire in his eyes. "May I cut in?"

Shaniel glances at her. She shrugs and takes Evan's hand, slightly surprised when Shaniel leans in and whispers something in Evan's ear before returning to the table.

Evan's eyes widen slightly, but he quickly recovers. He guides her through the seven-step dance, a little slower than Shaniel. He smells of mint and cloves, and Mara has to force herself not to breathe too deeply. Soon, Alec and Kimala are dancing nearby, and Mara marvels as they waltz through the moves with the grace and poise of two individuals who had grown up dancing.

Evan glances over Mara's shoulder at Alec and Kimala who hurriedly stare at one another. "It seems as though your friends still do not trust me with your well-being."

"I can take care of myself," Mara dismisses. "Kimala doesn't realize how well I can adapt to the situation."

"Really?" Evan chuckles. "So you're used to the heels and the corset, as well?"

Mara winces. "Those… might take a little bit more time."

They both laugh. "So did your father teach you how to fight like that?" he asks.

Mara's expression sobers. "Somewhat," she admits. "I mostly learned at dojos, though."

"Dojos...?" Evan ponders over the word. "I have never heard of them."

Mara smiles secretively. "I guess it's something Earth has that these realms do not."

Evan raises his eyebrows. "Oh, I see how it is." He sweeps her into another bow. "So what can I do to help you open up to me?"

Mara's eyes widen slightly. "What?"

Evan brings her up and pulls her in close. His lips quirk upward. "You have been quite formal to me this whole time, though I would like to get to know you a bit better." She shifts uncomfortably.

"Pardon me. May I have a turn?"

Mara's breath hitches as she recognizes the voice. Turning, she nearly gapes at Thanos who stands off to the side in an ornate gold mask, his green-and-gold suit a splash of summer against the autumn colors of the ballroom's guests. His ice-blue eyes contrast sharply with his gold-edged green mask.

Mara immediately reaches for him, but Evan frowns and pulls her away. "Who are you?" he demands, his eyes full of... fear?

Mara glances between Evan and Thanos, wondering if they know one another. However, Thanos seems just as surprised as Mara at the visiting duir'ne's reaction.

"Ah, my apologies." He bows slightly. "Do you no longer wish for me to be here, Mara?"

Mara reaches forward again, grasping Thanos's hand tightly. She gives Evan an apologetic smile. "I'm sorry, Your Grace. I honestly didn't expect my friend to show up; I asked him to come," she quickly fibs as

Thanos pulls her towards him. "If you don't mind, I'll dance with him for a bit."

"I won't keep her too long," he assures Evan, winking. Before Evan could say anything, Thanos spins Mara into the seven-step.

"I never expected you would be here," Mara admits as he admires her from head to toe.

He chuckles. "After your comment last night, I couldn't just stand by and watch the paro'stra dance with you all night."

Mara blushes. "I-I didn't say anything, though."

He leans in close, his lips nearly brushing her ear. "'I wish you were coming,'" he repeats, grinning.

Mara hangs her head, avoiding his gaze. "I must have been half asleep," she mumbles.

"You were." He tips her backwards, exposing her red cheeks. "I will say, though. It was a surprise when I heard you announced as Mara Danarko."

Mara rolls her eyes. "As if."

"It did! Just as much as seeing you all dressed up." He holds her at arms' length and examines her again. "Highlords, Kimala must be brutal. That thing looks awfully tight. How can you breathe?"

Mara laughs, clutching his forearms for support. "That's what I asked her!" she gasps, grinning. "You look quite handsome, yourself."

< * >

At the table, Shaniel frowns as Evan approaches without Mara. "Where is she?" he demands, his voice harsher than intended.

Startled, Evan stares at the Highlord with a dazed expression. "A... a masked man came up and asked her to dance. She seemed to know him, so..."

Shaniel frowns, noting the duir'ne's odd reaction. "What did he look like?"

"He…" Evan glances back and points. "There he is."

Kimala, Shaniel, Codi, and Alec glance in the direction of Evan's finger and see Mara laughing with the tall, white-haired young man in the green and gold Quasalan colors.

"I've never seen him before," Codi says first, his brows creased in concern. "However, it does look like she knows him."

"White hair…" Shaniel murmurs, something nagging the back of his mind. He notices Evan's odd expression of recognition and confusion. "Do you know him?"

Slowly, Evan shakes his head. "I don't… think so." He sees everyone staring at him. "Really, I don't. He just… reminds me of someone." His face darkens. It is all Shaniel needs to be wary of the white-haired man; after all, if the tyrant's son is wary of someone, who knows what that means for the rest of them.

Shaniel pivots on his heel, staring through the crowd to where Mara and the stranger stand. The young man notices and gives a lazy wink. "Carc'ra," Shaniel curses, striding into the throng of dancers.

< * >

"It looks like your instructor saw us," Thanos murmurs, pulling Mara deeper into the crowd.

"Why don't you want to meet him?" Mara asks. "I think you two would get along."

He beams at her. "Oh, I'm sure we would. But really, I'm stealing his pupil away! Why would he like me right now?"

Mara blushes. "We're not like that. I'm like a sister to him."

"Hmm." He pulls her out of the crowd of dancers and near the balconies that face the palace courtyard. "Do you mind?"

Mara gazes at the open bay door, wondering what Thanos is up to now. "Not at all. What is it?"

He leads her into the cool autumn air. She takes a deep breath, enjoying the space. "I figured you would like the fresh air," he says, "after being in that stuffy dress all evening."

Mara squeezes his hand, grateful. "Thank you."

Thanos grins, placing his hands on her hips and swaying in the slow-dance version of the seven-step. Mara puts her hands near his neck, glad for the darkness to hide her embarrassed expression.

"I can't stay long," he murmurs, leaning in close.

Mara's fingers tighten on his shoulders. "Did you sneak in?" she demands halfheartedly. "That sounds like you."

"You caught me." His breath is warm against her neck and ear. "I'll be out of town for a while."

"Thanos – "

"Please forgive me." He presses his lips against hers in a soft, tender kiss.

Mara's hands move on their own, wrapping around Thanos's neck and pulling him towards her. Her lips part, and she kisses him back as he slides his arms around her waist.

Her heart hammers in her chest as he holds her, his fingers skimming along her waist. She wants to push him away and cling to him at the same time. When he finally does break off the kiss, they stare at one another dazedly.

"I wasn't expecting that," he admits. He strokes her cheek, smiling slightly. "When I get back, I'll give you a better kiss."

Mara slaps away his hand. "When you get back, I expect you to resume training me," she says, but her voice is slightly out of breath.

He chuckles, kissing her forehead. "Of course, Mara. My little workaholic."

She slaps his chest, pushing back slightly. "I'm not anyone's."

He laughs. "Of course not." He moves closer. "May I have another before I leave?"

"Forget it!" Mara snaps, pressing her palm against his chest to keep him at bay. She stares at her hand. "How long will you be gone?"

"Hopefully, no more than a week or two," he says, lifting her hand and kissing her fingers. "I will let you know when I return."

He leaps over the banister, strolling through the courtyard and whistling to himself. Within seconds, he is gone.

Mara touches her lips slightly. *That idiot,* she thinks to herself, not daring to speak out loud. *He knows I could have punched him and broken his nose. He still did it, though.*

She looks up at the twin moons peeking from behind the clouds. *And I... kissed him back.*

"Mara!" Shaniel gasps, leaning against the balcony doors' frame. He glances around the little area, not seeing anyone else. "Who were you with?"

Mara buries her confused emotions and smirks at Shaniel. "What, do you not believe I have a social life?"

He watches her as she strides by him. "It *is* hard to

believe since you love to train so much," he grumbles, following her back into the ballroom. "So who was that white-haired guy?"

Mara glances at the hand Thanos had kissed and smirks slightly. "A... friend."

< * >

In her black intern robe with green, red, and blue accents, Mara rushes through the palace and into the fields behind it. The leaves on the trees are turning brilliant shades of red, orange, and yellow, the air cooling as autumn sets in and winter draws closer. She slides to a halt in front of Codi who is practicing his sword skills with Alec. Kimala lounges off to the side, having breakfast underneath a wide-leafed tree.

"Codi, Alec," Mara gasps, holding onto two books with one hand and leaning on her knees with the other. Her colorful intern robe gapes open, exposing her simple black camisole and loose slacks. "I need your help."

"Sure thing," Codi says. He thrusts his sword into the ground. They wonder what the mage intern needs so badly for her to sprint all the way from Cerlail Academy to the palace.

Mara holds up the two books. One reads *Optical Illusions: Intermediate Scene-Oriented Illusionist Techniques* and the other *Battlefield Strategies: How to Defend a City from a Siege.* "Which one should I focus on for my first mage robe?"

Codi laughs. "That's why you ran here?"

"Knowing you, you could do both," Alec points out, chuckling.

Mara blinks. She glances between the two books. "I never thought of that... Thanks. You're a genius."

"According to your mentors, *you're* the genius," Codi comments.

Mara blushes. "No, I'm not."

Alec smirks at her. "You finished the magelet and intern ranks faster than the average person. Of course it is impressive."

"Why defense?" Codi asks, examining the books. "No offense?"

Mara shrugs. "Why make me even more deadly and weaponize my Source?" Everyone stares at her oddly. "Why are you looking at me weird?"

Kimala picks up her tea and takes a dainty sip. "You've changed since coming here."

Mara rolls her eyes. "I know, I know. I've stopped calling it magic."

"No, since coming to Cerlail," Codi specifies, stepping forward and staring into Mara's face. He comes within centimeters of her nose. "Is that... belief? Belief in – oh, my – something you can't see?"

Mara smacks his arm. He grins and ruffles her hair. She throws him over her shoulder, but he drags her down with him. They collapse next to each other.

Kimala sighs. "Barbarians," she murmurs, disappearing into her teacup again.

"I *can* see it, though," Mara argues with Codi's earlier statement. Codi turns his head to stare at her, surprised. "It's right here."

She holds out her hand. A golf-ball sized sparking orb floats above her hand. The sparks are spaced out enough to clearly see the roiling black core underneath.

Codi's eyes widen. "You're controlling the density."

Mara shakes her head. "I still don't know how to

determine how much is okay based off of how it feels, though. I'm just lucky the 'density' can be physically seen. I reduce it until Shaniel or Gerard tell me to stop, and this is what remains." She closes her hand, snuffing the Source out. "But it breaks so easily."

Codi chuckles. "Only you would think that."

Mara sighs, sitting up. "I guess I need to get ready for the graduation ceremony."

"Where is it? I would like to attend," Alec says, giving her a hand up.

Mara pats at her robe, removing stray grass. "The fifth floor's ceremony room."

Codi brushes off her shoulder. "You better hurry back over there, or Mom will be mad at you for all eternity."

Mara rolls her eyes. "No kidding."

"Mara! Here you are!" Shaniel's arm snakes around Mara's shoulders and traps her in a headlock. He fakes looking depressed as Mara struggles to flip him over. "My little magelet is growing up!"

"Get off me, you oversized cat!" Mara cries, using one of the techniques he had recently taught her. Focusing her Source into her arms, she finally finds a good hold and flips Shaniel over.

He wheezes, the breath knocked out of him. He is in his Highlord robe, the magenta splashing over the grey fabric. The stiff collar protects his neck, the Common'Lord's symbol of a magenta lock and key resting over his left breast.

Leaping to his feet, Shaniel tries to brush off the grass and dirt. "Aww, and here I was trying to look nice…"

"Oh, shut up. Let's get going." She strides to the

palace, wishing Thanos was there to see her. After all, he is one of those who has been teaching her during these past couple months.

Off to the side, Aeserast chuckles, also dressed in his purple and blue Highlord robe. "Up to your usual antics, I see."

"Star!" Mara hugs him tightly. "So you're no longer on realm lockdown?"

"Yes." He pats her head, smiling. "How are you doing, Mara?"

"Great!" She beams at him. "Darion taught me a lot when he was here, and Shaniel isn't too bad of an instructor."

He laughs. "I am glad you are having a good time."

"You're not allowed to steal my student," Shaniel warns Aeserast, poking the Dream'Lord in the chest. Mara nearly blushes as she remembers Thanos's comment a week ago during the Sonatheia Ball.

"I wasn't planning on it." Aeserast pats Mara's head affectionately. "As long as she's enjoying herself, I am happy."

Mara smirks at him. "I am, Star."

Aeserast sighs heavily. " Please call me Aeserast..."

< * >

Mara kneels in the middle of a large room with no windows and only a single pillar-like table in front of her, still in her black camisole and loose cloth pants underneath her colorful intern robe. She stares into the water-filled indentation in the top of the pillar, wishing she could look around, but the custom dictates she needs to stare into the reflective water throughout the whole ceremony to express her 'dedication and desire to become a mage.'

Because using Source or Source-based trinkets is prohibited during the ceremony regardless of an anchoring spell, she had to give her illusion band to her mother for safekeeping. The bruise-like Hemius stretches over the right side of her body, looking as if she had taken a nasty beating on that side. The Source coursing through her veins had sparked a heated discussion amongst the higher-ranked individuals; it is considered a spell since it involves her Source, even though she does not consciously maintain it. However, she could not stop the flow because the repercussions could prove fatal. They had finally decided to give her an exemption since it would be too dangerous for her well-being to stop it for any length of time.

Headmaster Gerard Folion opens a book and speaks in Xharos over her. She recognizes a few of the words as she watches the reflection of Headmaster Folion's proud face in the water. He reads aloud for several minutes.

He snaps the book closed and beckons Shaniel from the side. He is in his traditional Highlord attire from earlier that morning, although he has on strange blue-grey gloves that reach all the way to his elbow. A neatly folded black robe is draped over his arm, not touching his skin at all.

He steps forward and takes off her current intern robe as she gazes into the bowl. He positions the new robe over her carefully.

As soon as the stiff material touches her bare shoulders, Mara's mind goes blank.

A silver bolt ignites between her skin and the cloth, racing along the black robe and activating the Source-sensitive material. The hem flares out behind her and settles gently over her shoulders.

She is no longer looking at the headmaster's reflection. Riveted by the image in the bowl, she leans forward, watching the swirling kaleidoscope. The silver entwines around a multitude of colors, braiding them together in a chaotic jumble of power. They fall into the abyss, looking like an exotic, strange waterfall.

"Mara Ariela Danarko." Gerard Folion's voice rocks through her core. She snaps back to the present, careful not to look away from the bowl. "Starting from this moment, you are now a part of the tacticians that protect the realms from anyone who dare defy the wishes of the Ecalains."

Ecalains. A mysterious family who supposedly could speak to Voyana directly. The most famous and prominent was the Alamir family; they had made the 'laws' of Source.

"Do you swear to uphold the Ecalain law and lay your life down for the people of these realms?"

Mara hesitates. She hadn't known this is a part of the initiation. She stares into the bowl. "I swear," she whispers, barely audible to her own ears. It is as if her voice is not her own.

"Do you swear to protect any Ecalain refuge with your very soul?"

"I swear."

"Do you swear to use your power only for the greater good and to never repeat the mistakes of long past?"

"I swear."

Inside the bowl, a silver crown flickers, held by an old man. Mara blinks, and it disappears.

"You may look up."

Mara slowly turns her gaze directly on Gerard Folion, slightly dazed at the images she had seen in the bowl.

Gerard beams, holding his hands wide. "Welcome to your new family, Mara. Vara tir'rani er thana baro."

"Vara tir'rani er thana baro," the other people in the room repeat before cheering loudly. *Fair weather and safe travels.*

Mara slowly looks around the room as if seeing her friends and family for the first time. Ezra and Codi beam at her, looking the happiest out of all of the people. Ezra scrubs at her face, trying to wipe away the two rivers racing down her cheeks. Even Codi tears up a little bit. Kimala smirks, nudging Codi to get him to clap for his sister.

Shaniel holds Mara's old robe over his arm, the odd Source-blocking gloves resting on top of the plain cloth. His eyes show his excitement and pride for Mara as he cheers.

Aeserast's grin is so big Mara fears his face will split apart. His purple eyes nearly spark with his barely contained excitement. She is happy he managed to make it to her graduation ceremony after his 'realm lockdown' punishment for disobeying the Highlord laws.

Darion smiles gently and claps, looking the calmest out of everyone in his brown slacks and grey tunic; apparently, Shaniel had dragged him away from his work just for Mara. *I'll have to apologize for the inconvenience later*, she thinks.

Even Wizard Narbundel, dressed in his silver robe with dark grey accents, borders, and shoulder bands, had shown up to witness her official indoctrination into the tactical wing.

"Congratulations, Mara!" Aeserast cheers, patting her back as he tugs her to her feet.

Mara smiles shakily at him. "Someone could have warned me about all of that stuff about the Ecalain laws and swearing to protect everyone," she admits in a low voice. "It felt more like I was being crowned instead of graduating to a higher rank."

Aeserast gives her a strange look. "What are you talking about, Mara? He was just telling you what the tacticians do."

Mara blinks. She glances at the bowl, realizing it must have been a figment of her imagination. "Oh. Sorry. Guess I zoned out during it or something."

"Maybe..." Aeserast watches her closely, noticing a faint blue ring in the middle of her burnt gold eyes slowly fading away.

Mara looks down at her robe, twisting to look at the sparkling green accents on the back. Even though the color is the same as the beginner magelet robe's green accents, it has a different sheen to it on the mage's robe as if it is of a higher quality. The fabric whispers around her ankles, and silver bolts flicker across the cloth.

"It's so pretty..." Mara murmurs absently. "Reminds me of Ruaguni Cliffs..."

"Mara, you've never been to Quanaris," Aeserast says, alarmed. Darion's and Shaniel's eyes widen at the Dream'Lord's raised voice.

Mara glances between them, rubbing her forehead as a small headache begins throbbing at her temple. "Ah... sorry. I must have seen a picture in a book," she passes off, smiling at them reassuringly. "I've been trying to study up on all the different places, after all."

"Mara," Darion murmurs, placing his hand on the Aeserast's shoulder as if to calm him. "How about we visit Timian and tell him the news?"

Mara gives him a quizzical look. "I was planning on it..."

Shaniel links his arm around hers, hauling her out of the ceremony room with a tense grin plastered on his face. "Great! Let's head there now, then."

She hears Darion and Aeserast making excuses for the others not to follow and wonders what the big deal is. *My imagination just got away from me,* she passes off in her head, although the realisticness of the daydream does bother her slightly. The colorful kaleidoscope of power and the shimmering crown that she had seen in the bowl of water flash through her mind, and suddenly, she is unsure of her own excuses.

"I'm sorry you got pulled into coming to my graduation," Mara apologizes to Darion as Shaniel leads her through the corridors towards the connecting path between the tactical and sorceral wings. "Shaniel can be a bit of a push-over."

Shaniel raises an eyebrow at her. "Darion told me to let him know when you graduated. Plus, he needs a break, too; he overworks himself more often than you, Mara."

People scatter to the sides when they see the four of them walking along the corridor. For a moment, Mara wonders why they look afraid – and then remembers that her Hemius is uncovered.

"My illusion band – " she begins.

"My apologies," Darion murmurs, handing it to her. "Ezra told me to give it to you."

Mara quickly slips it on, watching her skin lighten

to a normal color as the illusion takes hold. She laughs nervously as they cross the crystal bridge between the two buildings. "I think I scared some people... though I'm not quite sure why they would be afraid of a Hemius-infected patient."

All three of them stare at her as if she had said something condemning. "Mara, you..." Shaniel murmurs, trailing off.

"What?" She glances between them, confused.

"Your skin is glowing brighter," Aeserast says, staring at a pulsing artery in her neck.

She glances at her hand and swallows. Even in the direct sunlight, she can see her veins shining a pure silvery-white. She balls her fist and stares straight ahead, not saying anything.

What is going on with me? Mara thinks, not noticing the looks the three men are exchanging. *First weird dreams, then recognizing people I've never seen before, having strange deja vu moments, now this...*

CHAPTER 18
THE ESSENCE

Within minutes, they are on the lowest floor of the publicly available portion of the library. They approach the heavily guarded platform that leads to the restricted area of the library; the four guards, each wearing odd glimmering armor, snap to attention and slide open the platform door for them without a word.

The rounded panels on the inside of the platform are an opaque, soft gold color. Mara touches them, asking, "Where exactly is Uncle Timian's office?"

"Down a floor," Aeserast responds simply.

Shaniel shakes his head. "Not even. It's more like... between floors."

Mara tilts her head to the side, contemplating that. *It will be nice to finally see where he works,* she thinks as the platform opens onto a short hallway ending on a single door. A yellow parchment paper insignia is embossed on the smooth, dark wood, slightly different than the Time'Lord's typical symbol. Mara wonders if it is just a stylistic choice.

Aeserast knocks on the door. "Timian, we're here."

The door slides soundlessly into the wall on its own. On the other side, the walls are replaced with bookshelves packed full of loose-leaf folders, notebooks, thick volumes, and notes. The floor is a maze of stacked books and piles of paper. In the middle of the room, Timian sits at a huge wooden desk with papers and books scattered all over it. Two chairs sit across from him. Mara is shocked; she always thought the Time'Lord to be more organized than this.

Just then, Timian looks up and beams at her. "Mara! What a momentous occasion. I hope the ceremony went well." He sets down his pen and stands up, walking around his desk to give her a hug.

Mara grins at him. "It did. And the robe fits well!" She glances around as he moves behind his desk. "I'm surprised. I always thought you would be more organized than this."

Timian ruffles through the volumes along the back wall. "Ah, I usually am. However, I recently received all of the Highlords' annual reports; my office always becomes so chaotic around this time of the year." He returns with an inch-thick book and hands it to her, frowning at Shaniel. "I would prefer it if you start using a notebook instead of scratch paper, Shaniel." Shaniel rubs the back of his head, a bit embarrassed.

Mara is a bit surprised at Timian's first show of irritation, even though it *is* directed at Shaniel. She examines the book he had handed her; the title reads, *The Four Ancient Sisters and the Fall of the Alamir Family.* "So what is this for?"

"You have not been taught the history of this world, correct?" Timian asks, sitting back down at his desk and lacing his fingers together. Shaniel slumps against a bookshelf, examining his nails as Aeserast browses the volumes near the front door. Darion eases into one of the chairs across from Timian.

Mara sits in the remaining seat, resting the book in her lap. "Actually, I've read a little on it."

Shaniel stares at her. "When?" he demands.

"Whenever I felt like reading." She glances at the laig'hius. "I like learning through the written word, too."

Shaniel crosses his legs and plops onto the ground, grumbling to himself. Timian smiles in amusement. "So what spurred you to learn about the Alamir sisters?"

Mara shrugs. "They seem to be a major part of history, so I thought I should know about them."

"That is a good assessment. You are correct; their history plays a crucial part of today's circumstances despite the six thousand year difference. So what exactly do you know of them?"

Mara sighs. "Is this a quiz?"

"Of a sort."

Startled by his quick response, Mara straightens in her seat and frowns. "Well, there were four sisters. The oldest was in line for the throne, but the third sister killed her for it, banished the second sister to another realm, and wiped the youngest sister's memory." She snorts. "It was a really wicked plan. If it wasn't for the youngest regaining her memory and creating the first Highlords, the third sister – Rinali, right? – might have actually gotten away with it all."

The four men stare at her in stunned silence. Shaniel gapes at her, Aeserast looks appalled, Timian's eyes are narrowed and calculating behind his linked hands, and Darion looks as though he is about to jump out of his seat and drag her to the psych ward. The tension in the air makes her temple ache sharply.

She glances around nervously. "W-what?"

"That is an interesting way to put it," Timian admits, his voice quiet and emotionless. Mara, eyes wide, watches him slowly lower his hands and take a deep breath. "What do you know of Eliara's death?"

"That's the oldest sister, right?" Mara asks, and Timian nods. "I understand that Rinali stabbed her with her own sword, but..." She shakes her head, confused. "Then it went into some weird stuff about her splitting apart. I didn't quite understand it, and I couldn't find anything to explain it better."

Timian's lips quirk up in a small smile as Aeserast chuckles slightly. Mara feels the atmosphere in the room lighten, and she exhales slowly, her headache easing a bit. She wonders what had made them so tense.

Timian leans back in his seat, explaining, "When someone dies, they go to Eleth. However, when Duir'raz'ne Eliara was killed, her very presence – some call it a soul – shattered into seven fragments. Three are her swords and the Alamiran crest you are wearing, infusing the items with the will to protect and defend."

Mara lightly touches the pendant, stunned. *This was Eliara's? Why would Darion give me such an important pendant?*

"Only one of the two in Carni has been found, the Danti Ien." *Silver Garden,* Mara mentally translates as Timian continues. "The memories of the princess are in Eleth, keeping any other part of her from entering the death realm since no two of the same can exist in the same realm."

Timian's eyes flick to Darion momentarily. "The seventh is called the Essence; it is different than the others. It is the power hub. It contains all of the needed knowledge to survive in the realms, such as how to speak and hunt, as well as control the Source coursing through the vessel's veins. Some even argue that the Essence is made purely of Source and should be called as such: Source."

She frowns. "You're talking as if the Essence is still around."

"It is," Timian says simply. "Alkinians have known that souls from Eleth return to the living realms in a cycle of life and death; however, because the memory portion of Eliara is already in Eleth, this has disrupted the Essence's ability to truly die. Thus, it constantly reincarnates within an individual that can contain its power, unable to rest like the normal dead."

Mara tilts her head to the side, calculating. "Wait, so the Essence can no longer become whole with the memories or any of the other parts of Eliara simply because one is already in Eleth and the other is still floating around?" Timian nods. "Well, that's not fun."

Shaniel sniggers, but quietens at Aeserast's glare. Timian smirks a little, asking, "Do you have any other questions?"

Mara rubs her chin. "Yeah. Back to the four sisters." Timian frowns, and Mara laughs nervously. "I-it's actually something I've been meaning to ask one of you. Is the Dark Warrior... Rinali?"

"Yes." Timian looks at Darion again.

Mara glances at the bronze-haired elf, wondering why Timian keeps looking his way. She meets his green eyes and is startled by the intense look he is giving her.

"The Dark Warrior was originally the title given to Rinali as the third sister," Darion slowly explains, his green eyes penetrating into Mara as if looking for something. "There was Duir'raz'ne, First Heir Eliara; Duir'toa'ne, Second Heir Carni; Da'ruha, Dark Warrior Rinali; and Da'neka, Light Warrior Kyrina."

Mara's head spins slightly at the titles. "D-Duir'raz'ne? That's a bit long…"

"There have been longer titles," Timian says, chuckling. "As for Rinali, she tends to appear around the same time the Essence comes of age. Despite our attempts to lock her away in Hariana, our prison system, she somehow manages to break free. We have yet to find her outside accomplice in all of these years."

"Whoever it is is a master at covering his or her tracks," Aeserast adds in, his jaw tense. "I am the best mind-weaver of the Highlords, yet even *I* have not figured out what species they are from."

Mara's head throbs. She rubs her temple, wishing the pounding would stop. "So you're saying the Essence must be back since the Dark Warrior is here."

They stare at her silently.

She glances between them, noticing the expectant looks they are all giving her. Her eyes widen as it slowly dawns on her. "Wait. You don't think – I am *not* this Essence thing."

"Mara," Aeserast steps forward, concern creasing his brows. "Ever since the trip to Cerlail Academy, you have been acting oddly. You've been using techniques no one has taught you, and at the graduation ceremony – "

"Stop."

Aeserast's jaw snaps closed in surprise. Mara glares at him, silver bolts crackling around her hands in controlled anger. "I know you would only worry if I told you, but I've been training with someone after my daily lessons with Shaniel and Folion. He's taught me a lot, including styles I've never learned before. I

342

didn't realize using those would lead you to believe I'm this-this reincarnated version of some ancient princess."

Shaniel's eyebrows jab one another. "Mara, is he — "

"As for the graduation ceremony," Mara interrupts Shaniel, "I've been reading a lot late at night and falling asleep." Her cheeks flush a slight pink color. "I tend to dream of things related to whatever it is I am studying that day. It's how my mind processes new information."

Timian watches Mara closely. "The Essence tends to recollect through dreams. How are you certain you are not actually remembering past lives triggered by whatever you are doing that day?"

Mara stands up, snapping, "I'm not the Essence! I'm just Mara, no one else." She stalks towards the door.

Aeserast grabs her wrist, barely flinching as her erratic Source shocks him. "Mara, at the ceremony, you said something about the Ecalain laws and swearing to protect everyone. What was that about? Did you study about the crowning process of an Ecalain royal before you went to bed last night?"

Mara's face pales. *I didn't,* she realizes, *I had been studying what I needed to do for the ceremony the next day. How did he even know about the crown?*

Aeserast's lips part in realization at Mara's pale face. "Mara, we're just worried — "

She pushes past him, rushing out the door towards the platform. The walls feel as if they are closing in on her; she needs to leave before she suffocates.

Essence? I'm nothing like that, she tells herself, slapping her hand against the lift's operating system and nearly cracking the Source-operated mechanism with her potent power. *I can't hold that level of responsibility. I couldn't protect my father when he died; I couldn't keep Codi from being kidnapped; and when Mom was being attacked by Bryce, I couldn't do anything. I can't take care of others, let alone all of the* realms.

Darion darts onto the platform just as the door slides closed. They stare at one another as the platform slowly rises via Mara's raised hand.

"Mara," Darion begins.

She turns away from him. "Just leave me alone."

He sighs. "What about your robe made you think of the Ruaguni Cliffs on Quanaris?"

Mara slowly turns towards him. He is leaning against the platform wall with his arms crossed over his chest, looking relaxed. She glances down at her robe, pulling the design around so she can see the green markings better.

"The curves remind me of the picture I saw," she admits, remembering falling asleep over the book a few nights ago. "The black stone with the green felorna... it just stood out to me, how it grows on the side of the cliffs, especially in the smooth areas."

"That is not in the textbooks." She stares at his calm expression. "By what I know, felorna grass does grow on the cliffs, but I do not remember reading anywhere that the plant preferred the smoother sections."

Mara's breath catches. The platform door slides open, and Darion moves aside to let her through. "It was probably just my imagination, then," she mumbles as she hurries out of the lift and past the guards.

Darion stays right with her. "But they do grow on

the smoother areas."

Mara whirls around, staring at him. "What?"

"Felorna prefers the smoother rock," he repeats.

"Don't be ridiculous." Mara turns away, but Darion grabs her hand, stopping her. "L-let go!"

"Mara, please." He squeezes her fingers gently; she can see her Source is hurting him, but he doesn't let go. "We are only trying to help you."

"I-I'm not that person," she rambles, her eyes blurring as she fights to remain calm. "I don't want to be important. I can't be..." She swallows the lump in her throat.

They both hear the platform rising. Darion lets her hand go, nodding to the shelves. She can see a couple small red marks along his hand where her power had injured him. "Go; I will stop them."

"Thank you," she whispers, hurrying around a bookshelf.

She only makes it a few feet before she leans against one of the shelves, trembling. She stares at her hand, watching the silver sparks flit across it. *I hurt him,* she thinks, appalled. *I couldn't control my Source, and I... I hurt him. If I really am this... Essence... shouldn't I be able to protect those I care for?!*

"Do not follow her, Aeserast."

She whips around, staring at the end of the row. It is empty; they must be just around the corner.

"But Darion, she – "

"We have done enough. Do you not see what this is doing to her?" Shocked, Mara listens to Darion's defensive tone. "Do you want another incident like the last?"

Aeserast's breath sucks in. Mara frowns. *Like... the last? What is he talking about?*

"You think…" Aeserast trails off, his voice wavering.

"We should give her time to adjust; this is not something you can tell someone and expect them to accept it right away, especially someone like Mara." There is a brief moment of silence. "Do you understand?"

Aeserast sighs. "Yes. But what about the Shasta family? What if they find out?"

"We do not let them find out."

Mara stares at her silvery veins, watching them pulse. Something stirs deep within her, nagging the back of her mind like an omen. She pushes it back, afraid at what it could be – afraid it might confirm what they were telling her in that room.

She escapes the library, barely managing to keep herself in check as she runs to the medical wing. The medics move out of her way as she rushes through the curving hallways; the black and silver bolts racing along her robe and twining around her limbs probably gave plenty of warning that she is unstable right now.

By the time Mara makes it to Kimala's typical studying area, her cousin is already facing the door, mouth open in shock. "Mara, what – "

Mara slumps against the wall, staying as far away from her cousin as the room permits. Tears streak down her face. "I-I need – " She bites her lip, forcing the words out. "I need your help."

Kimala, thankfully, does not approach Mara immediately. "What's wrong?" she asks, reaching into her bag.

"D-don't call Mom," Mara quickly says, her breath catching. She holds her pounding head. "I… I have a migraine," she admits. "I just… I ran here. Uncle

Timian and the others were saying weird things, and my head was hurting, and I... I just..."

A blue bottle enters her vision. Mara's head jerks up; she hadn't noticed her cousin moving closer to her. "Drink this," Kimala says quietly, trying to smile. "It's a muscle relaxer; you probably have a tension migraine. It might make you sleepy."

Mara snatches the bottle and knocks back the liquid. Kimala sits next to her as her eyes grow heavy and her mind feels slightly drugged.

By the time Darion arrives, Mara is fast asleep with her head on Kimala's lap, the silver bolts mildly wrapping around her body in an odd aftereffect of her agitation. Kimala rests her hand on Mara's head, the soft silvery-blue glow of her Source easing away the tension as Mara sleeps.

Mara's silver lightning bolts tame under the gentle glow of Kimala's silver-blue light. The two silvers perfectly match and nearly meld together, revealing a link between the two girls that goes deeper than any blood relation ever could. A link that reaches their very souls.

< * >

Mara walks down a narrow path through the woods with an empty basket over her arm. She hums a lovely tune as the sounds of the animals and wind surround her. The bright blue sun filters through the trees, illuminating her pathway towards a field of strange-looking blue flowers. She plucks them, gently placing them in the basket.

She hears a thump nearby as if something heavy had fallen. She pushes through the weeds and tall flowers to look down at a girl cloaked in a dark reddish-black aura. She stares straight at Mara.

Her pupils and irises are a reddish-purple; the whites of her eyes are pure black. She has shadowed skin that shifts, the black and red swirls twisting and churning.

Mara stumbles backwards. The girl looks like a walking Hemius monster.

The girl grins, exposing shadowed red teeth. "Uthu morla a ik'te, Duir'raz'ne," the shadowy humanoid girl murmurs in Xharos. I found you, First Princess.

Mara screams and scrambles away. The girl reaches forward and grabs her ankle; a searing pain radiates up Mara's leg, distinctive and acute. She falls to her hands and knees, trying to crawl away.

The girl pulls herself closer and grabs the other ankle, sending more flaming sensation up her legs. Mara feels the Hemius creeping its way through her body. She weakens from the extreme pain, and the girl hovers over her. Mara whimpers as the girl grins and grabs the sides of her face.

Mara passes out from the pain, sinking into darkness. However, even there, she is not free from the Hemius girl. She follows Mara into her mind. The Hemius girl hammers her Source — a sickly reddish purple color — into Mara's very being. Mara screams from inside her mind, suddenly becoming trapped deep within herself.

Belatedly throwing up defensive walls, she defends what she can. The girl tears through them as if they are flower petals. Mara could feel the glee radiating off the girl's presence invading her body, infusing it with the Hemius poison — a side effect of the sickly Source coming from the girl.

"Stop, please," *Mara begs the presence with her mind.*

A mad cackle emanates from the presence that has taken up over half of her mind. "This vessel is mine now, Essence."

The presence continues to beat against the walls Mara had thrown up to protect the most valuable part of her: her Source, the very thing that allowed her existence. A single tendril breaks through the wall and strikes straight through the core of the silvery waves of Source strands. It shatters from the inside, turning into little silvery fragments.

Mara's mind breaks and dissipates. She feels as though she is being erased from existence.

It is worse than death itself.

The feeling of her core being eliminated from her own mind, of her very soul being shattered and scattered across the realms, consumes her very existence.

She is everywhere and nowhere; she registers everything at once but nothing at all. She wanders, blind, in a million particles. She searches, barely registering that she is looking for something to keep herself together.

Eventually, she finds it – a tiny life form. An empty vessel. She molds it to fit her Source and to contain her very essence. She finally finishes and slips into the form, sinking into blissful unawareness and ignorance. The tiny life trembles at her presence, greeting her with a feeble touch as it develops. She remembers no more.

Mara's eyes pop open and she sucks in huge gulps of air, struggling to free herself from whatever is grabbing her legs. Tears stream down her face as her eyes flit around, taking in her familiar yet foreign surroundings. The blankets tangle around her body, giving her the sensation of feeling trapped.

What was that?

A sob escapes from her lips and she curls into a ball, the sheets still entwined with her legs.

Was that… a memory?

She tries to muffle her sobs into the pillow. Someone knocks and enters the room, closing the door gently. She buries her head into her pillow to hide her tear-streaked face.

"Mara? Are you awake?" Darion murmurs, and Mara feels the bed shift as he sits on the edge.

"Go away," she says into the pillow, her voice cracking.

She could sense his alarm. He touches her arm, worried. "Are you all right? Was it a nightmare?"

Mara hesitates and then nods slowly.

Darion sighs. Mara feels the bed shift as he stands up. "I will call Aeserast – "

Mara reaches out and clings to his shirt, swallowing hard as she tries to control her terror. "No," she pleads. "Don't. Please."

Darion sits down, gently prying her hand off his shirt. She grasps his fingers tightly, and he squeezes back. She leans forward and rests her forehead against his upper arm. Surprised, he does not move.

"I'm sorry," she whispers, barely audible. "Just... give me a moment."

They sit like that for a few minutes. Finally, Mara takes a couple deep breaths, no longer filled with that sense of overwhelming sensation.

"Better?" Darion asks.

She nods.

"Do you want to tell me about it?"

She shakes her head.

"Will you look at me?"

Mara slowly meets his sympathetic gaze. Her eyes fill with tears again, and she blurts, "Why did you help me in the library?"

He stares at her, confused. "I saw how upset you were with the others and knew you needed to be alone to think about it. Are you feeling better?"

Mara leans forward, resting her forehead against his arm again as she takes another steadying breath.

"You're so easy to talk to," she rambles, "I just don't get it. How can I be so comfortable around you?"

Hesitantly, he rests a hand on her back. "I... am not sure."

"It was awful," she admits into his shirtsleeve, her fingers constricting around his hand. "She reminds me of Hemius. She-she forced her way into my mind and did something to me."

"It was just a dream," he says, although it doesn't sound reassuring.

"I've had more dreams." She closes her eyes. "I've been called different names in them, a-and the Essence. That girl shows up in them sometimes, too."

"Do you want to tell me about them?"

Mara laughs weakly, suddenly exhausted. "Nah, I think I've shared enough..." She shifts her head into a more comfortable position. "It felt good to finally tell someone, though... Those dreams freak me out..."

"You are still Mara regardless of the Essence," he murmurs, rubbing his thumb over her hand. "Just do not allow this knowledge to change your personality."

When she doesn't say anything, he tilts his head forward slightly to peer at her face; her eyes are closed and her expression looks relaxed. Darion smiles, easing her onto the pillows. "Sleep well, Mara."

Darion knocks softly on the open door, peering around the corner to see Mara tossing a change of clothes and several overnight items into her bag. She is dressed in comfortable clothes underneath her new mage robe.

He watches her for a moment before stepping in.

"Where are you going?"

"Lunesh'kun. Might as well check out the city my father had built." She shoves the last item – an extra pair of socks – into the bag and snaps it closed with a little bit more force than needed.

Warm hands encompass hers, turning her away. She reluctantly meets his jade-green eyes, noticing the flecks of gold looking like sunlight seeping through leaves. His gaze is filled with concern and worry. "Why the sudden decision?"

Mara swallows, looking away partially because of the topic and partially because his gaze is just a little too intense for her right then. "I-I just need some time to think," she mutters, pulling her hands out of his. "Get away from all of this crazy stuff about the Essence." She laughs, but her voice trembles slightly.

He stares at her for a moment before nodding. "War'Lord Riley will be leaving tomorrow, so if you visit, now would be the best time."

Startled, Mara meets his gaze to see a gentle smile on his face. She had thought he would try to keep her from going, but here he was, encouraging her.

"Thank you," she whispers, her hand wrapping around her bag strap. She bites her lip, her cheeks turning a little red. She doesn't notice his eyes widen at her subconscious move. "Could you... come with me?"

His hand pats the top of her head. She looks up just as his hand slides down to her shoulder.

Bzzz. Bzzz.

Darion yanks his hand back and digs in his pocket as Mara quickly turns away, trying to pull her frazzled nerves back together. What had she been thinking by *inviting* him? He is a busy elf who barely has time to drop by for a graduation, let alone spend a couple days in Danarkana.

In his hand, a crystalline oval glows softly as emerald Source pulses through it. He listens to some message in another language, his expression darkening at the frantic tone on the other end. He responds curtly in the same language before tucking the odd device in his pocket again.

"My apologies, Mara, but I have to return to – "

"It's all right, I was just being a little selfish," Mara brushes off, forcing a smile on her face. "I was planning to ask some other people, anyway."

Darion pauses, examining her face. He nods as if reassured by what he sees there. He strides to the door, calling back, "Have fun at Lunesh'kun."

"I will," she responds, taking a step towards the door. She slings her backpack over her robe and snatches Gamerog's sheath off the end table next to her bed.

As she steps out of the room, though, a furious Aeserast stops her. "When were you going to tell me of this trip?" he asks in a low voice.

"You're not going to stop me," she says, gripping the strap to her bag.

Aeserast trails after her as she walks through the palace. "Mara, please reconsider this. It's dangerous – "

"I'm going, whether you like it or not!" Mara snaps, pausing to glare defiantly at him. "It's a short trip. I won't even be gone that long!"

"That's not the point, Mara!" Aeserast huffs, his hair balled in his fist. "Danarkana is *right next* to Alamirana. What if they try to kill you? You're a Danarko, and Naiya hates Danarkos."

Mara rolls her eyes. "Riley is still there, isn't he?"

"Well, yes, but he leaves tomorrow – "

"Then if I want to visit Lunesh'kun while he is still there, I need to go *now*." She pushes by the Dream'Lord and walks down the stairs.

Aeserast rushes after her. "Mara, you need to think about – "

Mara shoots him a glare. "No." For a brief moment, she wishes Darion is there to distract Aeserast so she can escape. However, the handsome elf is nowhere in sight.

Aeserast follows her to Cerlail Academy, remaining a few paces behind her. At the entrance to the tactical wing, Mara whirls around and demands, "Are you planning to go all the way to Lunesh'kun with me?"

Aeserast crosses his arms. "If I need to, then yes."

Shaniel drapes his arms around Mara's shoulder, resting his cheek on his arm. "Aww, are you going on a trip? Why didn't you invite me?"

"Get off of me, Shaniel!" Mara exclaims, trying to slip out of his grasp. He hugs her shoulders tightly before releasing her with a grin. "And I was going to invite you."

Shaniel blinks, surprised. He points at his face before glancing at the flustered Aeserast. "Why just me?"

Because you won't nag me about this Essence stuff, she thinks, but doesn't say it out loud. Reluctantly, she turns to Aeserast. "I'm fine with you tagging along under one condition."

Aeserast narrows his eyes. "What is it?"

"Don't bring up yesterday's conversation in the library."

"Deal."

Mara is taken aback by his quick response. Why did he agree so quickly? "O-okay, then. Let's go."

"What about Codi? Wouldn't he like to go, too?" Shaniel asks, glancing at the sorceral wing.

"I was planning to ask him and Kimala."

Shaniel's eyes widen. "Wait, were you going to ask me first?" She nods; he pumps his fist. "Awesome!"

Mara finds Kimala easily enough, although convincing her takes longer. Finally, her cousin agrees to the day trip on the promise that they will return tomorrow morning. As she runs to tell Lilly and pack, Mara steps over to the sorceral wing and searches for her brother. Luckily, he is with Narbundel, so it takes less time.

The transportation platform is nearly as big as a basketball stadium; the frosted crystal floor clicks underneath Mara's shoes as she taps her foot impatiently. Aeserast is talking to the portal engineer while Shaniel glances at Mara. Both of them are in their colorful Highlord robes.

I should have told them I wanted to leave before lunch. Mara glares at the swirling oval of warped air, squashing her fear of passing through the portal by examining the small strands of light holding open the edges and anchoring the dimensional hole against the raised platform.

Codi and Kimala finally show up, Rick tagging along behind them in the Quasalan green and gold armor.

She smiles at him. "Haven't seen you in a while. How's it going?"

Rick bobs his head respectfully. "Well enough. I hear you are going to Danarkana for the day; I hope you do not mind me accompanying you."

Mara quickly shakes her head. "Not at all."

Aeserast approaches them. "Perfect timing. The engineer has it set to Danarkana's front gate now. Are you ready?"

Mara's eyes flick between the engineer and the portal. "It took that long?"

Aeserast nods. "Anchored portals are easier to maintain, though it does take some fine-tuning to get an exact location."

Shaniel grabs her arm, grinning. "Let's go first."

Mara clutches at his hand in reflex, nervous. "What do we do?"

"Just walk through!"

Before she could object, Shaniel tugs her into the portal. She has the odd sensation of water passing through her very being, but unlike the first time, she does not feel any tearing sensation inside her mind.

Her knees nearly buckle as her feet strike a paved road on the other side. Shaniel supports her as she regains her balance. "Huh. That wasn't so… bad…" she trails off as she looks up at the looming wall. The perfectly smooth, sand-colored stone towers several yards above her, making it difficult for intruders to scale it.

Codi and Aeserast exit the swirling portal next, quickly followed by Kimala and Rick. Aeserast and Shaniel share amused looks as Mara slowly lowers her gaze to the open gate.

Unlike the sand-colored wall, the gate is made out of a glimmering grey metal with pictures etched onto the huge slabs. By the looks of it, it is the story of how the city was created. Standing just inside the entrance is Riley, his beard trimmed close as his red hair is pulled into a tight ponytail. He is in a simple black shirt and light brown pants, the symbol of a light brown raven embroidered on his shirt.

"Welcome te Danarkana!" Riley booms, grinning.

CHAPTER 19
DANARKANA

Mara stares past the Scotsman into the convoluted streets. Just from the entrance, she can see the two layers of the city splitting into multiple levels the deeper into the city they went. The ground slopes upwards, the buildings edged and flat on top to give the defending city's troops a vantage point.

"I don't have much te do before I have te leave, so how 'bout a tour?" Riley asks.

Mara's eyes spark in excitement. "That would be awesome!"

As they begin walking up the uneven road meant to trip intruders, Codi, Kimala, and Rick introduce themselves to the War'Lord. Mara marvels at the uniform buildings, arching pathways, hidden passages, and twisting alleyways. The air smells different here, like sun-warmed stone and freshly baked pastries and bread. For lunch, they have Danarkana delicacies – a special pie made with fruit and bread grown and made in the city – as they walk around.

Riley shows them the lesser-known sights, taking them deep into the underbelly of the multi-leveled interior. He shows off the illusionary walls, the shifting pathways, the top view of the inner city, the hydraulics system, the river running underneath the city, and more. All of the diagrams Shokain had made of Lunesh'kun for the games she used to play with him had obviously been a simplified version of this vast, convoluted city built to confuse and even completely deter attackers. Mara is awed that her father had built such a complicated, intricate structure in just a few years.

She is not surprised when they end the tour on the top floor in the center of the city. However, she *is* surprised that the central hub of the city is a mansion and not something bigger, such as a palace. *I guess Dad didn't care much for the big and grand... after all, he might have been able to have a whole castle built here if he had wanted it.*

Riley nods to the guards as they approach the simplistic doors to the mansion. "Hinrei is eager t' meet ya both." He eyes the three young adults up and down. "Did ye bring somethin' nice te wear?"

Mara's face pales as both Codi and Kimala nod. Seeing her reaction, Kimala rolls her eyes. "I have a spare, Mara."

We're here for one day and night, and she brought two dresses, Mara grumbles internally. *No wonder it took so long for her to get ready.*

Riley chuckles. "Shaniel, Aeserast, you know where the rooms are. I'll inform Hinrei." He pats Mara's and Codi's shoulders. "He's a young lad, but a good sital'fu. You'll get along."

Before Mara could ask what he meant by that, he disappears. Aeserast and Shaniel lead them through the twisting corridors that are almost as confusing as the city itself. Once in the rooms, Kimala lends Mara a beautiful shimmering blue dress and puts up her hair for her. Before Mara leaves her room, she moves the Alamiran crest to her ankle, still self-conscious about wearing it out in the open.

When Riley picks them up for the evening meal, he does a double take on Mara. "My, my. Aren't you turnin' into the fine young woman."

Mara blushes slightly as he leads them through the mansion. Finally, they arrive at a large yet simplistic room. Weapons line the walls, and a long, narrow table laden with food takes up a good portion of the space. At the head of the table, a man with rounded ears and the stocky frame of a Blazhreian stands and bows deeply to them.

"It is an honor to meet Shokain's descendants. I am Hinrei Piras, the current sital'fu in charge of Danarkana. Please, sit wherever you would like." The sital'fu gestures around the table.

Mara sits down near the head of the table, Codi beside her. *Sital'fu,* she mulls over the title, *similar to a mayor… so odd Dad would assign that level of a position to someone over his own city.*

"Are both of you attending Cerlail Academy?" Hinrei asks, and they nod as they sit down. He smiles slightly. "What are you studying?"

"Illusions," Mara murmurs, poking at the food in front of her.

"Elemental tactics," Codi announces, grinning. "I would love to see some of Lunesh'kun's materialized walls if you don't mind, Sital'fu Hinrei."

"Not at all; I can show you the nearest one as soon as we are finished with dinner." Hinrei glances between Mara and Codi. "So which of you is the oldest?"

Confused, Mara points at her brother. "Codi is."

Hinrei beams at the dark-haired boy. "So you will be the one to take over Danarkana one day?"

Both stare at the sital'fu, stunned. Codi stammers, "Ah, well, I'm actually adopted – "

"As long as you're recognized as Shokain's son, it

shouldn't be a problem. Do you have his crest?" he asks, glancing between the two siblings expectantly.

Mara glances at the ring on her right pinky, a bit overwhelmed. The golden sunstone glints in the Source globe lighting.

Hinrei notices the ring. "Whoever has that has control over the city's defense system. Shokain programmed the security system to respond only to the one who wears that ring; it is used for recognizing the heir. If you have it, then – "

Mara expressionlessly takes off the ring and hands it to her brother. "You're the oldest."

Codi shakes his head. "Dad wanted you to have it."

"I am *not* taking over Lunesh'kun," Mara says firmly, using the original name for the city. *What was Dad thinking?! I can barely take care of myself. Why does he think I'll be able to manage a whole city?*

"But – "

"If you don't take it, I'm chucking it into the next body of water I run across."

Codi finally accepts the ring and puts it on. It resizes to his finger.

Hinrei looks a bit uncomfortable by the exchange. "I guess that settles it."

The conversation switches to more comfortable topics. However, after dinner, Riley receives a message telling him to head straight to his next assignment. He hugs both Mara and Codi before leaving. Hinrei offers them a tour of the mansion, and Mara is stuck wandering around the castle in the borrowed dress. Kimala sniggers, knowing that Mara is very unhappy right now.

Hinrei opens yet another door, leading them into a

wonderful room filled with weapons and pictures of battle scenes along the walls. Short bookshelves border the entire room, only three feet tall. In the middle of the room, a very large table glows softly.

"This is Shokain's strategic room," Hinrei announces, sounding as though he, too, is growing weary of the tour.

Shaniel side-steps around him and runs his hands over the surface of the glowing table. "This is a tactical table. It's often used for strategy and tactical planning." He thumps the surface of the glowing table with a fist. "Fae'reth, show a map of Saheir," he commands.

The glow brightens into a steady light. Slowly, a colored landscape appears, fully detailing the layout of the country.

Mara recognizes the Xharos words for tactical table. "Wow. What else can you do with this?"

"You can create new maps, mark pathways, design buildings, and put troops down," Hinrei explains as Shaniel copies a segment of the map and enlarges it.

Shaniel circles a section and draws a little stick person on it. "You can just say it, too. Fae'reth, show me Danarkana layout."

It shows Danarkana from the air, exposing the confusing labyrinth. Mara examines it closely. "Fae'reth, zoom in on the palace," Mara orders, trying it out.

The map zooms in on the palace. There are no soldiers or stalls; just the building itself. "It's just a rendition," Mara murmurs, disappointed.

"Definitely not Google Earth," Shaniel snickers quietly.

Mara glances at him. "You've been to Earth?"

Shaniel rolls his eyes. "Of *course* I've been to Earth."

"I wonder if we could play a game of Siege on this..." she murmurs almost absently. "That would be fun."

Shaniel and Codi grin. "Yeah, it would be!" Codi agrees.

Shaniel rubs his jaw, leaning over the table. "It should be possible... want to try it out?"

Mara shakes her head. "Not now; maybe some other time. We're only here for tonight, after all." She glances around the rest of the room, her breath hitching as she stares at the portrait of Shokain Danarko on the back wall.

Shokain's chestnut brown hair curls around his face, nearly reaching his shoulder. The crinkles around his golden eyes on his tanned face show his laughter while the small smile hints at the storyteller in him. He poses in a black robe with grey accents and silver shoulder bands – the tactical mastery robe with a focus in illusions. He holds a book of tactics in one hand and a simple katana in the other. The silver ring with the goldstone is on the pinky of his right hand.

Mara glances down at her pinky where, up until earlier, she had been wearing her father's ring. *So small*, she realizes. *Still so small when compared to Daddy.* She sighs and stares up at his golden eyes. "I miss you," she whispers.

"Did you say something, Mara?" Aeserast asks, leaning over the table.

She forces a smile on her face and turns around. "It's nothing. Let's go."

Mara is relieved when she makes it back to her

room, almost rudely closing the door on her friends. She knows Codi wants to join Hinrei in the library to talk about the city, but she is tired of walking around in the heels. She kicks off her shoes and throws open the balcony doors, staring up at the two moons. The urge to spar with someone creeps up on her, and she quickly shakes away her thoughts of Thanos and all the different moves he had taught her.

A light fog twines its way through the streets, rising from the lower levels of the city. Mara frowns. Is it common for the river below to produce so much fog?

She leans against the balcony, suddenly feeling heavy. She rubs her head, trying to shake off the sleepiness as she turns back to her room.

Three silhouettes approach Mara from the side of her balcony. "Who are you?" Mara demands, raising her arms in defense.

The intruders lunge towards her, attacking as one. The fog disguises their features and movements; Mara struggles to defend herself as her body only grows more sluggish. *I should have changed,* she regrets instantly as her dress tangles around her legs and restricts her movements. At this point, she cannot even see Gamerog's sheath inside her room, let alone reach it so she could summon the ancient sword to her aide.

One of the intruders slips behind her and wraps a cloth over her face. Suspecting the cloth is drugged, she does not inhale as she struggles against her assailants, but a sharp kick to her gut has her sucking in air in surprise.

Her vision wavers as her captors press cold metal against her wrists and ankles, clicking the cuffs into place. She coughs against the sickly sweet smell, finally passing out.

< * >

Something presses against Mara's neck uncomfortably, dragging her out of her heavy slumber. Breathing deeply, she barely recognizes the smell of cold stone beneath her. She shifts her hands, but her wrists are heavy from the metal cuffs wrapped around them.

She opens her eyes and stares at the inch-thick metal cuffs. She touches a bigger one around her throat.

Aeserast's pendant is gone.

She sits up, shaking the grogginess out of her system. She is in a white room made out of quartz-based rocks, faint Xharos runes appearing and disappearing over the surface of the walls.

She looks down at herself. She is on a granite cot with only a thin blanket between her and the cold stone. She shivers and rubs her arms, the sleeves of her blue dress barely enough to banish the chill of the room.

She shifts her feet to the edge of the cot, feeling an odd sense of emptiness and wincing as something tugs against her anklebones. She lifts the hem of her skirt, seeing two matching cuffs encircling her ankles. There is absolutely no trace of silvery veins anywhere on her body.

Dread creeps into Mara. The silver dragon crest is not on her ankle, although from the looks of it, her illusion band has not been discovered. She glances around, hoping the crest had just fallen off, but it is nowhere to be seen. Suddenly, a sharp pain pierces her right hand.

Horrified, Mara fumbles underneath the cuff on her ankle, taking off the transparent band to examine the Hemius stretching across the right side of her body. It sluggishly writhes in response to her anxiety. She takes a deep breath to calm her nerves as she puts the illusion band on her ankle and focuses inward.

Her Source is oddly calm, as if sedated; the black is eerily still as the silver sparks barely creep across it. She tries to coax some of it into her system to stop the Hemius, but the silver sparks do not respond to her request.

Gasping, she opens her eyes and examines the room for an exit. She needs to escape somehow; if not, she may just die here.

A seamless door and table in the opposite corner catch her attention. She stands up and takes a step forward; a sharp pain lances up her right leg and through the bottom of her foot. She winces, realizing the Hemius is more active than she originally thought. She steps forward with her left foot, but the same thing happens.

She glances down, alarmed. Tiny wires crisscross the floor, blending in with the off-white stone. Mara scrambles onto the cot, bile rising in her throat.

Mara pulls her legs up, carefully examining the bottom of her feet. A wave of dizziness rocks through her when she sees a thin wire still lodged in her foot. *How... how do they know?!*

It isn't the pain. It isn't even the objects themselves. It is the sensation of something thin, small, and sharp worming its way through her foot, cutting her into pieces from the inside. She can't stand it.

She claws at the collar around her neck, intuitively knowing it is restraining her Source. She sucks in air, her eyes riveted to the floor. Tears gather in the corners of her eyes in frustration. She wants to blast away those little strands of metal, but she can't. She wonders if she can use the blanket to sweep them away, but as soon as the material touches the strands, they shred the flimsy fabric into ribbons.

Creeaak. The seamless door opens. Evan walks in, wearing a simple grey tunic, tan pants, and thick black boots. "I brought you some food," he says, placing a plate on the small table. "How are you feeling?"

"Why are you doing this to me?" she gasps, her fingers wrapping around the band around her throat. The Hemius shifts underneath the illusion, sluggish yet active. She feels as if the metal cuff – or the Hemius – is choking her.

He frowns. "Are you all right? The Source inhibitors aren't too tight, are they?"

Source inhibitors. Mara tears her eyes away from the floor and stares at Evan. "Why?" she demands, her eyes watering. Her right eye nearly closes from the sharp ache of the active Hemius.

Evan's eyes widen. He looks down at the floor, finally noticing the thin wires. "The phobia manifestation," he spits in disgust, grimacing. He kicks some of the wires away with his boot; they snap under the slightest pressure. He stomps over with the plate and squats in front of her.

"Get away from me," Mara gasps, flattening herself against the wall. The metal collar clangs loudly against the quartz stone, but neither are damaged by the harsh impact.

Evan holds out the plate. "Here, I brought some

breakf – "

Mara knocks it out of his hand. The food scatters. "Get away from me!" she screams hoarsely. She buries her head in her knees, unwilling to let him see her in this weakened state.

Evan stares at her for a moment before slowly cleaning the mess. He pauses before leaving. "I'm sorry," he whispers. "I didn't want to do this to you."

The door shuts. Mara curls into a ball on the cot, her sniffles echoing in the tiny chamber as she finally releases the tears. The Hemius writhes underneath her skin, threatening to kill her with a single touch. She becomes very aware of her situation: a stone room that cannot be opened from the inside, threads of razor-sharp strands on the floor ready to cut her into ribbons, and a deadly living poison slowly eating away at her. No matter how many scenarios she thinks of, she cannot think of one that could get her out of here alive. Sure, she could pick up some of the wires and make a deadly rope with it, but how far could she get before either they dragged her back or she collapsed from the Hemius?

She presses her cheek against the cold stone, watching her tears form a small puddle.

"Someone... help me..."

< * >

Aeserast opens his eyes slowly, frowning at the bright sunlight filtering into the room. He struggles to focus on it, his vision blurry. He sits up and grasps the end table, nauseous from the sudden movement. "Sleeping spell," he slurs, clutching the side of the bed.

After the world stops spinning, he staggers to his

feet and barely makes it into the hallway and to Mara's door. He knocks, but there is no answer. He rattles the handle and the door swings open, unlocked.

The balcony window is shut tight. There is only the bed, a small dresser, a table, and a handful of chairs decorating the room. A bundled lump resides underneath the covers.

He collapses on the bed's edge in relief and pulls back the covers. "Mara, wake – "

He freezes, staring at the pillow in the place where Mara's head should be. He pulls back the comforter all the way; pillows are lined up in the shape of someone sleeping. "No. No."

Hoping it is just a prank, he scours the room. Her backpack is still on the chair near the balcony door; Gamerog and her knives rest on the table, untouched since yesterday. She is nowhere to be found.

He stumbles out of the room and bangs on the door next to Mara's room. "Kimala. Tein'stra Kimala!"

No response.

The Dream'Lord, not having the same skills as the Common'Lord, kicks open the door. Kimala is collapsed on the bed, still in the dress from last night. Aeserast slumps onto the mattress and rests his hand against her forehead, carefully coaxing her slumbering mind to consciousness. "Kimala, wake up."

"Highlord Aeserast…?" Kimala murmurs sleepily, staring at him through half-opened eyes.

He presses a finger to his lips. "We've been drugged. Can you clear it out of your system?"

She lurches upright, her eyes wide. She moans, clutching her head as she leans over the edge of the bed. "I-I think so."

"Hurry." Aeserast checks the balcony window before walking to the door and monitoring the hallway as Kimala's soft silvery blue Source washes over her entire body.

Once done, she stands up and joins him at the entrance. "I don't understand," she whispers to him. "Who would send such a spell? How did they do it?"

Aeserast shakes his head. "It must have been the fog from last night. I've never seen it that thick before." He smiles grimly. "I should have expected this."

He steps into the hallway and passes Mara's door, striding to Codi's chambers. Kimala glances at her cousin's door. "Shouldn't we..."

"She's been kidnapped."

She freezes, staring at the lavender-haired young man. "What?" she asks stupidly.

Aeserast's poker face falls. He grits his teeth and balls his fists in his hair, spinning in a tight circle. "It's my fault. I was on sleeper spell watch. I should have seen through this."

"Aeserast..." Kimala starts, utterly confused. "What's going on? Is someone after Mara?"

"We need to wake the others." He moves to break down Codi's door, but Shaniel appears and grabs his shoulder. "Shaniel?" Aeserast says, stunned.

"So you're awake, too," Shaniel murmurs, scarily serious. His jaw muscles twitch. "I saw that Mara is not slumbering like a good little duir'stra."

"We need to wake the others," Aeserast gestures to the door. "Get that thing open."

Shaniel raises an eyebrow. "You're always so strict about the rules. What changed?"

"You idiot. Think about it," Aeserast growls. Shaniel's eyes widen at the ferocity in his glare. "We need to find her. Now."

Shaniel's gaze darkens. He quickly picks the lock. "I'll gather intel."

Aeserast and Kimala stare at him. "You don't think..." Aeserast stops himself, his fingers tangling in his hair anxiously.

Shaniel slowly nods. "If the same ones who had summoned *her* just kidnapped Mara, it's only a matter of time before they figure out who she is. How long do you think that ritual will take?"

Aeserast pales, his face turning as white as paper. "No..."

Shaniel jogs backwards. "If you don't hear anything from me in two days, gather the other 'Lords."

Aeserast's back thumps against Codi's door. He slides to the floor, his hands covering his head. "I'm the worst guardian ever... Shokain should have picked Darion, not me..."

Kimala stares at the Dream'Lord with wide eyes. "What is going on? Why would someone kidnap Mara?"

"Wake up Codi," Aeserast sighs in resignation, his head bumping against the stone as he shifts to the side. "It would be best for both of you to hear this."

< * >

Mara shivers on the cot, staring across the room at the door. The Hemius writhes, more active than earlier that day. She buries her head into the pitiful representation of a pillow that Evan had brought in earlier.

Someone knocks on the door softly. Mara doesn't look up as Evan enters and walks towards her. "Come on," he coaxes, touching her arm.

She slaps his hand away.

Evan sighs. "Desdemona," he calls.

Mara glances at the doorway, startled. A black-haired girl with silver streaking through it saunters in, wearing leather pants and a jacket over a purple top. Her boots crush the wire threads. She sneers. "You're pretty pathetic without your Source, aren't you?"

"Stop it, Des," Evan sighs, gesturing to the door. "Mother is waiting."

Desdemona glances at him. For a second, disgust flits across her face. "You're the one she is angry at," she informs as she tugs Mara up by the arm. "You're pretty weak. Didn't you eat earlier?"

"She refused to," Evan says, gritting his teeth.

Desdemona rolls her eyes as she pulls Mara across the floor.

Mara bites her lip hard. The coppery taste of blood fills her mouth as the wires dig into her feet, unseen. She tries to block out the sensation of the almost invisible wires slicing deep into her feet and lodging there, continuing to cut into her with every slap of her soles against the ground.

They walk through a stone passageway, passing by other windowless doors similar to the one they had just come from. Desdemona yanks Mara through various corridors and up a set of wide stairs.

Mara barely registers the crystal hallways glistening in the evening sun through huge bay windows. Everything has a dark tinge to it as if a thick miasma had settled over the castle.

"Stand up straight already," Desdemona huffs,

stopping at the foot of a long staircase climbing several flights to a set of huge, heavy ornate doors. The steps stretch fifteen feet from left to right.

Mara stares at the steps, dreading the long trek. Her legs are already about to cave on her from the walk from the dungeons; how is she supposed to climb all of these stairs?

Evan notices something on the floor behind them. He kneels down and examines it. "Her feet are bleeding," he notices, alarmed.

"You're kidding me." Desdemona throws up her hands. "Why didn't you say anything?"

"Why do you care?" Mara rasps, cradling her right arm as it throbs.

Something knocks against the back of her legs. Mara squeaks as Evan lifts her and begins the long climb up the stairs.

"O-ho, trying to make up for all of your mistakes?" Desdemona teases him. "I bet you won't be able to make it to the top."

"Shut up, Des." Evan continues to climb. He notices Mara staring at him. "What is it?"

Mara turns her head, ignoring him completely.

Desdemona laughs. "Still has some spine. Nice!"

Why is he carrying me? Mara wonders as she glances at his face inches from her own. The heavy metal shifts against her collarbone, reminding her once again that her Hemius is active and could kill her at any moment.

Mara focuses inwards, trying to access her Source again. She fights to pull out even the tiniest of flickers, but to no avail. She tries again and again as they near the huge silver-flecked lapis lazuli doors at the top. She doesn't pay attention to the intricate carvings on the doors as two guards in red and black livery open them.

Evan puts her down, and she collapses to her knees on the huge black rug. Mara quickly glances around, analyzing her surroundings.

An enormous, sparsely furnished circular room the size of a moderate house is dimly lit by Source globes scattered around the walls. Along the rear of the room, eight chairs are perfectly lined up and covered by black cloth. Burgundy drapes keep the setting sun's light out of the crystal throne room.

A woman with jet-black hair, pale skin, and soft blue eyes stands by one of the bay windows and peers past the heavy drape. She glances at them before touching the red and blue amulet around her neck softly. Her movements are slightly wobbly as she glides towards them, her pointed ears peeking out from her black wavy hair.

Desdemona and Evan kneel and bow their heads to the approaching woman. "Mother," they chorus.

Mara stares at the woman, stunned. *Impossible*, she thinks. *She's way too young.*

"What happened?" Paro'ki Naiya asks softly, concerned. She catches sight of Mara's bloody feet and reaches forward.

Mara pulls back, refusing to be touched by this woman. Something felt... off about her. Her movements are too irregular to be a laig'hius or an elemental, and she lacked the flowing grace of the elves and fey. The amulet glistens a bloody red around her throat.

Evan glances sideways at Mara. "I believe she cut her feet in the phobia manifestation cell."

Naiya's head tilts to the side. "That is simple

enough to rectify. Mara Ariela Danarko," Naiya murmurs as if tasting the name. "Such an interesting choice for a name. Do you even know what you are?"

Mara grits her teeth against the burning pain in her throat from the writhing Hemius, refusing to speak.

Naiya frowns and grabs Mara's chin, staring into the girl's eyes. "Something else is wrong," the woman says as she examines Mara's right eye. "She has an illusion on."

Desdemona and Evan glance at one another, startled. "Her Source is completely restrained, though," Evan says.

"A band, then." Desdemona taps her chin. "Maybe on her wrist or ankle?"

Naiya waves her daughter over. The teenager's fingers are rough as she searches, finally wrapping around the clear band on Mara's right ankle. She snaps it off, and Mara's smooth skin ripples to expose the writhing Hemius.

Naiya's eyes widen as Desdemona stumbles backwards. Evan nearly topples over as he moves away, shocked. "How are you still alive?" Naiya demands, shaken.

Mara smiles bitterly. "My Source, which you so rudely cut off. Who knows how long I'll live now."

Naiya glances at the bay window as if someone is speaking to her. Her jaw muscle twitches. "That takes an enormous amount of Source. Evan, you told me the Highlords have taken an interest in her? Is there anything else you witnessed about her specifically?"

Evan searches the carpet as if it held the answers. "Um… her skin had a silvery sheen at the Sonatheia. I just thought it was some type of powder."

"Silver…" Naiya's stormy blue eyes widen and her

hand flies over her mouth. "Are you the Essence?"

Mara stares at her stonily. "I don't know what you're – "

Naiya slaps her. "Do not play with me, child." Mara glares at the black threads in the rug, flexing her jaw. "What color is your Source?"

"Black," Mara reluctantly admits, going on a hunch. Perhaps the 'Essence' is silver.

"Hmph." The paro'ki turns to her son.

Evan fidgets nervously. "I-I saw silver bolts around her once."

Naiya lets out her breath slowly as she faces Mara. "Trademark of the Essence," she murmurs, smirking. "Which means it is black and silver, is it not?"

Mara refuses to speak.

Naiya grabs Mara's face, a strange light flashing through her eyes. "If you will not tell me, I will find out for myself," she hisses.

Mara shrieks as a slimy purplish-red presence shoves its way into her mind. As soon as the tyrannical queen finds Mara's subdued Source, she withdraws.

Mara falls to the floor on her hands and knees, gasping as cold sweat runs down her spine. Naiya steps back, looking contemplative. "It does not seem as though the Sources have merged yet," she murmurs out loud and glances at the curtain again before waving a hand over Mara.

The cuff around her neck falls away in two pieces, thumping onto the thick black carpet.

Mara rubs her neck, immediately trying to drudge up enough Source to create one of her explosive spheres. Evan and Desdemona scramble away from her, their eyes wide.

Mara stares at her hand, watching the silver fuzz weakly disappear. Her black Source barely responds to her touch, sluggish and still heavily restrained. She glares at Paro'ki Naiya.

"I hope that is enough to stop the Hemius," Naiya purrs, a small smile on her face. "We cannot have the Essence dying on us, despite you being a Danarko."

Mara hangs her head, focusing all of her mental power on coaxing her Source into her body to drive back the Hemius. She winces as the Hemius fights back. The silver Source calms it down, but it does not completely stop.

Mara gasps, a bead of sweat rolling down her face. She opens her eyes to find Naiya across the room and sitting in one of the chairs.

"Oh, how beautiful," she coos, clapping as she stares at Mara's faintly glowing skin.

Mara tugs on the cuff around her wrist. "It's not stopping. I don't have enough to control."

The elven woman tuts, waggling her finger at Mara. "I am afraid I cannot remove any more than I have; you are simply too powerful unrestrained. I will make sure a Hemius suppressant drug is put in your food and drink."

"Mother, may I speak?" Evan asks, stepping forward.

"Go ahead." Her voice is ice cold, completely different from when she was talking to Mara.

Evan swallows hard, staring at his mother's feet. "You placed a phobia manifestation spell within her room. However, it has already brought bodily harm to her." Evan waves his hand at Mara. "She has multiple lacerations on her feet."

Naiya raises an eyebrow. "You know that it is not

my spell to undo, son."

"But – "

"Silence." Naiya throws up her hand, her pendant glowing softly. "Desdemona, take her to the sick ward and have the medic check her feet. Under no circumstances is she to escape."

Desdemona grins. "Of course, Mother." She lifts Mara to her feet and hisses in her ear, "I'm not babying you like my brother did."

"Evan," Naiya calls out as Desdemona leads Mara to the door. "Come over here."

Mara glances over her shoulder in time to see the curtain along the far wall tremble slightly. The door closes with a deep boom, blocking Mara's view.

Desdemona holds true to her word. If Mara stumbles or trips, Desdemona lets her fall to the ground. If she doesn't get up fast enough, she drags her across the quartz pathways until she manages to stagger to her feet again. By the time they make it to the destination, Mara is utterly exhausted and trembling.

"Duir'ne Desdemona." A tall, scrawny man in a white robe with blue bands – an intermediate medic – quickly bows to Desdemona. "What can I do to assist you?"

"Her feet were injured in the phobia manifestation cell. Treat them." Desdemona shoves Mara at the man.

He quickly catches her as she falls. "Sorry," Mara automatically rasps out as he helps her to a cot.

"I'm Medic Salanski," he introduces himself, smiling shakily as he tries not to stare at her Hemius-covered skin.

"Mara," she offers warily as he examines her feet.

"Quit getting friendly and finish up." Desdemona picks at her nails with a knife. "I want to return to the training fields before supper."

"Could you lie down, Mara?" Salanski asks, frowning slightly.

Mara slowly stretches out, wincing. She cradles her right arm as Salanski examines her left foot closely. He turns to Desdemona, grim. "I apologize, Your Grace, but I must request your assistance."

"Wh-what's going on?" Mara demands, sitting up and drawing her legs to her chest. She ignores the sharp painful bite in her feet.

Salanski prepares tweezers, a Source globe, and several other utensils and solutions as Desdemona stands next to Mara's cot. "Your Grace, I will need you to restrain her with your Source. Seeing as she acquired these wires from the phobia manifestation room, she will most likely not like what I am about to do."

Desdemona grins at Mara's panicked expression. "Oh, this will be fun," she purrs, shoving Mara flat with her mahogany-colored Source.

Mara squeezes her eyes shut, hoping it does not last long. Salanski carefully removes the snapped wires out of her skin. She whimpers, wishing she could bite her hand in order to distract herself.

Clink. Clink. Clink.

Even Desdemona's face pales as Salanski pulls out the long wires one by one.

Clink. Clink.

Mara's whimpers grow louder as she is slowly driven into a frenzy by the metal sliding underneath her skin coupled with the inability to move. Tears stream down her face as she struggles against the mahogany constraints; they keep her perfectly still, though, as Salanski digs the strands of razor-sharp metal out of her feet.

Clink. Clink. Clink.

CHAPTER 20
THE DARK WARRIOR

The door opens and Evan walks in, his boots crushing the wires still coating the floor. He sighs at the sight of Mara curled up on the cot, staring blankly at the wall across from her. "Mara, you need to eat."

Mara pulls herself into a tighter ball, keeping her concentration on her mental barrier. She has slowly been feeding it her Source throughout the entire night; it is nothing when compared to the one she had built against Darion, but it is better than simply giving up.

Evan glances at the floor covered in wires and drags the table to the edge of her bed. The water sloshes in the cup and the bread nearly falls off of the plate in the movement.

"I do not know why Mother continues doing this," he admits as Mara hesitantly unfolds herself just enough to reach over and grab the water. "Eat. You need your strength. Did you sleep last night?"

"No," she rasps, hungrily chewing on the bread. Her jaw methodically works as she continues the process of reinforcing her mind from any impending attacks.

"What is it, then?" He picks off one of the broken wires that cling to his boot. "Do you not like wires?"

Mara winces at his question but doesn't say anything.

Evan sighs. "At least you finally ate." He stands up. "Come. Mother wants to see you."

Mara shrinks against the wall. "No."

"You must, Mara. My mother will not take no for an answer." Evan grabs her arm, pulling her away from the wall. She is too weak to resist him.

She shakes her head fervently. "I can't – "

"I'll help you. Come on." Evan lifts her off the cot, carrying her like he did up the stairs.

She leans her head against his shoulder, closing her eyes briefly.

"Uh... Mara?" he stammers, his arms briefly tensing.

"Thank you," she breathes, biting her now-healed lip. "You're... nicer than your sister. I'm sorry."

Evan pauses at the entrance to her cell. He takes a deep breath and expels it. "I wish it didn't have to be this way," he murmurs as he sets her down.

She limps next to him, her feet still sore and her Hemius causing her body to ache. He takes her arm and guides her through the corridors.

This time, Mara glances around in wonder, noticing the nuances in the material used throughout the castle; nearly everything is made out of some form of semiprecious stone. "Where... are we?"

"Alamirana Castle," Evan replies.

"It's beautiful," she admits. They start up the marble steps to the throne room.

When they enter the circular room, Mara glances at the curtain that had shifted right before she had left. It doesn't stir, although she intuitively knows someone had been standing there yesterday.

Queen Naiya sits in one of the two central chairs, staring into a crystal on her lap. Several servants in the red and black livery prepare a table with a variety of materials and bowls, including a strangely shimmering knife. Mara shivers.

"Mother, I brought her," Evan announces, stopping only a few paces into the throne room.

Naiya looks up, slightly dazed. This time, her amulet looks like a blue and red dragon's breath fire opal. "Ah, thank you, Evan. You may release her." Her voice is softer today, and her eyes seem gentler.

Evan lets Mara go and stands off to the side. Naiya rises and glides towards Mara, her movements smoother than they were yesterday.

Naiya gives her a strange sad smile. She strokes Mara's face. "I am terribly sorry for this," she whispers, looking sincere. "But I must know. How much do you remember?"

Mara's body jerks. She stares at the queen, her eyes wide.

Naiya continues to smile solemnly. "We have spies in Quasala, dear Mara. I know you have begun the recollection phase."

Mara gulps. She looks anywhere but at Naiya. "Why do you even need to know?"

"The Dark Warrior can only enter the Essence's vessel when she is near or in her recollection phase. Tell me, how far are you?"

She remembers the slimy sensation of the paro'ki picking through her mind. *I guess she didn't see that, then,* she thinks as she swallows hard. "People say I'm the Essence, but I think they're wrong," she admits truthfully. "I don't know anything other than my own life."

Naiya's face falls. Mara refrains from showing her hopeful look. "It is not too early, then."

Mara blinks. Shouldn't the queen be happy?

Naiya's voice is quiet as she wanders back to the

throne. "Evan, return her to the cell and find Desdemona; we will perform the ritual this afternoon."

Evan bows and leads Mara through the castle once again. This time, they pass through a long hallway. Mara spots a large door that looks suspiciously like the entrance to the castle.

"Is that the way in?" Mara asks.

Evan glances at it and then up at the long staircase now behind them. "Yes. The ancients seemed to not think it was a bad idea to place the throne room in such close proximity to it."

"Doesn't seem too smart," Mara agrees, contemplating using her stored Source to break free and make a run for it.

Evan's hand tightens on her arm as if sensing her intentions. "Don't even consider it," he warns quietly. "If Mother found that you tried to escape, I can assure you that all of this will go much more painfully for you."

When they reach her cell, Mara allows Evan to lift her into his arms. She squeezes her eyes shut, refusing to look at the floor. He sets her down on the cot and releases her.

Slowly, Mara opens her eyes. Startled at Evan's close proximity, she backs up, but her head thumps against the quartz-stone wall.

Evan's smile wavers slightly. "No need to hurt yourself," he attempts to joke, his voice cracking.

Mara stares at him. "Why are you helping me so much?"

Evan shrugs, staring at the floor. "I know what happens to the Dark Warrior's vessels." He bites his lip. "I wish it didn't have to be you."

Mara wraps her arms around her legs, staring at her now torn dress. "I just wish I had been wearing something a bit better than this."

Evan pats Mara's head. She stares at him, startled at the show of affection. "If... if anyone can escape, you can," he whispers.

He leaves before Mara can ask him what he means by that.

Several hours pass by as she focuses on the mental shield she has been working on, trying her best to reinforce it. It isn't even as strong as the one Aliyah had made before the Dark Warrior had crushed her Source. She needs to be prepared for anything, though.

The door bangs open and Desdemona stomps in. Mara's eyes widen, her mental barrier nearly shattered by the shock. "Come on, girly," Desdemona snaps, yanking Mara off the cot.

Mara's feet slap against the floor. The thin wires slice into her soles, digging new marks into the tender skin. She sucks her breath in, pain searing through the bottom of her feet.

She fights against Desdemona, but she is weak from not eating or resting properly. Her feet leave a bloody trail throughout the castle.

Desdemona drags Mara all the way to the throne room, ignoring Mara's pleas to slow down. She throws Mara onto the carpet a few feet away from the long table in front of the throne.

Mara wipes at her face, trying her hardest to ignore the sharp pain in her feet from the thin wires. Desdemona snickers off to the side; Evan is nowhere to be seen.

Paro'ki Naiya tinkers with different items on the

table. Her movements are no longer fluid like earlier. She turns around and stares at Mara, the amulet at her neck glowing a soft red with no trace of blue at all within its depths.

Naiya reaches forward and strokes Mara's face. Mara flinches away, and the woman pouts, acting almost like a different person now. "You are so young. I dislike doing this so early."

Mara glares at the queen. "Why are you doing this?"

"My precious warrior needs a body to move in," she says as she returns to her vials. "Desdemona, guard the doors with your brother."

"But you agreed I could help you, Mother!" Desdemona whines, pouting.

Naiya whirls on Desdemona, a sickly purplish-red aura emanating from her. The amulet glows a blood red color. "*I* do not want your assistance," she insists more forcefully.

Desdemona bows her head, not looking her mother in the eyes. "I understand." She shuts the doors behind her.

Naiya returns to her tinctures as Mara glances around, searching for a way out. However, the only exit is the door she entered through – and she is pretty sure Desdemona would not allow her to just stroll right by and leave.

Naiya's hushed voice draws her attention to the table. Four large bowls encircle a huge basin in the middle, containing sand, salt, water, and a viscous, pulsing red liquid that Mara doesn't want to think too hard on.

Naiya murmurs in a strange dialect; Mara almost does not recognize the Xharos words. The woman slowly pours the salt and water together and the consistency begins to smoke.

Naiya lifts the bowl full of red liquid next, pulling out a human heart that pulses within her hands. Mara stares in horror as the queen pours the blood into the basin before carefully placing the heart on top.

The mixture slowly coalesces, rising from the basin to meet her hand. She pats the nub affectionately, smiling.

Mara's hand covers her mouth as she tries not to make a sound at the sight of the rising form in the basin. *It looks like Hemius,* she realizes in horror, all of her hard work on her mental barrier nearly broken from that single thought.

She struggles to yank her Source free, forcing it to meld with her defensive mental wall. She needs to be ready before that creature touches her. The mental spherical wall slowly grows a little brighter, almost to the same level as Aliyah's. It needs to be much stronger. Tears form in Mara's eyes as she tries to keep calm while watching the summoning ritual; becoming upset only draws out the reinforcement process on her barrier. She needs to stay focused.

A huge, elongated form slowly rises from the basin. Naiya picks up the bowl of sand as the form grows taller and taller, extending limbs and developing curves.

Mara senses the dark energy radiating off of the form. Aliyah's life tells her everything; this creature is the embodiment of hatred itself. Mara stares at it, horror wrapping around her core like an icy coat.

Naiya tosses the sand over the creature's head. It rolls down, forming a layer similar to skin and sinking into the being. It morphs into a rough interpretation of a body, pale and featureless.

Mara frantically tosses her Source against her mental walls, coating them in as much power as she could. She pulls all of her Source away from her skin and tolerates the Hemius aching painfully as she forces the reserves to meld with her mental barrier.

She has to be ready. If she isn't, this creature will end her in the worst way imaginable.

"Come, warrior," Naiya beckons, stepping away from the basin. "Merge with the Essence's vessel."

"*Where is she?*" The voice speaks to the mind, rocking through Mara's core and nearly shattering her defenses. It must be blind.

Mara closes her eyes, stabilizing her hard work and trying to focus completely on it.

Naiya bows to the featureless form that has a vague resemblance to a girl. "She is in front of you, Da'ruha." Mara vaguely remembers the Xharos title for Dark Warrior.

The creature floats towards Mara, setting down in front of her. It squats, and she has the odd sensation the faceless monster is staring at her.

Creepier than the monster she had met in Quasala, this creature bears almost no resemblance to the Hemius girl in her dreams. *Are those two things really the same?* she wonders.

"*You are different,*" it comments, and Mara picks up on the faint inflections. Is it... male? "*Are you the Essence?*"

Mara, a crazy idea crossing her mind, stalls for time to build her defenses. "I'm not quite sure. Who are you?"

The form turns its head to the side. Something moves under the surface of the featureless face and indentations form where the eyes should be. Mara watches in horrified fascination as the spots darken and two swirling black, red, and purple eye-like things form on the creature's face. *"I am the one who killed Eliara nearly six thousand years ago."*

Mara continues to feed as much Source as she can into her mental wall despite her fear of the creature. "What are you?"

"I am all that is left of me," it responds. This time, it sounds more feminine. *"I am the mind, soul, and Source of Rinali Alamir. My body was destroyed thousands of years ago."*

Mara stares at the form, barely maintaining her Source supply to her mental barriers. "You're... a ghost?"

"That is one way to perceive me," the Dark Warrior admits, leaning forward on its odd representation of arms and approaching Mara. The inflection changes again. *"I need a body; this one never lasts long. Will you help me?"*

Mara eases backwards, weak from lack of sleep, her injuries, and the awakening Hemius. "Why should I help you? You'll only cast me out. I'd rather die than experience that agony."

"Then you understand how I feel. I exist like that for centuries on end. I suffer the agony of having my very being ripped into shreds and unable to completely bring it together even in my prison. The only time I feel whole is when I am inside a real body."

Mara stares at the creature, pity slowly creeping into her. She actually understands its pain of constantly drifting and feeling as if the whole universe is trying to destroy her. Every second feels like an eternity. "It's the worst kind of torture," she whispers out loud.

"*Please; end my suffering.*" This voice sounds more feminine. The creature shakes its head to the side as if dispelling something and reaches for Mara's face.

Mara struggles to back away, but something solid stops her. Startled, she turns her head and finds the wall of the room. She stares at the advancing hand, doubt and fear creeping into her mind.

Can she really stop such a creature?

In a final act of desperation, she closes her eyes and focuses all of her concentration on her Source, building up her wall's defenses as fast as she possibly can within the few seconds remaining.

She feels the cool touch on her cheek, like wet sand on a beach. It leaves a bloody streak on her face.

The attack begins.

A brutal blow lands on the weakest part of Mara's mental sphere, and an obvious crack forms. Mara quickly mends it, but the Da'ruha attacks other weak spots, keeping Mara on the defensive.

She frantically pulls from her sluggish Source and reinforces her wall, desperate and rushing. The Dark Warrior presses down harder.

Mara's defenses slowly crack.

Tendrils of the Dark Warrior's will slip through and barrage Mara's mind. Mara screams in defiance and pain.

The Source inhibitor on her left wrist flies off, striking the far wall with a loud clang.

Power surges through Mara, finally giving her enough Source to truly fight back. She grabs the Da'ruha's hand against her face and struggles with the creature's grip. Her other hand wraps around its neck.

Her fingers squeeze tightly even though she knows

it won't faze it at all. She shoves back on the mental weight, slowly gaining ground.

The vague representation of eyes widens and the face splits apart in a breathy shriek. Sand sprays across Mara's face. She stares into the stringy, bloody mouth, the various movies of banshees and vengeful ghosts with stretched faces and dangling skin flitting through her mind.

"*No! No! No!*" it wails. Mara winces at the shrieks inside her mind. "*Impossible! Stop it! Stooop iiiit!*"

"Have a taste of your own medicine," Mara growls, shoving the mental force out of her mind and pushing into *its* mind.

Darkness swirls around her, consuming the world in a haze. Everything, right down to Naiya's blue eyes, are tinged red.

Mara looks at the Dark Warrior and sees a young girl of about sixteen with her face contorted in rage and agony. Her reddish-purple eyes spark as her dark hair is thrown backwards from the force of Mara's hand shoving against her neck.

It is the same girl from her dreams.

"*Go ahead and do it,*" the girl whispers telepathically, a sick grin on her face. "*If you dare.*"

Mara enters the girl's mind.

Dark, corrupted images float around Mara. She fights to ignore them, but some of them still catch her eye. A family stabbed to death; a young girl tortured for weeks on end; a whole village slaughtered mercilessly... Mara turns from the images, nauseous. She finds an odd chaotic ball of color.

Red, pulsing veins suffocate an ocean blue ball, squeezing and subduing the water-like substance. Mara remembers Shaniel's words when he had looked into her mind; a possession looks like two Sources in the same mind. Was this what he had meant?

"What will you do now, Essence?" the Dark Warrior asks, mocking her – though Mara hears a faint trace of fear in it. The red veins whip around the blue sphere tauntingly.

Mara gathers her Source – still difficult because of the cuffs. She fights against it, forcing her Source to come free. *Move*, she orders, dragging it free with all of the force she could muster. The cuff on her right ankle flies off and bangs against the stone wall.

Her sparking Source gathers around her like a cloak. She aims it at the core.

A single blue wave escapes the roiling red veins and floats feebly towards Mara's consciousness. Reflexively, Mara mentally reaches out and catches it.

"Do it..." Mara hears a clear yet weak female voice, young and weary. *"End me. I do not want you to hurt anymore because of me, Dan'te."*

"Who are you?" Mara asks, hesitating at the familiar nickname.

The red veins pulse rapidly and constrict around the blue core. *"Shut up, shut up, shut up! You should not speak!"*

Another blue tendril narrowly escapes the throws of the red veins and collapses against Mara's mental presence. *"Destroy me,"* it begs, sounding desperate. *"Before I destroy you. Free me..."*

Mara hesitates. Why would this presence actually ask for such a horrible fate?

"No, no, no! Do not kill us!" the Dark Warrior screams, shoving against Mara's mental mind and trying to force her out. *"Get out! Get out! Quit talking!"*

"End it. Please," the strange female voice begs,

desperate.

Silver tears slide down Mara's face. "*I'm sorry,*" she apologizes to the blue presence. "*I... I can't do it.*"

The cuff on her right wrists snaps and her power rushes out like a snowstorm. A silver lance pierces the center of the blue Source.

Mara sucks in her breath. She doesn't have any recollection of forming it, yet there it is, stabbing into the mental heart of the sorrowful presence.

She stays inside the mind of the Dark Warrior, watching the Source fracture into a billion pieces before shooting out of the mind at lightning speed.

"*Thank you...*" the female voice whispers as the Source vanishes to all the corners of the world – no, the universe.

Mara opens her eyes to find her hand within the chest of the creature. Horrified, she stares into its face.

It releases an inhuman shriek, clawing at her madly as its form oozes to the ground as if losing the ability to hold itself together. Sand and blood spew from its gaping maw to coat her in a gruesome paste. "*Die! Die! Die!*" it screeches, its aura now a pure blood-red. It rips her dress with long claws, tearing into her skin.

It's not dead.

The shreds of Mara's control snaps.

She screams in terror, throwing raw Source into the creature with her one free hand until it blows up. Sand and blood shower over her, covering her in a gory muck.

Mara's entire body trembles violently. Her back thumps against the wall as she stares forward, her eyes tearing up. *Is it... gone?* she wonders, cautiously looking around.

Naiya tumbles out of her chair, clutching her head with one hand and clawing at the amulet with the other. She screams in agony, writhing in pain as her amulet glows a bright blood-red. It sears into her skin, burning her. Mara stares at it, her eyes widening.

Something shifts in Mara's hand. Horrified, she looks down at the bloody lump in her palm.

Thu-thump. Thu-thump.

Bile rises in her throat. The heart tumbles from her fingers.

Thu-thump. Thu-thump.

Mara stares at the heart, petrified. Its thumps slow down until it moves no more.

"*No!*" the same voice of the monster screams. "*Noooo! All of my hard work – gone! Wasted!*"

Pure terror pierces through Mara's heart. She stares at the glowing amulet around Naiya's throat, realizing the creature is using the woman as an anchoring point to remain here. A small sound escapes Mara's lips, sounding like a shriek cut off by a sob.

Mara struggles through the sand and blood surrounding her, tripping and falling to her hands and knees in the sticky muck. She crawls out of the goo, scrambling to the door.

Naiya's agonized screams stop as if someone had pressed a mute button.

Trembling, Mara slowly glances over her shoulder to see a blood red aura oozing out of the amulet and wrapping around the now unconscious paro'ki. It slowly sets her on her feet.

"*You will pay...*" the creature's voice whispers through Naiya body, deadly and ominous.

Mara staggers to her feet and lurches for the door. She shoves on the heavy stone, but it doesn't budge.

She glances at the floating body of Queen Naiya drawing closer to her. The bloody Source manipulates her arm, raising it. A red, dripping sphere forms at the fingertip.

Mara blasts the door with raw power. It flings outwards, banging against the walls and narrowly missing Desdemona and Evan standing just outside it. Their eyes widen at her filthy blood and sand-coated appearance.

Mara dives to the floor between the two of them, feeling the deadly ball of Source skim over her back. It leaves a fiery hot trail of pain in its wake as it barrels over her and straight for Desdemona.

Desdemona instinctively throws up a multilayered shield. The Source sphere explodes against the shield, but the impact throws the tall girl against the wall and knocks her out.

Mara coughs as she struggles to her hands and knees. Her back burns as if the Hemius had spread over it.

Evan grabs her arm, pulling her to her feet. He stares at his mother in contained horror and hatred as if he had seen this before. "Go!" he urges.

"I – can't," Mara chokes, blood dripping out of the corner of her mouth. She feels the Hemius calming under her Source, but it had already damaged her lungs, causing internal bleeding. Despite having control over her Source again, she does not know how to heal herself.

Evan glances between the floating monster controlling Naiya and the fatally injured Mara. "Carc'ra..."

"Run," Mara forces out, pushing weakly on his shoulder as the monster raises Naiya's hand again.

Another blood-red sphere forms at her fingertips.

Evan scoops Mara into his arms and takes off down the staircase. "You kept it out of your mind, didn't you?" he asks rhetorically as he sprints down the stairs and weaves through the side tunnels of the castle.

Mara wheezes against his chest, clutching his shirt. She stares at her bloodstained hand, and her eyes tear up. "I…"

Evan glances down at her. "Hang on, Mara."

Mara's vision blurs. *I'm dying…* she thinks. An image of her friends surrounding her around a huge tactical table flashes through her mind. She remembers the feeling of the armor on her skin and the determined looks on multiple faces as she swore to them she would not give in to the enemy during the battle. Mara registers the memory as her own, although she cannot remember where she had been for it. *I'm sorry, everyone… I couldn't keep my promise.*

She slips in and out of consciousness as Evan escapes the castle through the servants' quarters, hiding in the alleyways of the city. Gasping, he sinks to his knees, gently cradling Mara against him. He peers at her back in the dim light, gritting his teeth as he sees the severe burns and the writhing Hemius stretching to cover nearly all of her back.

Closing his eyes, he holds his hands over Mara. A deep blue-purple wave cascades over her body. Her breathing slowly regulates as the burns on her back heal and the slashes on her stomach close. He takes off his outer tunic and carefully drapes it over her, preserving her modesty. Cradling her in his arms, he staggers to his feet.

"Hold it right there, li'l boy."

Evan slowly turns around to face a woman in her twenties with black, wavy hair and glowing silver eyes. Distinct, elongated ears point to the sky as she raises a perfectly sculpted eyebrow at him. Her deeply tanned skin blends with her dark, grimy clothes. Behind her, two elves, one being Aeserast in his disguised form as Ace Narweun, gasp when they see Mara.

"Heh." Evan collapses to his knees, relief seeping into his veins. "Thank the Highlords. You're safe now, Mara."

< * >

All Mara can see is the bloody sand-monster clawing at her, trying to rip her to shreds after she had destroyed the blue core. Its bloody tendrils sink into her, piercing her body in vengeance. She jolts upright, screaming.

Two sets of strong arms catch her flailing limbs while a hand covers her mouth to muffle her screams. She fights blindly against them, hysterical.

"Mara, stop it! Your Source will call the paro'ki here!" Aeserast's mental voice breaks through as he enters her mind.

Mara panics, feeling his presence as a threat. She erects a barrier and throws him out of her mind. The three sets of arms are suddenly gone, and Mara curls into a tight ball, sobbing into her legs. "No, no, no, no, no..." she repeats over and over. She rocks back and forth, unable to block out the shrieking monster's screams. She does not notice the others lying in heaps several yards away from her.

A black-haired elf blinks his brown eyes several times, his vision blurry and head throbbing from the impact with the alleyway wall. "Carc'ra..." he curses, rolling onto his side and coughing. "Is everyone all right?"

Ace runs his hand through his blonde hair, taking deep breaths as he checks his head for lumps. "I seem to be."

Evan groans, lying flat on his back down the alleyway. He had been lucky not to hit a wall; however, being sent airborne and then landing on the hard stone pathway is not a much better alternative. "I... I think so."

"Wha' the bloody Mavi was that?" a thick Xharos-accented woman exclaims, rubbing her head gingerly. She bares her teeth at Mara, her pointed elf ears twitching in irritation. "Tryin' to help ya, an' ya go an' throw us all over tha place!"

"I don't think she recognized us, Erimentha," the black haired elf groans as he crawls towards Mara. He stops about a foot away. "Mara, can you hear me?"

"Stop... just stop..." Mara's hands are covering her ears. She rocks back and forth, oblivious to her surroundings. Evan's tunic covers most of her ripped dress, although the hem is absolutely ruined from the sand, dirt, and blood.

The elf frowns, listening to her ramblings. "Mara, what happened?"

"Stop screaming... just stop..."

Evan creeps forward and hears her muttered words. His jaw clenches, grim. "It must be what happened before we escaped."

They stare at him. "What happened?" Ace asks.

Evan closes his eyes, steeling himself. "Mother summoned the Dark Warrior."

Their heads whip towards the muttering Mara. "Then..." Ace starts.

"She's fightin' tha Da'ruha," Erimentha breathes.

Evan quickly shakes his head. "No, it hadn't possessed her. I-I think she blew apart its temporary body, forcing it to possess my mother. We escaped before it could catch us."

The black-haired man stares at Evan. "Blew it apart? How?"

"I don't know, but…" The duir'ne points at the blood and sand still coating Mara like a second skin. "Those look like the ingredients Mother was preparing before the ritual."

Suddenly, Mara goes quiet. They all hold their breath and watch her, wondering if she truly is not possessed.

Mara had heard something beyond the screams, something familiar and comforting. She focuses on it, pushing past the screaming. Nothing; whatever she had heard had stopped. She whimpers, the creature's screaming echoing in her head again.

"Mara?"

Mara's eyes snap open at the familiar voice. She turns to the side and stares into the elf's brown eyes that widen at her terrified expression. "You're safe," he quickly reassures her.

Mara reaches out with a trembling hand. *Shaniel,* she knows intuitively, *it has to be him.* He takes it gently, surprised as she collapses against him and sobs. "It… it never died. It just kept moving. Kept shrieking…"

"Shh," he comforts, stroking her hair. "You're all right, now. We'll protect you."

"We need to get movin'," Erimentha warns in a low voice, handing the disguised Shaniel a silver ring with a labradorite stone in the middle. "Have her wear this, Neil; it will mask her Source."

Neil nods as Erimentha stands up and grabs their bags. "Mara, you need to wear this," he murmurs, pushing her back some so she can see the ring. "It will hide your Source from Naiya like how the amulet did."

Mara takes the ring with shaky fingers, fumbling to put it on. Ace reaches forward and steadies her hand, slipping the ring onto her left pointer finger. He smiles shakily at her. "Better?"

Her eyes tear up. "Thank you."

He pats her hand, his smile a little stronger.

Mara nods as she pushes away from Neil. As she pulls back, he gently grabs her arms and inspects her chafed wrists. "What happened?" he asks softly.

"Questions later!" Erimentha hisses, knocking Neil over the head. "We need'te *move!*"

"I'm going to pick you up," Neil warns, lifting Mara into his arms. Mara clutches his shirt tightly, sucking in her breath as her entire body aches. He runs with the others through the city, dodging patrols and escaping into alleyways. Finally, after what feels like a long time, they slow down and stop at an abandoned, half-destroyed building.

"Li'l duir'ne," Erimentha barks, and Evan straightens. "Try any weird moves with her, an' I'll cut you into ribbons. Got it?"

"Make that three of us," Ace mutters, openly glaring at Evan.

"Yes," Evan squeaks. Erimentha walks out, mumbling about a fire stone and hot water.

Neil sets Mara against the wall, kneeling in front of her. "How's the Hemius?" he whispers, concerned.

Mara smiles shakily. "Better." She takes a slow,

deep breath that calms her nerves. "Evan saved my life."

Ace raises an eyebrow. "I will admit, it was a shock seeing him healing you. We didn't even know he knew any medical knowledge."

Evan sulks over and slumps next to Mara. "You're Ace Narweun, right? The Quasalan spy and ambassador?" he asks the disguised Dream'Lord.

Ace slowly nods, wary. "I apologize if I have acted improperly, Your – "

"Don't worry about it," Evan cuts him off, not noticing Ace's shocked expression as he leans towards Mara. "How are you feeling? I tried the best I could, but I don't really know much…"

Mara smiles at him. "I feel much better. Where did you learn how to do that?"

Evan's cheeks turn pink. "I would watch Salanski heal the soldiers Des beat in matches. I would try to emulate what the medic did anytime my brother or I got injured. After a while, I started picking up on it."

Mara tilts her head to the side. "Amazing. You're self-taught, then?"

Evan nods. "My family knows my Source is weak. My brother, Jayden, has even less; he can do a few things, but nothing like Desdemona. It's because our mother did not remain faithful to our father. Mother protects my brother and I from his wrath." His lips quirk up as if he had said something ironic.

CHAPTER 21
SKY AND GROUND

Erimentha stomps into the crumbling room, her smooth and angled elven face contorted in irritation. Mara wonders what had happened for her to act so... inelegant. Up until now, Mara had never met an elf who acts anything but graceful and refined.

"Got ye some food," she exclaims, throwing a bag on the floor. "Along with medical supplies. Never ask me to do that again," she directs at Neil as she sits cross-legged in the middle of the room. She throws a stone onto the ground and holds her hand over it.

A silver lightning bolt shoots from her hand, activating the firestone.

Mara jolts upright, staring at Erimentha with wide eyes. "Who are you?" Mara demands, shaken at how much the elf's Source resembles hers.

Erimentha raises an eyebrow. "Ye don't know who I am?" She turns to Neil and Ace. "She doesn't know who I am?"

Ace sighs. "I apologize, Erimentha. Mara is still learning of our realms and customs."

Erimentha snorts, glaring at Mara in boredom. "Why do you ask?"

"My Source... it's the same." Mara holds out her hand. Source collects in the shape of an orb, and she is not surprised when the black doesn't move; the Source inhibitor on her left ankle still mostly suppresses it. However, the silver miniature lightning bolts dance across her hand before coalescing into a controlled spherical lightning storm.

Erimentha stares at it, her expression slowly turning into one of stunned shock. "I've only met one other with that same Source... the Essence."

Mara frowns. "Then what about you?"

Erimentha shakes her head. "Mine is not the same as the Essence's," she answers cryptically.

"Why is there only silver?" Neil asks, examining the spherical storm.

Mara gently touches the Source inhibitor on her ankle. "I... I think it's this."

Ace stares at the metal cuff. "That's..."

"A Source inhibitor," Evan says quietly. "Mother had put five on her, but had to take off one of them so Mara could regulate the Hemius."

"Five?" Ace squeaks.

Mara shakes her head. "It didn't work, though."

They stare at her.

"I didn't have enough Source to stop the Hemius's movement completely." Mara touches her temple gently. "Instead, I... I formed a wall in my mind shortly after she had taken off the cuff. I spent all night reinforcing it with Source. If it wasn't for that, the Dark Warrior would have possessed me." She trembles, rubbing her arms.

"That's why you didn't sleep," Evan breathes, realization dawning on his face. He bites his lip. "I apologize I couldn't help you sooner."

Erimentha picks through the bag she had brought in and plops in front of Mara. "Yer feet are injured, right? Let me see them."

Mara's breath hitches. "No," she gasps, holding her knees tightly.

Evan touches Mara's shoulder lightly. "What if I

try to channel the pain?"

Mara stares at him with wide eyes. "How is that possible?"

Ace glances at Mara's feet. "It's a method often used with patients who can't tolerate pain. A trained mind weaver interrupts the signals being sent to the brain and, instead, cause it to register into their own body." He stares at the prince. "How did you learn that?"

Evan smirks. "Salanski taught it to me after my brother fell from a tree and dislocated his arm. He can't stand pain, so Salanski had me channel it. He and my brother are the only two who know I have medical knowledge."

"It's worth a shot," Neil admits, still wary. "Do you think that will help?"

"It isn't the pain," she breathes, barely audible. She squeezes her eyes shut, finally admitting her fear. "It's... the sensation."

Evan grits his teeth. "I have an idea. What if I channeled *all* of the sensation from her foot?"

Erimentha and Neil stare at him. "But that would mean..." Neil murmurs.

Mara stares at her bloody toes, still able to feel the wires in her feet. "What do you have to do?"

"Well..." Evan chews on his bottom lip. "The most effective way is from inside your mind."

Mara's blood turns cold. She pales significantly, and her stomach churns. Ace grabs her hand. "If you would prefer, I can do it."

"Yeah." Swallowing down bile, she takes a deep breath and smiles shakily at Ace. "I... I think I can tolerate someone being in my mind better than those things in my feet," she tries to joke, although she can

404

tell everyone saw through her attempt.

"Think about what you're saying," Neil hisses, grabbing her arm. "I know Ace is good, but even he could mess up and accidentally change – "

"You weren't there."

Her quiet voice shuts him up. He leans back, stunned.

Ace pats Mara's arm before placing his fingers on her temples. "Are you ready?"

Mara nods. "Let's get this over with."

She fights to keep calm as her mind becomes crowded. Mara sucks in huge gulps of air as Ace leans closer, nearly touching his forehead against hers. She senses his worry at her sudden spike of panic, and he soothes her with his odd ability.

"*I have to access your Source,*" he says directly into her mind.

Mara steadies her breath, fighting her urge to shove him out of her mind as he draws closer and closer to the core of her power. He pauses, though, as fear spikes through her again. "*Why can't I see what you are afraid of?*"

Mara reigns in her emotions yet again, trying not to panic over his presence in her mind. "*You don't want to know.*"

His gentle presence finally makes it to her Source's core. The black tendrils in the middle are barely moving, the silver bolts nudging at it as if trying to wake it up. Occasionally, whenever a spike of fear shoots through Mara, it leaps up and crackles soundlessly in defense.

Ace frowns, examining it. "*I knew from Shaniel's reports that you have an unblended Source, but I was not expecting this... Mara, do you feel any different?*"

"*Not... particularly,*" she admits as his lavender presence approaches the ball. The silver sparks rear up in defense. "*I can't really use the black one, but the silver one is nearly unfazed.*"

"*Fascinating.*" He withdraws from her mind, turning to the others as she quietly recovers from the reeling aftereffects of him entering her mind. "It's possible," he says. "I'll just have to be careful. Part of her Source is still under the effects of the restraint; it's holding it in just enough so she isn't giving away our location. I just have to make sure not to get sucked under the effects."

Neil and Erimentha nod as Evan stares at Ace. "You're not a servant, are you?"

Ace rubs the back of his neck, laughing. "Ah, no, I am not. Both Neil and I are special guards sent with the group. When it comes to Mara, we already know about her Source."

Evan frowns. "What's wrong with her Source?"

"I have two," Mara says quietly. Neil and Ace glance at her and she shrugs. "It's not really a secret, is it?"

"Two..." Evan repeats, a flicker of fear flashing over his face. "Like... a possession?"

Ace and Neil shake their heads. "Not exactly," Neil quickly explains. "They are both hers."

Ace turns back to Mara, placing his fingers back on her temples. She forces a smile onto her face. "Let's get this over with," she whispers, and he nods, entering her mind slowly. Again, he notices how she flinches and struggles not to throw him out.

"*Mara, please tell me what happened,*" Ace begs, his growing concern seeping into her.

Cautiously, Mara opens herself up to him a little

more. "*Naiya... forced her way into my mind. And then... the Dark Warrior did the same.*" She shows him the brief memory of Naiya's encounter, but not the one of the creature.

His focus nearly slips at her mental words and the brief memory, pausing in front of her Source. "*I apologize. We can stop —* "

"*No.*" She takes a deep breath, steeling herself for whatever it is he will have to do. "*What do you need me to do?*"

"*Allow me access to your Source,*" he says simply. "*Going through the Source core is the fastest way to gain access to the nervous system since it connects to everything. However, it is very intrusive on your privacy; I can potentially see what is in your mind.*"

"*What about you?*"

"*I know how to block my memories and thoughts from seeping into others. I will try to separate the two of us, but because you do not know how to control your mind to the same extent as a mind weaver, a bit of memory-sharing will be unavoidable.*"

The bolts around the core intensify briefly, rearing up and sparking defensively. Mara takes a deep breath, calming herself. The lightning bolts settle down, hovering over the core's surface like lingering electricity. "*Do it.*"

The Dream'lord's lavender Source washes over the sparking silver bolts. Mara tries her best to reign in her anxiety and fear, but she senses his pain as a few bolts strike him in defense. Soon, her entire Source is wrapped in the soothing cool-colored energy, entwining itself with the bolts and seeping into the black tendrils.

Mara has the odd sensation of feeling trapped yet

expanding at the same time. She can tell when Ace experiences her encounter with Da'ruha, as well as the growing awe as he accidentally runs across the disjointed fragments of other lives.

"So this is what the Essence looks like..." she catches his thought, and feels his embarrassment as it reverberates back to him. *"I apologize. I shouldn't – "*

"What now?" Mara asks, cutting him off. She has the odd sensation of being herself but separate at the same time.

"I am going to separate your mind from your nervous system. It will feel uncomfortable, but it shouldn't hurt," he informs her. *"You may get reverberations through me, though, so prepare yourself."*

Suddenly, Mara cannot feel her body; all of her aches disappear, and she doesn't even sense her own weight. She vaguely senses Ace's struggle to maintain both of the bodies. *"Are you okay?"* she asks.

"Yes."

Mara feels as though she is observing herself through a glass wall: unable to affect anything around her. She does get 'reverberations,' but they are odd. Since she no longer had sensation of her own body, they feel foreign and strange.

"She's ready," Ace says aloud, and from the others' perspective, his forehead is touching hers and both of their eyes are closed.

"I did not realize your phobia was this bad," Ace murmurs directly to her as Erimentha begins digging out the thin wires. He blocks out the pain, dealing with two minds and bodies at the same time.

"It's a stupid fear," Mara tries to brush off. *"I've tried to get rid of it. I can look at thin objects; I just still can't stand anything sliding underneath my skin like that. Thank goodness*

I haven't needed IVs in my life."

She hears his odd mental chuckle, and then senses his curiosity as another memory floats by him. *"Who is… Thanos?"*

Embarrassed, Mara explains, *"He's… been training me in the evenings these past two months. I didn't want to tell anyone because they would just say I'm overworking myself."*

His disapproval and amusement washes through her. *"You are right. You are overworking yourself. When we return, I want to meet this Thanos person; we need to make sure he is not trying to use you."*

Indignant, she snaps, *"He has been nothing but helpful. I do not understand what you are concerned about."*

"I'm sorry. I'm just worried – " His attention snaps towards her Source, examining it intently. *"They need to hurry. Our minds are melding too fast."*

Mara senses his concern; in his dialect, he would have said 'I apologize,' while she would not have been so formal with her speech. *"I didn't know it was possible for minds to meld together."*

"I believe it is because of the Essence's influence; after all, it is meant to merge with another." He pauses as another of Mara's thoughts flickers across his consciousness. *"You suspect the silver Source is the Essence?"*

"You tell me," she grumbles. She watches the silver bolts flow separately through the purple ocean, not merging with it at all. *"I guess it is; I mean, it's not even touching your Source. Plus, it acts on its own most of the time."*

"And yet I have full access to you… maybe it's dormant." She has the odd sensation of looking through her eyes but unable to control her gaze. *"They are done. Thank goodness."*

Ace slowly withdraws his presence, but suddenly, the silver sparks rear up and encase him, blocking his path out of Mara's mind. Still linked with him, she senses his panic.

"*No! Stop it!*" she orders the sparking sphere that now contains him, restraining him inside Mara's mind. She feels Ace's fear become her own. "*Let him go!*"

"*Protect her,*" another voice orders him. Mara recognizes the fragmented speech from when she had walked through the silver door in her dream nearly three months ago. "*Do not allow – Da'ruha – control over – Mara. All Highlords – should – protect her.*"

Suddenly, the sparking silver sphere shoves the Dream'Lord out of Mara's mind. He falls onto his back and stares at the crumbling ceiling, silver sparks flitting over his body as he gasps. A single phrase trails through his mind, fragmented yet authoritative. "*Tell no one – of what – you experienced. Especially – Timian. It is not time – for his – involvement.*"

"Mara?" Neil asks as Erimentha leans over Ace.

Mara rubs her head. "Highlords, that was odd..."

Ace covers his eyes. "I am not doing that again for you."

Erimentha and Neil glance between them, alarmed. "Which of you is Mara?" Neil asks.

"I am," Mara says tiredly, leaning against the wall. "He said we were merging. I'm tired..."

She dozes against the wall as Ace sits up, looking exhausted. "We should return to the Academy before Naiya or Desdemona finds us."

Evan rubs his chin. "I can distract them to give you time to escape through the northwestern gate." At their stunned looks, he snaps irritably, "If you think I'm on their side, you're wrong. I'm dead weight to them; I'm surprised they haven't kicked me out before now."

"Thank you," Ace whispers. "I saw what you did for her. If you think you can give us a few extra minutes – "

Neil peers out the broken window, his jaw set. "We need to go now." He turns to Evan. "Would you object to us tying you up?"

Evan stares at Neil, realization sparking in his eyes. "Good idea. Go ahead."

Neil nods, scrounging in his bag and pulling out a thick cord. "Pardon me, then, Your Grace."

The disguised Common'Lord ties up Evan and they leave him in the building. As they escape through a back door, they hear when the guards find Evan and interrogate him.

Mara stirs in Ace's arms. She stares groggily up at his tense face and immediately asks, "What's wrong?"

"Desdemona and the paro'ki's soldiers are after us," Ace explains quietly. "Can you stand?"

Mara nods, wobbling to her feet. She glances around their small group. "Where's Evan?"

"He stayed behind under the pretense that we used him," Ace quickly explains as they race after Erimentha down the narrow streets.

As soon as they reach the outer wall, Neil rushes through the unattended guardhouse to take care of the guards and start anchoring an emergency portal outside the wall. Erimentha scouts the streets, making sure the guards haven't caught up.

Several agonizing minutes drag by. Erimentha approaches just as Neil pokes his head through the doorway. "It's done. It will only be open for a few more minutes, so we need to hurry."

Erimentha pats Ace's arm. "Thana baro, old

friend."

He grins at her. "Thank you for all your help, Erimentha. If there is anything we can do for you, just call one of us."

She nods firmly and pushes them through the doorway. As soon as her hand touches Mara's bare arm, a spark ignites between them.

"I-I'm so sorry," Mara apologizes, horrified. She had thought the single remaining restraint on her Source would have stopped such antics.

Erimentha stares into Mara's face and smiles secretively. "You did not hurt me, my little fletchling," she murmurs. "Leave before the others catch up."

"But what about you?" Mara blurts out, suddenly concerned for the woman.

"I cannot leave this city, and even if I could, I wouldn't. Evan still needs my help to escape." Erimentha rubs Mara's arm, igniting several silvery sparks and tendrils. "Go, Mara. Live. And know... know that you are no monster."

She vanishes.

Mara slowly expels her breath as she turns away, her eyes stinging with tears. She barely knows the woman, but she feels an odd connection to her. She shakes off the lingering urge to chase after her and steps through the abandoned guardhouse. Neil and Ace wait for her on the other side, holding out their hands to her.

"Let's get out of here, Danarko," Neil says.

A tension she had not been aware of drains out of her. She smiles tiredly, reaching for them.

"Seize her!" Desdemona roars on the other side of the wall. "Do not let that woman escape!"

Neil and Ace grab Mara's hands, yanking her through the portal. They tumble onto the rainbow-colored crystal pathway inside of Carni, the colorful swirls of clouds and mist clearing away for the path.

Ace reaches forward and grabs something, tugging downwards in a hard jerk. The very air rips like cloth, and he drags them through the hastily-made portal.

They tumble onto the teleportation platform of Cerlail Academy. Mara stares down through the semi-opaque glass, her eyes wide as she takes in the ground far, far beneath her.

Neil and Ace pull her to her feet, and she takes in the surprised expressions of Codi, Kimala, and Rick waiting on the platform.

"You found her!" Kimala exclaims in relief as Codi rushes forward to help support Mara, eyeing her bloodstained, filthy dress.

"Get out of here," Ace orders, taking a defensive posture in front of the portal. "Rick, draw your sword."

Neil whirls around and whips out his knives, crouching down in the familiar laig'hius pose.

Kimala's and Codi's eyes widen. They quickly drag Mara away, but she twists around to stare at her friends. "I need to help – "

Desdemona steps through, a bladed whip in her hand. She grins at Mara. "Uthu morla a ik'te, Essence," she purrs, and a chill races down Mara's spine at the familiar phrase.

The whip snaps, and blue-purple blood scatters. Ace falls onto one knee, crying out in pain; he cradles his side, bleeding freely.

"No!" Mara screams, struggling weakly against her cousin and brother as they drag her across the pathway. "We need to go back. *We need to go back!*"

"Mara, for once in your life, will you just *listen* to us?" Kimala snaps. Mara stares at her, stunned. In her cousin's expression, there is fear, of course, but there is also a fierce determination that Mara has never seen in her before. "You're too important to go back and risk – "

The crystal pathway trembles. Below them, a huge ball of mahogany Source crashes into the side of the building – right where the descending platform is.

"Carc'ra," Codi curses, swinging his sister's arm over his shoulder. "Kimala, get to the medical wing and tell Lilly what is going on. We'll head to the rooftop stadium and cross over that way to try to avoid Desdemona."

Kimala nods, her face pale. She takes off down the pathway, her white robe flaring out behind her as she turns the corner at the end, narrowly missing the caving floor.

Mara glances behind them just in time to see Neil flung across the transportation platform and smack into the side of the glass, knocked unconscious. "Run," she hisses at Codi, grabbing the hem of her skirt and stumbling forward.

They dart up the emergency stairs into the rooftop stadium, quickly traversing the park to the corner where there is a lift leading down to access the medical-tactical wing walkway.

"You can't run from me!" Desdemona calls out, and Mara nearly trips at the sound of her voice. Codi steadies her and they continue along the edge of the park, running as fast as they can to the lift on the other corner. They skirt the edge of the building, having the most cover yet a direct route despite the dangerous proximity to the plummeting edge.

Codi glances into the park and suddenly pushes Mara in front of him. She sprawls on the ground, glancing over her shoulder.

A mahogany-colored lance pierces through Codi's chest.

He chokes, staggering backwards. "*No!*" Mara cries, leaping forward to grab him.

Desdemona yanks Mara by her hair, snarling with glee, "You stay here." She throws Mara against a tree, and her head strikes against the wood with a thud.

Mara's head spins. She struggles to stand up, blinking away the dizziness. "Codi," she rasps.

Desdemona grins wildly. "Mother said nothing about keeping *you* alive."

She shoves Codi off the building.

"*No!*"

Raw, unchecked Source blasts out from Mara. The ground trembles.

Desdemona crashes against a tree, knocked unconscious by the pressure of Mara's Source.

The silver metal around Mara's ankle melts, sizzling in the grass as it drips off of her. It does not leave a mark on her skin.

Mara strides towards Desdemona, a dark, sparking aura coating her like a small thundercloud. Her skin shines a vibrant silver. Desdemona's head lolls as she slowly regains consciousness.

"Unforgiveable," Mara whispers.

Desdemona's eyes widen as Mara grabs her neck with one hand and slides her up the tree. Her feet dangle above the ground.

"You killed him," Mara says in a dangerously quiet voice.

Desdemona forces a smile. "You... killed the Dark Warrior," she chokes out.

Mara slams Desdemona against the tree. It cracks, fracturing under the sudden pressure. Desdemona coughs blood, wheezing.

"*She* isn't dead! Codi is!" Mara screams in her face, and Desdemona passes out from the pressure of Mara's chaotic Source.

Someone grabs Mara's shoulder. Her silver Source whips out and knocks the person away.

Mara glances over her shoulder, gasping in horror.

Aeserast's lavender hair is stained with fresh blood; his right eye looks half-closed. He slowly sits up, wiping away the blood dripping from his ears as he smiles at her. "I'm all right, Mara," he reassures her, his voice rough.

Mara's vision blurs and she collapses onto her knees. "I'm sorry," she chokes. Suddenly, Shaniel's arms wrap around her as he pulls her into a hug. "I'm so sorry..."

Aeserast limps forward, glancing at Desdemona. She lies on the ground, still unconscious from the brutal pressure of Mara's Source. "Shaniel, could you —"

"Got it." Shaniel stands up and disappears.

Aeserast kneels next to Mara, hugging her tightly. She pushes him away, crawling to the edge of the building. "Mara, no!" he calls out, trying to grab her arm. Her rampant Source keeps his hand from making contact.

"Mara, don't do it!"

Mara peers over the building's edge. Far below, a small crowd gathers around Codi's body. Medics put him onto a stretcher and take him into the medical wing.

Tears well up and blur her vision again. "I… I can't protect anyone…"

"*Yes, you can,*" a small voice whispers, sounding like hers.

Mara shakes her head. "Everyone… everyone around me always gets hurt."

"*It takes time. Time to – learn how to control – the power – before you can – protect those you love.*" Absently, she recognizes the disjointed, fragmented way the Essence speaks.

Mara leans forward, reaching for Codi. "But I couldn't save him…"

Aeserast wraps his arms around her, trying to pull her away from the edge of the cliff. "Mara, *snap out of it!*"

"*Then learn. Learn – all you can – so you may – protect those you care for. Once you are ready –* "

Two cool objects slide around her wrists, cutting the voice off. Mara stares at the metal Source inhibitors and slowly looks up at a haggard Shaniel.

He stares into her dazed eyes. "Mara," he gasps, collapsing next to Aeserast. A sparking purple and magenta dome swirls around them. Outside of the dome, mages and sorcerers put Desdemona in Source inhibitor cuffs before putting her onto a stretcher. "It's over."

Mara's gaze shifts to the edge of the building. "I… I don't want this to happen ever again."

The Dream'Lord coughs and sits upright. "Who were you talking to?" he asks, wiping blood away from his ears.

Mara's eyes tear up and she reaches out to him. "I'm sorry… I hurt you."

They stare at her. "Uh," Shaniel starts, wiping blood away from his nose. "Did her Source's pressure get to me or are you seeing what I'm seeing?"

"... I see it."

Fresh tears spill down her face. "What?"

"Mara," Aeserast begins, touching her face lightly. "Your eyes..."

Two thin rings of gold cradle a vivid lapis blue band in both of her irises. Her right eye has no trace of Hemius within it despite Mara not having an illusion on, exposing two clear, beautiful eyes. Silver tears glimmer as they race down her face, splashing on her Hemius-covered hand and shining brightly before disappearing.

Mara slaps away his hand, staggering to her feet and swaying towards the direction of the medical wing. "I... I need to see..."

He can't be dead. He... he can't be dead.

In her mind, a red flower blooms over her father's chest as the life slips out of him.

Not again.

Shaniel and Aeserast help her through the medical wing. As soon as Ezra sees her, she frantically tries to get Mara to sit down, but Mara just pushes by her.

Finally, she sees it.

A medic is holding the wrist of someone underneath a black sheet. He turns to the assistant and shakes his head.

No.

The medic notices her and walks towards them. "Do you know the boy who fell from the building?"

No.

Mara pushes by him and grasps at the edge of the cot. Her fingers tremble as she pulls back the sheet.

Codi's moss green eyes are closed. To the entire world, he could be sleeping.

"No..."

"Mara, come over here," Aeserast urges, gently tugging on Mara's arm.

Mara shoves him away, blindly racing out the door and into the woods surrounding the outer edge of the Academy. She collapses against a tree, sobbing loudly.

I failed. I failed to protect him.

She doesn't know how long she kneels there in the grass, choking on her own tears in her sand and blood caked dress. Seconds? Minutes? Hours? All she can feel is the pit left in her from seeing her dead brother.

I can't save anyone.

Someone approaches and touches her arm lightly. She turns around.

Thanos's eyes widen at her tear-streaked face and bloody appearance coupled with her Hemius infection. "Oh, Mara," he breathes, hugging her tightly. She clings to him, wailing into his shirt.

"He-he's dead. He fell. I-I couldn't... I couldn't help him."

He strokes her hair, soothing her. "It wasn't your fault," he murmurs as he leans against the tree, pulling her with him. "It wasn't your fault." Pain flashes across his face as if he had caused her brother's death himself. Closing his eyes, he buries his face in her hair.

XHAROS-ENGLISH DICTIONARY

~ ana	The marker for "city" in old Xharos. For example, Danarkana = Danarko City; Alamirana = Alamir City.
Adul'ne	King/queen. Gender neutral.
Aihalia	The second Alkinian city; it is situated in the Gwynhavo mountain range. The Alkinians had terraformed the basin into a livable area. It is the second-largest city in Saheir.
Alamirana	The Alkinian city of the Ecalains and Highlords; it is currently under the tyrannical rule of Paro'ki Naiya. It is the largest city in Saheir, as it was originally meant to hold the remainder of the Alkinian population 6,000 years ago.
Alkina	Home world of the Alkinian (elf) species.
Blazhreia	A world much like Earth in size. However, because of Alkinian influence, its technological advancements have been drastically different.

Bloody Mavi	Used the same way as the British expression; however, it is not a derogatory or religious term. Mavi is slang for Elethavi, which is the Death Gate ("Mavi" means gate).
Caclar	Black-colored coins. Represents the equivalence of $5.
Carc'ra	Curse word; the literal translation is "kranluk manure."
Carni	The corridor between realms; also known as the Realm Corridor or Dream Realm.
Cerlail Academy	A place specifically designed to provide a central location for everything learned about Voyana and Source in order to more efficiently put it to use.
Da'neka	Light Warrior; a title given to Kyrina, the youngest of the Four Ancient Sisters.
Da'ruha	Dark Warrior; a title given to Rinali, the second youngest of the Four Ancient Sisters.
Dan'te	A slang word that means, "silver-blood." Danti = silver; Ute = blood.

Danarkana	Originally named Lunesh'kun, it was built next to Alamirana. It is a labyrinthian city built on top of multiple layers. It is considered the third-largest city, although many argue it should be the second largest.
Danlar	Silver-colored coins. Represents the equivalence of $100.
Duir'ne	Prince/princess. Gender neutral.
Duir'ne Ien	Princess Grove.
Duir'raz'ne	First Heir/Princess (referring to Eliara, the firstborn of the Four Ancient Sisters).
Duir'stra	Child of a prince/princess. Gender Neutral.
Duir'toa'ne	Second Heir/Princess; a title given to Carni, the second-born of the Four Ancient Sisters.
Eleth	Death realm; all those who are deceased go here.
Evula	Rapier.
Fae'reth	Tactical table; it can show holograms and 3D images of structures. It is meant for building and designing large-scale projects, though it has

	also been used to strategically plan wars and end skirmishes.
Felorna	A green plant that flourishes along high cliffs and along the edges on Quanaris. Ruaguni Cliffs is renowned for its wild felorna and its steep drops overlooking the ocean.
Forlar	The smallest form of currency; coppery-orange. The equivalence of around $1.
Garular	Gold-colored coins. Represents the equivalence of $25.
Goindun	(Dragonir language) An esteemed title given to individuals who are not dragonkin yet are considered in such high regards by the dragonkin to be one of them.
Hariana	An advanced prison system that is linked to Eleth and Carni; its physical location is in Carni, although it only has one entrance through the Elethavi. It is an artificial realm that had been created for the sole purpose of locking up the Dark Warrior (Da'ruha).
Heakalius	Living Curse Storm.
Hemius	Living Curse Poison.

Heramus	Living Curse Scar; A section of land to the west of Veera infected with Hemius puddles. Ecalain War II had occurred in this area.
Kareia	Living metal; it holds a strange symbiotic relationship with its owner. At the expense of feeding it Source, the owner gains a reliable blade that lends power and strength.
Kranluk	A six-legged creature often used for travel and heavy hauling when teleportation hole travel is unavailable or inconvenient.
Le fora cauna.	Old Xharos; this way of speaking is highly respectful and formal. The phrase means the equivalence of, "You are spectacular."
Mind-weaver	An individual with the ability to manipulate someone's mind in some way; usually, they can manipulate thoughts or even memories and can cause people to hallucinate or dream of a specific thing. In special circumstances, mind-weavers can be used to aid someone during a mental illness or time of grief.
Nari	The feeling people get from someone's Source; based off the theory that Source can actually

reflect the ideals and goals of a person. Some Earthling cultures may call it aura or charisma.

Neivir	A razor-sharp crystal that grows like a weed. Used in assassination tools; it is an illegal substance.
Neka	Light (as in Light Warrior). Can also mean the side that receives sunlight, such as the Neka Coven, the sun elf coven, which is on the side of Alkina that always receives sunlight.
Orica	Hemius ointment; numbs pain and slows down the spread of the infection.
Paro'ki	Tyrant.
Quasala	The capital of Saheir; the fourth-largest city in Saheir.
Raz	One; first.
Ruaguni Cliffs	A section of Quanaris where the land juts high into the sky and drops down into the ocean in a dizzying drop. A common weed, felorna, grows there that can be used for all sorts of tinctures.
Ruha	Dark (as in Dark Warrior). Can also mean the side that does not receive light, such as Ruha Coven, the moon

	elf coven, which is on the side of Alkina that never receives sunlight.
Ruicov	Grandfather.
Runkare	An individual mixes their Source with raw Voyana to amplify and strengthen their energy usage.
Saheir	A country in the northern hemisphere of Blazhreia; it is a large island with a mountain range in the north and coasts in the south, with fields and forests in the middle.
Salev'i	Scimitar.
Salev'ra	Shorter, chained version of the scimitar.
Scio'thi	Katana.
Sera	Of course.
Sonakonu	Autumn (season).
Sonatheia	Autumn festival.
Source	The personalized Voyana within an individual whose ancestors had been affected by the initial release of Voyana.
Tav'luk	A bipedal creature native to Quanaris. It has extra joints and can

harden its skin to be as tough as rock. Some of the stronger tav'luk can harden their skin to be like strong metal. They are a fighting-based primitive species that was influenced by Alkinian involvement.

Tein'fu	Equivalence of a duke or duchess. Gender-neutral.
Tein'stra	Duke/Duchess's child. Gender-neutral.
Thana baro	Safe travels.
Thanos	Chamber; large enclosed space.
Therakare	An individual who can use their Source without amplifying it with Voyana. Some people naturally have this affinity.
Tick	A measurement of time; approximately a minute. There are sixty ticks in a tock.
Toa	Two; second.
Tock	A measurement of time; an hour. There are twenty-six tocks in one day on Blazhreia.
Tora	First month of the Blazhreian-Alkinian calendar. In the middle of

summary.

Uthu morla a ik'te	I found you. Uthu = I (gender neutral); morla = found; a ik'te = you (However, this form is very gender and species neutral. It refers to someone/something that the individual was talking about but had no name for them.)
Vara tir'rani er thana baro	A common phrase in ceremonies and large gatherings; it means "Fair weather and safe travels."
Veera	Fifth-largest city in Saheir; also one of the easternmost cities from the capital.
Voi' ~	Added to the beginning of a title to signify the recognition of or adoption into this rank without proper ties.
Voyana	A biochemical energy supply that had developed a conscious mind when it was released. Expands exponentially and devours chemicals/hazardous fumes in the atmosphere that would otherwise kill life.
Xharos	The Alkinian language; used as both a language and also a way to focus Source.

Xhavio	The equivalence of a soulmate; not many people believe of this superstition nowadays. It is an old term that fell out of style over 2,000 years ago.

CALENDAR NAMES

Days*

Zanuni	Monday
Bruanuni	Tuesday
Denuni	Wednesday
Koranuni	Thursday
Wionuni	Friday
Senuni	Saturday
Xhenuni	Sunday

Seasons

Torakonu	Summer
Sonakonu	Fall
Alorakonu	Winter
Fuakonu	Spring

Months*

Tora

Eona

Vuva

Sona

Maua

Kenza

Alona

Rawa

Pina

Lefa

Fua

Zua

Owa

*Seven days in a week; four weeks in a month; thirteen months in a year.

ABOUT THE AUTHOR

Maxina Storibrook grew up in the military life, constantly moving and traveling all over the world. She loved it so much that she wasn't satisfied by merely traveling to all of the unknown places across the Earth; she has to discover new places, write about other worlds, and meet amazing, adventurous people.

She graduated from University of Georgia with a bachelors in English. A little over a year later, she finished her masters in Creative Writing for the Entertainment Industry through Full Sail University. Now, she is living in Alaska, her home state. She works at night and writes even later at night. Sometimes, when she is especially fueled on creative juices, she writes during the day, too.

Visit her Facebook page:
www.facebook.com/MaxStoribrook/
Danarko Facebook page:
www.facebook.com/DanarkoBook/

Support Maxina on Patreon:
www.patreon.com/maxstoribrook

Made in the USA
Charleston, SC
02 December 2016

THE SOUL SPEAKS

Printed in the United States of America
Published by Imprint Productions, Inc.
First Edition 2022

THE SOUL SPEAKS

D. L. STATON

FOREWARD

An Acknowledgement to the Author
by his Mom/Arlina Staton

'Our deepest fear is not that we are inadequate.
Our deepest fear is that we are powerful beyond measure.
It is our light, not our darkness that most frightens us.

We ask ourselves, who am I to be brilliant, gorgeous, talented, fabulous?'
But God says; Who are you not to be?

The words spoken in the poem by the great Marianne Williamson gave me a vision of how God made you. You were always meant to shine, yet for so long you tried to bury your light. Your experiences have now taught you that light can shine through the darkness.

Never dim your light, as you feel it will blind others. You are a child of God, so you must shine because God is light. Playing small does not serve the world. It is the light that frightens us more than the darkness.

There is nothing enlightening about shrinking so that others don't feel insecure. Your beam can help ignite others.

Don't be haughty and proud, but humble yet mighty. The Glory of God is within you. You were born to manifest the gifts you have been given. Never dim your light for those blinded by your light; in time they too shall see. This is your season. Liberate yourself from your own fear.

You are brilliant, strong, gorgeous, talented, insightful, intelligent, gifted, intuitive, and creative. You were made great in the likeness of our creator. My son, you are POWERFUL BEYOND MEASURE.

Go forth and Manifest the Gifts.

Smooches,
Mom

INTRODUCTION

The poems you read in this book are more than just rhyming words on paper, more than just words in my head, these words are life: My Life. The Soul Speaks, tells a story of a young man trying to find himself. Since the age of two, he's been in and out of the system and now approaching age thirty, he is poetically telling of his journey. This book tells of his pain, betrayal, heartbreak, and hope for a future.

If you've been through pain and still fought to rise above it, you should be able to relate to my words. If you have ever been betrayed and still held your head high, my words will feel familiar. If you've experienced heartbreak then maybe you can relate to me.

I believe a soul is a hard thing to keep. It's kind of like faith, which you can't see, but you know you need it. Both can be lost. This book tells of a young man who sold his soul to vanity and lost hope in humanity. He had forgotten the true value of love and family and adopted a lust for the world. BUT! If you read this, you will hear his desire for these things to be back. You can tell he's learned that only GOD gives true satisfaction and nothing can compare to His love and the love of family.

TABLE OF CONTENTS

HOW INCONSIDERATE

How inconsiderate of me!!!

To waste all my family's hard work
Cause them unnecessary worry and pain
By not thinking of anyone other than me
How inconsiderate of me

To think about selling a substance of death
To confiscate what others have worked hard for
Just because of my own greed
How inconsiderate of me

To waste my education

To take advantage of positive opportunities

Because I'd rather live in a masquerade of negativity

How inconsiderate of me

To consider to sell my soul to the devil

To give my love to the world

Instead of My GOD who created me in his image

How inconsiderate of me

TRUEST FRIEND {DEDICATED TO MY MOM}

This is for my truest friend
That was there till the end
Whether I won or loss
She always supported her team like a boss

She was there when I couldn't even stand
Always willing to lend a helping hand
Even when I was too immature to comprehend
Her love withstood every bend

She never tried to preach
But always did teach

Without her, I would have never had a chance to be a man

Never have learned to walk on my own two feet

Never would be able to rock to my own beat

I would have just kept falling

Never able to stop crawling

But thanks to her lessons

I have received many blessings

You are the only one I have ever met with this unfailing love

That you would do this could only come from above

So for that, I say Thank You God

For providing me a rod

This statement is really true

This love, only a mother can do.

TRUEST FRIEND (PART II)

Now you inspire me to move on
When everything else feels like it's gone
You are my motivation to conquer fears and foes
To keep fighting through all the woes

You are the reason I hold my head high
I have the guts to look men right in the eye
You are the reason why I never succumbed to anger
Yet, I do not shake or shiver in the face of danger

You are the reason why I have a positive view of life
Even through all this strife
You were the first one to ever really love me
Only because of your guidance will I become what I'm meant to be

This can only be GOD's love for me

HAVE YOUR WAY

I'm tired of living the world's way

I surrender, God have your way

Give me Your spirit

So I can stay sane in this insecure world

Give me Your strength

So that I don't become weak and fall victim to temptation

Without You I am nothing

But with You I am something

Through You my smile reaches my eyes

Through You laughter comes from my heart

Without You all I do is live and lie

I would be impersonating a satisfied person

But my happiness would never be real

This I realize

This I know

Through You, I can be satisfied and have true joy

Lord I accept you

I surrender

Have Your way in me

SIN SLAVE

I'm a slave to this sin I live in

Thanks to it, I'm held down and separated from my GOD

It has me held down with chains

Doing things I love, but hate to do

It's like my mind's screaming freedom

But my body is unwilling to flee

Been doing it so long even though I know it's so wrong

It's like....It's only right to continue

Why switch venues when it pays so lovely

I'm a slave to this sin I live in

So I'm unable to stop drinking and smoking

Having frivolous sex on a daily basis

Just about a different woman every night of the week

Conscious level is on zero

So don't try to be no hero

Someone might end up missing.... You

Ten Commandments I grew up......on/off

But I fell to temptation....so GOD forgive me

FIX

Pain is embedded into my mind

Stained by weakness

Cloaked by darkness

Sprinkled with hope

That this black hole

That captured my heart will release me to the light

Hate strains my muscles

Weakness clogs my veins

Darkness comes on me like a fog

A dim light seems to shine through

But not enough to save me

HE DID IT FOR ME

He came for me
He died for me
So now I have the opportunity
To live a life free of sin
His death didn't make mankind perfect
But it gave us a chance to foresee heaven
A chance of the true repentance through Him
His death wiped our slate clean
Perfect blood was shed for our lives
One man-God's son paid the price
--------For all our sins

He came for me
He died for me
His death showed mankind a true example of love
So now I have the responsibility
To show love to all
It doesn't matter if they're a sinner
A convicted felon, a government official, or homeless
Whether I agree with their lifestyle or not
I must and I will show love
As Christ has shown....

He did it for ME

TRIUMPH

I see triumph in my future
Forget the sin and depression of my past
God is my cure
He has fixed my brokenness
Done took the scales from my eyes
So now I see

I see triumph in my future
I see the Angels fighting for me
I see demons crying out Jesus' name
No longer do I yearn for fame
The shackles from sin have been broken
Self-gain means nothing
My life is no longer mine
I have offered it away
GOD has claimed me - as his own
Through the spirits eyes I see
Triumph is in my future

WHAT'S TRUE?

Man I must've been dumb

To believe the fantasies

The fairytales that they had on the rack

This so called American dream

Of liberty, peace, and justice

Man I was a fool to believe that could be my life

Things could be sweet and easy

All colors and races are equal

I guess I was a fool

Cause all these things are untrue

What is true? Only God has peace

And justice is a myth

There is none under the sun

Only heaven has justice

Liberty that's funny

Even the innocent aren't free in this world

And equal rights are so false.......untrue

Minus a wail, a cry, boo hoo

What is true?

Only God gives peace

Serves justice and shows liberty

I HAVE A FUTURE

I have a past
That wasn't always pretty
But I also have a future
That has the potential to be bright
If only I follow the light
So I pray to GOD to show me the way
So my days will be long
My nights will be safe
So that my mind will be filled with
Knowledge, understanding and wisdom
That I will be shown mercy and grace throughout my existence
Let my tongue be humble
And my heart at peace
Even though life hasn't always been fair
God has always been with me
When I didn't realize He was there
So I know my future is bright
It may be hard, but I just have to believe
Reach it, grab it, and grasp it.

HINDSIGHT

In hindsight, I see the mistakes I've made
Decisions, that in plain sight, I never thought wrong
I never thought they would have been consequences
That the reaction to my action could affect so many others
BUT, equally it has, and did
Due to my actions, I have lost many
Some to this world and some to the grave
Some have latched on and still follow
Others have stepped back but still watch
Some were swallowed whole due to my actions
I was a leader, but I lead blindly
I didn't recognize I was being followed

Leading others besides myself
I thought I was sharing my goals
But I was truly deceiving myself
By doing so I was hurting others
If I knew then, what I know now, from hindsight
Would I do anything different?
I won't say yes, I won't say no
But I will say-
Because of hindsight
I will no longer lead blindly

HOPE IN A HOPELESS SEASON

Many days I wake up feeling forlorn
My life is being wasted in a reclusive state
I stand without my heart
My heart is at home, but I'm gone

If you were watching my life
You would've seen all the life being squeezed out of me
Like juice from a lemon
Bitter and tart without sugar

So I sit pensively staring ahead; but I see nothing
I'm bereaved 'cause In the obituary someone else is gone
But still I try to have hope
Even if this seems like a hopeless season

Without faith
I will rot away
Like flowers uncared for
Starving for a few drops of rain

I lifted my head higher
With everyone I devoured,
But the Lord delivers the hopeful
Even in hopeless seasons

TREASURED

I once treasured all the wrong things that life had to offer
Not items of real value
But I kept processing the things of this world
Things that would one day deteriorate

I put J's on my feet
Chains on my neck
-All before my education

I gave the streets and my homies

My time and my respect

 -Instead of my family

Lots of females that were fast

Relationships that didn't last

Got in the way of the joy God gave me

I only treasured material items

Which only gave me joy for a second

Never completely filling the void in my heart.

PRIDE

Pride is
The destination of one zealous in himself
Overconfidence is destruction
The prideful are just a minute away from being humbled.

So me
I'm humbled
Waiting to be exalted,
My come ups are not in my name but GOD'S.

Big headedness was my destruction
I gained my throws
But I gained it in all the wrong motives
So it came and left like a thief in the night,

Here for a second and gone the next
Like a flower in the wind blown away
My pride was my downfall,
I was my own worst enemy
My humbleness in Jesus
Will be my redemption,
I'm hidden in the Lord's pavilion
Where HE is making provisions

With him I'm nothing less than a conqueror

Pride is defeated

In His name, diminished

Pride is no longer an issue

It's nonexistent

Pride is dead

Humbleness has risen

NEVERMORE

Nevermore shall we be captured

Our Spirits broken

Hearts troubled

Soul aching

Wishing our own death,

Nevermore shall this be me

Trapped in a cage with hate and rage

Filled with anger

One step from danger

'Cause of one devastating mistake

Nevermore, shall I be called incompetent

Incapable of greatness

Outsmarted out of my dreams

Hopes, and ambitions

Nevermore, will my fears immobilize me

Hold me back from accomplishing my goals,

Nevermore, will they be capable of devastating my community

Depriving us of food and withholding life

Using Tasers on our children

Controlling our schools

Nevermore, I claim

Nevermore, shall this be

Nevermore, shall we let this government undermine our people

Enslave our society,

Control us by their curses

Claiming we have no say

Nevermore, shall we let this be our life

Our circumstances

Nevermore, can we let this be our punishment

Letting them reign over us, saying this is our destiny

I say Nevermore.

Nevermore again!

Nevermore can we be stopped

Soaring with wings

I will fly to great heights

Never to be held back again !

SORRY, I DON'T BELIEVE YOU

You say you love me
Sorry I don't believe you
You say you want to see me do better
Sorry I don't believe you
How can this love be real?
You never supported Live Fly Die Free
You said "I want you to succeed."
Yet you never offered better options
Said "I want you to do better."
But you watched me starve
You'd call for a plug
But never bought my book
Claimed you'd be there
But where were you?
When I had nowhere to go
When the commissary was low
The lawyer bills were high
That love was so fake
My heart beat was a constant ache
So I'm sorry I don't believe you.
I swear I ain't mad though

All the lies made me stronger

I'd rather have ones I can count on one hand

Than 100 false friends

The hunger made the thirst for my dreams insatiable

I have loved and lost friends

I Have loved and lost brothers

I have loved and lost family

Those with whom the love was mutual, remained

Though they were disheartened by my mistakes

They weathered the storm

Withstood the pain, with me

Stood in the rain, with me

Held it down till the sun began to shine again

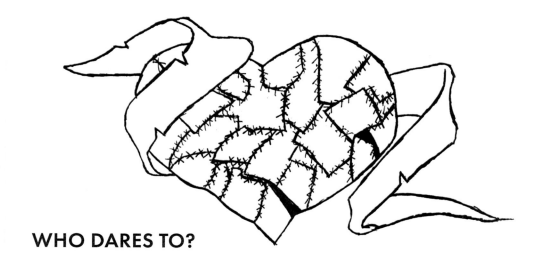

WHO DARES TO?

Who dares to show love
To a stranger
To an enemy

Who dares to hope for a brighter day
For justice
For deliverance

Who dares to let go of the past
Of pain, of hurt
Of sin

Who dares to open up their heart
To feel
To care, to love

Who Dares To?

LAST DAYS

Death is near I can feel it in my veins
My whole body pains
I'm held down by iron chains

My body aches from lack of nourishment
My muscles strain from failure to administer treatment
It's as if the walls are caving in
Seems like my world is coming to an end

There is no light in sight
No one's willing to listen to my plight
My spirit is crying out

My mind doubts whether anyone cares that these are my last days

Can this be my final resting place?
My spirit will not stay another day, I will not face.......
So, I surrender to my captors
I bow my head to my master
I recognize these as my last days

ON THE VERGE

Seems like freedom keeps eluding me
Even when I'm free, I'm still not free
On the verge of a breakdown

Trying to find my way through this maze
But I can't, I'm constantly in a daze
Days and months pass by
No matter how hard I try
My breakthrough escapes me
As if I'm incapable of being free...

On the verge of a breakdown
Who would have thought the pen
Would become my best friend.

SICK AND TIRED

So sick, so tired of these games
Of my own bull with all these females who surround me
The ones who told me they love me
All the ones I spoke those same words to
When we both knew it was never meant to be
It was only lust, a misleading attraction
Even so, we put our time and bodies into a relationship
To only end up empty

So sick, so tired of these games
Of these relationships, was it only about sex?
Waking up in the morning and not even remembering her name
No love involved, not even once
And to me as a man it's not enough
As a child, I didn't mind
But now grown up
I realize that love is better than lust

So sick, so tired of games
Of being left without love
My hand out there in the open
Coming up empty-handed
Left where I stand.... By myself.

RAIN

Heavy rains remind me of the tears I cry

Cause of these lonely nights with no one to depend on

Puddles surround me from the tears I cry

But they're not blue they're red

It's like I forever wear the mask and cry later

I constantly bask in my sorrows

Walk around with my head down

In this storm that surrounds me, I hear thunder

In this storm I'm left with no umbrella, no jacket, no covering

My only companion is the water that surrounds me

So once again I'm surrounded by puddles but this time they're blue not red

So my question is will this rain ever cease?

FAR AWAY

Peace I have not seen since you left

Ever since that morning my heart has not been at rest

I'd give up money and the fame

Cause without you it's just not the same

Not only did you take my joy

You left me seeking redemption

Due to that, I fell to temptation

You left my heart ripped

Left my spirit chipped

I am now only one half...incomplete

A man with no peace

FAITH IS DEAD

I don't understand why there's so much pain
Why so many young people are being slain
The government claims to be making laws
To solve the problem of deaths jaws
But nothing changes
Everyday another person dies in vain

I swear every day I wake
It seems it's just the same....
Don't put faith in man
Only GOD'S promises stand
While questioning you, they have a hand on their gun
Telling you to calm down son
They just waiting for you to take the bait

So they can put you in the grave

The government's solution to the problem is homicide

Society's youth is committing suicide

What happened to faith?

There is none

Everybody's got a gun

The sun has ceased to shine

Men have lost their spine

As pain racks through their bodies

They lay shaking and quivering

Faith has died,

It was all a lie

This is genocide.

WALK AWAY

You ever felt like walking away?

Well I do everyday

Cause every day I wake up, its stress filled

A Dude, Quan-Quan, just got killed

So R.I.P., I'll see you in heaven above the skies

His baby mother got tears in her eyes

Big Bro got locked back up,

Beef on the streets are at a high

Everybody's got a gun

Everybody's trying not to be the next one that dies

Crime is on the rise

Penitentiary yard,--- they stare at the sky

You ever feel like walking away?

Every day clouds are gray

Thinking about telling the streets good day

Even though I love the hustle

And the fast pace of the bustle

But it's tearing my family apart

I'm losing many that are close to my heart

I need a new start

Before I end up in an early grave

Or serving life in someone's prison

It's time for me to walk away

WHEN I DIE

When I die, celebrate

Pop a bottle for the kid

Cause I'll be in a better place

Where I no longer have to wake up knowing there were gunshots and arguments

So when I die don't cry

'Cause you know Shaun lived life to the fullest

He wouldn't have wanted you to waste a single tear

So many tears were already wasted during my years

You see it shouldn't be a sad day

But more like a day when you look to the sky and yell hooray

Be happy now, you got one more angel

I'll be watching over you

I will be there for you till the end

When I die——---

I'm going with a smile

STAND, GOD FORGIVES

Felons stand with your heads high
Gangsters stand with your heads high
Hustlers stand with your heads high
Addicts stand with your heads high.
Why? Cause you still living every day
You wake up you still breathing
Don't close your eyes and die
Put you faith in the most high
I know it's hard but if you just believe
I promise his grace will relieve
Just depend on Him
He will come in your life and change you
He will give your life a new purpose
He will put you in front of every opportunity and need
Just His word you gotta heed

Felons stand with your heads high
Gangsters stand with your heads high
Hustlers stand with your heads high

Addicts stand with your heads high.

I know we got trouble, I know we got problems but if you lean on Him

He will be the problem solver, your trouble dissolver

Even when you're in the depths of solitude, feeling nothing but desolation

All that can be conquered....just put your faith in the creator of all creation

I know better days don't seem likely

Our old lifestyles came more naturally

But....With Christ the supernatural becomes natural.

I've done been around real gangsters

I've done hustled with the best of them

I've done seen a million and one addicts

But I rather see CHRIST

He forgives even us

And he will if you just believe

So felons, gangsters, hustlers, and addicts stand with your head held high

Cause God will redeem

IF...you let Him in

God. Makes. Everything. Possible.

STRENGTH COMES FROM GOD

I place my faith in my God

I stand by His strength

I'm protected by His power

I receive mercy and grace from Him

He is my Father

I have been adopted into His family

Thanks to His son's death

I have Salvation

Due to His son's Resurrection

So I strive to imitate Jesus Christ

TIME DOESN'T WAIT

Time waits for no one

Stand still and get left behind

Move too fast and you'll miss something

There has to be a balance

Trust, whether you wake up or not

The world will keep spinning

People will go on with their lives if you get incarcerated

The sun will still rise and set

Music will still change

People will move on

New styles will be created

The world will keep on spinning

No ones impact can stop time

Time waits for no one

PAST DAYS

What happened to the past days?

When brothers and sisters would come together for a cause

This generation has lost all unity

They would rather kill one another

Than stand face to face with Uncle Sam

Where did all the Rosa Parks', Martin Luther King and Malcolm X's go?

The ones who had the heart to stand and fight

Like Nelson Mandela, Harriet Tubman, Frederick Douglass

The ones who didn't just lie down and comply

But fought for their rights

Went to jail for their rights

The ones who were willing to die for their rights

No longer do we get incarcerated or die for those reasons

Now it's killing or turning our own into addicts

What happened to the Black Panthers?

The ones who fought those that oppressed us

Those who stopped the burning down of our houses

---------and hanging of our young men

Those who lifted their fist in the air with pride

Why are they no longer here?

Now what's left? or who's left to represent us?

Gangs and dope boys.....That's what the youth are dreaming of being

What happened to pride, to the fathers, to mothers, to families?

To Love,

To Unity,

To Black Pride

Are all these things just from past days?

IT'S INEVITABLE

Why sweat it?
It's going to happen anyway
You can't stop it
It's inevitable
It's omnipresent
Always at the end of the race
Stop worrying
It's one bullet you can't duck
So just live life
Take advantage of every opportunity
They won't last long
I mean life's only a vapor anyway
So why not enjoy it
Spoil yourself
Treat yourself
Indulge in everything life has to offer
Cause it goes by quick
Only here a second, like the wind
Death's always at the end
It's inevitable

STRICTLY BUSINESS

I'm not interested in companionship

Or seeking friendship

For me it's strictly business

My only endeavor is to stack this paper up

No emotions involved unless you play with my confetti

Me, I'm about my business, no time for games

Save those for the lames

Steadily we on the hunt for the money

We don't laugh cause ain't nothing funny

Our job is to get paid

And know, by the end of the night, we getting laid

Other than that

It's strictly business

STILL MINE

People were praying for my downfall

Facebook dudes were saying....... "Hope he's gone for the long haul"

Others asked, "When your boy coming home?"

Mama didn't have the heart to reply

Police were claiming he's hated by many,

It's easy to get someone to turn rat

Me, I was laughing like it couldn't happen

Well won't I

Wrong!~

Someone did rat—but with a lie

So now they got me in a cage

I'm thinking none of my team was true

Young dudes left me on my own

Broads carried it like I had too much time for them to ride

It's ok though, because I'm going to make it through

So... to those who smiled at my downfall

To all the females who forgot how to pick up when I called

To the police who worked so hard to make me out to be a menace to society

Don't worry I'll be home soon

--and trust.... the world is still mine

AFRAID....

I'm afraid of attachment
I'm afraid of entanglement
I'm afraid of entrapment
I am afraid of relationship
But most of all I'm afraid of love

Afraid of waking up and being alone
Of you getting tired of all the struggles
It's just becomes too much for you to deal with
As it did for my mother as only a baby she left me to another
Being a mother became too much for her
The first female I allowed my heart to be entangled with
Up and left me for some other dude
Shorty left me stuck and then tangled in lies and corruption
Now I run from attachment
Cause everyone I ever latched on to left me high and dry
Due to that my heart has subsided to trust
I disapprove of entanglement cause that would mean I have to trust some-
one
Someone to guard my life....to hold on tight
To give me advice when I'm broken
Love makes me afraid cause to allow it into my life
I would have to allow my heart to be revived
And that...makes me more afraid than anything

BETRAYAL

Betrayal is what I'm facing

Seems like individuals all attack with daggers

They're all sitting on the stand

Speaking words that have sharp points

What makes it even more deadly, I once trusted them

To never abandon me

To be continually faithful

But instead you manipulated my heart and my emotions

To the point where I told you my deepest and darkest secrets

At night you slept in my bed

By day you told all my stories

You held nothing back from these people

Like I thought you did with me

I called you my queen and you took my crown

I gave you independence and you abused me, and it at the same time

Thinking only of dollars and nobodies heart

In a single moment you destroyed our empire

My heart

My soul

My spirit

NEVER DID

Happy though sad that we never

I use to really wish that we did,

But if you would've had my kids

We would've never been rid of each other and ended up with another,

But we never did have that chemical balance, between me and you

it was more an imbalance; odds and ends

No matter how hard we tried, the pieces just never did fit quite right

I always told you that you was that —itch

You promised that you would never ditch

But you did, you switched,

I use to wish that you never did

I used to think that you never would, that we would never be rid

I mean we made vows to walk down the the aisle, though we never did

They say time heals but it never did, I tainted you though I wish I never did

You showed your true colors, you switched

Curse after curse

I swore I still loved you, I wish I never put anything above you

You know I cherished you

But I never did

I never did enough to nourish your mind

I only did enough to waste your time

To rid of you, you of me, I wish I never did,

You was supposed to have my kids but never did, we never did

Lies upon lies

Skipping rocks across the pond

A bond destroyed, issues never expressed, hidden so deep

Problems so real that we should've weeped,

We held each other, divulged in one another

Tried to heal each other

But we never did

Instead, we creeped, we hid then ran off to another

Did our bidding in secret, I wish we never did, I wish they never did

But secrets never stay dormant for long

For wrong always comes to the light

Even though we wish it never did!!!!

DISTANT LOVER

I admire you from afar
You are more beautiful than a star
If only I had the heart to speak
Instead of standing in the corner taking a peek
Don't take me as a stalker
I just don't have the heart to approach you
I'm just not up to the part
If you would reject me from the start
But I hope you hear me from this stage
Please do not look at the difference in our age
Only because of you that I speak from my heart
I wish I would have told you how I felt from the start
Just come straight and offer you my heart
But here I am now on bended knee
Asking you to be my Lady, please

GOOD-BYE

It never feels good to say goodbye

But I done took too many loses with you

So now I think it's time to get up and walk away

I don't have the time to keep looking back

Reminiscing on the past..... thinking about the times we had

It's time to bury those memories and leave them at the grave

Too much pain and too many regrets

Don't get me wrong, I'm not saying we didn't have good times

But the price was too steep

So I've got to say good-bye to this relationship

I can't keep getting hung up on your allure

Cause it's leading me to an early grave fast

I'm not trying to be like TUPAC----R.I.P.

THE GAME'S NOT FAIR -BYE

I'm so sick and tired of getting burnt by your flames

You keep trying to include me in all your schemes

Just to attain more fame

You were using me, like a dummy

Had me out there in your playground...doing your dirty work

I thought in the end you would make me an equal

But the whole time, I was just another pawn on your board

I realize, I'll never be an equal to you

I'll always just be another person for you to use ....till you're tired

So I think it's time for me to say goodbye

While I'm still here

Cause you don't play fair

PRICELESS

If I've ever seen one thing in this life

That was invaluable {precious} it was the emotion called love

The only thing I noticed that could not be bought or took from under someone's feet

It has to be truly earned

An item that proved true, that could not be manipulated

No matter what I shoot at it, it did not budge

I could not buy this mutual feeling, this affection that's so dear

I continually search for a price tag

Yet respectfully rejected of this item that proved to be truly priceless

It's called love and you can't buy love.

HOW COME?

Why are Black youth blamed for the high rates in homicides?

When it's not even Blacks doing mass murders in schools and movies

Is it because racism is still alive?

How come if a group of young White men rape or rob someone

The courts just turn the other cheek, just show them pity?

But a group of Black man, who do the same crime, you can kiss their lives goodbye

There is no mercy in sight

How come even though schools are no longer segregated

Students only hear about Black History once a year?

How come even when Obama was in office blacks were still being oppressed?

The government's tearing down the projects and turning them into government housing

They're giving us rules and guidelines on how we can live in our own houses.

Well, How Come?

TOO MUCH

Maybe it's too much for me

All this so called changing and rearranging my life

Giving up everything I once held dear

Maybe it's too much for me

Cause it hasn't been 3 years yet

I'm already ready to go back to a sinner's lifestyle

I'm starting to think none of the progress is real

Maybe it was all a facade

I tried to act like who I used to be…

But it wasn't really me acting out, dressing out or impersonating

It's like now, I really have a mask on

People say they can see the cracks in what I'm trying to portray

And what I'm trying to portray is the life of a changed man

So maybe this is too much for me….to change

Or maybe I just really don't want to do it

Or maybe the sense is, I'm only halfway changing for self

The other half for others

Maybe that's why I can't seem to change

I don't know how much longer I can keep this act up

My mind battling between right and wrong

Battling between who I used to be, and who I think I want to become

Maybe I'm just letting my mind get befuddled by the past

Seems like my carnal side is going to get the best of me

Maybe it's too much for me to change

Cause I'm ready to give up

THE THINGS WE FIGHT FOR

The things we fight for
Are they worth your life?
All the stress, pain and strife
Is the gain worth the loss?

EMBRACE

It's time for me to embrace my fears

Stand up and be a man

Can't run no more

Got to face these problems

This, the last race right here

It's either succeed or fail

Win or lose

Me, I'm tired of losing

So it's time

Time to strap up my J's and go to the starting line

I've been ducking it for a while now

Claiming I was preparing myself but really I was too nervous

See, I didn't think I would amount to the expectations

I thought if I just didn't do it, I wouldn't be letting anyone down

But by not trying to move on in life,

I let everyone down including myself

So now I must put all my worries behind me

Stop wasting life

Stop not amounting to my potential

I have to embrace my fears

Push ahead to the winners circle

At heart I'm a winner, and it's time to show it

Watch the world embrace me

A man who landed on his own two feet.

WHY IS GOD MAD?

Instead of cherishing God's creation

All we do is bring upon devastation

We participate in tearing each other down

We enjoy bringing tears to other's eyes

We destroy this world that was generous to us

We misuse other peoples trust

We do these things without even a second thought

Then, we wonder why God is mad at us.

TELL ME

Can someone please explain?

How do people put the ones they love through so much pain?

How blaming another one is the name of the game?

Why is it so easy to do wrong?

I constantly ponder this idea

It's so complicated to do right

Like we don't think twice to commit crimes

Though we would think twice to do a good deed

Yet still we wonder why there are only hard times

Why is the world so full of greed and sin?

We look for an end before we even begin

Tell me why schools are steadily getting' shot up

Kids are steady dying

The government stops nothing

They cause destruction and bring about corruption

They say pray to God

But they take him out the picture

A FALLEN STAR

What do you do when a star falls?
When it is found all on its own
With no friends to depend on
Feels like you can't even count on a higher power
It feels like it would be devoured
Who do you look to – to restore it?
Who do you depend on to build it back up?
Or, do you just let it stay in its stump?
Letting its light die out

No, you help it get back up
To soar once again
To places it's never been
To be brighter than all lights
To be the best it's ever been

Now that is what you do.
Dedicated to all those that fell and someone reached down to help them
get back up

MUST BE NICE

Even when your street life days are done
She'll be right there holding on
Even when the streets dry up and everything flees
She'll still be there.
Must be nice having a chick who is always by your side
Must be nice having someone that's always down for the ride
Must be nice having someone there through the storm
Even when it subsides
Have love for someone who stands by everything you do
Still waiting to be your boo -
Throughout all the car chases and all the court cases
Must be nice having someone who, is with you all day and all night
through
Must be nice having that chick as your queen
Having this makes life so serene

HARD HEADED SON

The sad thing is I ruin everything that I love, friendships and relationships

Pain turned my heart cold,

Childhood stolen, soul broken

Lessons learned left me trusting none

Being a hard-headed son led to incarceration

Delusional, failing to accept reality

Stuck in a childhood state of mind

Trying to shine in all the wrong lines

Had me experimenting with drugs

Like acid dripping down my spine

Couldn't accept love so I was refusing hugs

Lacking empathy had me ruining relationships

Problems with authority made it hard to maintain employment

Refusing to understand; you can't buy feelings

Had me lacking financially... which drove me to depression

Made me repeat the cycle

Being a hard-headed son

I CRY

Sometimes I cry for the ones who are brokenhearted
Sometimes I cry for the ones who have departed
Sometimes I drop a tear for the youth incarcerated
Sometimes I cry out for the ones sexually degraded
Sometimes I cry for the ones I'll never see again'
The ones who are never getting out of the pen
The ones who no longer have a choice
The ones who cannot express their voice
I cry because we no longer have political speakers like Tupac anymore
Who was more likely to knock down the governments' door.

I cry for my situation
Sometimes I cry for my own pain
Sometimes I cry 'cause It was really all in vain
I cry for my situation
I cry because of the uncaring administration
Now these tears I cry are bittersweet
They come out in an unorganized beat
I cry ....Because my heart is held captive

Wishing I had a love one to express my feelings to

Someone who understands or even had a clue

But it seems like no one cares to understand

No one, even offers me a hand

They'd rather leave me sitting on the ground

With nothing but a frown

They act like they can't hear a sound

Just keep walking around me while I am down

I cry....... and no one cares to know why

U.S.A.

In this country all you see is devastation
In every abandoned house there is molestation
Poverty triumphs all
Everyone waits for another man to fall
Nobody will even care
All people just seem to walk away and stare
Nobody offers any help

They all act like it's a deadly disease

But this is the land of the free and home of the brave?

I don't understand why so many people crave..... To be

Isn't this the land of the free?

There are more fathers in jail that children can't see

But this is the country where everyone wants to be?

The great U.S.A.

DAYS/DAZE

They ask me why I believe in God

"He's going to forsake you anyway"

And I say

'Cause he's the only hope I got now a days

I was looking for God all around the city

It was such a pity

I couldn't find him and I looked everywhere

From the church to the pulpit I still couldn't find him there

So I called mother on the phone

She said "You got to come home

Jesus is not where you said he'd be

I really need to converse with you immediately.

She asked, "Boy what's wrong?"

I said mama I need help, let me tell you in my song.

Sometimes I feel like I've already died

Because I see Angels fly as people die

Before, when I tried to sleep at night

It's like a fight, it makes me want to cry

As my soul drips from my eyes

It rips my heart, I pray for it to be repaired

It's like a bomb was dropped on my life.

I lost trust in everybody

It's like metal rusts and dust collects

They say I'll be there; but that was fake

It makes me mad

I lose control and then get sad

Walking on a path where time has passed me by

A life, I've never had

DARK AND LIGHT

By the light we walk

By the dark we creep

Out in the open in broad daylight

We try to commit acts in secret

To try to impress others

We try not to get caught

How high and mighty we are

We still lust in our own pride

The things we do by day or by night

We hide

But the evil is still there when closing of eyes

MIND CONTROL

They lock us up, throw us in cages

Governmental figures try to kill our minds

Politicians say we should be satisfied with minimum wages

They try to enslave us, put us in a bind

Their goal is to destroy our creativity

Trying to demolish the people's voice

Their war is to kill all positivity

Make you think you only have one choice

This government that we are ran by, tries to make it like they care

They want to take your intellect from you,

But if you ask me, that's very rare

They force you to sit down and listen to the madness that they brew

They don't listen to your concerns because they don't care about you

They killed Tupac for speaking his mind

They crucified Jesus for speaking the truth

The man was constantly on his grind

Now see they didn't want to believe Jesus –The Truth

Why would anything differently happen to you?

OLD LIFE BEHIND

Farewell to this life
It's time to move on without thinking twice
I won't look back at these horrid times
Or think about my deceitful ways
I won't reminisce on the past
I'll just take the lessons I learned with me
As I move onto this next plateau of life
I'll do so with my head held high
Looking only at the sky
Don't look at it as daydreaming
This is just me moving on
Leaving the old life behind

MY GENERATION

I cry for this generation

A generation of children growing up too fast

They all want money that won't last

Some too lazy to work hard

They don't even want a 9 to 5

They just want to be slaves to this system

The money they get has them hypnotized

But the trance breaks as soon as the cuffs clasp

They think the penitentiary is the answer

But they are either transmitting young boys or gorillas

There's few in between,

$8.50 an hour wasn't good enough for them

Now .38 cent an hour makes them a slave to working

I cry for this generation

A generation of children growing up too fast

Young girls at 15 shaking in the clubs

Got grown men buying them drinks

Too young to know their limit

Thinking that they're grown

Not knowing men are seducers

They wake up in a hotel room

Not seeing the man they left with

She wakes up knowing that something went wrong

A generation growing up toooooooooo fast.

THE MURDER CASE

Murder they conspired
The plans didn't include a gun
No contact with poison
But still the man died
He didn't die of old age
He was murdered
His flesh stiff
His mind and soul evaporated

First they crushed his confidence
Made him believe he was nothing
This destroyed his hope
His ambition was discarded
His motivation was smashed
As they publicly crushed him
Stripped and raped of all he was
The only potential he had left was death
They masturbated on his dreams
And spat on his face
All that inspired him was taken
All that was lost ate him up from the inside
He was left as a shell

LIES

Trying to run from my problems

Hiding in solitude, repeating the cycle, refusing to listen,

Refusing to follow God

I been feeling like Jonah, I wasn't ready to face my future

I've been running this marathon, in and out of this hell, in and out of this cell

I lost sight of my ambition, of Living Fly, Dying Free

Had to reclaim my motivation,

Had to get down on my knees and pray to God for inspiration

Been at the bottom of a bottle for way too long

It's time for me to find my way home

Been with the strays in the streets, carrying heat

Running with cleats

No field, no goals,

Just poles, no role models

It's dice, snake eyes

Just me and my guys, we was supposed to be down for life

Lies, surprise

Tables turned, bridges burned, lessons learned,

Just cause they in the car don't mean they gonna ride

I fell for the deception, now I gotta stand tall, RISE

Waving goodbye, time, a New Year, a reason to chill

So many years lost, but brighter days ahead

I'm raising my head- God help me please

I'm in need. I'm tired of this greed

These sins, hateful ways

It gave me no wins

Left me with no friends

Ends running low

Can't keep running from my problems

Asking God to hear my plea

I'm in need !!!

RISE

See me rise

See me fall

I'll always stand up tall

Even when I fall my head is still held high

I still got my eyes on the prize

If all lose trust, I will rise once more

My ambition can't be killed

I may get caught slipping

But it's ok

I'll get back on my feet to stay

Never let struggling show a frown

Never let strife slow me down

Through it all I sit back and build my mind up

To prepare to rise again

So if you see me fall

Just know I'll rise again.

I PRAY

I pray God is with me as I walk through this stifling world
Searching jewels and pearls, beauty unseen
Something that's been lost for a long time now
Something you just don't see anymore
I'm not talking about worldly passions
This is about the truth, I'm trying to accumulate
I pray for this cause I'm sick and tired of being lost
Tossed and turned like a ship in a rough sea
This craziness I'm living with is mind boggling

The something that has been lost for a long time now is me

So pray that God allows me to find myself

Cause these masks really aren't my reality

When people see me

You can see they're thinking

Who is he going to be today?

I pray that God lets me become a constant person

'Cause these multi personalities aren't cutting it

God, I pray to you that I find wisdom in myself

In your son Jesus' name I pray

Amen

CONCLUSION

I would like to thank everyone who purchased and read this book. Your support is greatly appreciated. I now challenge all you dreamers, hustlers, and entrepreneurs to find a way to express yourselves positively. To live knowing all dreams are worth fighting for. That all can fly, if you open your mind to believe. Live to die a blessing, not a burden. Remember you are as free as you allow your spirit to be. No one should have power over your spirit or mind other than you.

Yours Truly,
Mr. LFDF!!!!!!!!!!!!!!!

Live* Fly* Die* Free *